He found Tully on
living-room floor.
Tully, for the mess that someone had made of his face and head would have made recognition difficult even for his own mother.

Blair knelt down beside the bloodstained body and cradled the ravaged head in the crook of his arm. The gurgles eased somewhat and eyes tried to open against the rivulets of blood.

Tully was trying to say something. Blair bent his head down close to the swollen mouth.

'It's the . . .'

'Yes, what?'

'. . . the . . . phone . . . phone . . .'

An arm lifted weakly and pointed across the floor.

'Yes, I'll phone,' Blair assured him, then looked round to where Tully had been pointing. Lying on its side in the corner was another body. That of Mickey Mouse. From the blood and hair still adhering to the novelty telephone, Blair realised with a sickening thud that Tully had not been exhorting him to use it, but warning him about the use to which it had already been put.

Also by Neville Steed

Tinplate
Die-Cast
Chipped
Clockwork
Black Eye
Black Mail

Hallowes' Hell

Neville Steed

First published in 1990
by HEADLINE BOOK PUBLISHING PLC

First published in paperback in 1991
by HEADLINE BOOK PUBLISHING PLC

A HEADLINE FEATURE paperback

10 9 8 7 6 5 4 3 2 1

ISBN 0 7472 3451 5

Typeset in 10/11¼ pt English Times
by Colset Private Limited, Singapore

Printed and bound by Collins Manufacturing, Glasgow

HEADLINE BOOK PUBLISHING PLC
Headline House, 79 Great Titchfield Street, London W1P 7FN

For my wife, with love

For all those calls
we may never hear . . .

Chapter One

The shock, this time, stunned rather than surprised. And whilst her body jerked away like some choice victim under the slaughterhouse stunner, her fingers seemed welded to the tailgate handle. Pain lightninged up her arm, yet still she couldn't seem to let go.

Mary Stride looked up and around, but there was no one in sight. The cul-de-sac was living up to the estate agent's description of 'an oasis of peaceful seclusion, tucked well away from the bustle of the town'. For a second she felt an awful sense of isolation, an awareness of her own vulnerability that was almost stifling. She shut her eyes tight and tried to tell herself not to behave like an idiotic child. After all, she should be used to it by now. Both her own Corolla and her husband's Bristol were constantly shocking them with releases of static electricity. It was nothing new. That's why her husband, John, had arranged for both their cars to be fitted with rubber straps that dangled from the rear bumpers. They were a fairly common sight in the Hallowes area. Like little puppy dogs' tails wagging away, as if pleased to see any following vehicles.

The childishness of the thought calmed her and, opening her eyes, she found she could now remove her fingers from the handle. The telescopic struts of the hatchback seemed to sigh with relief as they expanded to lift the door. Mary Stride smiled to herself rather self-consciously as she looked down at the big cardboard box full of Sainsbury groceries she'd bought on her way back from taking her son, Mark, to school. The familiar sight of the weekly shopping was comforting, but at the same time, a sharp reminder of what a fool she had been in getting so up-tight about such a trifling phenomenon as a touch of static from a handle – even if, this time, the electrical charge seemed rather more powerful than usual. Powerful enough to cause pain.

As she leaned forward to pick up the heavy box, a blush spread across her tanned and still young features – not from the exertion, but from the thought of what her husband's patients would think of her minor panic this morning. Not that they would ever know, of course. But doctors' wives were always expected to be pillars of sanity and strength, soft enough to comfort, yet robust enough to lean and rely on. And so far, in the nine years she had been a GP's wife, she prided herself she had been just that. Her husband, John, maintained – much to her satisfaction – that his good standing in the practice was as much due to her reassuring character as his own bedside manner and professional skills. A belief which modesty made her deny, but which, privately, she reckoned might have some truth to it. After all, whilst John was undoubtedly a fine, hardworking GP, they had only moved to Hallowes some two years ago, yet he had already become the second most asked-for doctor in a five-man practice.

She put the box of groceries down on the drive and shut the tailgate. This time the handle held no surprises. With her foot, she kicked at the little rubber strap.

'Do your job properly or I'll take you to the vet,' she muttered at it, smiling. Just after she had picked up the box again to carry it indoors, she heard the telephone ringing inside the house. Half stumbling under the weight of her load, she humped her way as fast as she could to the porch, terrified she might miss some life-or-death call from some desperate patient or other. In her experience, it was always the calls you missed that turned out to be the urgent ones.

Though the sticking lock on the front door hardly

aided her, she managed to get to the telephone before the dring-drings ceased.

A somewhat childish voice she didn't recognise asked bluntly, 'Doctor in?'

'No, I'm sorry,' she answered, as sympathetically as her shortness of breath would allow. 'Dr Stride is out on his calls right now, but if you . . .'

'When will he be back?' the girl's voice cut in.

'Well, you could try the surgery and they will make an appointment . . .'

'Don't want the surgery. Like to see the doctor at home. It's personal, see.'

Mary Stride was starting to get the message. It was not the first time she had taken such a call from an anxious young girl.

'I'm afraid Dr Stride won't see patients at his home. But if you'd give me your name and number, perhaps I can get him to call you.'

She heard a sharp intake of breath. 'No. No. That's all right. No need to ring me. Really. I'll ring him.'

'Do you know the surgery number? If not, I can . . .'

The line suddenly went dead. Mary Stride held on for a moment or two longer, then made to replace the receiver back on its mount. It didn't click first time. It was starting to become one of those days.

Rick Rickett's beady eyes looked up at the crunch of gravel, then with a sigh looked back at his copy of the *Sun*. It was only the vicar in what rust had deigned to leave of his Morris Marina. The portly nurseryman had been hoping it would be some beaming, plant-potty matron in, say, a BMW or, perhaps, the lady who ran the health food shop, after some flowers to add fragrance to its ambience, or even, dare he think it, the gushingly attractive Annabel Craven, the estranged wife of Hallowes' most successful property developer, around whom he, Rickett, had spun many a hot fantasy many a time. Anybody, in fact, with a little spending money in their pockets and purses, for his modest nursery would have gone bankrupt years ago on a diet of impecunious occupiers of manses. Besides, the reason for most of the Reverend Meek's visits to his nursery was to purchase neither plant nor flower nor tree, but in Rickett's view, to take advantage of the ever growing religious devotion of his wife, Thelma.

'Sorry. She's out, Vicar.'

The nurseryman hardly looked up from his paper, which, by now, he had taken the precaution of turning to page four.

'Ah, a very good morning, Rick,' the Reverend Meek enthused and the glass panes in the conservatory seemed to rattle with the decibels of his delivery. For the pastor had never seen any need to change the volume of his voice to suit the numbers of his audience, their status, their environment, be it at home, street or church, or his physical distance from them at the time of the utterance. All was equal in the sight of the Reverend Meek, which, while it made him avidly popular with the deaf or those about to become so, also rendered him somewhat of an embarrassment to those with all their faculties – especially if their living rooms were none too generous.

'Morning, Vicar. I told you, she's out. Shopping.'

The Reverend Meek insinuated his thin gangling frame into one of the canvas chairs the nurseryman kept by the side of his counter; chairs he had bought five years ago when he had still been thinking of branching out from plants to garden furniture.

'A very good morning to you, Rick,' the pastor continued, licking his lean lips, as if to revive them, 'because, for once, I haven't called to see your dear wife, but your esteemed self.'

Reluctantly, Rick set aside his newspaper.

'Oh yes, and what can I be doing for you, then? Some nice arrangements for your altar, perhaps? Thelma can make some up directly she's back. You know how good she is with those big sprays of flowers. Like the ones she did for you at Easter, remember? Or maybe, you'd like a nice bunch of flowers for yourself?'

He pointed a stubby, grubby finger towards some cut flowers arranged none too decorously in buckets on the floor by the door.

'Got some really nice chrysanths in fresh this morning. Or if you don't fancy those, how about some dahlias? All colours and every bloom guaranteed earwig-free . . .'

The Reverend held up a rather blue and bony hand and smiled beneficently.

'All very admirable, Rick, I'm sure. You seem to have a fine selection for the time of year. Very fine. But this morning, I've just dropped by to . . .'

'I've told you, Vicar, she's gone out,' the nurseryman muttered.

'No, no, no, you've got me wrong, Rick. I have come about flowers, but not for today.' He leaned forward in the somewhat rickety chair and pushed his frameless glasses back up his nose. 'And not quite in the quantities, perhaps, you have in mind.'

Rick sat back from the counter and patted at a loose thread in his faded sweater.

'Don't sell singles. Except roses, that is. No profit in it.'

'There'll be plenty of profit, my dear chap, in what I have in the back of my mind.'

The nurseryman frowned. 'What would that be then, Vicar?'

Meek ferreted in a side pocket of his fading black jacket and took out a newspaper cutting which he carefully unfolded and handed across the counter. Rickett perused it for a moment in silence, then, still frowning, handed the piece of paper back.

'Read all about that some time ago, I did. It's really my wife who'll be interested in his coming, not me.'

Again, the blue hand was held aloft.

'Now don't be so hasty. I know you and your wife

hold rather different views on our Beloved Saviour and the importance of the work of our little church, but what I'm about to say now has little or nothing to do with religion or worship.'

The nurseryman prodded his finger towards the piece of paper now reposing on the Reverend's lap.

'But you can't tell me that clipping's not all about religion, now can you? The famous Bobby Quick coming to Britain for the first time.' His small, but fleshy, mouth broke into the semblance of a smile. 'Unless, of course, Vicar, you don't really reckon evangelists like him and that there Billy Graham. Think they're more show business than religion, eh?'

Meek sat back in his chair and was starting to regret having called in at the nursery. If it hadn't been for Thelma Rickett, who helped him organise so many of the church events during the year, he probably would not be sitting here about to offer her husband what could well be a lucrative opportunity. For he had never liked the man. He couldn't really think of anybody who did. Uncharitable thought, but that's just the way it was. Everyone said that the reason Rickett's nursery had never really prospered – it was the same very modest size now as when it had started some fifteen years before – could be traced to the disagreeable personality of its owner. It was no real wonder his wife had found her salvation in church affairs. So Meek guessed he owed her husband something, for the parish of St Matthew would certainly be the poorer without the good works of the devout Thelma.

'No, no, my dear chap, I'm afraid you misinterpret me. Of course, I have to admire phenomena like Bobby Quick and Billy Graham. They have spread the word of our good Lord to more people across the world than probably any before them. If it requires an element of show business to attract the uncertain, the unhappy, the lost, into the wide, comforting arms of Christ, then I am the last person to object or criticise. Each of us carries out God's work in our own distinct ways. Mine is but a humble parish compared to theirs . . .'

By now Rickett had lost all interest in what his visitor was saying and impatiently toyed with a chewed Biro that lay on the counter. The tapping, as intended, brought the vicar back to his point.

'. . . but that's another story. Ah yes. But now let me get back to why I came by . . .'

'I'm not stopping you,' the nurseryman muttered, half under his breath.

Meek sat forward in his chair once more. 'Flowers, Rick. Masses of them. When Bobby Quick comes down to hold his big rally in Hallowes, he will undoubtedly appreciate the finest floral arrangements we in the South West can offer. Indeed, I have already been in touch with one of his aides, who is already in London and he has accepted my little idea with enthusiasm – that the parish of St Matthew should be responsible for finding and providing the flowers for the great day. It is the least we can do to welcome such a famous evangelist to our town.'

Rickett looked up. 'And you thought I might be able to help.'

Meek nodded. 'Maybe not for everything, you understand. The rally field we have in mind is vast, as you know. And the aide tells me the platforms they will be bringing down are of Hollywood size and magnificence. They'll take some decorating.'

The nurseryman chewed at the end of the Biro.

'Think I'm not big enough?'

'Well . . . you know . . . we're talking a lot of flowers.'

'You mentioned funding. Just who's going to pay for all this, then?'

'Ah yes. Well, for a start, I'm hoping my parishioners will turn up trumps and reach deep into their pockets. It's not every day we have a chance like this. Then, I plan to hold a number of special church events, jumble sales and the like, before and after the rally, which should raise . . .'

'You're talking hundreds, Vicar. The amount of flowers you've mentioned could set you back thousands.'

Meek held up his hands in mock horror.

'Oh, indeed. I do hope we don't let things run away to quite that extent. It's one of the reasons I thought of you, Rick.'

'I ain't cutting prices for no one. Can't afford to. Barely cover me expenses as it is. That Bobby Quick is as wealthy as ruddy Croesus. Seen a picture of his house in California in a magazine. Makes Buckingham Palace look like a mud hut.'

He wagged his pen at the visitor. 'What's more, Vicar, if I get involved, I'll need paying in advance. I can't wait for no jumble sales after the rally. Cash up front, or I'm afraid it's no go. Sorry and all that.'

'I quite understand. I wouldn't ask you to provide anything for which money could not be found.'

Meek unfolded his bones from the chair. 'So can I take it, you'd be prepared to supply some of the flowers for this momentous event?'

'If I know what you want, yeh. And cash with order. Do me best.'

The vicar moved towards the conservatory door.

'Many thanks, Rick. I'll let you know. Meanwhile, do give my respects to your wife and say I was sorry to miss her. I'm sure she will be delighted you may be supplying the flowers. And no doubt she'll be anxious to do some of the arranging, when the time comes. It's not long now.'

'Yeh. Okay.'

The nurseryman watched through the window, as the vicar graunched his Marina into gear and shuddered out back to the road. Then he looked at his watch. His wife would be back in under an hour, so he just had time to make the phone call he had been planning.

Locking the conservatory door, he went into the

cottage. From a broom cupboard he took out a long bamboo spider broom with feathers on its end. Then he mounted the narrow staircase and went into a small spare bedroom. Using the bamboo handle of the spider broom, he prodded under the shallow legs of a menacingly large Victorian wardrobe until a magazine with a half naked girl on its cover slid across the carpet. Picking it up, he turned to one of the back pages, made a mental note of one of the telephone numbers mentioned in a lurid advertisement, then, replacing the magazine, made his way quickly downstairs to the telephone.

It took some moments for the call to connect. Rickett used the time to prepare himself. These calls were far too expensive to waste a second of them.

Whilst Thomas Tully was busy reloading, Annabel Craven looked around the bland walls of the tiny studio. Really, she wouldn't be seen dead in a tatty place like *Click* – it's very name made her cringe – if it weren't for the rapidly growing reputation of its young owner. Certainly, the portraits he had taken of some of her female friends, none of them beauties, had been both dramatic and surprisingly flattering, quite clearly due to his creativity rather than that of God, their maker. Due to his insistence on always photographing his female models in black and white – 'the crudeness of colour I reserve exclusively for the cruder sex,' he always jibed – and using heavy contrast lighting, Thomas Tully succeeded in endowing his subjects with a mystery and allure that used to be the preserve of the great Hollywood portrait photographers in the thirties and forties. What he did not confess to his female clients was that the use of black and white film enabled him to retouch away on the prints almost every imperfection they might possess, from spots to scars, to lines and bumps and even excess avoirdupois. Indeed, were it known, his professional magic lay more in his skill with an air-brush than with camera or lights, though his professional charm certainly aided putting his subjects at their ease and giving of their, albeit imperfect, best.

'Right. I think we're ready to go again.'

A broad smile surfaced from below the Hasselbladt – a smile whose undoubted challenge somewhat unnerved Annabel Craven. She wasn't used to one of the main weapons in her own armoury being used against her.

'Same kind of thing?' she asked, rather lamely, re-adopting the languorous pose on the *chaise-longue*, her head against the scroll of the bolster and her long bleached hair caressing its side.

'May need a comb now,' she added, but he was by her side before she knew it. A hand brushed against the top of her thigh and she was acutely aware he had little need to actually touch her.

'Move across a little, can you?' He looked down at her and she knew the plunging neckline of her black, silk evening dress was at its most revealing from that angle. But she didn't really mind. Quite the reverse. If a young man, who couldn't be more than twenty-four or five, rather fancied her at thirty-two, then what the hell. It wasn't as if he were unattractive and unable, as her husband would term it, to 'pull' anyone young or beautiful. Again, quite the reverse. In her book, and that of many others, Thomas Tully was loaded with both impudent charm and looks and, like his photographs, reminded her of the movies. His dark hair was as oiled and sleek as any Tom Cruise, his eyes as brooding as those of Jeremy Irons and his large mouth with its coldly amused slant, as wicked as any Douglas, father or son.

'Like this?' she asked softly, shifting her slim body further across the *chaise-longue*.

This time his hand touched the bareness of her shoulder.

'Further down.'

Fingers increased the pressure. She did as he bid, the silk of her dress riding up to reveal more leg.

'Far enough?'

She saw him nod, then he disappeared, to re-emerge

kneeling beside her, his face now dramatically close to her own.

'It needs stroking,' he whispered.

'Stroking?' she repeated, her eyes showing a glint of alarm. 'What . . . ?'

'Your hair,' he smiled back. 'Needs stroking. Rather than combing, I mean.' He went on, 'Combs leave sort of railway lines in hair. Too regular. Too unnatural. Mechanical. When I'm in this close, I want hair to look . . . like merging strands of silk, woven rather than regulated, soft and sensuous . . . do you know what I mean?'

She had a distinct feeling she knew what he meant.

'But the comb first,' he went on, 'just to arrange your tresses over the edge of the couch. Then comes the stroking.'

He used the comb as smoothly as he used words and, as he did so, his eyes hardly left her own. Annabel wondered how many of her friends might have ended up using this *chaise* for rather more than posing. After all, most of their husbands had long become bores and there was no denying the virile attraction of this young and talented man. As for herself, had she not been currently up to rather more than her ears with her lawyer, why then . . . ? But the thought was idle and very soon she had a suspicion she might have to close her shutter on Thomas Tully, before things developed too far. But for the moment, the biplay held a certain amusement.

'Doing well, Mr Tully?' she smiled.

'I like to think so.'

She bet he did.

'I meant your business. You're getting quite a reputation in Hallowes.'

He put the comb back in his pocket and proceeded to stroke her long blond hair with practised fingers. Each movement was hypnotic in its slow deliberation, as, no doubt, he intended it to be.

'I get by.' Again the Rhett Butler slant of a grin.

Annabel sighed to herself. Oh, it would really be all too easy. And besides, she and Sebastian, her lawyer, had not had a chance to be together for well over a week now. Whilst there weren't too many things physical that Annabel Craven baulked at, making love in the back seat of an XJ6 or indeed any car, was one of them. Sebastian had to be kept waiting until he could spare a few hours to take her away from Hallowes to a hotel – which was not often enough for either of them. But in her book, sex was like money. It was too good to waste on a five minute fling.

Tully's fingers stopped stroking and descended to rest on the bareness of her shoulder.

'Your hair is almost as smooth as your skin . . .' he began, but she stopped him.

'I have a lunch appointment soon. Shouldn't we be getting on? Don't forget I have to change out of this little number before I go.'

He removed his hand.

'You should stay as you are forever. There are just a few women who are made always to be in the most elegant of clothes . . .'

She laughed. 'What a delightful male fantasy. The languid beauty who never does a stroke of anything, save luxuriate and recline on equally elegant furniture, waiting for . . .'

She stopped suddenly, as she realised where her words were leading. Tully, however, pursued the thought to the end.

'. . . her lover to return.'

She reached out and touched his shoulder. 'Or a photographer to return to his camera. I've told you I have a lunch date.'

Tully rose from his knees and reluctantly returned behind his camera.

'You could have lunch with me,' he observed, as he scanned the viewfinder. 'Then it would give us more time to try out some different poses.'

She could imagine what some of those positions might well be like.

'Let's see how these come out first, Mr Tully, before we try anything else. I'm not so vain, I need myself photographed in every pose under the sun.'

He didn't look up from his camera.

'You look divine. You have an incredible face. The camera will love you. It can't help but do so with those incredibly dark eyes, your high cheek bones and . . .'

'Pouting mouth,' she interrupted.

He looked up. 'Pouting? Rubbish. Who said it pouted? Your look is made by your mouth. It's full and sensual, yet very . . . how can I put it? . . . classy.'

'Thank you, kind sir. It's not what dear husband thinks.'

'He the "pouter" man?'

'In the main.'

'He doesn't deserve you.'

'He's not going to have me much longer. We're getting divorced.'

She detected the glint in Tully's eyes. The glint she had noticed in the eyes of almost every man to whom she had imparted news of her divorce proceedings. It was as if the word 'divorce' triggered the start of some open mating season in the male imagination.

'When's it come through?'

'Oh, not for some time yet. I have only recently started proceedings. Still living in the old family home.'

'But I thought,' he began, but she cut him off with a smile.

'Separate rooms, don't worry. Now would you please get on? I'm stifling under these lights.'

After she had gone, Tully took his reels of exposed film to the dark room, but found he was in no mood to start work on the protracted task of developing. Annabel Craven had disturbed him too much. More than he'd like to admit to himself, for 'older' women – that category started early for him, around the age of twenty-eight to thirty – did not normally interest him and certainly did not leave him feeling distinctly frustrated, as now. For Thomas Tully liked his conquests to be younger than his own twenty-six years and, preferably, much younger. Indeed, sometimes as young as the law would allow.

His present girlfriend was, in that way, almost ideal. At least, physically. Bettina Blair was, in fact, still at school, having just taken her GCSE examinations that summer. Though still only sixteen and a virgin when he had met her at a local dance held in aid of an Ethiopian Appeal Fund, she had proved to be a speedy and avid learner of every sexual trick he had to offer. To such an extent that sometimes, now, she shocked him rather than the other way about. And it wasn't just her seeming insatiability or her constant willingness to experiment. It was her whole attitude. Whilst he was delighted in a way with the open pleasure she displayed during their love-making, her accompanying language, of late, had become almost gross in its crudity and, on occasion, he had been terrified lest her shouted expletives and injunctions would be heard through the walls of the modest flat he occupied above his studio in Hallowes' Fore Street.

Still, Bettina suited Tully well, for the moment. That is, unless she opened her big mouth to her parents, or . . . He crossed his fingers at the last thought, then looked at his watch. After twelve. She should have got in touch with the doctor by now. That is, if she'd kept her word and feigned illness that morning, so that her parents would let her stay home from school. They both went out to work, her mother to serve behind the counter of a fancy goods shop, her father to Payless on the industrial estate, where he was the warehouse manager. So no one would hear Bettina pick up the phone or hear her conversation. Or, indeed, the phone ringing, for that matter. He decided to work out a little of his frustration by making it do just that.

'Oh, it's you, Tom.'

Precocious as her body and physical practices might be, her voice was still that of an immature schoolgirl.

'Who did you think it might be then?' he chuckled.

'You know.'

'No. Tell me.'

There was a pause, then she whispered, 'The doctor.'

'Why are you whispering, Bettina? Aren't your parents out?'

'Yes, they're out.'

'So, why . . . ?'

'Because . . . that's why.'

'Not like you to be so . . . shy. What's the matter?'

'Nothing. Yet.'

'What do you mean?' he asked anxiously. 'Something go wrong?'

'Not really. It's just that when I rang the doctor's home, he wasn't in and his wife answered.'

'So, where's the worry, love?'

'Nowhere, I suppose. But she said Dr Stride never sees patients at his home. Only in the surgery.'

'So you rang the surgery?'

'Not yet.'

'Why not?'

'I'm a bit, sort of, embarrassed at going in there. There'll be people and nurses and things. Besides, someone might see me.'

Tully thought for a moment. 'Did you tell the doctor's wife why you wanted to see him?'

'No.'

'Why not?'

'I don't know.'

'You should have.'

'Well, I didn't, that's all.'

'Why don't you ring her again and explain what you want?'

A pause. Then. 'I'd rather speak to him, than her. She might disapprove.'

'Not her business. You're over sixteen.'

'Yeh, well . . . er . . .'

'So what are you going to do? We can't go on like we are. It's too risky. You hate rubbers and you can't get the pill any other way but seeing a doctor, so . . .'

'Couldn't we just go on the way we do now? I mean, most of the month I can't get into trouble anyway. And the other days . . .'

Tully's tone changed. 'Now, pull yourself together, Bettina. This isn't like you. Ring the surgery at lunch time and make an appointment for this evening. Tell your parents you're going to the movies or round to a friend's house or something. If you like, I'll pick you up at the end of your road and take you to the surgery and wait outside.'

Her mood brightened. 'You will?'

'Scout's honour.'

'But still, someone might see me.'

'So, if you meet someone you know in the surgery, tell them you've hurt your wrist or something. They will never know otherwise.'

She sighed. 'Oh well, if you think it'll be all right.'

'It'll be all right.' He changed the subject. 'What have you been doing?'

'Sitting around. And you?'

'Had that Annabel Craven woman in. You know, the wife of that property developer. The one whose latest plans are causing all the ruction.'

'She's not bad looking. I remember seeing her picture in the local paper, when they opened the new telephone building.' Then she added, 'Was she good looking?'

'Not bad. For her age.'

'And for your age, you dirty . . .'

'Ah, ah. None of that. Strictly professional, me. Business and pleasure.'

She laughed. 'Don't give me that. Don't forget I've seen some of your pictures – the ones that don't get in your window. By the way, you said you'd take some of those of me one day.'

'So I will.'

'When?'

'Tell you what. If you can get the whole evening off tonight, we'll have a session after we come back from the surgery.'

'Promise?'

'Promise.'

'Want me to bring anything with me?'

'Such as?'

'Well, you know . . .'

'Oh, I see what you mean. No. Just come as nature made you. All the rest of the . . . er . . . props, I'll be only too happy to provide.'

Chapter Two

Priscilla Marsh arranged the last avocado in its tissue paper and stood back to admire her work. She had to admit that her employer, Penny Seymour-Jones, was right in insisting that higher priced items needed to look special and there was nothing like tissue paper to lend that special touch. Especially as the higher priced items in Hallowes Health Farm were, in Priscilla's view, astronomically priced. Indeed, everything in the shop cost well over the odds. But, surprisingly, it did not seem to affect trade. Hallowes was that kind of town. It was renowned for the high proportion of its inhabitants who were into 'alternative' just about everything – medicine, food, education, culture, crafts, entertainment, dress, you name it, it had to be alternative to the norm. So organically grown food was *sine qua non* and had been for years before it had become the fashion elsewhere. And the sticker 'organic' didn't come cheaply – especially in Penny Seymour-Jones' establishment.

Priscilla went back behind the counter and wiped her hands on a damp flannel that she kept for such purposes. For her employer frowned on her continually going into the back room to wash. She didn't really know why. Maybe Penny thought she would pry into the account books that were kept there or maybe take the occasion to make private calls on the shop telephone. Either way, Priscilla felt a trifle hurt. After all, she was not like any ordinary employee. She had known Penny for years. When her own husband had been alive, they had gone to each other's houses for dinner. Played tennis together, croquet on the lawn. Even, occasionally, gone to the theatre together. And not just in Plymouth or Exeter either. Twice they had gone in her husband's car all the way up to London.

But since her husband's death two years ago and, out of loneliness Priscilla had offered to help out in the shop, their relationship had changed. Oh yes, she realised there would have to be some adjustment because, after all, one of the two had to be the boss, but somehow the payment and receipt of wages had taken all the warmth from their friendship. She had spent many evenings trying to figure out why and the nearest she could get to a possible explanation rather hurt her – that it was the departure of her husband rather than her arrival at the shop that had triggered the change. Penny was still only just a shade over forty, fifteen years younger than herself and as Priscilla was the first to admit, her friend was considerably more attractive than she had ever been.

She had always known that her husband liked Penny's company and that she always displayed pleasure in his. But Priscilla did not consider for a minute that their relationship had ever gone further than friendship, not so much because she was so certain of her husband, as her suspicion that Penny was probably rather a cold fish at heart. And, in her experience, cold fish liked to swim in the warm ponds of other people's misapprehensions as to their true nature – misapprehensions they'll do everything to engender but . . .

'Finished the avocados?'

Penny Seymour-Jones swept in from the back room, strands of her over-long hair, as almost always, masking one eye.

Priscilla held out a slightly liver-spotted hand to the display.

'Yes. They look quite a good selection today. Only two that were rather bruised.'

'Two too many,' her employer retorted. 'I'm thinking of changing my supplier.'

'Goodalls? But they're always so helpful if you ring up with a problem.'

Penny went over to the display and, quite unnecessarily, started fussing with Priscilla's arrangement.

'They're getting too expensive.'

Priscilla smiled to herself. Whatever any supplier charged, Hallowes Health Farm almost doubled to the consumer, so she suspected the objection to Goodalls lay somewhere other than in their prices.

'Who are you thinking of instead?' she asked.

Penny turned back towards the counter.

'You wouldn't know them.'

'I might do. I've got to know most of the organic suppliers now.'

'New people.'

'Oh? Just started up?'

'Been going a bit, but . . .' Penny's eyes turned to the door. 'Oh my God, look who's coming in.'

Priscilla looked. It was the Drench fellow. Neither of them much liked him. His offices were only three shops down from the Health Farm, so that their chances of avoiding contact for long were slim.

'Afternoon, ladies.'

'Afternoon, William,' Penny replied coolly. 'No one buying any houses today?'

Drench came over and sat at the counter. Even seated, he was almost as tall as Priscilla, a large awkward lump of a man, whom Penny had once described as a bean-bag with legs. A somewhat twisted smile played across his florid and, compared to his body, curiously thin and pointed face.

'Don't see too many people in here jostling for your overpriced merchandise.'

Banter was always the overture to every Drench purchase in their shop and had to be got out of the way as quickly as possible.

'Besides,' he went on, 'what's the good of having

assistants, if you can't take a break every now and again?'

'Anyway,' Penny smirked, 'from what I hear of your plans, William, you'll soon be coining so much money, you will be able to shut up your estate agency for good.'

'Never count my chickens,' Drench retorted, in a tone that clearly indicated he wished to draw a curtain over that particular subject. But Penny was in no mood to oblige.

'Little bird told me that your mother is planning to get up a petition against . . .'

Drench closed his rather blood flecked eyes and cut in, 'My mother is a law unto herself. The whole world knows that.' He looked up at Priscilla. 'Now, if you ladies don't mind, I'd like to get back to why I came in here.'

'Nuts, William?' Priscilla offered, knowing Drench's strong partiality for chewing peanuts at every opportunity.

'Not this time. I'm not buying for me. It's for the old dragon. I'm going up to see her this evening, so she rang and asked me to get her some stuff.' He took a short list from his pocket.

'A jar of that coffee substitute she has. Don't know the name, but if it's any guidance, it tastes like sewage water. Then a packet of that special muesli, a jar of honey, oh, some organic potatoes, a cauliflower and, what's this, oh yes, a can of ozone friendly plant spray. Hell, it's people like my mother who keep you people in the lap of luxury.'

Penny stroked the lank strands from her eye, so that Drench could appreciate the coldness of her stare in full measure.

'You are the one with the BMW and the large house, Mr Drench.'

Priscilla took Drench's list from him and busied herself amongst the shelves, putting up his order. Arguments with customers were not part of her style.

'Come on, Penny. You don't do so badly. You can't do, with the prices you charge. And I bet, if truth be known, half your ruddy stuff is about as organic as a Wimpey hamburger. One day the penny will drop with your customers.' He chuckled and looked across at Priscilla, her employer having retired smartly into the back room at his remarks.

'Get it? "Penny dropping"? You know. Penny, Penelope . . .'

Priscilla forced a smile and bent down to get a carrier bag for Drench's order.

'I think I've got it all, William. Do give my regards to your mother when you see her.'

After he had taken the carrier bag from her, she stopped him, 'By the way, did I hear you say your mother rang you? Does this mean she's on the phone now? If so, she can telephone in her orders direct and we can deliver the stuff in the 2CV. Save you bothering.'

Drench sniffed.

'Well, as you know, she's never wanted the blasted phone. Doesn't hold with any mechanical contrivance that makes life easier. Never has. But now she's over eighty . . .'

Priscilla shook her head. 'My, my, is she really? You'd never know to meet her. She always acts so lively and looks so brown and . . .'

'. . . I insisted she had it put in,' Drench went on as if Priscilla had never spoken. 'Lord, the fight I had to get her to agree. But none of us are getting any younger. I'm the wrong end of my forties now and can't always be traipsing up to her place just to see if she's still alive and kicking. Isn't as if I've got a wife or anything to check on her sometimes during the day. And she won't have anyone living with her. Not that I'd wish that fate on anyone, God knows. Anyway, long shot is, she finally agreed to have one put in. But only if it was a certain model. You just won't believe which, either.'

He shook his head, then leaned confidentially across

the counter, his breath speaking of the pints he had absorbed over lunch.

'Donald flaming Duck. Gor . . .'

'Love a duck,' Priscilla beamed. Drench, once again, ignored her sally.

'Muttered something about, "At least it is a bird. But why don't the telephone people make phones in the shape of real birds, like owls, eagles and seagulls?" I can tell you, she comes out with some priceless gems sometimes.' He tapped his head. 'Senile dementia, wouldn't wonder. But they've got a new name for it now, haven't they?'

'Alzheimer's disease,' Priscilla offered quietly, 'but I can't think your mother . . .'

'Got it in one,' Drench chuckled, as he made for the door. 'Can't think, my mother.'

Sebastian Fanshawe moved away from the french windows. He had never liked storms and the evening sky was now threatening what the weathermen had definitely not mentioned in their forecasts for the South West.

As he sat down, opposite his wife, in an over-stuffed armchair made in the days of easy living, the first rumble of thunder rolled round the hills that surrounded Hallowes. His wife, Prue, looked up.

'Not another one,' she sighed.

'Sounds like it,' her husband replied and settled back to finish *The Times*, which, due to an unexpectedly prolonged court hearing, he had not had a chance to catch up with all day.

'I wish Sophie wasn't out,' Prue fretted. 'She's worse than you are with storms.'

Fanshawe did not bother to comment. In his view, his wife was always fussing inordinately about their ten-year-old daughter. Indeed, she fussed over just about everything. He should have noticed that before he married her. On reflection, all the signs had been evident even then. But he'd cared to interpret her over protective attitude as evidence of a girl who really cared about life, her fellow man and woman, and especially about him. He'd found her solicitous attentions flattering, as an impecunious young man articled to a Hallowes firm of solicitors. For, after all, she came from a much better-found family than his own, the Montagues of Dartmouth, who could trace their land-owning pedigree as far back as the sixteen-fifties and who still farmed over a thousand acres along and around the River Dart. And her rich, red hair and pale-skinned beauty had attracted, to his knowledge, more eligible suitors than himself.

He cast a quick look at his wife, from the top of *The Times*. Though she was still only thirty-six, two years younger than himself, her pale and now heavily freckled and lined features could be those of a woman ten years older. He should have taken heed of a remark made many years ago now by an old school friend of his; 'Redheads don't make lasting bedheads'. But he had to admit, she had been devilish attractive in their early days. And better in bed than any girl he had known before her. How was he to have known that her ardour would fade with her beauty, until now about all they enjoyed together was their daughter, Sophie.

'Do you think I should ring?' his wife persisted. Really, she found her husband's indifference quite maddening.

'What for? Sophie is perfectly safe over at the Stride's house. Anyway, it's under an hour until they'll be dropping her back. You know how she likes being with Mark. Don't spoil their fun.'

'I'd rather she was home, if there's going to be another storm.'

Fanshawe put down his paper irritably. 'Come on, Prue, don't be silly. Even if Sophie does get a bit frightened, she couldn't be in better hands than those of a doctor's wife. Hell, Mary must have had enough experience with her husband's patients.'

For once, she had to admit, her husband might have a point. She looked across at him. Drat, now he was spoiling everything by wearing his smug, 'I told you so' look. In the last few years, since success had come to Fanshawe and Grebe Solicitors, her husband had developed a whole series of looks and phrases, all of which, however, were based on smugness. There was the smug 'Oh, I wouldn't say the practice was doing that well', the smug 'Oh, yes, I suppose it is a nice house, now you mention it' look, the even smugger 'Ah, don't be fooled by appearances, my dear. Inside I sometimes feel a thousand years old.' This last was unfailingly accompanied by a dry chuckle and inevitably followed by her husband paying an indecent amount of attention to the decorous prompter of the knee-jerk reaction.

And what pained Prue Fanshawe more than somewhat was that her husband had, indeed, kept a good deal of his youthful attraction. His lean handsome face bore hardly a line, his hair nary a streak of grey. He was like those actors you view on the screen year after year, but who never seem to change. Prue took some malicious solace in the thought that maybe, when the physical decline came, it might be as total as had been the case with some of her screen idols. One day they're juvenile leads, the next senile has-beens.

She was startled out of her thoughts by a crack of thunder that rattled the french windows.

'Won't be long before it's overhead,' she said, watching for his reaction.

Her husband rose from his chair.

'I think I'll get a drink. Would you like one?'

She shook her head.

'No, thanks. I'm fine,' she smiled.

Fanshawe went to the Art Deco cocktail cabinet by the door and poured himself a stiff Scotch. Storms unnerved him. Had done ever since, in his childhood, he'd seen a cow struck by lightning in a field. He could still smell the burning flesh.

'I don't know why we're getting all these thunder-storms. After all, it's late September. Not August any more.'

'They're probably only local. Mary Stride told me that last week's storm didn't even reach Torquay. No one in Torbay, apparently, had a drop of rain. Just saw the lightning over our way, that's all.'

As if on cue, a vivid flash zigzagged from the dark clouds outside the window and was almost immediately followed by a crack of thunder that seemed to make the whole house shake.

Fanshawe gulped at his Scotch and looked away.

'Hope the rain isn't too bad this time,' Prue said, reflectively. 'Last week's almost put paid to the last of the flowers. And I'm a bit worried about the dahlias.'

'Blast the dahlias,' her husband muttered. 'They can look after themselves.'

She shrugged. That had rapidly become her husband's philosophy. Everyone and everything could look after themselves. Self-sufficiency. Stand on your own two feet. Chin up. Back straight. Don't look back.

Suddenly, she heard the telephone ringing in the hall. She got up from her chair.

'I'll go. Bet that's Sophie, saying she wants to come home. If so, I'll go and fetch her. Save Mary turning out in this weather.'

Fanshawe went back to his chair. If his wife was fool enough to get the car out on an evening like this, so be it. After the long day he'd had in court, he was in no mood to offer to go himself.

To his surprise, Prue came back into the room almost immediately.

'It's not Sophie,' she said quietly.

'Who is it?'

'It's . . . er . . . Mrs Craven.'

Fanshawe did his best to hide his shock.

'Mrs Craven? What does she want?'

'To speak to you. She apologises for interrupting our

evening, but something has just occurred to her that might affect her divorce proceedings.'

Fanshawe unfolded from his chair as nonchalantly as he could. He did not dare let his wife detect his impatience to get to the telephone.

'Damn. I hate clients who phone me at home. That's the trouble with a small place like Hallowes. Everybody knows where everybody else lives.'

He went out into the hall, being careful to shut the sitting-room door firmly behind him.

'Seb?'

He cleared his throat. 'Mrs Craven, I must point out I make it a rule not to receive professional calls at home.'

'What's the matter?' Annabel whispered. 'Can your wife hear you?'

He cupped his hand over the mouthpiece and whispered back, 'I told you never to ring me at home.'

'I know, I know,' she said hurriedly. 'But when the storm started, I thought of you. Remember last week?'

He remembered the last week only too well. The storm had broken just after they had checked in at the motel outside Exeter. They had only been in bed a few minutes . . .

Fanshawe glanced back at the sitting-room door.

'Mrs Craven, perhaps now you have phoned, you could give me just a brief account of what is troubling you and we can make an appointment to discuss the rest, maybe tomorrow or the next day.'

'She is listening, isn't she?'

He cupped his hand once more.

'No. But she's in the next room. Now hurry up, Annabel, and tell me what's the trouble.'

'Nothing's the trouble, Seb. Except we're not together . . . It's just that now I know how much thunderstorms upset you . . .'

The scene of last week came disturbingly back to him. She had been surprisingly good about it. Even joked, after one particular loud crash of thunder, that if she'd known he suffered from the clap, she'd never have agreed to go to bed with him. But none of her comforting words or manual or oral efforts made any difference. Their love-making, like the weather that afternoon, had proved a wash-out.

'I just wanted you to know I was thinking of you.'

He looked again at the door. 'That's kind of you, Mrs Craven, I appreciate it.' Then he whispered close to the mouthpiece, 'Love you, Annabel.'

'Love you. By the way, I had my photographs taken this morning. Should see some prints tomorrow. I'm getting Tully to print a small one for your wallet.'

'All right, Mrs Craven. I'll look into that tomorrow.'

'What time? I can't wait.'

'It won't be until very late in the day, Mrs Craven, I'm afraid. I've got to go to Exeter.'

'Same motel?' she breathed. 'The storm will be long over by then and we can make up for last time. Hell, Seb, I wish they'd get that video facility finished at the new Telephone Exchange. Then we could see each other too. Guess where I am at the moment?'

'Look, Mrs Craven, I'll bear in mind what you've said and I will try to see you about it tomorrow.' Then he whispered urgently, 'That's quite enough, darling.'

But she ignored him and went on, 'I'm in bed. And guess what I'm doing with my other hand . . .'

He took a deep breath. 'Good night, Mrs Craven. I would hold everything until you've seen me.'

As he replaced the receiver, he heard her breathe, 'Too late . . .'

Chapter Three

William Drench switched his wipers to fast mode. But even so, the screen still became almost opaque between their now manic flicks from side to side. The groan and click of their cranking irritated him. In fact, everything about his evening's expedition irritated him. For he knew that when he reached his destination and was indoors safe from the rain, he was in for another giant storm that wouldn't blow away in a hurry.

Lightning lit up his thin, sparing features, as it flared across the hills around Hallowes. Drench heard the thunder roll above the sound of his wipers, and the splashing of his tyres in the fast-running streams that now coursed down each side of the road, desperate to find a river into which to rid themselves of their force.

'Hell,' he muttered under his breath. Why the hell had he been afflicted with the curse of a mother like 'Dotty Enid', as she was known in the town. A woman, nay dragon, nay witch, who had cast rocks in his path ever since he could remember. And rocks were not the only things she could cast, according to some.

'Hell and damnation,' Drench spat out, as he could feel the BMW's rear wheels lose grip and slide on the bend. He eased back on the accelerator and the car, after a twitch, resumed its correct line. It would be just his luck to have an accident, before he had a chance to do battle with his mother. God, he could just picture her in her dilapidated and unkempt cottage, her rheumy eyes alight with malice, willing and willing and willing some hellish event to intervene and stop their night's meeting.

But he was going to beat her this time, as he had beaten her over the sale of the land for the new telephone building. No threats of mounting petitions or cutting him out of her will would cut any ice. Nor, her favourite trick, of bringing down every curse upon his head, if he proceeded. After all, she had long since overplayed her card of his 'going to Hell', if he went against her wishes.

Even in his childhood, he had never really believed her prophecy of fire and brimstone; even so he had looked behind his back on occasion, after having transgressed one of her 'Hell bent' rules, like lying to her about any subject. School results; where he was going; where he'd been; why he was late; even whether he'd washed behind his ears. Or swearing; being unkind to animals, people, even ruddy plants in the garden. Or most heinous of the tickets to Hell – stealing. He could still feel the heat of her curse, when she had discovered a shilling too many in his school trouser pocket. Well, he smiled to himself. I've made many an extra shilling since then, despite her. And the old fool still called it stealing. Well, that was her problem. But tonight, unfortunately, she was to be his . . .

He swung the BMW off the road and down an unmade-up track to the right, flanked by high and untrimmed hedges. For a quarter of a mile the car thudded into water filled pot holes, before the silhouette of a small, low cottage cast its outline against the storm-illuminated sky. Drench stopped outside, hunched his raincoat collar up around his head and ran from the car to the worm-holed front door. To his anger, he found it locked, so he pounded on the ancient oak with his fist. As usual, his mother kept him waiting.

She said nothing as she opened up. He brushed past her and hung his now sodden raincoat on a hook on the back of the door. When he looked back at her, she said in her croaky voice, 'You can see what the heavens think of you.'

He followed her tall and still surprisingly upright figure

into what passed as her sitting-room – a stone flagged area on which lay two threadbare rugs. Across one corner was an open fireplace, in which smouldered the remains of some logs. Pulled up in front of it was an old Lloyd-Loom settee that had, at one time, been pale blue. On its faded and none too clean cushions reposed a dark and hairy bundle that perked up its ears at four human footfalls rather than two. It gave a disdainful stretch, then flopped on to the floor and disappeared into the hall.

Drench caught his mother's expression.

'Don't say it,' he said irritably, then mimicked her voice. 'Cats are choosy.'

She ignored him and sat back at one end of the settee, trying to stifle a groan. She had no wish for her son to detect how bad the arthritis in her hip had actually become.

Drench remained standing and looked out of the small latticed window at the stair-rodded rain.

'Well,' she began, 'you've got me to see you. Aren't you going to say something?'

He glanced back at her. In the soft glow from the old oak standard lamp – the only illumination in the room – his mother's face had lost some of its severity and whilst its expression at no time in her life could ever be termed truly soft or benevolent, tonight it suddenly seemed as near matching those adjectives as he could ever remember. In a moment, he was caught off balance, until he remembered how subtly clever his mother could be, especially when she feared that she might be facing defeat.

'It needn't take long, Mother. There's little to discuss.' He took a deep breath. 'The development of Widow's Field is going ahead. Craven and I had assurances from the council this morning that no amount of agitation – from any source – will cause them to change their minds. The planning permission stands.'

With a shrug, he came to stand by the settee.

'So that's that.'

A slow smile grew across her lined face, as she looked up at him.

'So you've done your sums, have you, William?'

'Sums?' he queried. 'Well, of course we've done our sums.'

'I mean *you*, William Drench. Not you and George Craven.'

'Of course I've done my separate calculations. If you're trying to snipe at me for making a bit of money out of the development, then just remember the houses we'll be building will be of benefit to more than just me and Craven. Hallowes is crying out for more and better housing. There has been precious little development in the town since the sixties. And then there wasn't goddamn much, as you well know. People have got to have somewhere to live, Mother. Otherwise, Hallowes will just die away as a town and on its bloody gravestone will be written, "Killed by Enid Drench and all those demented conservationists like her".'

He ran out of breath and inspiration. She looked up at him.

'Have you finished?'

He turned back to the window and drew the curtains to try to shut out the storm. But whilst he had dimmed the lightning, the thunder still orchestrated their conversation, like drums in the orchestra.

'I take it by your silence that you have. In which case, if you'll allow me, I will explain what I meant by your doing your sums.'

His mother's voice had taken on a tone he recognised only too well from childhood and he was ashamed of the pang of fear that ran through him.

'You've weighed things in the balance, haven't you, William? The profit you will make from developing Widow's Field and the money you estimate you might get from me upon my death.'

He didn't dare to look at her.

'Now, don't be absurd.'

'And you reckon it's no contest, don't you? Look at me, William. Don't you?'

'Mother, I'm not going to be dragged into that kind of crazy argument tonight. I only wanted to see you to tell you that the council will not be swayed by anything you and your cranky friends might organise.'

A crack of thunder right overhead loosened some flakes of plaster from the cracked and bulging ceiling. The descending dust lent the room an eerie light.

His mother laughed. 'Is that a good enough answer for you, my son?'

'Oh hell, Mother, don't begin pulling all that mumbo jumbo about us offending the gods or whatever you believe in, by plonking a few houses on a ruddy field.'

She looked hard at her son. 'Know what ruddy really means, William?'

'Oh God, what are you on about now?'

'Ruddy means red, William. Red, do you understand?'

Drench threw his arms in the air. His mother was obviously further round the bend than even he had realised. He could see it would not be long before she would have to go into an old people's home and join the rest of the cracked brigade.

'All right, William,' she went on, 'you'll see. You'll see. I just pray, by then, it won't be far too late. I've told you time and again, Widow's Field isn't any old field . . .'

'You say that about every bloody piece of land around Hallowes. You said it about Starlings Meadow. You more or less said that the world would come to an end if we sold it for the new Telephone Exchange.' He laughed across at her. 'Well, we're all still here, aren't we? More's the pity.'

He pointed across to the Donald Duck telephone standing incongruously on a bamboo table in the far corner.

'What's more, you've personally benefited from it being built too. Push buttons, a hundred number memory, even a damned volume control, so that you can hear us all better. And if you'd bothered, you could have had a video set built in, so that, in a year or two's time, when the system is finished, you could see us all, when you're phoning. And we could see you too. What a bloody treat!'

'I did not want the phone. It was you who persuaded me,' she observed quietly. 'I wanted nothing to do with what happened to Starlings Meadow.'

'All right. All right. But it makes no difference. You're against progress, pure and simple. You're against any kind of development. Anything new or adventurous. You know you are. You'd like Hallowes to be fossilised in the nineteen-thirties or forties. A sort of museum town, where everything is in the past and nothing is in the future.'

He swept his arm around the room.

'Why, look at the way you live. Other than that damned Donald Duck, the last mechanical thing that entered this goddamned place was electricity. Oh, and perhaps that great wooden wireless of yours. You have no Hoover, washing machine, tumble drier, television, video, micro-wave, you name it, you won't have it in the house.'

He went up to her and grabbed her wrist. Pointing at her old fashioned watch, with its scratched and discoloured face, he went on, 'You're like this ancient Ingersoll of yours. You stopped years and years ago. As far back as the war, I wouldn't wonder. What happened, Mother? Did a stray bomb rattle your works about? Snap your hairspring? Or loosen a few too many screws?'.

He let go as he saw her close her eyes, and moved away.

'I'm sorry,' he muttered. 'But you really ask for it sometimes.'

'It's not I who's asking for it,' she murmured, then looked up at him. 'You know, William, you're quite a phenomenon. The older you get, the harsher you are becoming. Usually, time tends to mellow, soften the edges a little. Maybe you would be a bit different if you had someone other than yourself to think about.'

He sighed. 'Oh no, Mother, don't let's get up on that little hobby-horse of yours.'

'You'll regret it one day.'

He laughed. 'I'll regret everything one day, according to you. You just won't believe I'm happy the way I am, will you? I like living on my own. I like having no one other than myself to think about. I'll, no doubt, relish it to my dying day. Living on my own is the secret of my success. I could never have built up my estate agency so fast or so well,with a nagging wife or screaming kids to distract me any second of the day or night. Some people need other people around. I don't. Never have, never will.'

He had never revealed the whole truth to his mother. That he wasn't quite like most other men. Even in the latter days of school, he knew he was different. When other boys started to be lewdly fascinated with everything and anything to do with sex and girls, he had remained as before, aloof and disinterested. In fact, as the years had rolled by, his lack of interest in sex had been compounded by a certain distaste for any expression of sensuality in others. It was the only thing that worried him about George Craven – besides Craven's wife, that is. Her obvious sexuality unnerved him and Drench was thankful when he heard they were to be divorced. However, he doubted whether Craven would remain unattached for long, after his divorce came through.

'So you won't listen to me at all, is that it? The great self sufficient William Drench is hell-bent on developing Widow's Field?' his mother asked, her eyes now turned from him.

'No, great prophet of doom. Hell has nothing to do with it,' he snapped, as he moved towards the door.

'That's as we shall see,' she sighed, but thunder drowned her words.

'Want to see any more?'

Walter Blair looked across at his dumpy wife, who was, as always, knitting away as if her life depended on it.

'Oh, I quite like Michael Caine,' she said, without looking up from her clacking needles. 'Thought you liked Michael Caine.'

Walter Blair picked at a callous on his hand. He had thought he'd left behind humping stuff around in the Payless warehouse, the moment he became manager, but for the last week two of his men had been off ill and he had been obliged to take over some of their manual work. Not that the actual physical effort irked him. After all, he was a big man – 'the John Wayne of Payless', as the cheeky little telephonist had dubbed him and the name had stuck. For even his face had that lean and slightly off-centre look so typical of the Hollywood star – and he had always been very careful to keep himself in good physical condition. If, occasionally, he drank overmuch with his mates, he would always try to compensate for it by working out in his bedroom before going to work. All much to the amusement of his wife, who called his press-ups 'making love to the carpet'. And she'd often threatened to insinuate herself between him and the floor, so that she could occasionally 'get a bit of the benefit'.

Walter looked back at the screen.

'There's Michael Caine and Michael Caine, isn't there? The good stuff they put on earlier than this, my love. I thought this might be a bummer, starting so ruddy late.'

'Well, I like it,' his wife persisted. 'Calms my nerves, it does, after that awful thunderstorm.'

Her husband chuckled. 'That's because you haven't seen any of it.'

'Yes, I have.'

'No, you haven't. You haven't looked up from your knitting once. I've watched you.'

'Can hear, can't I? Anyway, I look up enough to know what's going on.'

Walter picked once more at his hand.

'Well, I think I might go up.'

She looked up for the first time. 'What, and leave me here all on my own?'

'Well, come on up to bed too.'

She resumed knitting the bright pink sweater she was making for her daughter, to go with her skin tight ski-pants.

'You know one of us should stay up until Bettina's back.'

Her husband sniffed and looked at his watch.

'It's past eleven now. She should be back before we've had a chance to go to sleep.'

Margaret Blair pulled at her wool. 'That's as may be. But I'm staying up until she's back. But you can go up, if you want to, seeing as how you've had all that extra to do today at work.'

Walter sighed and relaxed back once more in his over-foamed, over-patterned armchair, which they had bought as part of a suite from a mail-order catalogue.

'No, I'll stay up. Probably fall asleep over this ruddy film, any road.' He folded his arms in front of him to be prepared for just such an eventuality. 'Where did you say she's gone?'

Margaret started another row. 'The Rooks.'

'Rooks?'

'Yes, you know. Her new friend at school. Charlene Rook. She's at the parents'.'

'Oh. They dropping her back, then?'

'So she said. Around eleven, eleven-thirty.'

'Too late, I reckon, on school nights.'

' 'Tisn't a school night, Friday. She can lie in tomorrow.'

'Wish I could.'

'Wish you'd shut up, so that I can hear this film.

Either that or give me the control box, so I can turn the volume up.'

He shut up, then closed his eyes. After a few moments, he started to realise the film did sound better than it looked and that his wife actually did have a point. Mind you, she wasn't often wrong, his Maggie. He reckoned not many men could concede that about their wives – especially after seventeen-odd years of marriage. He was lucky really. Maggie hadn't changed too much in all that time. Character, that is. Still chirpy and energetic, despite the few extra stone she must have put on over the years. But somehow, her roly-polyness suited her. She'd always had a round face, a bit like one of those balloons with big smiles painted on them and now her body kind of matched it. Anyway, Walter rather liked a mother figure of a woman, rather than a matchstick. He couldn't understand why girlie magazines didn't sometimes feature big, bouncy types, instead of the, to him, monotonous diet of slim and characterless nymphets.

He was woken from his reverie by the sound of the phone. Opening his eyes, he groaned up from his chair, turned the volume down on the remote control, then went over to the portable phone on the window-sill.

'That'll be our Bettina, wanting to be picked up, I'll be bound.'

'Just as well we haven't gone up, then.'

He picked up the phone and extended the aerial. His wife watched his face for a clue as to who it might be. But after a few seconds, all he did was raise his eyebrows and give the phone a shake.

'Bad line?'

Walter nodded. 'I can hear a voice. Could be Bettina. But I can hardly hear it for all the ruddy crackle.'

'That you, Bett? . . . Bett, that you . . . ?'

'Give it another tap. Maybe something's loose. Never had this trouble with the old phones.'

He followed his wife's suggestion then, with screwed-up eyes, listened intently.

'Anything?'

He waved a hand. 'Sshh. I'm sure it's Bettina, but with all the crackle . . .'

She waited as patiently as she could and even, for once, stopped knitting, in case her needles made too much noise.

'Bett, I can't understand what you're saying . . . there's too much interference.'

'Get her to ring again.'

'Can you ring again, Bett . . . ring again . . . can you hear me, Bettina? Put down the receiver and . . .'

He looked anxiously across at his wife.

'She won't stop talking, Maggie.'

'What's she saying?'

'Can't make it out. It's like she's talking to someone else.'

His wife got up from her chair and went over to him.

'Well, what's she saying, then? Can you make any of it out?'

'Hang on . . . well, I can only make out bits. She seems to be talking to someone else, like I said, only . . . well, you can't hear the other voice.'

'Crossed line?' She held out a hand for the telephone, but her husband held on to it.

'There . . . I caught that. "Dr Stride", she's just said . . . and now something about being embarrassed . . . about nurses . . . oh, now it's all crackle again.'

This time she managed to take over the phone from her husband.

After a moment or two, he asked anxiously, 'What's happening now?'

'I don't know . . . all seems crazy. Bett. Bettina. Can you hear me? It's Mum. Can you hear me, darling?'

Walter touched her arm, but she shook her head.

'I don't understand it . . . now she's going on about someone might see her and then she said something like, she was sitting around.' She tapped the telephone smartly with her knuckle. 'Here, Bett, it's a terrible line. Now if you can hear me, get off and dial us again.'

'Can she hear you?'

Margaret shook her head. 'Doesn't sound like it. She's just going on about "pictures in windows" or something.' She looked at her husband. 'I don't know what's going on.'

'It has to be a crossed line. You'd better hang up and . . .'

His attention was suddenly diverted by a noise from the direction of the hall. A second later his daughter, Bettina, put her pretty head around the corner of the sitting-room door.

'Sorry, I'm late, folks, but I was watching a video.'

It was at that point that the phone slipped from Margaret Blair's trembling hand and smashed her favourite mail-order vase.

The Hurricane's wings wiggled nervously as John Stride adjusted the radio controls.

'Whoops,' he smiled down at his eight-year-old son, Mark. 'Got to try to be smoother than that next circuit.'

But the small boy, with his mop of blond hair, didn't really hear his father. His whole attention was riveted on the exquisite model fighter he had watched his father make over the months and which now had started to bank, the morning sun glinting off the red, white and blue of its roundels.

'Bring it in low this time, Dad,' he urged his father excitedly. 'So that it just skims our heads.'

His father slightly tightened the Hurricane's bank with his miniature joystick.

'Want me to crash it?' he smiled.

'No. Don't be silly, Dad. Just bring it in low.'

'Right, squadron-leader, I'm starting my run-up now.'

With a steady and skilled hand, Stride brought the

aircraft back to straight and level, preparatory to its run across Widow's Field. He had always adored making and flying his own radio-controlled aircraft and his face betrayed his pleasure. A face that many of his patients described as handsome, but which, in reality, defied almost all the rules that normally shape the definition. The nose too long, the eyes too hooded, the mouth, perhaps, too broad, too deep a cleft in the chin. But somehow, as an amalgam, his features seemed to enhance each other and, certainly, as a result, lacked that hint of weakness that casts doubt on many a handsome man.

The effect of his looks was such that many a friend of his wife, Mary, had intimated that were she to be John's wife, an eagle eye would be the order of the day - and night - to see that he didn't fall prey to any predatory patient. But Mary felt she had no fears on that score. She trusted her husband implicitly, and the only cause for jealousy was, curiously enough, his hobby. Sometimes, she felt he spent just too much of his so valuable and rare spare time on his beloved aeronautical creations. Their garage loft was, after all, now stacked to the roof with flying models, from four-engined Lancasters and Flying Fortresses to Blenheims and Marauders and Mustangs and Spitfires. The Hurricane was only the latest in a long, long line.

But Mary had never said anything. She knew he cared for her deeply and would give it all up, if she asked him. But she would never do that. Besides, their son, Mark, would be heartbroken if the Stride Aviation Works shut up shop. He was spellbound, whether his father was just assembling ribs to spars or stringers to bulkheads, or starting up the aircraft's glow-plug engines and flying them into the wide blue yonder.

'Now duck if I make a mistake and it comes in too low,' his father shouted, as the high-pitched noise of the Hurricane grew louder by the second.

Mark saluted, then kept his hand up to his forehead to

shield his eyes from the sun. The miniature fighter plane crossed over them, almost before they knew it. They both spun round and watched as the camouflaged shape soared upwards to clear the clump of bushes in the middle of Widow's Field. Almost immediately, Stride started the aircraft into a bank, so that it would remain well inside the telegraph wires that bordered one side of the field, on its return flight.

'That's great, Dad. Let's have another one, only lower this time,' Mark urged, a mischievous smile across his tanned face.

'Any lower and it'll take your head off,' his father joked.

'Not mine. Yours. You're taller,' his son joked back.

'Hang on. Let's get it back round first.'

With deft precision born of long experience, his father guided the small fighter around the inside of the perimeter of the ten acre field, until it was little more than a black speck against the blue sky.

'We're lucky the weather cleared up,' John observed. 'I'm on call tomorrow, so today's our only chance.'

His son didn't reply. At eight years of age, he took each day as it came and weather didn't really worry him. Besides, his memory, like all children's, was selective. And in childhood, weren't most days sunny anyway? Even the previous night's storm was now stashed away in his 'Forget' file.

Mark watched intently as he saw the now tiny silhouette turn towards them, its wings straight and level.

'Really low, Dad,' he shouted. Even from that distance, he saw the nose of the fighter dip and from the higher-pitched scream from the glow-plug engine, he knew his father had put on the power for a high speed run.

The head-on silhouette seemed, at first, to grow in size very slowly, then, suddenly, with a scream that made Mark clap his hands to his ears, the plane was almost upon them, but, for some reason, still in a descent. The boy threw himself to the ground, but only just in time. He swore afterwards he felt the slipstream from the propeller on his face.

Rolling over, but still keeping well down, Mark searched for a sight of the Hurricane. To his amazement, the plane had not crashed, but was climbing away at a crazy angle. He heard footfalls approaching him and then his father's anxious voice.

'You all right, Mark?'

' 'Course. But what are you doing, Dad? Trying to crash it?'

He saw his father frantically operating the joystick.

'*I'm* not doing anything. It just won't respond.'

Mark looked back at the plane, which had now flattened from its climb and was screaming towards the edge of the field.

The boy got up quickly and stood by his father, a look of panic across his young face.

'Quick, Dad. Do something. Gee, look where it's heading.'

But John Stride did not need his son's warning. He could see only too well where the Hurricane was hell-bent. But he seemed to be powerless to stop it. Every control on his handset seemed to have gone dead and the Hurricane was now clearly on its own in free flight.

'I can't stop it,' he exclaimed breathlessly, and swung the aerial of the remote control in a wide arc to try to renew contact with the now rapidly diminishing silhouette of the Hurricane. But to no avail. The plane continued screaming towards the telegraph wires that bordered that end of the field, as if, somehow, it was being inexorably drawn to them.

'It could fly through them, Dad,' Mark said hurriedly, more in hope than expectation. 'There's room between the wires.'

But, for some weird and dreadful reason, his father was certain that it would not. That the plane had, somehow, exchanged his guidance for that of some other power . . .

Both father and son stood as if transfixed to the spot, as they watched the final seconds of the fighter's flight. Then, as the whirring propeller hit a wire, Mark hid his face in his hands. But he heard the explosion and his father, for a split second, saw the flash, before he too had to cover his eyes against the incredible intensity of the zigzagging light.

When they dared look up again, all that could be seen was a tiny dark blob on the wire. And even this seemed suddenly to disappear before their eyes.

It was a moment before they started to run towards the spot. When they arrived beneath the wire, they started to look for the remains of the plane. It was Mark who spotted it in the long grass by the hedge.

'Look, Dad, it's over there.'

He looked where his son had pointed and, to his amazement, saw that the Hurricane seemed to be more or less in one piece and relatively undamaged.

Mark ran over, picked it up and brought it back to his father. A quick look confirmed their impressions. Incredibly, the plane's structure was intact and the only damage seemed to be to the propeller which had been broken, blackened and half melted by the impact.

'Gee, Dad, you'll be able to get this back in the air in no time,' his son said excitedly. 'All it needs is a new prop and away we . . .'

But John Stride was no longer listening, but looking up at the telegraph wires above him. They were gently swaying as the air currents played through them. And the whistling of the wind across the wires seemed almost like some siren's call . . .

'What's the matter, Dad? Aren't you pleased?'

His father at last looked round at him, then pointed down at the plane resting in the grass.

'I'm afraid the prop isn't the only thing wrong, Mark,' he said quietly.

'Why? What else?'

He knelt down beside the plane and pointed inside its cockpit. Mark saw immediately what his father meant. The fuselage was completely empty.

'The receiver's gone, Mark. There's no trace of anything . . . anything at all.'

Chapter Four

The Reverend Meek looked across at his guest.

'Well, Mr Friend, if you really think that we in Hallowes may not be able to handle even the flower arrangements for Mr Quick's visit, then . . .'

'That's not quite what I said,' the American evangelist's aide replied, in a surprisingly thick Bronx accent. Surprising, only for its juxtaposition with reasonably sophisticated phrasing, vocabulary and concepts. The Reverend Meek could only assume the tubby and undersized Mr Friend – who reminded him so much of a round and stubby actor he had noted once, a few decades ago now, in the only London musical he had ever seen, 'Guys and Dolls' – either had an ear for education but not accents or had deliberately retained the reminder of his upbringing as a useful tool for making others feel immediately at home with him. Well, as far as the vicar of St Matthew's was concerned, such a tactic might go down well in Albuquerque or Auburn, Indiana, but dear Hallowes still preserved a certain respect for quiet dignity, not to mention class.

'No, Arthur . . . I may call you Arthur, I'm sure. And as I told you, I'm Homer. We're all Christian names in our great Christian movement.' The Reverend Meek's stomach turned, as the little man beamed at him and went on, 'Even our great inspiration and leader, Bobby, hates being called Mr Quick. You might warn everybody about that, so that they're prepared for when he arrives.'

He took a breath and any moment the vicar expected the centre button of Friend's loud check jacket to give up the struggle. 'Anyway, Arthur,' another beam, 'what I actually said was that, over the years, we have analysed every aspect of our expenditure on each and every rally, each and every big occasion. And we know to the last dime, what pays off and what doesn't. What is a good investment and what is dollars down the . . .'

There was a pause and the Reverend Meek was pretty certain the hiatus, in some other company, might well have been filled by 'goddamned' or similar.

'. . . drain. And that goes for every aspect of our presentation, from what visual aids pay off, the degree and range of sound amplification we need – we don't want to pay for what's not necessary. We're not a pop concert.'

The more Meek was learning about the selling of Bobby Quick, the less he was really convinced about Friend's, sorry, Homer's, last statement.

'Then there's the amount and arrangement of the seating. We don't want too many or too much. Just enough for the old and infirm, the disabled, the sick. Would you believe, we've even cross-related the ratio of standing to seating with the degree of hyster . . . religious enthusiasm we generate. There, I admit, we have learnt something from the pop movement. There's nothing like thousands of souls standing and swaying to stoke up the fires of their fervour . . . get those hands clapping for Jesus. Oh yeh. Amen, I say.'

He took another deep breath. Meek's eyes never left the button.

'What I mean to say. After all these years, we know our business. Down to the last . . . nut and bolt. *And* flower. Get too many flowers around the platform or around the stadium or rally field, and people think they're coming to a wake, not a great awakening. I'll tell you, the blooms at a Bobby Quick event aren't just brought in wholesale.' He gave a squeaky laugh. 'Only thing wholesale about our flowers is how we bought them. Yeh, too true, Reverend. I'll tell you we now do the same flower arrangements at every rally. Platform-wise, anyway. Stands to reason, the actual flowers vary according to the . . . season, but their numbers don't. Nor does the way we set 'em out. We have three lovely ladies on staff, who do almost nothing else, praise the Lord.'

He cleared his throat and put on an expression as near modesty as he could muster.

'One happens to be my beloved wife, Winnie, matter of fact.'

'I had been hoping that one of my parishioners, a Thelma Rickett, might have been of some service to you. At the actual flower arranging, I mean. She's so clever. The way she makes even the most humble flower . . .'

'So you can see, Arthur,' Friend cut in, as if the vicar had not opened his mouth, 'the degree of . . . professionalism that permeates every aspect of our beloved Bobby's operations. *Everything* is calculated beforehand. I could normally tell you right now how many people we can expect at the Hallowes' event and how many lovely people will offer their lives to Christ. Yessir. But not this time. You people down here are highly privileged to witness the first use of a great new advance in our staging techniques. Wow! We aim to really wake you all up down here in the South West. Get that ball rolling for Christ like it's never rolled before.'

Whilst another breath was drawn, Meek took the opportunity to offer, 'When you say . . . Homer . . . that everything is "calculated", what do you quite mean by that? I mean, do you start your calculations with the number of souls saved, so to speak, or . . . ?'

Friend, being street-wise to a major fault, immediately detected the drift of the vicar's 'or' and why he might have put his 'or' in. That's always the . . . trouble with dealing with the Brits, he thought. They're always so . . . pure and precious and pretend that they're above such fundamental facts of life as dollars and dimes and what you get for a cent. No wonder their silly little island always seemed to be up some financial gumtree or other. But then, how can you get lazy snobs to learn anything?

He looked at the glitzy gold watch bisecting his wrist like twine round a pudding.

'Excuse me, Arthur, I had no idea how late I am running.' He rose from the chintz of the chair, but seemed little taller standing than he had been sitting.

The Reverend Meek unfolded from his own chair and stood beside his visitor, head bowed and blue hands clasped in front of him, like some tubercular cupid hiding his genitals from drinkers at a fountain.

'Well, Homer . . . as I say, there's not one of my parishioners, indeed, I would go so far as to say, not a soul in the whole of Hallowes, who has not heard of your Bobby Quick's visit to our little town. And, certainly, everyone who has spoken to me has expressed absolute delight that he has chosen Hallowes as the key town for his tour of the South West.'

Homer Friend held up a childlike hand.

'Keep spreading the good word, Vicar.' He shook his head with pride. 'My goodness, we aim, with God's good help, to really make this day a day to remember for all time. A holy day that will go down in the history of your sweet town, that you and your children and your children's children will talk about and marvel over for ever and a day, amen. By Jiminy, Vicar, your town will be envied by every other town in the South West, I'll bet my good life on it.'

'And Hallowed will be its name,' Meek smiled beneficently.

The aide double-took, then forced a smile of his own.

'Oh yes. Mighty clever. Yessir. "Hallowed" be its name. I must remember to tell that to Bobby. It'll go down fine in his initial words of greeting.'

And with that, he strutted towards the door, then at the last second, turned.

'Remember, leave the flowers to us. Leave everything to us. All you have to do is spread the good word, Arthur. Get 'em really hyped up and on the day, get 'em marching towards that holy field.'

* * *

The Reverend Meek felt exhausted after he had waved the big Cadillac out of the weed-covered drive of the vicarage. The last time he had been so drained had been after a long religious sermon on the merits of double glazing delivered by a door-to-door salesman, who, the vicar could see now, had little to learn from Homer Friend and his ilk.

He went back into the chill quiet of his study and sat down at his desk. After a while his spirits somewhat revived, as he compared the slow pace and serenity of his own life and parish with what he imagined must be that of the great and famous Bobby Quick. At one time in his career, Arthur Meek had rather fancied the idea of climbing the clerical ladder and becoming a name to conjure with in his church. His wife, when she was alive – the good Lord had seen fit to clasp her to His bosom rather early, it seemed to Meek, at the tender age of forty two – had done her best to fuel his ambition and had worked energetically, if not subtly, on her uncle, the Bishop of Trentham, to better prepare the way for his advancement.

But as the years slipped by, Meek had grown to love the small and self-contained world of rural parishes and revelled in its relative simplicity. At the same time, he had developed an antipathy to the over-political atmosphere that he gathered from many of the bishop's remarks, surrounded the steep slopes leading to the summit of his calling. This evaporation of ambition, he knew, had hurt his wife, who had nursed visions of moving away from the sleepy South West to some hub of the nation and, thus, enjoying the prestige and privilege her aunt revelled in as a bishop's wife.

So there was not a trace of envy in Meek's soul, when he contemplated the success of the phenomenon like Bobby Quick – though as he looked round at the faded and crumbling décor and fabric of the vicarage, he did rather wish his church could afford him a mere thousandth of the luxuries and comforts of the evangelist's home, a vast mansion set in the Hollywood Hills, that he had seen depicted in the press.

His thoughts were interrupted by the telephone. He rose wearily from his desk. He knew who it was likely to be and he was proved right.

'That you, Arthur?' the thin voice enquired.

'Yes, indeed. How nice of you to call, Bishop. And very timely too. Our friend's chief aide has only just left.'

'So he's been? I thought I might be a little late, but I couldn't ring sooner. I've had this . . . lady . . . on the phone from America.'

Meek knew only too well to whom he was scathingly referring. The latest in a line of transatlantic females, who had now been ordained as bishops.

'Objects to my article in the *New York Times*. I daren't repeat, Arthur, some of the comments she made. Really, heaven preserve me from militant women, whether they be Christian or heathen, devout or devious.'

'Quite so, Bishop, quite so. Now would you like to know all the arrangements that are being made for Bobby Quick's visit?'

'Not right this second,' his caller said, impatiently. 'First of all, just tell me if the rumours are true.'

'What rumours?'

'That Quick seems about to turn his whole visit into a . . .' he hunted for the right words. '. . . circus, a vast vulgar show business extravaganza that even Barnum and Bailey would have blanched at. Arthur, we have just got to see that we don't get so associated with him, that our beloved church is seen to be supporting such cheap methods of . . .'

Meek cleared his throat and interrupted. 'Quite so, quite so, Bishop. That would never do. But from my conversations with Mr Friend – that's the aide I mentioned – we in Hallowes are not being asked to contribute very much to the occasion. The Bobby Quick organisation seems to have everything already "buttoned up", as they say across the water.'

'Did he tell you about the giant screens?'

'Pardon?'

'Giant screens, man. From what I've just heard, they are intending to put giant video screens all around the rally site.'

Meek suddenly realised that the screens must be the great new development in presentation techniques to which Friend had referred.

'No, the aide did not mention them specifically. But he did hint that . . .'

'Well, they're happening. I tell you, Arthur, the whole event is deteriorating into a revolting glorification of Bobby Quick. And will have as much to do with the glorification of our Lord as a pop concert or Disneyworld.'

'But the Quick organisation has always used show business methods to get the good message across. Surely screens are only an extension . . .'

'Do you know what they say they're going to show on them?' the bishop rapped.

'No, as I said, Mr Friend only mentioned the use of some new techniques. We didn't get into any details.'

'More's the pity, Arthur. I told you to be careful about this Quick visit. You should have probed more. After all, it's your town that's acting host.'

Meek cleared his throat once more. 'So . . . er . . . what are they planning to show on the screens?'

'What *aren't* they, would be a better question. Let's start with pop stars rocking for Jesus. Arthur, can you imagine, "rocking for Jesus"?'

Meek wisely let the question go.

'Then there's something called "Rally to Jesus", which, apparently, is highlights of other rallies that Quick has held across the world, then a series of interviews called "Sinner Winners". I hardly need tell you, Arthur, what all that's about. And for one of the biggest moments in this dreadful side-show, there's going to be a film humbly entitled, "Bobby Quick, soldier for Christ". It's the great man's life story in glorious hyperbole. But wait, Arthur, guess what little gem they're going to play up, just for all you people in Hallowes. From what I've heard, it's even mentioned in the film.'

'I can't imagine, Bishop. Something especially for Hallowes, you say?'

'Extra specially, Arthur. Apparently, would you believe, they're going to claim Bobby Quick was actually stationed near Hallowes during the war . . .'

Penny Seymour-Jones rolled on to her back and grinned.

'You've certainly picked some partners in your time, George.'

Craven reached across and rested his hand on her breast.

'That's a bit unfair, Penny. Any man can be forgiven one mistake.'

'I wasn't just talking about wives.'

His fingers teased her still erect nipple.

'So what else have you been hearing, Mrs Jones?' he grinned. 'You don't want to believe everything you hear. Hallowes is a hot-bed of gossip.'

'Emphasis on the bed,' she grinned back.

He gave her nipple a slight twist, enough for Penny to frown a warning.

'So what have you been hearing?'

She rolled back on to her side and perused her bed companion. It was curious. They had known each other for years and yet had only become lovers in the last two weeks. Perhaps 'lover' was really too romantic a word for their new-found relationship. 'Screwer' Penny reckoned would be a far more apposite word. 'Only become serious screwers in the last two weeks.' For she recognised that the property developer had no real interest in her, beyond bed. Even her undoubted ardour and skill between the sheets, she knew would not hold him for long. She was a distraction. Not a destination. From his divorce, from his business worries, from boredom, from . . . ? She didn't know and she didn't really care. She'd had many lovers before and would have others after him. Not so many of the latter, more's the pity, now that she had passed the big Four O. She smiled to herself. The same age as the dear George beside her. But with his kind of looks, a kind of chiselled ruggedness that would not crumble with age, George Craven had many more lover-years ahead of him, whilst she . . . she was already on the slippery slope. In only a few more years, she would be reduced to making do with her husband. The dear, sweet bore, who never suspected a thing. And who, thank God, spent more time abroad representing his employers, a large marine equipment operation, than queering her pitch at home.

'Nothing much. Nothing concrete, that is. But bags of speculation - especially since we heard about the divorce.'

Craven reached forward and lifted her long, straight hair away from her face.

'There, that's better. I can see who I'm speaking to.'

'Amazed I'm still worth looking at.'

He indulged her poaching for a compliment.

'You look fine to me.'

And it was almost the truth. For he had to admit that Penny Seymour-Jones had retained both her looks and figure remarkably well. Only the slight sag of her slightly overripe breasts and a trace of slackness on her stomach really betrayed her age. And maybe her waist had once been nearer that of an hour glass than it was now. But for forty, she was in almost as trim a shape as his estranged wife, Annabel, who had only just turned thirty-two. But then, dear Annabel was as lazy as Penny was energetic and preferred lying in bed to exercising with Jane Fonda or the Green Goddess - video tapes of whose exercises he had spotted in a video cabinet in the Seymour-Jones' large sitting-room.

'So why the dig about my partners, if you haven't really heard anything?'

She snuggled into the crook of his arm.

'I chose my words carefully. I said partners, didn't I? Not wives or girlfriends or . . .'

'Okay. So what are you getting at?'

'Can't you guess?'

'Drench?'

She nodded.

'Got it in one.'

'You don't like Drench, do you? Why, because he hasn't made a pass at you?'

She dug her elbow into his ribs.

'One more like that, Craven, and you'll find yourself out of the front door, if not the window.'

He stretched his arm reassuringly down her body until his fingers met the moist darkness of her curls.

'Sorry. But all I meant to say is that Drench isn't bad. You shouldn't condemn him because he's not quite made like the rest of us. He is just not interested in women. Or men, for that matter. Or anything, it would seem, except his business. And you have to admit, he's a damn good estate agent.'

'There's no such thing,' she smiled, and put her own hand down to encourage his.

'Okay. But he's more than just your average estate agent. That's why I like working with him. He's got an uncanny sense of his market. A nose for a bargain, an eye for seeing opportunities others miss, or can't even recognise.'

'Or recognise but don't want to exploit at the expense of others or the environment or . . .'

His hand stopped playing. 'Oh come on, Penny, don't give me all that alternative style crap. You of all people.'

She turned her head towards him. 'Why me of all people? Don't I run a health food shop?'

'Sure you do. But not for the good of society, don't tell me that. You saw a niche in this stupid town's market and were the first to fill it. Not to contribute to your consumers' physical well-being, I would hazard a guess, but to contribute to your own financial health. You like the good life as well as I do, Penny Seymour-Jones. Exploiting the gullibility of this town's surfeit of long skirted, lank haired, limp-brained lefties is no more praiseworthy than . . .'

'. . . what you want to do with Widow's Field?' she interrupted, now more than a little annoyed at her new-found lover's line of argument.

George Craven removed his hand and sat up, resting on one elbow.

'Oh come on, Penny. I didn't expect that when I came up to your place, we'd spend half the time at each other's throats.'

Her pained and rather severe face softened slightly.

'But most of the time on quite another part of the anatomy.'

He leant across and put his mouth to hers. She let his tongue explore for a moment, then she drew away and said, 'Don't get offended, George, but there's trouble brewing over Widow's Field.'

'There was trouble over the siting of the new telephone building. But it all died down, once people realised we were serious and there was no alternative site, anyway, that wouldn't have caused even more objections.'

'Widow's is different.'

'It's just another field.'

'No, it isn't,' Penny said quietly. 'It's special. It's where all the children play. Always have done. I used to go up there, as a kid.'

Craven was surprised at her sudden display of sentiment. For sentimental was certainly not one of the adjectives friends and acquaintances ever used about Penelope Seymour-Jones. And as for her now exhibiting an affection for children – why, everyone knew she had no time for them. After all, wasn't that why she had chosen not to have any of her own?

'There are plenty of other fields around Hallowes.'

'Then buy one of those to put up your little square boxes.'

He frowned. 'Do you mind – "executive and starter homes".'

'Is that what your friend, Drench, is going to call them?'

'Probably. They'll sell whatever they're called. Hallowes has a crying need for new housing. The town will slowly die on its feet, if it doesn't provide it.'

She took his hand. 'Look, George, I'm not denying we need more housing in the area. All I'm against is your choice of site.'

'Too late now. In fact, I've got a digger going in tomorrow to dig a test section, so that we can test how deep the shale is.'

He cupped her breast. 'Anyway, sorry to be desecrating your childhood memories.'

'Not just mine, George. And all the fuss isn't just about losing an innocent playground, as you well know.'

'Hell, Penny, you don't believe all that superstition about the site, do you? You of all people.'

'Watch it, George. That's the second time you've said, "you of all people". And yes, I do sort of believe it. Over the years, too many queer happenings have been reported, for all of them to be figments of the imagination.'

He raised his dark eyebrows. 'God, Penny, Devon has always been the home of dark mystery and wild folk-lore. The stories have got embroidered more and more over the years, as the tourist boards have realised there's money in them thar tales. That ruddy field is a prime example. Drench and I did quite a bit of homework, before we applied for planning permission, because we anticipated some cranky *brouhaha* or other. And you know the bit about its name – that it was called Widow's Field because some of the dead from the Napoleonic Wars were buried there? All a complete fabrication. It was called Widows after a farmer who bought it at the end of the last century. An Isaiah Widows. It's all in the parish records. I've seen his gravestone – it's lying in some long grass at the edge of St Matthew's graveyard.'

She sat up and his hand slipped away from her breast into her lap.

'Damn you, George, for killing another little romantic illusion.'

He looked at her with a wry smile. 'What was the first one?'

She didn't answer his question, but continued, almost as if to herself.

'But what about all the sightings over the years of queer lightning flashes and ghostly shapes and unearthly groans . . . ?'

He laughed. 'You sound like Drench's mother. She's big into all that supernatural crap. Even tries to frighten poor old William into giving up the project by hinting that ghouls and ghosties will grab him by the goolies if he doesn't watch out.' He chuckled. 'That is, if dear William has actually got any goolies, which I sometimes doubt.'

'You know Enid Drench is organising a march through Hallowes.'

He looked across at her in surprise. 'Who did you hear that from?'

'Enid rang Priscilla last night and asked if she'd join it. She said yes, then rang me to see if I would.'

'Are you going to?'

'I don't know, yet,' she smiled.

His fingers entwined themselves in her pubic curls.

'Don't you?'

She didn't reply.

He gave a tug. She wasn't sure whether she liked the sensation.

'I'm my own mistress,' she said quietly.

He suddenly let go and pulled her down under him.

'You're mine right now,' he smiled. 'I'm not divorced yet.'

For a moment, she resisted, but only for a moment . . .

* * *

He stopped in mid-stroke. 'Ignore it.'

She lowered her legs and pushed at his chest.

'I can't. It might be my husband. He said he might ring about now.'

'So you were out.' He plunged back into her, but she froze.

'I said I wouldn't be.'

'Oh, goddammit, Penny, so you changed your mind.'

But he could feel the moment had now gone, so he reluctantly withdrew and rolled off her.

She got up from the bed and smiled back at him.

'You won't believe how many times this happens. I've often thought that the telephone people would have gone bankrupt years ago, if they could be sued for coitus interruptus.'

She went out to her dressing-room and he noted she closed the bedroom door behind her.

But she returned, even before his erection had fully died and got back into bed beside him.

'God, if I'd known it was only Priscilla, I wouldn't have bothered.'

'What the hell did she want? Didn't you tell her you would be caught up this afternoon?'

'Yes. But something came up. The telephone in the shop seems to be playing up.'

He frowned. 'But she got you all right.'

'I know. But she says it keeps ringing in the shop and when she answers it, all she gets is a load of crackle and what sounds a bit like my voice. So finally she rang to see if it had been me. When I said no, she suggested that she had better get on to the telephone exchange and report a fault. So I said, get on with it, and not to ring here again, as I didn't know whether I would be in.'

Craven pulled her hand down towards his groin.

'But I hope you didn't add that you *did* know who would be in you . . .'

Chapter Five

Homer Friend pushed at the quicks atop the bitten remains of his fingernails.

'Well, I didn't think . . .' he began, but his lord and master cut him off curtly.

'You should have thought, Homer. That's what I pay you for.'

Bobby Quick eased his lean, yet muscular, frame out of the reproduction Louis the Sixteenth chair and started to pace the over-ornamented and gilded sitting-room of his hotel suite.

'I'm starting to think, my dear Friend, that you may be taking your privileged position in my organisation a mite too much for granted. Maybe I brought you on too fast. Maybe I should have held back the keys to Bethlehem, until you'd proved yourself abroad, as well as back home.'

The mention of Bethlehem – one of the most prized properties on the Quick estates just north of Los Angeles, a ten bedroomed mansion in the neo-colonial style, into which Friend and his family had only moved some six months before – made Friend's football of a face break out in a sweat. For he knew that the evangelist had a track record of withdrawing his favours as impulsively as he bestowed them. And if he ever lost Bethlehem . . . the thought did not bear pursuing.

'Now, Bobby, there's no real harm done. I can take care of everything. I can get back down to Hallowes this afternoon . . .'

His voice trailed away, as he saw the smile grow across

the tanned and etched leather of the evangelist's face. The smile that had mystified and mesmerised millions. The smile that was the very essence of the Quick appeal. Hypnotised every passer-by from advertising hoardings across America, reached out to the hearts of television audiences from Mississippi to Medicine Hat, from Washington DC to Washington, Oregon, from Santa Barbara to Santa Fé. The smile that said, 'Come to me', 'Unburden your soul'. The look that promised, whatever the size of the problem, the complexity or the depth of the hang-up, there would be a Quick solution. And the smile that, to his aide right that second, sent shivers up the spine.

The evangelist combed his snow white hair from his forehead with his fingers – a gesture equally known to millions, and as calculated as each and every inflection of his Orson Welles' voice.

'I'm sure you will, Homer, I'm sure you will. Better late than never.'

'But I promise you, Bobby,' Friend offered, the expression on his face rather belying his words, 'that I always had it planned. My next trip down there. You see, you may not realise, Bobby, how very careful you have to be dealing with the British. It pays to take things real slow. Spell things out real clear. And not try to get too much over to them at a time. They're not like us. Why, you just won't believe the pace at which they live down there. It's almost like, well, going back a century.'

Quick frowned. 'Don't tell me they're going to be like the Amish.'

Friend shook his head vigorously. For he remembered only too well the disastrous evening in Pennsylvania to which the evangelist was referring, when the rally had been interrupted time and time again by followers of the Amish sect objecting to the mercenary methods and conspicuous life styles of Bobby Quick and members of his organisation.

'No, nothing like the Amish. They'll love you down

there, Bobby. Eat you up. That's a promise. They will have never witnessed anything like it before. It's just that they're not like us. They're very . . . British, that's all. Reminds me of *Upstairs, Downstairs*, remember?'

Bobby Quick remembered. He had tapes of every episode of the old British television series and re-ran them time and time again, much to the boredom of his over-polite entourage, as if, somehow, he desperately wanted those clear cut days to return, when the world was divided into masters and servants and everyone kept to their place without quarrel or query.

For the first time, he had a feeling that he might like his time in Hallowes.

'Think a grand is enough?' he queried.

'Should be. The British don't earn very much, you know. Especially down there. There's no real industry or anything. Just farms and fields and Bed & Breakfast places and . . .'

'Bed and Breakfast places?'

'Yeh. They're ordinary homes that make a buck from letting people stay the night.'

'Don't they have enough hotels, motels?'

Friend grinned. 'They don't have enough money.'

The evangelist shrugged. 'So a grand's okay? I don't want any comeback.'

'There won't be.'

'Remember, make it an old lady, not an old man.'

'Whatever you say.'

'No one ever suspects little old ladies of lying. Just old men.'

'Right.'

The evangelist came over to Friend's chair and towered above him.

'And for Pete's sake, get the story right.'

'Got it.'

'Sure I don't need to go over it again? Though, saints be preserved, we've been over it often enough.'

Friend shook his head.

'Okay. You'd better have. And you'd better stand over that little old lady until she's so word perfect, she actually believes what she's saying. If you tell me she's good enough, we'll play her right at the start of the rally and give her a seat on the platform.'

'She'll be good enough.'

Bobby Quick looked at the Omega on his tanned wrist.

'Okay, Friend, I've got some things to do now and you'd better be off to Hallowes.'

The aide was on his feet and making for the door of the magnificent suite in no time. For when Bobby Quick called an end to an audience, it ill behoved his entourage or hangers-on to do just that.

'I'll report back tomorrow.'

'You do that,' Quick said wearily, but by now, he had his back to the door.

It took at least ten minutes before he could get through and, by then, the evangelist had started to understand what his aide had been saying about the British.

He stretched his lanky legs out on the *chaise-longue*, telephone in lap, and waited impatiently for his call to be answered. After what, to him, seemed like an eternity – patience was certainly not a Quick virtue – the ringing stopped and a female voice, barely stifling a yawn, replied.

'This is Malibu . . .'

'Forget the number, honey,' he cut in. 'This is you know who.'

'Bobby!' the female voice exclaimed with obvious surprise and delight. 'Gee, I never thought you'd ring. And in the middle of the old night too.'

'Didn't intend to, honey, but I just couldn't resist it. By the way, it's morning here.'

'Miss me?' she cooed.

'Sure do.'

'Wish I was with you,' she breathed in her well practised Goldie Hawn little girl tone.

'Likewise, honey. This great mausoleum of a hotel could do with someone like you waking it up a bit.'

'Oooh,' she drawled. 'There ain't anybody quite like little ole me, is there?'

'Now cool it a bit, honey. You don't know who might be listening.'

'Yeh, I know. That's why I was so surprised you phoned. You don't ever call me when you're on a trip. And you've always forbidden me to call you.'

'Well, I guess this'll be the one exception that proves the rule.'

He rested further back on the *chaise-longue* and put the telephone on the floor.

'But it'll have to be a quick one.'

'I thought you didn't go for quick ones,' she teased.

'That's enough of that, Betty-Lou.'

'All righty. So how are you getting on? What's little ole England like? I'd love to go over one day.'

'Forget it. It's just as boring as you just described it, hon. "Little and old" sure sums up its excitement.'

'They'll love you all the same, Bobby. One flash of that old smile and they'll fall over backwards . . . Just like I did, I guess.'

'What are you wearing, hon?' he asked huskily.

'What I always do in bed, silly.'

'Tell me.'

'I'm nude as a slug. Just like you like me. Gee, I wish you were here beside me . . . well, not exactly beside me, more . . .' She hesitated.

'. . . inside,' he whispered.

'Right on, lover. Gee, Bobby, I do miss you. Ever so. Much, much more than when you go off over here. Somehow you seem so very far away. Over all that land and water. Feels like almost you're on a different planet.'

'Soon be back.'

'Yeh.'

'Come on, sound a mite happier about it. What's wrong?'

'Well . . . you know. You'll be back. But not really with me.'

Quick sighed. 'Don't start that again, honey. You know the way it is. There's nothing I can do about it.'

The line went silent for a moment, then she said, almost as if in a trance, 'Maybe God will do something about it.'

Bobby Quick sat up smartly.

'What d'you mean?'

'Oh, nothing.'

'Come on, Betty-Lou. Out with it.'

'Well, your wife's none too well, is she? It's awful, Bobby, but I sometimes lie and dream that God has taken her and then you and I . . .'

'Yeh . . . well . . .' he stuttered, 'just you quit thinking that way.'

'I can dream, can't I? Don't you ever wish that old lady wife of yours out of the way, sometimes?'

'That's as maybe,' he said quickly, deciding it was time he killed the call. 'Now I've just gotta hang up. There's some guy coming to see me.'

'Love you, Bobby. Love you heaps. Now you just look after yourself and come back real quick.'

Quick swung his legs to the floor and carried the telephone back to the table. 'You too, hon. Can't wait to get out of this joke, backward, boring, one horse little island, you just gotta believe it.'

The Telecom van pulled up just short of the inspection cover, at the entrance to the short cul-de-sac, known as Drake's Avenue.

Ted Bailey, the engineer, picked up the clipboard from the passenger seat and with a sigh, perused his work sheet. It was well past seven in the evening and though he appreciated the extra that overtime brought with it, that evening he had promised himself he would keep free for a night of snooker with the lads over in Paignton. It was not often his wife went out after he finished work, but tonight she was babysitting for her sister in Babbacombe and wouldn't be back until at least midnight. So he'd cursed under his breath when his supervisor had presented him with his overtime task of checking out the lines at both Drakes Avenue, where someone called Blair had reported a fault, and in Fore Street, where some shop called the Hallowes Health Farm had done likewise.

With a groan, he opened the door of the Escort van and eased his fourteen stone out of the sagging front seat. He did not bother to take any of his test equipment with him, as he was pretty certain what he'd find once he'd opened up the inspection chamber. Nothing more than what he had discovered on numerous other calls of this nature over the years. For telephone complaints followed thunderstorms like night follows day. And with all the rain that had fallen on Hallowes recently, there was little question that the first thing that would meet his beady eye would be the glint of water. And all he'd have to do tonight would be to file an instruction back at headquarters for the pumping crew to turn out in the morning.

The inspection cover, once unlocked with his special tool, lifted with comparative ease. For, after all, the whole of Hallowes' telecommunication system had been totally renewed and updated only in the last twelve months and was, in fact, the prototype of a revolutionary new system that eventually would spread across the whole of the United Kingdom. Already built into it was not only the most advanced use of fibre optics seen in Europe, but also the facility for video telephone relay at a later date, probably not more than five years away.

But the engineer's prognosis proved, for once, wrong. No glint of water met his eye and even when he shone his torch around the chamber, he could not even trace any sign of damp, let alone standing water.

He cursed his luck. Now he'd have to probe further and run through his long manual of testing procedures. Every ruddy test meant he'd be missing another frame of snooker over in Paignton. Before he got up off his knees and went back to the van to get his equipment, he ran his torch once more over the slim and multicoloured cables that traversed the chamber, hoping to find some obvious break or interruption in the lines. But nothing seemed to be out of order and he was about to switch off when . . .

Mary Stride looked up at her husband.

'You look tired.'

John pushed aside his now empty plate and sat back from the kitchen table, where they had just had lunch.

'I've had one of those mornings,' he smiled wearily. 'I thought the surgery would never empty.'

His wife rose and came round to stand behind his chair. Soon her slim, yet strong, fingers were massaging the muscles at the base of his neck.

'You've never lost the knack,' he said quietly.

'Why should I? Had lots of practice.'

She was referring to her young days in nursing, when she had specialised in physiotherapy. Indeed, it was how she and her husband had first met. John had suffered whiplash in a minor shunt in his car and had been sent to Mary for a twice weekly course of treatment. It was not long before they were seeing each other rather more than twice a week and outside the hospital walls as well as in.

'If it's like this in late September,' her husband sighed, 'I dread what the winter will bring, when the 'flu and cough brigade start sniffling in.'

She stopped her massage and put her arms around her husband's neck.

'You should take a holiday. A real one. Not just the odd day here, odd day there.'

'Yes. You could be right.'

'I know I'm right. We haven't taken a proper holiday

since we've been in Hallowes. Very soon I'll start regretting we ever moved.'

He held her clasped hands in his own.

'No, you won't. You love it here too much, my darling. You, of all people, can't ignore your roots. Where you were born and raised.' Grinning, he went on, 'When I first knew you, I thought I'd never met anyone who went on so about their childhood and home town. I sort of guessed, if we got together, we'd end up moving down here, sooner or later.'

She did not comment. He was right, of course, she did love Hallowes. Despite everything; her father's desertion of the family and her mother's early death, when pregnant with a second child. Reminiscent indeed of her own grandmother, who had actually died when giving birth to her mother: born not of wedlock, but of a brief and passionate affair with a GI, who had been stationed in the town and who had been reported killed on D-Day, his body never having been recovered.

Mary's upbringing by a kind and loving aunt, her mother's sister, was the source of so many happy memories, that the pain of her mother's death, whilst never wholly exorcised, was made both bearable and somehow, at one remove from her day to day experience. But now even she was gone; killed by a lorry whose brakes had failed on the precipitous hill that led into Hallowes. So now it seemed to Mary that she clung on to the very place itself, rather than any one of its five thousand or so inhabitants. As if, somehow, the folds and sweeping arcs of the green hills that held Hallowes in its midst, were the soft curves of some all embracing earth mother, that would comfort and protect her and her family for ever.

Her husband tilted his head back and looked up at her. Even upside down her face still looked as attractive as when he had first met her. For high-cheek-boned beauty such as Mary Stride's so often shrugs off the onslaughts of life and age with impressive, but to other less fortunate women, downright annoying, dexterity.

'Don't stop. Your fingers were just starting to work a little magic.'

She resumed the massage of his neck, but muttered, 'It's not my magic touch you need, darling. But the magic wand of a travel agent. I bet you recommend holidays to all your rotten patients, but you never think of prescribing one for yourself and your family.'

He laughed. 'Funny you should say that. The last patient I saw today got a holiday as the only medicine.'

'Nothing really wrong with him that getting away wouldn't cure?'

He frowned. 'So it looks. Checked him up, down and every which way, but couldn't find anything, really.'

'Anyone I know?'

'No. He's a telephone engineer. Apparently he was found last night collapsed over some man-hole or other, where he was doing a bit of overtime.'

'And it's a case of over-much overtime?'

'Maybe. He has certainly put in a helluva lot of hours this year. Apparently a lot of their engineers have, since the new telecommunication system was built.'

'So you told him to use a bit of his overtime pay on a ticket to paradise?'

'More or less. But I don't think he'll do it. He swears he's got the constitution of an ox and it's not overwork that caused his collapse last night.'

'So what's his own diagnosis?'

John Stride stilled his wife's hands and got up from the chair.

'You wouldn't believe it if I told you.'

She grinned. 'Try me.'

'Well, he claims . . .' he hesitated, and looked away from his wife. 'Oh, it's just too ridiculous even to bother with.'

She put a hand on his shoulder. 'No, go on. You know I love to hear the wild things some of your patients come out with. I reckon it's what helps keep doctors' wives sane.'

'Okay, you asked for it.' He took a deep breath. 'He claims that when he was working on that inspection chamber . . . hell . . . he saw things.'

'What kind of things? Devon pixies, hobgoblins?'

'Not quite, but something just as fanciful and absurd. He says the telephone cables or optic fibres or whatever they're called, suddenly started to glow, then, well, move . . . You know, on their own.'

'Move? What do you mean, move?'

'Well, I must say he gave me a helluva graphic description of it all. He said some of the lines . . . well . . . "pulsed" was the word he used . . . then went red and then brilliant white.'

'That all? As if that isn't enough!'

'No, that's not all. He said he was too scared even to move and somehow, he felt as if the lines were trying to draw him down into the chamber.'

She held her hands high in the air. 'Shock, horror! It's lucky Mark is at school and can't hear all this. He wouldn't sleep for a week. Do go on.'

'Well, then he said the lines seemed to be trying to unfold themselves - I didn't quite follow all of his ramblings, you understand - and then, still glowing white, try to leap out of the man-hole, as if to somehow lasso him.'

She laughed, disbelievingly, 'My God, how much had this man had to drink last night?'

'Nothing, apparently. I asked him.'

'So then what happened?'

'Nothing.'

'Nothing?'

'Not that he knows of. Next thing he remembers, he was in an ambulance being taken to hospital, where, of course, other than a high pulse rate, they couldn't find anything wrong with him. They just advised him to take today off and get in touch with his own doctor. That's yours truly.'

John looked at his wife. 'Needs a psychiatrist, more than a doctor, wouldn't you say?'

Mary Stride did not answer, but posed a question of her own.

'Have you heard whether anyone has checked that inspection chamber since?'

He frowned. 'You don't mean you believe any of this twaddle, do you?'

Again she did not answer him. 'But has anyone?' she asked quietly.

A slight smile replaced his frown. 'Yes, they have, Mary. The engineer says it was checked this morning and they found nothing apparently wrong with it. Okay?'

She smiled weakly, then started to clear away the plates.

'But surely there must have been something wrong with it, otherwise the engineer would not have gone there in the first place. Unless, of course, it was just a routine inspection.'

'Someone had reported a fault on a line, as far as I could gather. Perhaps the recent storms have upset the system a bit.'

'Yeh,' she said with a sigh.

He took the plates from her.

'You don't sound very convinced.'

She looked up. 'Don't I?' she said, then after a moment, added with a shrug, 'Anyway, let's forget all that. And get back to where we started. If that deranged engineer won't take his holiday, how about us all taking one for him? Over Christmas. When Mark breaks up . . .'

Chapter Six

She reached up and ran her fingers through his oiled hair.

'Tommy, I'm not sure I want to do it in here after all.'

The photographer put his finger to the schoolgirl's lips.

'Sshh. Be quiet. You know I don't like to talk when we're making love.'

'But, Tommy,' she protested, raising herself from the *chaise-longue* on one elbow, 'I'd much rather we went upstairs. All these lights . . .'

He stilled her mouth with his own, then whispered, 'But you didn't mind it the other day.'

'That was different. You were taking photographs of us then.'

Tully's eyes flicked towards the far wall.

'Anyway, Bettina, just this once. Please. I like doing it under the lights. They make me feel warm and . . . sexy.'

She lay back once more, as Tully cupped her firm, budding breast with his hand. Soon his lips were teasing her nipple and she parted her legs to allow him to get on top of her. But to her surprise, Tully still made no effort to do so, but continued to kneel by the side of the *chaise-longue*, his erect member casting a shadow across her face.

'Tommy,' she breathed. 'Come on . . . I've never known you take so long. What's the matter?'

He did not dare tell her and he knew if he continued the foreplay too much longer, she might start smelling the rat he was being.

'Just a little longer,' he whispered, then swung his hardness towards her mouth, whilst his left hand parted her legs even wider. Her lips once more accepted him, but he could see from her eyes that he would soon be overplaying his cards. But for the moment, at least, he was keeping her too busy to talk.

As the video ended and the screen turned to snow, Tully looked at his watch. Twenty one minutes. It was barely long enough, but it would have to do. And he reckoned that by the time the boys in Soho had edited out her silly talk, the running time would be down to around seventeen minutes. He hoped their edits might help hide the fact that basically, the material was amateur in the extreme. Videoed from just one angle. Only one set up. And all in mid shot. But he guessed they would probably edit in a few horny close shots from their, no doubt, huge bank of porn material. For, after all, the basic act, shot really tight, is pretty anonymous.

He got up from his chair, switched off the recorder and took out the tape. Whatever its shortcomings, he didn't really care. For there was one thing he knew. Young teenage sex footage was always in high demand and Bettina Blair was ten times as pert and attractive as some of the tender-aged bimbos he'd seen in blue material. At least she wasn't all puppy fat bulges and bespotted with pimples. His girl had class. And not only in her looks.

Tully took the videotape over to his Mickey Mouse telephone and dialled a London number.

'That you, Benny . . . right, it's Tom Tully . . . yes, sure, I got what you wanted. She's sensational. Just sixteen. You wouldn't believe her body. Tits like big lemons. You know, all immature, with nipples . . . right, like walnut whips . . . sure, yeh . . . you'll flip when you see her giving me head . . . yeh, the whole goddamn works . . . I'll put the tape in the post, together with some stills I took of her on the job the other night . . .

no, she has no idea . . . told her the photos were just for us. She swallowed it hook, line and you know what . . .'

Call over, Tully replaced the receiver in Mickey Mouse's hand and went back to his chair. As he picked up a copy of Penthouse, he thought he heard a click. He looked up and around, but seeing no reason for the sound, he shrugged, then started to flip the magazine's pages.

'Is he bald?'

Prue Fanshawe smiled back at her daughter, Sophie.

'No.'

The ten-year-old girl went back to perusing the characters still left erect on her *Guess-Who?* board.

'Is he . . . ?' she began, but her mother cut her off.

'Hey, hang on, young lady, it's my turn now.'

Her daughter laughed and tossed her long blonde hair away from her face. She liked playing board games with her mother. Especially like now, when she had already changed into her pyjamas for bed and was being allowed to stay up a bit later than usual because her father was not yet back from his day in the Law Courts.

Prue Fanshawe shifted herself round in her chair. Recently, she had been finding it harder and harder to relax at the end of the day and she had rather grabbed at this opportunity to play games with her daughter, as it would help fill the void that somehow she felt her life was becoming. She could not or, perhaps, it was more dared not, put a finger on any one reason for her unease. It wasn't as if her own life had changed in any discernible way recently. She was still what she had always been – a typical middle class wife caring for her family, as best she could, and playing a modest role in some of the community activities in Hallowes, notably the WI, the local tennis club and the Hallowes Dramatic Society, where she was secretary and treasurer, rather than a leading light. But all the same, try as she might, she could not seem to still a growing restlessness within her. She prayed that it might be due only to the long hours her husband seemed to be working these days and, thus, their lack of quiet time together compared with before. Perhaps, when his work load lightened, so would her unease. It was really that hope that kept her going.

She looked down at her board and the erect gallery of her own characters, fewer of which were still standing compared with her daughter's.

'Does yours wear glasses?' she asked.

Sophie made a face.

'Yes.'

Her mother collapsed all her characters that did not wear glasses, then pursed her lips in thought.

Sophie tapped her fingertips on the table.

'Does yours have a moustache?'

'Yes.'

Sophie grinned, then collapsed all her own characters without moustaches. This still left her with seven, whilst she could see that her mother was now down to four.

'Right, Sophie,' her mother said, with mock determination. 'I'm going to make a wild guess, now . . . Is it Joe?'

Sophie giggled with delight.

'No, mum, it's not Joe. Now it's my turn.'

She perused her characters once more, but before she could ask her next question, their game was interrupted by the sound of the telephone from the hall.

Her mother rose from her chair. 'Hang on, Sophie. I won't be a minute. It's bound to be dad, saying he's going to be back later than he thought.'

Prue picked up the phone. 'Hello,' she said, smiling as she recognised her husband's voice, even though the line was by no means a good one.

'. . . but I can't make it, my darling. I've got to be in Court that afternoon.'

She frowned. 'Pardon, darling? What did you say? I don't quite understand.'

But her husband did not seem to understand her

either. For his voice droned on without stopping.

'. . . of course I do, my darling, don't you think I'd much rather be making love to you than defending some yobbo who drinks too much and punches policemen?'

'Darling, it's me. Prue,' she interrupted, raising the volume of her voice. But her husband still did not seem to react to her at all.

'. . . Friday . . . I don't know about Friday yet . . . hell, and I won't really know until the afternoon before . . .'

Prue took the receiver from her ear and stared at it for a second, as if, somehow, it had a life of its own. But she could still just hear his voice.

'. . . I know it's awful . . . it's awful for me too . . . no, I can't make any time at the weekend, you know that . . .'

She lifted the receiver back to her ear.

'. . . no, it's not because of my "bloody wife", as you call her. If it was just Prue, I wouldn't worry, you know it's because of Sophie. Now don't torment yourself. There's no need . . .'

'Seb . . .' she said weakly, 'Sebastian . . .'

'. . . I've told you a thousand times, I haven't made love to Prue for months . . . no, I promise . . . no, never. You have to believe me. I believe you, when you say you don't make love with your damned George . . .'

Prue felt for the chair by the phone and collapsed on to it.

'. . . all right, Annabel, I'll tell you what I'll try to do. How would you like us to stay over Friday night? But only on the proviso that I'm back at home by midday Saturday . . . what'll I say? Oh, that I have to go to Bristol or London or somewhere . . . just leave all that to me.'

Prue let the receiver slowly descend from her ear, then replaced it very carefully on its base – for fear if she were to be too definite in her action, her husband might somehow detect her presence on the line. Almost immediately, she heard her daughter's voice from the sitting-room.

'Mummy, are you coming?'

'In a moment, darling. I won't be long.'

She closed her eyes very tightly and prayed very hard that what she'd heard was all part of some nightmare from which she would very soon wake up. But the terrifying rub was, she had recognised the excuse her husband had seemed to be framing for his absence from home. It was identical to the one he had used the previous weekend.

John Stride pressed the button on his intercom.

'Send the next in, please.'

A moment later, a diminutive little woman entered his surgery, with a handbag over her shoulder that dangled down by her calves.

'Come in, Mrs Rickett,' the doctor invited, with as much enthusiasm as he could muster, then indicated the chair in front of his desk.

Thelma Rickett sat down, tucking her legs under the front rung of the chair and pulling her skirt well down over her knees.

Stride consulted the notes in front of him, then looked back at his patient.

'Last time was that nasty fungus you had growing in your mouth, wasn't it, Mrs Rickett?'

A more apt complaint for such a thin lipped, thin framed, mean 'excuse-for-a-woman' Stride could not imagine. Though the doctor had a reputation for being charitable about almost everyone he knew, he had, after many efforts not to do so, made an exception in the case of the local nurseryman's wife. And in so doing, had aligned his feelings with those of almost everyone in Hallowes who had come across Thelma Rickett – the only exception being the Reverend Meek and certain members of the congregation of St Matthew's church. Even they respected the tiny woman more for her good works for the church than for herself.

'Cleared up, has it now?' Stride continued. 'No recurrence?'

She shook her head very carefully, so as not to disturb the tight perm she had treated herself to only the day before.

'Haven't come about that, Doctor, I haven't.'

'So what . . . ?' he began, but she did not let him finish.

'Me head,' she said bluntly.

Stride leant forward.

'Your head? You mean you're getting headaches?'

'No.'

'Then what . . . ?'

'I dunno. You're the doctor, not me.'

'But, Mrs Rickett, you will have to give me more to go on than that. I can't diagnose if . . .'

'All right then,' she sniffed. 'It's like a great heavy lump is sitting right on top of my head. Sort of weighs me down, it does. Makes me depressed, good and proper.'

Stride came out from behind his desk and came round to her side.

'Head hurt anywhere? I mean when you touch it or lie down?'

'No.'

The doctor reached forward to examine her, but she tilted her head away from him.

'No. Nothing like that.'

He thought for a moment.

'So no headaches, no local pain, no . . .'

'No. I told you.'

'So it's not so much an ache or a pain, as a . . . feeling. That it?'

'Could be.'

'Do you suffer from it all the time or, say, when you wake up or in the evenings?'

'Now and again.'

'So it's intermittent?'

'S'pose so.'

Stride reached for her wrist. This time she didn't draw away - her wrist hadn't had a perm.

'My heart's all right,' she grumbled.

'I'm sure it is, Mrs Rickett. Just routine, that's all.'

He noted her pulse rate was on the high side, but nothing to cause anxiety.

He went back and sat behind his desk.

'Any troubles at home, Mrs Rickett?'

Her eyes flicked up, like a fox's when its lair is disturbed.

'No. Why should there be?'

'Oh, nothing,' he tried to calm her. 'I just meant perhaps you were working too hard in the nursery, or maybe, you have someone in the family who you are worrying about.'

'Like who, pray?' she queried sharply.

'I wasn't thinking of anyone in particular, believe me. I was just trying to pinpoint what might be causing this heavy depressed feeling of yours.'

She took a deep breath and seemed about to say something. Then she obviously changed her mind.

Stride tried another tack.

'Mr Rickett well, is he?'

She did not reply.

He waited a moment, then said quietly, 'Are you worried about your husband? Is that it, Mrs Rickett?'

Still no answer.

'Is it he who has the headaches, sorry, heavy feelings?'

'No,' she snapped. 'He's too healthy by half, he is.' Then she added under her breath, 'And he don't have no feelings, he don't, anyway. You've met him, you know what he's like.'

Stride had, indeed, met him. And he could certainly see something in what his wife was saying. The nurseryman could be said to be in 'rude health' in almost every sense of the phrase and was about the last person in the world he would have imagined Mrs Rickett marrying. But then he supposed, neither could be said to be a brilliant catch and many a marriage pairing was a last resort, anyway.

'But I have a feeling you're worried about him all the same. That right?'

Again no response. Stride decided it was time to plunge into the deep end and get it over with, one way or the other.

'You are forty-seven now, that right, Mrs Rickett?'

She pointed to his notes.

'Must be written on me cards, isn't it?'

'Have you stopped . . . er . . . ?'

'If you're trying to ask if I'm still having me periods, well, the answer's no.'

'Ah. Thank you, Mrs Rickett.'

She leaned forward in her chair.

'I know what you're getting at. You reckon I'm having these feelings 'cos of the change of life, aren't you?'

'Well, I . . .'

'Well, I'm not,' she cut in. 'So there.'

Seeing he was getting nowhere, Stride decided to return to the subject of the obviously detested husband.

'Mr Rickett wouldn't be, by any chance, . . . ?'

But again he was not allowed to finish.

'No, he wouldn't. 'Cos all that nonsense stopped ages ago. Really, Doctor, you men are all the same. All you seem to think about is . . .' She couldn't bring herself to say the word.

Stride leant forward over his desk and said quietly, 'So what's the trouble, Mrs Rickett? You can tell me. It's in our code, don't forget. We're sworn never to reveal our patients' . . .'

She looked up and said suddenly, 'Can't you give me some tablets?'

'Well, I can, of course. But I can't promise they'll cure you of . . .'

Yet again she cut him off. 'I don't want them for me, Doctor. They're for *him*.'

'Him? Your husband, you mean?'

'Who else?'

He frowned. 'I don't quite follow.'

'You know, tablets like they give them in the army.'

Stride kicked himself for not having followed her drift.

'Can I ask a question, Mrs Rickett? If you and he are no longer . . . well, why should he need tablets of that sort?'

'Because . . .' She hesitated. Stride came to her aid.

'Because he's showing some interest in someone else, perhaps?'

She stared down at her lap and her thin veined hands.

'He makes phone calls. I know he does. I looked at our last quarterly bill. It's much higher than it's ever been. And we aren't doing any more business than we ever did.'

'Is that your only evidence? The bill. Surely . . .'

'I've heard her, I have. Picked up the phone twice, I have and she's been on. Foul mouthed creature . . .' She shuddered. 'Ugh! You can't imagine the filth she came out with. Wouldn't stop, whatever I said to her. Just went on and on about . . . well, doesn't bear repeating what about.'

'You actually spoke to her?' Stride said, with considerable surprise.

'Yeh. But I don't know whether she heard me or not, so much blasted crackle on the phone.'

'So what did you do then?'

'Put the phone down on her, of course, having told her good and proper never to try to get in touch with my husband again.'

'Mentioned it to Mr Rickett, have you?'

She shook her head, then looked up, with a malicious grin on her face.

'Not yet. But if she tries it again, he'll know soon enough what I think of him. Oh yes, he'll know all right, don't you worry.'

'Darling . . .'

'Yes, dear?'

Prue Fanshawe did not need to look at her husband, for

she was pretty certain she knew what was about to follow his almost nonchalant 'darling'.

'About tomorrow night.'

'Yes, dear? What about tomorrow night?'

'Well, I'm afraid I won't be able to go with you to the Strides, after all.'

Still she did not look up from her book, *Hotel du Lac*.

'Oh?'

'Yes, you see I just have to go to Bristol again. I'm starting to regret that I took on this slander case now. Should have stuck to my old rule – keep your clients on home pastures.'

For the first time, she looked up.

'Couldn't you go earlier in the day, then you'd be back in time for Mary's dinner party?'

His eyes didn't even flicker, she noted, so practised had he obviously now become at his deceptions.

'The chap I have to see works all day. Can only see him in the evenings. Could be the vital witness for my client. I can't not go, I'm afraid.'

She looked back at her book. 'All right, dear.'

Neither spoke for some little time. Then Prue said quietly, 'Phone rang last night.'

Fanshawe got up and went over to the cocktail cabinet.

'Oh yes? Like a drink?'

She shook her head, then waited whilst he poured himself a Scotch and soda. She did not want to waste her next words on only a half-attentive husband.

When he had resumed his seat opposite her, she went on, 'The line was very bad.'

'Report it?'

'No.'

'Should do. One or two of my clients have complained to me recently that their lines seem to be far worse than under the old telephone system.' He grimaced. 'Price of progress, I suppose.'

'But even with the crackle, I picked up enough of what

the caller was saying to . . . get the message.'

Fanshawe sipped at his Scotch, then rubbed his mouth with his pale fingers.

'What message was that, dear?' he asked with obvious lack of interest.

'It was someone apologising for not being able to make a date.' She smiled weakly. 'A bit like you tonight, really.'

'Who was it? And what date are you talking about?'

She put down her book and looked at her husband intently. She did not wish to miss one iota of his reaction to her reply.

'Well, the problem of the date was soon cleared up. He moved it to Friday afternoon. Then suggested that perhaps he might be able to stay the night.'

He looked up from his Scotch. 'Someone staying the night? Here? What on earth are you talking about?'

'Oh, not here, dear, no. The last place I think he had in mind was here.'

Her husband put down his Scotch. She could see that now he could just have tumbled to the quite unprecedented fact that she might be playing with him.

'What are you going on about, dear? Who is this "he"?'

'Someone you know and love very well, darling.'

Her husband rose abruptly from his chair. 'Oh, come on, Prue. Out with it.'

'All right, dear, since you ask for it.' She took a deep breath. 'It was you.'

His mouth fell open.

'Me?'

'Yes, *you*, dear,' she replied calmly.

'What do you mean, me? I didn't ring you last night. You know I didn't.'

'That's right, Sebastian, you didn't ring *me* last night. But you did make a call to someone else, because I listened to it.'

'You listened to it?'

'Yes, dear.'

'But I didn't make any calls after office hours last night. It can't have been me.'

'It can't have been anyone else, dear.'

He came over to her chair. 'Come on, Prue, it's way past April the first, late September is no time for practical jokes.'

'I wish it were all just some practical joke, Sebastian.'

He had never seen his wife in a mood like this before and it worried him. He moved behind her chair and asked, hesitantly, 'All right. So what did . . . I say to this . . . someone else?'

Prue rose from her own chair and went over to the drinks cabinet. She slowly and deliberately poured herself a gin and tonic, enjoying making her husband wait. Then glass in hand, she went over to the french windows, then turned to face him.

Backlit as she now was, Fanshawe could not see his wife's expression, as she said, 'You arranged a dirty night away with your lover.'

He swallowed hard.

'My lover?'

'Yes, your lover. And client. Annabel Craven.' She tutted at him, like some gently remonstrating school teacher. 'What a naughty boy you're being, Sebastian. Never mind your marriage vows. Just imagine what the Law Society will think of your bedding one of your clients. Oh dear, oh dear, oh deary me.'

'That you, Annabel?'

She instantly recognised the urgency in his voice.

'What's wrong, Seb?'

'I don't know.'

'But there's something, isn't there?'

'Yes.'

'Oh God, don't tell me she's found out.'

'Well . . . the whole thing's crazy . . . unbelievable.'

'So she *has* found out?'

'Well, she has and she hasn't. It's all very . . .'

'Oh, drop it, Seb. If she has found out, just come clean, can't you? I'm not a child.'

'Now, hang on, Annabel. It's not quite like that . . .'

Fanshawe proceeded to recount the horror of the evening before and his story was followed by what seemed like an interminable silence.

'Annabel, darling. You still there?'

He heard a sigh. 'Just about.'

'Now you can see why I'm all totally confused. What happened, or what she *says* happened, is downright impossible. As you know, I didn't ring you last night. And as you equally know, the call she says she heard sounds like the one I made last week, not last night.'

Annabel Craven's somewhat shallow mind raced for an explanation.

'She must be lying. She must have heard about us from, I don't know, someone or other. And made up all this rubbish just to scare you.'

'Prue's not like that. Prue's always been . . .'

'Don't tell me,' Annabel cut in sharply. 'Loyal and honest, devoted and true. Aren't all deceived wives, goddamn them?'

'Sorry, Annabel, but I really don't think she is lying. I think she really did hear something on the phone last night. God knows what it was, or how it happened, but . . .'

'Oh, don't be an idiot, Seb. Pull yourself together. How can anybody get a call that's a week old and was, anyway, made to someone else?'

'I don't know.'

After a pause, she asked, 'So that's how it's left, is it? You denying you're having an affair with me and maintaining that the voice she heard was not you, but someone else who is arranging to screw some Annabel or other. And that it was all a crossed line and she was deceived about whose voice it really was by all the crackle?'

'Right.'

'And you say she quietened down a bit after that top of the head explanation?'

'She never got angry. That was the awful part. She talked about it all, as if she was describing her normal boring old day.'

'But you say you think she might have swallowed it?'

'*Might* is the operative word.'

'So let me guess, my darling. To further convince her that you're whiter than a bloody Daz-washed shirt, you're cancelling your night stop-over in – where was it you were supposed to be going – Bristol, wasn't it?'

'Sorry, darling. I had to. We'll refix something. Don't worry.'

'Worry?' She laughed derisively. 'Why should I worry? I'm only a mistress, after all. It's wives who worry; mistresses just grin and bear it. Or not "bare it", as will be the case this week.'

'Don't talk like that. I'll just have to let the whole thing die down in her mind for a bit, that's all. Then we'll refix . . .'

'Seb, you're daydreaming,' she cut in. 'Whatever the truth of last night, whether she actually heard that phone call or was just making the whole thing up to scare you – which is the most likely – she will be on the alert twenty-four hours a day from now on. And if we try any of your fake overnight trips again, I wouldn't be at all surprised if I suddenly saw her face at the motel window, whilst you're obliviously still banging away at me.'

'Oh God, Annabel, there must be a way.'

She laughed. 'Somehow, my dear Sebastian, I don't think God is going to bust a divine gut to help us through this little crisis. You'd be better off putting your call through to the Devil.'

Chapter Seven

Mary Stride felt herself blushing slightly, as she caught her husband's eye in the dressing-table mirror.

'Don't do what?' he teased, pulling the bedclothes further up around him.

'You know.'

She reached for her jar of cleansing cream and started to take off her make-up.

'Cat can look at a king. Sorry, queen.'

'Didn't know you were a cat,' she bleered back at him, as she rubbed the cream around her eyes. 'Bit of a dog, sometimes, maybe, but . . .'

'Hurry up,' he grinned, 'Otherwise I'll be asleep before I can be a bit of a dog again.'

She raised her now cream laden eyebrows and reached for a Kleenex.

'Talking of being in a hurry,' she remarked, 'did you notice how anxious old Sebastian was to go tonight? Not like him. He usually hangs on till all hours and we have to practically throw him out on his ear.'

'Thought both of them were a bit strange tonight, actually. Didn't you?'

She nodded. 'Did you notice Prue ate hardly anything at all? And after I'd gone to all the bother of cooking her favourite, or what she claims as her favourite, dish as well.'

'Never mind, darling,' he reassured her. 'It's one of my favourites too. I can never have enough of your lasagne.'

She laughed. 'You didn't have to say that, you know. I

saw you dolloping seconds like a half starved schoolboy.'

'Seb didn't overdo himself much either, so somebody had to oblige.'

She finished wiping the lipstick off her well defined mouth, then said, 'You don't think there's anything wrong between them, do you?'

He shrugged. 'There's probably nothing to it. Maybe they had a row or something just before they came out. I wouldn't read too much into their behaviour tonight. Anyway, you had a chance for a quiet talk with Prue, didn't you? She was gone ages after she'd said she was just popping into the kitchen to see if you needed a hand.'

Mary replaced the top on her cleansing cream jar and smoothed her face with her fingers.

'Didn't say much, really. Just sat on a stool and watched. I felt like one of those cooks on television, it's most uncomfortable with an audience.'

'So she didn't let anything slip or get to pour out her heart?'

'Nope. We spent most of the time chatting about Mark and her Sophie and how she likes the way they love playing and being together. Then the rest was just several bits and pieces. Oh yes, she did go on a bit about phones.'

He sat up on one elbow. 'Phones?'

'Yes, phones. She said theirs had been acting a bit funny recently and asked whether we had had any trouble with ours. I said, no.'

'Did she describe what was wrong?'

She turned on the stool to face him. 'Well, it was all a bit garbled, but from what I could gather, she's had a call or, perhaps, more than one call, where she seemed to be connected with somebody who just kept talking and talking and didn't seem to be able to hear what she said.'

'Nothing, surely, in that. Just a crossed line.'

'That was my reaction. And she said it was hers at first. But she said the more she thought about it, the less she felt it could have been a crossed line.'

Stride held out his arms towards his wife and she came over, shrugged off her dressing gown and, now naked, climbed into bed beside him.

'What on earth made her think that?'

'She said she recognised the voice, even though the line was, apparently, crackly. And it seemed to be talking about planning an event or whatever that she said she recognised as having taken place a week before.'

'Anyone we know?'

'No. She didn't say who it was. Just that she'd come to the conclusion that it must have been . . .' She stopped suddenly. 'Oh darling, it sounds absolutely ridiculous, when I think about it.'

'Never mind, get it over with.'

His hand moved across to her breast. 'I have other things in mind right now than listening to dear Prue's wanderings.'

'Well, she said she thinks she must have received . . . a call from the past.'

Walter Blair woke with a start and sat bolt upright in bed. In the distance he could hear thunder rumbling across the hills around Hallowes and at first, he thought it must have been the storm that had woken him. But as his brain warmed up, he suddenly realised there was a much more local sound – that of the telephone ringing in the hall.

With a curse, he got out of bed and pulled on a dressing gown. On the landing, he quietly opened the door to his daughter's bedroom, just to check she was still asleep. All was well, so he padded downstairs and answered the phone.

'Yes?' he said curtly. But the voice on the crackly line seemed to be already in full flight.

'. . . thank heavens old Stride came up with the pill,

otherwise, the way we're going, I'd always be counting the days until . . .'

'Hello, hello,' he cut in loudly. 'Who's there?' But the question was superfluous. If his two a.m. brain was not deceiving him, he would swear, despite the bad line, that the voice was that of his daughter.

'. . . hey, Tom, you sod, I hate you for making me shave for those photographs . . . every time I put my hand down to it, it feels all bristly and scratchy . . .'

Blair shook his head vigorously, as if to help wake himself up from this seeming nightmare. For now, there was not a shadow of doubt in his mind but that the voice was his daughter's. And yet that was impossible. He had only just seen her, curled up fast asleep in bed.

'Hello, hello. This is Walter Blair . . .' Suddenly he remembered the previous call. The call he and his wife had ultimately convinced themselves must have been a crossed line or a fault on their phone. Anyway, they'd reported it to the operator and left it there. For, obviously, the voice they heard then could not have been Bettina's. After all, she'd come home, hadn't she, while they were still on the phone?

'. . . but I tell you, Tommy, that's the last time I'm going to let you do it in that studio. It's upstairs or nothing at all from now on . . .'

'Hello, hello,' Blair banged the receiver with his fist, 'if that's some bugger up to some bloody unfunny practical joke, I'll tell you right now, if you try it again . . .'

'. . . I can't ring tomorrow, because . . .'

'. . . you'll find the police on your tail . . .'

'. . . we've got a hockey match and I won't be back until . . .'

'I'll tell you bloody for why. I'm reporting this to them first thing in the morning.'

'. . . mum's already home . . .'

'D'yer hear me? Don't think I can't work out what you've bloody done. You've gone and got my daughter to record . . .'

'. . . so don't waggle it at anybody else, you horny bastard, until I see you Sat'day . . .'

'. . . this filthy rubbish just to get us going, haven't you? Come on, bugger you, admit it . . .'

But his daughter's voice teased on, like the continuing rumbles of thunder.

'. . . otherwise, mate, I'll ruddy bite it off, I will, and that's a promise.'

'Oh come on, Dad,' his wife urged, her arm around her sobbing daughter. 'Now that's enough. Bett has said a thousand times she doesn't know anything about it.'

Walter Blair wagged his finger angrily at his wife.

'There you go, Maggie, defending her again. How can we bloody believe her? She's admitted now that she's on the pill. She wouldn't need the effing pill, if she wasn't up to something, would she? And that ruddy recording makes it bloody plain who she's up to something with. It must be that new photographer in the High Street. Tom Tully. I've heard he's a randy bastard.'

His wife looked at her watch. 'Walter, it's half past three in the morning. And Bett must get some sleep, otherwise she'll be no good at school. Can't we leave it now and go back to our own bedroom?'

'No, we bloody can't,' Blair snapped. 'I want it all out right now.' He moved towards his daughter, who was sitting on the side of her bed, shaking and with her head in her hands.

'Now, listen to me, Bett. If you don't know this prick, Tully, then how come anyone could make a recording like I heard? What would be the point of inventing all that about Tom and the studio and all that? What's bloody more, how can you go on claiming you've never made any recording, when I ruddy well heard it, didn't I? I'm not lying. Not like you ruddy are. And it's bloody unlikely anyone's imitating your voice just to get you into trouble, like you claim. I mean there can't be that many prize winning female impressionists in your school, now can there? Otherwise, I'd have bloody seen them on the telly in Opportunity Knocks.'

His wife pushed him away. 'Now shut up, Walter, and leave Bett alone. She's had enough for one night.'

'From what I heard tonight, she can't get enough.'

'Walter,' his wife shouted, getting up and confronting him. 'That's quite enough. Quite enough. I can understand you being annoyed Bett went off and got herself on to the pill without telling us. But you're letting it fuddle your whole ruddy brain, rob you of any shred of common sense.'

She put a calming hand on her husband's shoulder, as lightning flashed across the distant sky.

'Come on, Walter. We know our Bett. We know in our hearts, she'd never be party to making any recording to hurt us, let alone get up to what you said that recording was about. What's more, you say the line was crackly, so you could well have been deceived by some other girl thinking it funny or clever to imitate our Bett. How do you know there isn't a good mimic in her class? I've heard children do some marvellous imitations – sometimes quite as good as Mike Yarwood's or Faith Brown's.'

She took her husband's hand. 'So what do you say? Let's just leave everything to the morning now and let Bett get some sleep, if she can, after all this.'

'But I can't believe . . .'

'Yes, you can, Walt.' She turned back to her daughter, who, by now, had stopped trembling and was staring at the screwed up handkerchief in her lap.

'We're going to leave you now, Bett. Tomorrow you just find out which of the girls pulled this dirty trick tonight and I'll report her to the headmistress, before she tries it with someone else.'

But as she gently started to steer her husband towards the bedroom door, he suddenly stopped and pointed his finger back at his daughter.

'I've just remembered something else, Maggie, that

call said. 'It said . . .' He hesitated, then lowered his voice. 'It said that man had got her to shave.'

'Shave?' his wife queried. 'Well, men like smooth legs, that girl would know that, wouldn't she?'

'No, not her legs. Her . . .'

She looked back at her daughter in disbelief.

'Bett, you haven't, have you? Now don't lie. I can look, you know.'

Bettina slowly nodded, then her wet eyes, for the first time, slightly brightened.

'Yes, that's it,' she said, grasping at straws. 'I did it just for a lark and told the other girls about it. So everyone knew . . . everybody in the class. Some of them even saw it . . . me, when I was changing for netball practice. That's what must have given whoever is imitating me the idea.'

Maggie Blair gave a sigh of relief.

'Well, there you are, Walt. Nothing to get so worked up about, I told you. Now let's, for God's sake, get back to bed and grab a bit of sleep, if the ruddy storm will let us.'

Reluctantly, her husband turned back towards the door, but as he went out, Bettina heard him mutter, 'But I'll bloody have something to say to that doctor in the morning.'

'Who was that?' Penny Seymour-Jones asked, as the elderly customer pocketed her change and went out of the shop.

Priscilla Marsh bit her lip. 'Oh . . . er . . . I think it must have been a wrong number.'

She came out of the office and started to fuss around the well-shined aubergines in their angled tray.

'I don't know what's wrong with the phones recently,' Penny grumbled, staring out the window at the passing traffic. 'Can't blame it all on the stormy weather. Been nothing but trouble since they changed over to the new system.'

'Er . . . yes, . . . it would seem so,' Priscilla commented quietly. 'Personally, I've always preferred the old phones, where you had to put your finger in and dial round.'

'Press buttons are the only bit I like,' Penny commented. 'Save a lot of time and certainly your fingernails.'

'Yes, I suppose that's true,' but Priscilla's mind was not really on the present exchange with her employer, but still pondering on the strangeness of the telephone call. After a few moments, she decided she had to take her courage in both hands and do a little probing. Otherwise she knew she would fret about it all day and most of the night.

'Penny . . .'

'Yes?' her employer drawled, her attention now on a slim-hipped young man getting out of a TVR sports car in the street outside. To her disappointment, he did not even look towards the Health Farm, but went straight into the art gallery and picture framers' opposite.

'Penny . . . are you absolutely . . . sure about Griffons? You know, our new suppliers.'

Penny turned back to Priscilla, her eyes now coldly suspicious.

'What on earth can have prompted that question?'

'Well, it's just that . . . well, I just wonder sometimes, whether all the produce we buy from Griffons is quite as, well, "organic", as they claim.'

Penny came out from behind the counter and stood, hands on hips, in front of her.

'And what, pray, prompted that wild and woolly thought?'

Priscilla avoided her gaze, as she hunted for a plausible reason. 'Oh, it's just that, well, some of the stuff doesn't seem quite as fresh as we used to get from Goodalls.'

'We haven't had any complaints, have we?'

'No.'

'Well then . . .'

'But Penny . . .'

Her employer threw up her hands. 'Oh God, Priscilla, don't fuss so. If you have one failing, it's certainly that you're not happy unless you've something to fuss over.'

As she walked back to the counter, Priscilla suddenly came out with, 'That call. It wasn't a wrong number. It *was* someone complaining. I didn't like to tell you.'

Penny shrugged. 'So. You can't please all the people all the time.'

Priscilla smiled to herself at the aptness of the saying her employer had just misquoted, then went on hurriedly, 'In fact, it wasn't so much a complaint, as an accusation.'

'Accusation?' Penny's nonchalant indifference had now certainly evaporated.

'Yes. She said that we were selling produce as organic, when it wasn't . . . and . . . and . . .'

'And what?'

'And that it was all because we'd changed to Griffons as our suppliers and that . . . and that the Health Farm was charging fancy prices for goods that were no different from what you can get at under half the price at any ordinary greengrocers.'

Penny thought for a moment, then asked, 'You said "she". So it was a woman?'

Priscilla nodded.

'Recognise the voice?'

'Er . . . no,' she lied and turned her head away to hide any blush.

After another pause, her employer said, 'Well, if she comes through again, be sure to put her on to me. I think one threat of legal action should shut her mouth for good.'

Priscilla nodded, then adjusted an orange back into its neat display pyramid.

She did not mention the call again that day and made no attempt to warn her employer that someone must be recording her telephone conversations with the new, so called 'organic' suppliers. For in Priscilla's sober view, those who deliberately played with fire, deserved to be burnt.

John Stride put the morning newspaper aside and stretched his long legs out in front of him. He decided he had no intention of spoiling his one morning off by absorbing any more of the world's bad news in that morning's *Independent*. For he tended to take too much to heart the catastrophes, be they flooding, famine, kidnappings or killings, even when they occured in remote areas of the globe, far from his own world and experience. What's more, he became immensely irritated by journalists who reported such tragedies with a detached matter-of-factness that they would not dare to use were they reporting on an event a hundredth or thousandth of the magnitude in their dear old United Kingdom. That morning's edition was a prime example of this contrasting standard – a minor riot at a first division football match rating twenty times the column inches of a flood in Bangladesh, that had killed over two thousand people and left tens of thousands homeless.

Stride turned with relief to the weekly local paper, the *Hallowes Gazette*. At least, in there, the worst headlines were merely concerned with the recent storms and growing complaints about the standard of the new telephone service. He was halfway through a short report on the latter, when he heard a car pull up outside the house.

From where he was sitting, he could only see the car above its waistline, but he recognised it as an old, first model Vauxhall Cavalier. He turned back to the paper, assuming it was some door-to-door salesman, probably for double glazing – Hallowes had experienced a rash of them since the storms had begun. The double talk invariably included, 'You see, madam, the double glass not only cuts down your fuel bills, but even the noise from the traffic, your neighbours, aircraft and, of course, mindful of the thunder and lightning recently, lets you sleep through it all . . .' or maybe the electrician his wife had sent for to fit another couple of power points in the house.

But very soon after he had heard the doorbell ring, his wife, Mary, opened the sitting-room door.

'I'm sorry, darling, but I've got a Mr Blair in the hall.'

Her husband put down his paper. 'Oh hell, Mary, I keep telling my patients not to worry us at home. Really, we will have to go ex-directory if this goes on. Tell him to make an appointment at the surgery.'

'But John, he seems very upset . . .' But before Mary could explain further, she was pushed aside by the obviously fuming figure of Walter Blair.

'I'm damn well going to see you now, Doctor, and don't give me any garbage about your damned surgery.'

Stride got up from his chair and indicated to Mary that it might be wiser if she left the visitor solely to him. After an 'Are you sure you know what you're doing?' look, she went out, quietly closing the door behind her.

'Now, Mr Blair, it is not my practice to see . . .'

'I don't care what your bloody practice is,' Blair cut in. 'I'm here and I'm going to stay until I've had my say.'

Stride decided that further remonstration would only inflame his visitor, so indicated a chair.

'I don't need to sit, Doctor. There's nothing wrong with me. I'm not a ruddy patient.'

'So . . .'

Blair came right up to Stride and jabbed a thick finger almost in his face. Suddenly the doctor realised what might well have incensed him.

'So . . . I'll give you "so". What the bloody hell do you think you're doing putting my daughter on the pill?'

His guess had been right. It was about Blair's daughter, Bettina. But he couldn't imagine she would have disclosed what she had obviously wanted to keep a secret. So how the hell had her father found out?

'If your daughter is old enough in law to make love,' Stride replied firmly, yet quietly, 'she is, in my view, old enough to consult her doctor about the pill.'

'Rubbish. Bloody rubbish. First, my daughter's not a ruddy teenage whore like some of those school kids I hear about. So she doesn't need no ruddy pill. Second, if she did, you, as our doctor, should have bloody advised me or her mother, that she's come and asked you. Don't parents have any rights these days?' His finger stabbed the air once more. 'Eh? Eh? Or does everyone else know better than they do about their children? Eh? Tell me that, Doctor, come on, tell me bloody that.'

Stride was silent for a moment, then asked quietly, 'May I ask how you found out that I had prescribed the pill for your daughter?'

Blair looked taken aback.

'What's that got to do with anything?'

'I'd just like to know, that's all. In case someone may have been indiscreet at my surgery or . . .'

Blair's finger stopped its stabbing. 'Yeh, more than bloody likely. Could be how that ruddy girl . . .'

'What . . . "ruddy" girl? Are you saying some girl told you?' Stride asked, disbelievingly.

'It wasn't quite like that.'

For the first time, Stride saw that his visitor might be prepared to talk, rather than simply vituperate.

'Why don't you sit down, Mr Blair, and tell me all about it?'

He indicated the chair once more.

'Now, this girl . . . can you tell me who she is and how she came to tell you about your daughter?'

'Well, it's like this 'ere, Doctor,' Blair began as he, resignedly, moved towards the chair. 'Middle of the night, during the ruddy storm, the phone rang . . .'

Two figures moved away from the deep scar in Widow's Field, which the JCB had dug the previous afternoon.

'Well, William, that's not so bad. The shale's down deeper than I thought.'

Drench looked across at George Craven and sniggered.

'Worried you were going to have to shell out for top soil for their tiny gardens, were you, George?'

The property developer did not reply, but decided to ask an equally barbed question of his own.

'How's your mother then, William? There's talk around that she's managed to raise quite a rabble for her protest march through Hallowes.'

'Damn my mother,' Drench growled. 'She's no more chance of stopping this, than she had over the telephone exchange deal.'

Craven pursed his lips. 'I hope you're right, William. There's a helluva lot riding on this.'

' 'Course I'm right.'

Craven stopped and looked back towards the trench.

'Well, we've made a start now. Kind of reassuring, isn't it? Soon I'll get the big stuff in to level and terrace the site a little. Now I know the depth of soil . . .'

He suddenly pointed towards the telegraph poles that bordered one side of the field.

'My God, do you spy what my little eyes spy?'

Drench held his large but podgy hand up to his eyes and looked where his companion was pointing.

'Oh shit.'

'Now, now, William,' Craven chided with a smile on his squarely rugged face. 'That's no way to speak of the mother that bore you. Dragon she may be. Witch even. Mad as a hatter, in all likelihood. But shit, never.'

But Drench was in no mood for banter. For his mother had always been his Achilles heel and he didn't like anyone lashing out at his sorest tendon.

He grabbed at Craven's arm. 'Come on, George, let's get out of here.'

Craven shrugged himself free. 'Don't be childish, William. You're a big boy now. Now's your chance to tackle her about her crazy march. I'll be fascinated to hear what she has to say.'

Reluctantly, Drench complied and followed Craven as he started to walk back towards the trench – the spot towards which it had now become clear Enid Drench was heading.

She said nothing as she approached them and gave no sign of recognition. Both men watched her as she came up to the untidy heaps of red Devon soil piled each side of the trench, both seeming afraid to break the silence before she did. But as she eased her large frame gingerly down to kneel by the soil, the hills broke the spell by echoing a faint but recognisable roll of thunder.

'Just like you, Mother,' her son muttered. 'It had started out a sunny day, then you came on the scene.'

She did not even look up, but reached out with a large and liver spotted hand and grasped some soil between her fingers. She seemed to be wanting to feel each grain, before she finally let it slip to the ground. Still she did not speak, nor even recognise their presence.

'Mother, don't think I don't know what you're up to,' Drench said at last, now thoroughly unnerved by her behaviour. 'In a second, you're going to come out with some ridiculous mumbo-jumbo about the sanctity of the soil, each grain crying out against the rape perpetrated by our capitalist digger, or some such. Well, I tell you, Mother, that kind of crap may go down well with that loony society in Hallowes of which you seem to be the queen nut, but it doesn't cut any ice with the powers that be, no matter how many ruddy petitions or marches you organise.'

Enid Drench reached forward and picked up another handful of earth. As if by some uncanny arrangement, lightning zigzagged across the hills towards Dartmoor.

Her son laughed. 'How do you do that, Mother? I'll swear you must have some light or sound FX switch hidden under that big, black peasant dress of yours.'

But his smile instantly vanished, as she suddenly thrust her handful of soil up towards him.

'See, the red in the soil?' she intoned, the crackle in her voice reminding Craven of the old, scratched 78rpm recordings his own mother still sometimes played in her lonely room in the old people's home in Paignton.

'Oh God, here we go,' her son muttered.

'The good Devon soil is bleeding from the vicious wounds you're making,' his mother crackled on, letting the soil filter through her fingers, like some ancient, black befrocked Mother Time. 'Bleeding with the desecration.'

'For Pete's sake, Mother, the soil round here has always been red. It's red as a beetroot from here to Torquay and beyond.' He turned to Craven. 'See what I mean, George? How can you reason with anybody like this?'

She rose from one knee and grasping a fresh handful of soil, thrust it towards her son.

'Take a good look, William Drench. Red the soil may be, but not as red as this.' Grasping her son's arm, she raised herself up to her feet and held the soil in front of his eyes.

'Look. Look hard. Note it well, my son, before it's too late.'

He turned away, his florid face now almost vermilion with embarrassment.

'Oh, come on, George, let's get out of here, before we all go as batty as she is.'

Suddenly his mother lashed out and smeared the soil down his shirt and jacket. Drench, in his horror, took a step backwards. His foot slipped in the mound of soil and he felt himself falling. He held out a supplicating hand to Craven, but too late. He crashed down on to his right shoulder and screamed out with pain, as it protested against the impact of his considerable weight. As he twisted to try to get himself back upright, the soil beneath him started to slide back into the trench and a second later, he found himself following it, to hit the exposed shale with a sickening thud.

Craven switched to and fro from Enid Drench's look of avenging triumph to the red-besmirched body now recumbent in the trench, like some victim of violence in a rough and ready grave – the similarity was made all the more vivid by the soil that continued to fall downwards to form a shallow covering over his colleague's large frame.

Try as he might, Craven found it impossible to move to help. It was as if his feet were somehow being held by giant clamps hidden in the grass. As he shook his head at the impossibility of such a thought, he was suddenly blinded by an explosion of light and sound that seemed to blow every fuse in his befuddled brain.

He cowered down and hid his face in his hands. As the thunder of the explosion died away, there was an ominous silence. Then after a moment he heard a crackling sound that was vaguely familiar to him. Trembling, he removed a hand from one eye and looked around nervously. He could just see Drench's arm moving up to the rim of the trench. But of his mother, there now seemed to be no sign. It was as if she had disappeared into the ether like some witch on a broomstick.

He found the absence of the ominous black figure a considerable relief and his spirits started to lift. He kicked himself for having been so shocked by what had obviously been no more than a violent storm passing overhead, and so unnerved by the ravings of no one more deadly than a superstitious old fool. Finding he could now move more freely, he immediately moved across to the trench and making sure he had a good foothold in the loose soil, extended his arm downwards to the, now blood-red, figure of his colleague.

But when Drench shakily raised his own arm, it was not to grasp his, but to point way past him.

'What's the matter?' Craven asked.

But Drench's reply gurgled to nothing in his throat, as his eyes stared way beyond Craven. The developer whipped round. Instantly he saw the cause of both the crackle and Drench's terror.

The telephone lines, from pole to pole, were glowing

white hot and showering the ground with a million sparks, like the Devil himself was celebrating some Satanic anniversary. But even before Craven really absorbed the enormity of the sight, the sparking suddenly ceased, as the lines, equally abruptly, reverted through red to their normal greyish black.

It was not until the next afternoon that some children, playing in Widow's Field, found beneath the line of telephone poles the blackened shape of a giant cross burned into the grass.

Chapter Eight

The telephone rang almost immediately after Rick Rickett had left for the railway station to pick up a delivery of plants and shrubs coming up by rail from Penzance. Thelma Rickett put down her secateurs and stopped dead-heading the chrysanthemums. She let it ring for quite some time before she made any move from the conservatory back into the cottage. Somehow, she knew who it would be and she was terrified of what might follow if her guess should prove correct. Indeed, the last few days had been a nightmare for her, every dring-dring of the telephone had struck terror into her soul and the relief in her voice, when the call proved to be totally innocent, had promoted comment from many of her callers.

At last, when she realised that the ringing was unlikely to die unless she herself was its executioner, she went back slowly into the hall with an expression on her lean face that spelled both sadness and resolution. When she picked up the receiver, she did not even bother to announce herself or say 'Hello'. She knew there would be no need.

'. . . and I'm lying back on the bed, darling,' the now familiar girl's voice breathed on, 'naked as the day I was born and my hand is playing with the curls around my pussy . . .'

Thelma bit her tongue and for the first time, let the girl continue without interruption. After three or four agonising minutes, when she found the role of aural voyeur as near unbearable and disgusting as any experience she could remember, Thelma, to her added horror, found herself muttering under her breath, obscenities and injunctions that she was only just conscious of knowing, let alone had ever thought of using in private or public.

She put her free hand to her mouth and bit her finger hard, but rather to her surprise, the girl seemed now to be bringing her sexual monologue to some kind of conclusion.

'. . . and so, darling, if you'd like to make love to me again, all you have to do is get a nice big hard on and ring the same number . . . or I have other friends too, just ready and waiting, mouths and legs open, just panting for your call. You'll find their numbers in the same magazines you found mine. So remember, my darling . . .' she interrupted herself to blow some kisses '. . . exercise your instrument and put your finger in my dial real soon now. Whatever the time, day or night, remember little Busty Bloomer is always hot, wet and willing . . . Bye now.'

The voice stopped. Thelma Rickett's expression gradually turned from one of total disgust to one of malicious amusement. She slowly replaced the receiver, then went into the small, neat sitting-room and started to remove the cushions of the dralon covered settee.

Even though the cottage was small, it took her almost half an hour to find the magazines. Under the wardrobe was the last place she thought of looking. She took the pile of girlie magazines downstairs and arranged them in rows on the crudely over-patterned sitting-room carpet. Two copies of *Penthouse*, three of *Mayfair*, one each of *Men only* and *Club International*. Then five of the most crudely produced of them all, *Sextra*.

One by one, she carefully went through them, their monotonous parade of naked female flesh very soon anaesthetising Thelma's sense of revulsion. She noted that most carried advertisements for the kind of calls that she had recently been receiving. But it was not until she had already perused eleven of the magazines that she came across, in one of the *Sextras*, amongst a long list of telephone numbers to ring, an advertisement that obviously featured the morning caller.

'Busty Bloomer's Big One. Call 776590 99791.'

Folding the magazine at that page, she went out to the telephone in the hall and dialled the number. It took some little time for the call to connect, but after a series of clicks, she again heard the revoltingly familiar voice.

'Hello, darling, you'll never guess what I've been doing while waiting for you to come . . . on the line, I mean, of course (giggle) . . .'

She slowly replaced the receiver and went back into the conservatory. She sat down on the stool by the counter and started to rearrange the packets on the shelves behind her as she liked them. For after an hour or two of her husband in charge of the shop, she could often not lay her hand on anything quickly – for tidiness was not anywhere in her husband's rough and ready manual of life.

Just as her hand hovered over a packet of Pathclear, she saw their old Datsun pull into the driveway, tugging its trailer load of shrubs and plants. A moment later her husband was at the door.

'Give us a hand to offload,' he asked in his usual gracious manner. Then he noticed what she was doing.

'Hey, don't fuss around with those sodding weedkillers. I purposely keep 'em away from the fertilisers and pet foods just in case one day, somebody gets hold of the wrong bloody stuff and whoops there go the plants and bang there goes the canary.' He guffawed, then again beckoned for her to follow him out to the trailer.

'Yes,' she said quietly. 'Bang goes the canary. Mustn't have that happen to anyone, now must we?'

* * *

The bicycle took the curve into the short driveway too fast, the rear wheel lost its grip and slewed to the side: Bettina Blair fought to retain control and stay upright, but the bike collapsed sideways and threw her off, her right leg hitting the concrete path, her torso falling back against the rockery stones that bordered the tiny lawn.

She screamed out in pain, as the momentum dragged and scraped her against drive and stones, until the bicycle clattered to a stop against the fence, some feet from her, taking her left slip-on shoe with it.

Shakily she raised herself up, half expecting to find something worse than the vicious scrapes on her leg, which were now bleeding, and the bruising across her back and side, which made her wince at every movement.

'Fuck him,' she muttered, as she painfully got to her feet. Leaving the bicycle by the fence, she stooped with difficulty and picked up her school bag from the lawn. Extracting her front door key from its side pocket, she limped to the front door and let herself in.

At first, she was tempted to go upstairs and bathe her grazed leg, before making the call for which she had been rushing home; the call that she had been so pre-occupied with all day, she had several times been admonished by her teachers for inattention. But the thought of one of her parents perhaps getting home early, spurred her on. So instead, she held her handkerchief over the worst of the bleeding and angrily punched Tully's number.

The instant she heard the dialling tone cease, she leapt in.

'Hell, you bugger, Tom. What the hell are you playing at, recording what I say to you over the bloody phone? You wouldn't believe . . .'

She suddenly stopped, as she realised that the photographer was talking over her and had obviously not bothered to listen to a single word she'd said.

'Tom, Tom,' she shouted. 'Don't play any more fucking games! I'm dead serious, now . . .'

But Tully's voice droned on and what's more, as she

caught one or two of the sentences, it became obvious he was not talking to her.

'. . . glad you like it . . . More? . . . well, I don't know whether she will fall for it again.'

'Fall for what, Tom?' She vainly tried to interrupt, her tone now not so much belligerent, as almost pleading.

'. . . I may have to get another girl . . . well, it's hard to get sixteen-year-olds . . . I know teen-sex videos make a bomb of money . . . yeh, but just shaving them doesn't really make a twenty-year-old look sixteen.'

She slowly lowered the receiver, realising the terrible significance of what she had heard. Her other hand raised the handkerchief to her eyes, which left her cheeks smeared with her own blood.

The old Cavalier's suspension protested as the tyres bumped over the pavement kerb. But Walter Blair had enough pride to park around the back of the photographer's premises and not risk comparisons with the sleek black Camaro that was parked out front and which he assumed must belong to Tully. To Blair, such vehicles would only be bought in Britain by pimps and club owners and, generally, those up to no good. In such a category, by profession and by reputation, he firmly placed Thomas Tully.

Having locked his car, he walked back round to the front and peered in the photographer's window. Beyond the expected array of portrait and wedding shots, christening and anniversary pictures, he could see that the lights were still on in the small ante-room. Further back, in what he took to be the studio itself, he could discern lights reflecting off what looked like a silver umbrella. Plucking up courage, he tried the door. To his surprise, it was still unlocked, although it was now well after seven. He went in cautiously and closed the door behind him. He could hear no sound, save for a passing car outside. Almost on tiptoe now, he moved on towards the studio, but when he peered his head round the door, there was no one to be seen or heard there either. Just an array of lights shining down on a large and ornate tapestried chair – a chair that Blair recognised from one or two of the portrait shots in the window.

Thinking Tully seemed to be about to start an evening session of photography, Blair assumed that he must have gone out for a moment, maybe for a quick drink at the pub on the corner or, say, to post some prints to a customer in the post office box just down the High Street. He was just cursing his luck, when he heard an odd sound that seemed to be coming from above his head. He listened hard. The sound repeated itself. A curious gurgle, almost like water in a cistern or central heating pipes. But each gurgle was followed by a kind of dragging sound, a little like the noise the heavy sacks made on the warehouse floor, where Walter Blair worked.

He looked up at the ceiling as the twin noises continued at irregular intervals. Eventually he worked out that they seemed to be coming from almost above the studio door. Blair moved over to the spot and looked up again. The instant he did so, something wet and sticky struck his forehead. Taken aback, he put a shaky hand to his head. When he took it down again, he knew right away the red on his fingers had nothing to do with any painter's pot.

It was the work of a moment for Blair to find the rickety staircase up to the flat's modest landing. He found Tully on the polished pine boards of the living-room floor. Or someone he assumed to be Tully, for the mess that someone had made of his face and head would have made recognition difficult even for his own mother.

Blair knelt down beside the bloodstained body and cradled the ravaged head in the crook of his arm. The gurgles eased somewhat and eyes tried to open against the rivulets of blood.

'Tully . . . Oh God, I've got to go and get help.'

The head slipped around slightly on his arm and he

could see Tully was trying to say something. Blair bent his head down close to the swollen mouth.

'It's the . . .'

'Yes, what?'

'. . . the . . . phone . . . phone . . .'

An arm lifted weakly and pointed across the floor.

'Yes, I'll phone,' Blair assured him, then looked round to where Tully had been pointing. Lying on its side in the corner was another body. That of Mickey Mouse. From the blood and hair still adhering to the novelty telephone, Blair realised with a sickening thud that Tully had not been exhorting him to use it, but warning him about the use to which it had already been put.

The editor looked up from his paper-littered desk.

'Well . . . ?'

Sue Pike put down her portable tape recorder.

'It's bad . . .' she began, but her editor cut in impatiently.

'He's dead?'

Sue shook her head, her long dark hair falling across her intelligent, and by no means unattractive, face. In reality, it was her appearance, rather than her considerable writing skills, that had won her a reporter's position on the *Hallowes Gazette*. The editor, now in his late fifties, rewrote most of his reporters' copy anyway, so that dimensions other than the purely creative determined his judgement towards staff he employed. And he reckoned Sue's bright and yet sensual features and her long slim legs brightened up his day at the dark and dingy offices of his paper more than somewhat.

'So what is he? A cabbage or what?'

'They think he'll probably recover in time,' she said quietly. 'They just don't know yet. He keeps passing in and out of consciousness and doesn't seem to have any feeling below the waist.'

The editor took out his handkerchief and blew his nose noisily, like a trumpeting elephant.

'Sit down,' he invited, more to get a better view of his reporter's legs than for her comfort. But to his disappointment, she declined.

'No, I'd better not stay. I just came back to deliver the tape so far and now I plan to get over to the police station and interview the man who found him.'

'Do they know who did it?'

'They wouldn't say anything over at the photographer's this morning. By the way, we got some good shots of the inside and outside of the studio and even one of his sitting-room, where he was found.'

'Get a shot of the Mickey Mouse phone?'

'No. They had obviously taken it away last night.'

'Then see we get some pictures of a similar phone. The electricians at the bottom of the hill stock them. I've seen them in the window.'

'Okay. I'll tell Ted. He can go there while I go to the station.'

The editor fingered his fat and unkempt moustache, as if he were delousing it.

'By the way, Sue, get an angle on this Tully story. Don't just give me the straight attempted murder bit. All the South Hams and Torbay newspapers will do that to death.' He chuckled. 'So to speak.'

Sue cleared her throat. 'Well, I think I've already got a sort of idea for an angle.'

'So what's that?'

She looked across to the brand new hundred number memory telephone on his desk.

'I've been thinking. You know we ran that piece last week on all the problems the new telephone system seems to be bringing to Hallowes?'

The editor creaked back in his reclining chair and a supercilious smile tried to surface from under his moustache. 'Oh no, Sue, don't tell me you're trying to link an attempted murder with a Mickey Mouse phone, with humdrum consumer complaints about the service.'

She blushed and now regretted having revealed her

idea before it had been fully researched, both on the ground and in her own mind.

'I don't know for certain, yet, what I'm trying to do.'

He leaned forward, elbows now on the desk.

'But you're not such a complete idiot, Sue, as to come up with something like this without any evidence at all, are you? If you are, you shouldn't be working on a provincial paper at all, but one of the national tabloids. But if you know something you haven't told me, then out with it, girl. I'm your editor, not your competitor.'

She hesitated to answer, but knew it was too late now to remain totally silent.

'It's no great shakes, I'm afraid. At least, as yet. It's just . . . well, something a nurse said at the hospital.'

'All right. So what did she say? I'm not going to bite your head off, you know.'

Sue Pike looked away to the window. 'She said . . . Tully kept saying it was the phone, the Mickey Mouse phone, that attacked him.'

The editor threw up his stumpy arms. 'Of course it was the bloody phone that attacked him. It's who was holding it that we want to damn well know.'

'That's the problem,' Sue remarked softly. 'The nurse says that whenever Tully comes round, he keeps saying . . .'

'Yes?'

'No one . . . no one was holding it except him.'

Maggie Blair came out of the kitchen the instant she heard the front door close.

'Go all right?' she asked her husband, her eyes almost popping with curiosity.

'Yeh, I s'pose so,' Walter replied quietly and went through into the sitting-room, closely followed by his wife.

'Pretty girl, I thought, for a reporter. Was expecting someone, you know, older . . .'

She stopped when she saw her husband wasn't listening.

'Walter, what's the trouble? Did she ask some awkward questions, or what?'

He collapsed into a chair.

'It's what she didn't ask that's worrying me,' he muttered.

She went over and sat on the arm of his chair.

'What do you mean? Didn't she accept the story you told the police?'

'Oh yeh. She was quite willing to believe I went round to Tully's to arrange for our twentieth wedding anniversary photographs to be taken.'

'So why are you looking so glum? You're quite a hero, you know. Your turning up probably saved his life. Bet that's what the papers will say.'

'If it was worth saving.'

'Oh come on, Walter. His reputation can't be that bad.'

Her husband shrugged. She reached for his work-worn hand.

'Bad enough for someone to want to attack him.'

'How do you know it wasn't a burglar he caught in the act? Or some homicidal maniac or other? Needn't have been anyone he knew, you know.'

He sniffed, then suddenly, put his head in his hands.

'Oh God, if you'd seen him, Maggie . . .' His voice broke into sobs. '. . . his face . . . you could hardly recognise anything . . . nose . . . cheeks . . . it was just all one big, bloody pulp.'

She put her arms round his shoulders and hugged him to her.

'There . . . there . . . don't think about it. It's all over now. All over.'

He slowly looked up at her. 'How can you be so bloody sure, Maggie? It may just all be bloody beginning.'

'What on earth do you mean? They'll probably find out who did it in no time. With all that geriatric finger-printing, or whatever it's called.'

Her husband suddenly sat bolt upright, almost unseating her from the arm of the chair.

'Maggie, use your brain. Supposing they find something that . . .'

'. . . that what, Walter?'

He could not bring himself to say it outright.

'Well . . . I'm worried sick about Bett.'

Maggie breathed a huge sigh of relief. 'Bett? Why, she's all right. Bruises will go in no time and that leg looks a bit bad, but it's all on the surface, nothing deep, otherwise I'd have kept her home from school today. Kids are always falling off their bikes. Nothing to lose sleep over.'

He reached over and grasped her hand tight.

'Maggie, all last night I couldn't sleep thinking about . . .'

She smiled sympathetically. 'I know . . . I know . . . it'll take time for you to forget finding Tully like that.'

'No. It's not Tully. It's Bett.'

She squeezed his hand back. 'I told you, it's nothing to fret over. It's just rotten she fell off her bike, the same day you found Tully . . .'

He abruptly got up from his chair and turned round to face her.

'Maggie, listen to me,' he shouted. 'Supposing she isn't telling us the truth. And she never fell off her bike at all.'

She frowned. 'Then how did she get all those bruises and cuts . . . ?' But her voice died away in her throat, as the full implication of what he had said dawned on her.

Chapter Nine

'Can you spare a minute, Nurse?'

The rather thickly set blonde finished realigning the screens around the bed and with a self-conscious smile on her face, came over to Stride.

'Yes, Doctor? Is there something I can do for you?'

He took her arm and led her into the empty sister's room at the end of the ward.

'I don't know quite. You see, I'm interested in your new patient, that poor man, Tully.'

'Oh, you should see Dr Richards about him. I don't know too much about how he's responding to . . .'

He waved his hand. 'No, I don't really want to worry Dr Richards. He's got enough on his plate without answering silly questions from a colleague.'

She frowned up at him, fluttering her blue eyes. She had always rather fancied Dr Stride, as did more than a few of the nurses and she was quite flattered to be singled out by him that afternoon.

'Silly questions?'

Stride grinned. 'Well, not really silly. Perhaps I should have said questions that have nothing to do with medical practice or treatment.'

A look of relief came over her face. 'Oh, I see. That's why you think *I* might be able to help.'

They both laughed and Stride was glad he had selected her, rather than the severe but more elegant brunette with whom she shared vigil over the photographer.

'So what would you like to know, Dr Stride?'

He started to pace the small white ante-room.

'Well, it's all about something I overheard in the corridor this morning, actually. Someone,' he turned to her and smiled, 'who shall be nameless, was telling a patient she was taking to X-ray that Mr Tully, at the odd times he came round, was making a rather extraordinary claim. Or, not so much claim, as, I suppose, in reality, a rather incoherent and rambling statement.'

The nurse grinned, then shook her head.

'Shouldn't take any notice of what patients say when they're not fully with it she shouldn't. What's more, she certainly shouldn't be going around telling other patients what she's heard.'

'Quite right, Nurse. But nevertheless, what I overheard still intrigues me. Before I tell you what poor Mr Tully is reported to be saying, perhaps you could tell me if he is actually speaking coherently at all – at any time.'

She nodded. 'Oh yes. Sometimes when he does come round, he gets quite excited. Mind you, the words are often rather difficult to make out, what with his terrible injuries and all those bandages over his face. But all the same, the number of times he's repeated it . . .'

'Repeated what?'

She suddenly blushed. 'Well, probably what you overheard in the corridor, I expect.'

'Which is?'

'That he wasn't attacked by anyone. He says it's all the telephone's fault. Then he adds, if you'll pardon the language, Doctor, "that bloody Mickey Mouse".'

Stride turned away to the window, so that the nurse would not see his expression.

She innocently went on, 'I expect we and he will have a good laugh about what he's now coming out with, once he's back on the road to recovery, don't you think, Doctor? Patients normally are ever so embarrassed afterwards.'

Stride did not reply. For he had a gut feeling that time would not be confirming the nurse's prophecy. And what's more, that the future, if they were not very careful, might well prove quite the opposite of laughable.

The cat, though his eyes were closed, sensed his mistress's return across the room to her chair. Within a moment, he was back on her lap, now half forgiving her for having disturbed him to use that funny new thing that now lived on the bamboo table in the corner.

Enid Drench closed her eyes and stroked the cat's back affectionately. If only her son, she thought, repaid her love and care the way Merlin did. For she still loved William, despite what he had forced her to do now. In her mind, there was a complete divorce between her feelings for her son and what she had just asked her lawyer, Sebastian Fanshawe, to arrange. For she was convinced that her estate – consisting mainly of a portfolio of stocks and shares bought with money left to her by her father and, more or less, unchanged and untouched by her over the years – would, if left bequeathed to William, only go to further his heathenish and uncaring plans for Hallowes and the South Hams.

It was not solely the damage to her beloved environment that bothered Enid Drench. But much more importantly, the damage to what little was left of her son's soul. For she was being only too sincere when she threatened him with eternal damnation for the direction in which his life was headed. And her money could only help drive him further along that road.

She had made up her mind the dreadful day of the storm, when she had discovered her son and the other heathen, George Craven, appraising the unforgivable scar they had made in Widow's Field. As she had stared down at William writhing in the blood red pit of his own making, the soil starting to cover his smeared body, she had suddenly seen, when the bolt of lightning had bleached the world white . . . She sat bolt upright and shook herself vigorously to try to dispel the vision and Merlin cocked a disapproving eye up at her for the disturbance. As she had physically that day, she now mentally made her escape from the terror of the scene and tried to switch her mind back to . . . ah yes, Sebastian Fanshawe and the drawing up of a new will. The last will and testament of Enid Drench that would now leave everything to people she had never met, over the ocean she would never ever navigate.

Inspector Dudkin looked at his watch, then across at Constable Bradshaw.

'Look, I must go now,' he whispered. 'I can't stay here any longer waiting for another spell of consciousness.'

The overweight constable was quite relieved to get up from his hardback chair. Going up to the bed, he peered down at the dried blood and bandages that were Tom Tully's head.

'No sign, sir. He's been like this all the time. Comes round when you least expect it. No rhyme nor reason.'

The Inspector unfolded his six foot four frame from his own chair and smiled across at the, seemingly humourless, nurse seated by the door.

'Well, let me know immediately if there's any real change.'

She nodded and he turned back to his constable.

'Remember, Bradshaw, keep taking notes of everything he says. But don't bother me with any more of his ramblings. I'll only come back when he's recovered enough to start talking some sense. Mickey Mouse, indeed.'

The constable saw his superior to the door.

'Right, sir.' He cleared his throat. 'May I ask, sir, if the forensic boys have picked up any clues yet? I mean, like fingerprints or bits of clothing or . . .'

The Inspector frowned. 'Really, Bradshaw, you don't need to run through the whole gamut of possibilities. I can just about guess what you mean without all that, you know.'

Bradshaw blushed at the reprimand and regretted ever having opened his size twelve mouth.

'Right, sir. Good luck, sir. Sure you'll find him.'

He opened the door, and Dudkin made to exit, then turned back, with a supercilious smile on his lean face.

'So, Sherlock Bradshaw,' he whispered, 'you've worked out it's a *him*, rather than a *her*, have you?'

And before the constable's brain could switch to think mode, he added, 'Who knows, my friend, it might even've been Minnie Mouse!'

The Inspector was relieved to exchange the smell of carbolic and antiseptic for the aroma of cellulose, polished wood and plush upholstery in his brand new Rover.

The driver looked back over his shoulder.

'Where now, sir?'

Dudkin thought for a moment. 'Back to headquarters. I've been out too damned long today.'

The driver accelerated out of the hospital drive, then turned left into the long hill that led back down into Hallowes.

'Been a bit of bad luck, sir, I'm afraid, while you were in the hospital.'

Dudkin raised his eyebrows. He had more than enough on his plate right now, without bad luck adding to the problems of his modest force.

'All right,' he responded gruffly. 'So what the hell's gone wrong?'

The driver hesitated, but knew he'd gone too far to stop now.

'Well, sir, it's like this. There's been a bit of an accident, like.'

'Accident? What kind of accident?'

'At . . . er . . . the junction of Spelling Lane, it was, and Moor Road. You know, just by Widow's Field.'

The driver saw the Inspector glower in the rear-view mirror.

'All right. Don't tell me. It's that PC Weaver at his Ayrton Senna tricks again, isn't it? My God, someone should have him out of that cushy driving seat and back to pounding the bloody beat before you can blink an eye.'

'No, sir, no. It's not Constable Weaver this time.'

'Good God. So who's been the bad boy, then?'

'Well, I don't think anybody, really, sir, from what I can make out. You see, both the patrol cars . . .'

Dudkin sat forward in his seat.

'You mean *two* of our damned cars are involved?' he exploded.

' 'Fraid so, sir. But both the drivers are okay. Shaken but . . .'

'They should be bloody shaken – until their teeth fall out.' He took a deep breath, then said more restrainedly, 'How bad is the damage?'

'PC Armitage's is a write-off, they think, sir. But Higgins's seems repairable, as I understand it.'

The Inspector threw up his hands. 'Hell, as if we haven't got enough on our bloody hands, without losing the use of two of our precious vehicles . . . So what excuses have these two prize idiots come up with, eh?' He put on a childish voice. ' "Sun blinded my eyes", "A dog ran across the road", "I think my brakes must have failed", or was it a case of "It wasn't me, sir. It was him"?'

The driver braked, as it would happen, to miss a terrier running across the hill.

'No, sir. They're not blaming each other, sir. They're not blaming anything to do with their cars or the roads, sir.'

'Then what are they blaming? Their unmarried parents?'

'I think . . . er . . . it might be better, sir, if you waited until we're back, so you can hear it from them, sir.'

Dudkin punched the back of the driver's seat.

'I'm going to hear it from you right now, that's an order. What the hell are they blaming?'

'Er . . . their radios, sir.'

'Radios?'

'Yes, sir.'

'How can you blame a radio, unless you're a liar or a bloody idiot?'

'Well, sir, it seems they suddenly acted up, sir. In both the vehicles. Went sort of crazy, from all accounts.'

'Crazy, What do they mean, *crazy*?'

'Seems, sir, they started to make funny sounds, sir, then they started . . . well, sir, you're not going to believe this.'

The Inspector gritted his teeth.

'Try me.'

The driver sighed. 'They started to scream, sir. And scream so loud, sir, that the drivers felt, well, that they were going stark raving mad. So they couldn't help taking their hands off the wheels, sir . . . to block it all out and prevent their eardrums from bursting.'

He tried the latch and the door swung open. Drench smiled to himself. Just like his all-trusting dotty mother to leave her front door unlocked. He went through the hall into the living-room. But there was no one there but the cat, who looked up grudgingly from his sleep, stretched, then curled up again, but now with his back to the visitor.

'Mother, you upstairs?' Drench called out, but did not really expect a reply. Had his mother been resting in her bedroom, the cat would surely have been up there with her.

'Mother . . .' he tried more loudly, in case his voice was being swallowed up by the wealth of exposed timbers in the cottage. But again, there was no reply.

Drench cursed under his breath at what now seemed like a wasted journey. Wearily, he mounted the creaking staircase and searched the two bedrooms, but there was no sign of life.

Downstairs once more, he went back into the living-room and eased his big frame on to the well worn cushions of a chair. He decided to give her a maximum of a quarter of an hour to come home. If she had not returned by then, he planned to leave a note for her to ring him. One way or another, he was determined to make one last stab at persuading his mother to call off her now imminent protest march through Hallowes.

It was not that he feared the march would in any way alter events or influence the powers that be to change their minds about the development of Widow's Field. It was far too late for any of that. No, his reason for a last minute appeal to his mother was purely to protect the interests of his present business, not that of the future. The publicity and talk that his mother had been arousing through the mounting of the march, was starting to affect both his personal reputation and that of his estate agency in Hallowes. The last few days had seen more people coming into the agency to enquire about the march, and his own views about the event, than to solicit information about the properties he had for sale or rent. Indeed, business had fallen away just recently, which was contrary to the market trend, which was still climbing. The decline, Drench had concluded, could only be attributed to his mother's insane and well nigh calumnious campaign of protest over that damned field.

He looked round the small room, then sighed impatiently. It was just as well the melodramatic and absurd events that had taken place when his mother had discovered the trench they had dug in the field, had not been witnessed by anyone other than himself and George Craven. His mother's lunatic behaviour that day would have smeared his professional reputation as effectively as the old fool had smeared his clothes with red mud.

'Shit,' he muttered to himself, as he vividly recalled the shock of the storm and then the devilish sparking of the telephone wires.

'Shit. Shit. Shit. Why does the old bag have the power to frighten the living daylights out of people?'

But his mouthings were interrupted by the ringing of the telephone. He looked across at the absurdly childish Donald Duck instrument, which his mother had insisted on choosing because she claimed telephones were cold and inhuman things and that the Disney character at least was a bird and gave it some warmth and humanity. For a full three minutes he let it ring, then, when it was quite clear it wouldn't stop unless he acted, he got up, went over to the bamboo table and lifted the receiver.

As he was about to snap gruffly that his mother was out and that he had no idea when she would be back, he suddenly realised it was, indeed, his mother on the line. But she seemed to be already speaking to someone.

'. . . yes, that's what I said and that's what I want . . . no, Mr Fanshawe, I no longer wish to leave my son, William, anything, anything at all . . . I have no intention of disclosing to you the reasons that have prompted me to change my will, but . . .'

'Mother, Mother,' Drench attempted to interrupt. 'What are you saying? Where on earth are you? This is William. I can hear every word you're saying, Mother . . .'

But it was only too clear his mother could not hear him and her voice rattled on, in its only too familiar fashion.

'. . . yes, I know their names and addresses may be hard to trace, but I want you to get on to it right away. I'll pay you well for your time . . . Yes, in the meantime, that might be a good idea, if you think it's legal. I know my son, if the will isn't watertight, he'll try and sink it the second I'm gone . . .'

Then suddenly, the slight crackling that had been evident throughout the call, grew in intensity and volume, until it swamped his mother's voice. He held on for a further few minutes, but to no avail, for the interference only grew the more severe, until it seemed to make the very beams of the cottage ring with its screaming.

For once, being at the wheel of his old Bristol gave Stride next to no pleasure. His mind was still occupied with his unproductive meeting with the chief electronics engineer of the Telecommunications Centre, Ray Pedler.

Not that the engineer had not bent over backwards to be welcoming and co-operative from the very moment Stride had rung him to ask for a meeting. And it had soon become plain that he had already taken serious note of the many complaints about the Hallowes telephone service and had instituted an elaborate series of checks on both the system and on his staff to make certain that as far as could be ascertained, there were no technical or human reasons why his service should be displaying the present distressing symptoms of disorder. So far, with the checks almost completed, he had stated that they had discovered none.

'I guess you must be familiar with this kind of thing with your patients, Doctor,' he had smiled. 'Symptoms flaring up with no real discernible cause. And then one morning, the symptoms just disappear, go, just like that, with no treatment, no medicine . . .'

'I am, of course,' Stride had replied, 'but telephones are hardly humans. Surely . . .'

'Your TV, your car,' the engineer pointed out. 'Don't they sometimes develop faults, which before you have time to take them to an engineer or a garage, just right themselves on their own. Infuriating isn't it?'

'So you think that the Hallowes telephone system will just cure itself in time?'

'If . . . when our checks are finally completed, we have still found no faults, then what else can we do, but wait and see? Our fibre optic system may be new to you, but it's not new to science and one of its major advantages is its simplicity and therefore, overall reliability. So . . .' He held out his hands. 'Sorry, I wish I could say more, to you and every other Hallowes subscriber.'

'And you're absolutely certain that no one can be recording calls at the exchange and replaying them over the system?'

'Quite impossible. It's not manual, Dr Stride, with lots of girls pulling out and putting in plugs, you know. That went with the Ark. It's fully automatic and to tamper with such a system to effect what you describe is, anyway, quite impossible. If someone is recording calls, then playing them back, they're doing it from their homes and not from here, I assure you.'

'So you have no explanation for any of these phenomena?'

'Sorry, Dr Stride. Maybe we should blame it all on the recent stormy weather. We have no real explanation for that either, now do we?'

As he neared his home, Stride cursed to see another car in the drive. He looked at his watch. It was already ten past twelve. The meeting with the engineer had taken up more of his morning off than he had planned.

Stride parked the Bristol by the kerb, so that he wouldn't have to move his car when his visitor came to leave. He got out quickly, then made to slam the door. As his fingers made contact with the metal, a violent shock stabbed up his arm. So charged with pain was the static that he cried out and fell to one knee on the road.

For a few seconds, he felt too numb to move. He looked at his right hand. It was bloodless and ashen and trembling like an oscillator. He shook his head to somehow try to lessen the stabbing of the pain. At last he stumbled to his feet and, clutching his tingling fingers with his other hand, made his way up the drive towards the front door.

'I'm very sorry I'm late,' he smiled awkwardly as he entered the sitting-room.

'That's all right, Dr Stride.' The reporter smiled back. 'Your wife made me very comfortable with a cup of coffee.'

He went across and shook her hand. His fingers were still so numb he could hardly feel her grip.

'Sue Pike.' Her eyes suddenly showed concern. 'Doctor, are you all right?'

He moved away. 'Yes, yes, yes. A silly thing happened

just now, that's all. Bit of static from the car as I closed the door.' He turned back to her and waved his hand. 'Still tingles.'

'Mine do often,' she grinned. 'What is it about Hallowes that causes all this static? When I first moved down here, I blamed it on my old Mini. But it seems most people suffer from it, if you can believe the number of straps that dangle off rear bumpers. I've never seen so many.'

He shrugged and at his invitation, she resumed her seat.

'Anyway, Doctor, you rang the office and asked me to come round. How can I help you?'

Stride sat down opposite her and for the first time really appreciated just how attractive the *Hallowes Gazette* reporter was. He had been expecting someone older and somewhat fuddy-duddy. That was more in line with his image of local newspaper staff – an image created not from any direct experience, but from the dingy Victorian look of the *Gazette*'s offices. But now the quietly intelligent looks of Sue Pike reminded him that local newspapers must often prove the spawning grounds for some of the best national journalists.

He pointed to a coffee table on which lay a copy of the latest *Hallowes Gazette*.

'I read your article this morning.'

'Oh good,' she blushed. 'I'm glad to hear someone read what I wrote. Poor Mr Tully. I do hope he recovers. Is he a patient of yours?'

'No, he's not.'

She frowned. 'Oh, I thought, perhaps, you wanted to see me with regard to what I wrote about him.' She ran her fingers through her long dark hair. 'You know reporting what I gather he's saying when he comes round made my editor concerned that I might be going a little far, but he agreed to it in the end.'

'No, I'm not worried about anything you wrote about Tully.'

She sighed and sat back in her chair. 'Oh, that's a relief.'

Stride leaned forward. 'But I am worried about the connection you hinted at.'

'What connection?' she asked, but was certain she knew the answer.

'The telephone connection.' He suddenly smiled. 'No, that's not meant to be a joke. Far from it.'

'You mean the question I posed at the end of my piece on Tully?'

He nodded. 'Yes, where you said something like, "It's not the first time we've heard strange tales of telephones misbehaving in Hallowes recently, now is it?".'

'That's why you asked me to come and see you this morning?'

'Yes.'

She thought for a minute. 'What do you want to know, Doctor?'

'Was that ending just a . . . sorry . . . convenient piece of journalistic blah, or did it spring from something else you've found out? Have you some theory?'

'Not really. Not yet. But all the same . . .' She looked back at him. 'You know something, don't you, Doctor? Is that why you called me?'

'Not really. Not yet. But all the same . . .' He grinned self-consciously. 'Sorry to repeat your words.'

'But all the same, *what*?'

He rose from his chair and went over to the window. On the far distant hills towards Dartmoor, he could already see the gathering storm.

'There's something very strange happening here in Hallowes, Sue. I have enough evidence from three of my patients, let alone what that poor man, Tully, seems to be saying. What's more, I have seen something with my own eyes that defies all logical explanation.'

She rose from her chair and came over to him.

'So've I, Doctor.'

He looked round. 'You?'

She nodded. 'I've just come from Widow's Field.' She stopped abruptly. 'But maybe you have heard it already from the local children.'

'Heard what?' he asked anxiously.

'There is now a huge area of burnt grass.'

'But the weather has been too wet, surely?'

She seemed to ignore him and went on. 'Burnt in the shape of a giant cross, right by the . . .'

He completed her sentence, '. . . telegraph poles. That's what you were going to say, isn't it?'

She nodded once more.

Taking a deep breath, he said, 'Sue, we've got to do something.'

She looked at him. 'You feel it too?'

'Yes,' he said quietly. 'Look, Sue, we may both be mad, but will you help me?'

'If I can. What would you like me to do?'

'Well, reporters can ask questions without raising other questions, if you see what I mean. Now, if I or my wife went around probing, everyone would want to know what the hell the doctor and his wife were up to.'

She laughed. 'But everyone knows what reporters are up to, you mean – no good.'

'Well . . . er . . .'

'All right, Doctor. But you have to tell me a bit more about it all and what kind of probing you would like me to do.'

So he proceeded to tell her, starting from the day in Widow's Field, when his Hurricane went out of control.

Chapter Ten

Drench looked at his watch and then up at the bespectacled receptionist.

'How much longer is he going to keep me, for goodness sake?'

Once more she stopped her typing. 'As I said before, I'm awfully sorry, Mr Drench, but his previous appointment is obviously over-running.' She felt sympathy for anyone who had an appointment after Mrs Craven's – for they invariably over-ran.

'Well, I can't wait for ever,' Drench grumbled, then pointed to the intercom on her desk. 'Can't you buzz him to say I'm here.'

'I'm sorry, Mr Drench. I have strict instructions never to interrupt Mr Fanshawe when he's with a client.'

Drench subsided back into the chair and irritably flipped through the pages of yet another *Country Life*. But after a further five minutes, he suddenly got to his feet and came over to her desk.

'Look, I've been here now for three-quarters of an hour. If I ran my business like this, I'd deserve not to have a single sodding client in the world.'

The receptionist looked up at his towering figure.

'I quite understand, Mr Drench, but . . .'

He banged her desk with his fist. 'No buts, if you please. Just put your dainty finger on that button of yours and buzz him, or I'll . . .'

By now, the receptionist was becoming more than alarmed.

'But, Mr Drench, no one is allowed to buzz . . .'

To her surprise, Drench backed off from her desk. Holding up his hands as if in some kind of surrender, he muttered, 'Okay, okay. No one will press your little buzzer, don't worry. I don't want to get you into any trouble.'

Then just as she was starting to relax, Drench turned on his heel and was at her boss's door before she could stop him.

'No, you can't go in,' she shouted, but his hand had already turned the knob and opened the door.

A second later, she heard Drench say, 'Oh, I'm sorry, Mr Fanshawe. I was told you were with a client.'

The lawyer played with the papers on his desk, deliberately avoiding Drench's eye-line.

'I do apologise for keeping you waiting, Mr Drench. But you can imagine how upsetting divorce cases can be for the parties involved.'

Drench smiled. 'I can imagine.'

'That's why my appointment with Mrs Craven overran so much. I sometimes think that divorce lawyers should have some training in shock therapy or whatever they call it these days, so that we're more equipped to deal will all the traumas divorce produces.'

'You seemed to be doing all right,' Drench remarked and his grin, to Fanshawe's concern, betrayed his disbelief.

'Oh, an arm around a waist or a head on a shoulder is no substitute for . . .'

'. . . the real thing,' Drench interrupted.

Fanshawe cleared his throat. 'Yes, well, I'm sure you don't want to waste any more time with my problems, Mr Drench. Now, how can I help you?'

Drench leaned forward in his chair. 'Very easily, I would imagine, Mr Fanshawe.'

The lawyer prayed he hadn't detected a slightly threatening note in his client's remark.

'Fire away, Mr Drench.'

Drench relaxed back. 'Well, it's like this. I happen to know my mother has approached you to draw up a new will.'

Fanshawe swallowed hard. He could see what was coming.

'Oh yes?'

'Oh, yes, indeed. Now, Mr Fanshawe, I also happen to know, among other things, that she plans to cut me entirely out of her will.'

Fanshawe was silent for a moment, then asked, 'May I ask, Mr Drench, how you came upon this information?'

'Quite simple. I heard my mother making the telephone call.'

'Heard her, you say?' The lawyer frowned, for he knew Enid Drench well enough to know she would never make such a call if there was any chance of her son being within earshot.

'Yes. *Heard* her.'

'You were in the house, when she made the call, perhaps?'

Drench shook his head.

'Then how did you . . . ?' He stopped suddenly, as he remembered the inexplicable calls that his wife had received.

'Never mind about how I heard it, Mr Fanshawe,' Drench said gruffly, 'and let's get down to what you are going to do about it, shall we?'

'Well . . . er . . . I must obviously carry out your mother's wishes, whatever they may be.'

Drench held up his hand. 'Ah, now that brings me to another little question that I'm sure you will be able to answer . . . all things considered.'

Fanshawe waited with baited breath.

Drench continued. 'And that is to whom exactly my mother now plans to leave her modest estate?'

'So you did not hear the whole call, is that right, Mr Drench?'

'Never mind what I heard or didn't hear. The point is,

I want to know who the poor deranged soul now favours over her son.'

The lawyer shook his head. 'Mr Drench, you must know that a lawyer cannot possibly divulge information of this sort.'

A thin smile broke across Drench's mean face.

'I know a lot of things, I do, Mr Fanshawe.'

There was no doubt about the threatening turn of the interview and Fanshawe cursed his receptionist for not preventing Drench from catching him embracing Annabel Craven.

'Mr Drench, why did you come here?'

'You know why,' he grinned.

'If you've come here to try to stop me drawing up the new will, then I'm afraid . . .'

Drench suddenly leant forward in his chair. 'Look here, Mr Fanshawe, you know my mother. Everyone in Hallowes either knows or has heard of my mother. And you, no doubt, know what most of them think of her, don't you?'

'That is irrelevant, Mr Drench.'

The estate agent wagged a thick finger. 'No, it isn't, my dear fellow. You know the law well enough to know wills drawn up by people of unsound mind etcetera etcetera.'

'Are you trying to say that you consider your mother insane?'

'Oh, insane is, perhaps, too harsh a word. Let's leave it that she's thoroughly senile. I bet doctors would say she's suffering from, what d'you call it – Alzheimer's disease. Anyway, almost the whole of Hallowes considers her crazy as a jaybird, you know that.'

'So you're telling me that if I draw up this will, you will contest it upon your mother's death?'

Drench chuckled. 'Not quite, Mr Fanshawe. You see, I don't think it will ever come to that.'

'You mean, you won't contest it?'

'No,' he laughed. 'You won't bloody draw it up, if

you value your reputation in this town.'

'Could you tell me which room Mr Tully is in, please?'

The nurse-receptionist looked up from a letter she was reading, expecting to see either a female reporter or a policewoman. But the sight of the windblown and wet schoolgirl rather took her by surprise.

'Room two-one-seven,' she answered, then quickly added, 'But no one is allowed to visit him just now, without the permission of his doctor.'

Bettina Blair thought quickly. 'Oh, that's all right. I wasn't expecting to see him. I just wanted his room number so that I can send him a get-well card.'

'I expect he'll appreciate that, now I hear he's starting to get a bit better.'

'Oh, he's recovering, is he?'

'So I believe. Everyone is quite amazed at how well he is suddenly doing.'

Bettina smiled weakly. 'Well, thanks for his number.'

'You're welcome,' the nurse smiled back and idly wondered whether the young girl could be one of the many girlfriends she'd heard the photographer attracted like flies to fly-paper.

Bettina left through the swing doors, but waited just outside on the steps, from where she could still see the reception desk. After a few minutes, when she saw the receptionist's attention fully occupied by a fat lady trailing four less-than-clean children, she doubled back in and made her way quickly around a corner to where she had noticed earlier that the lifts were located.

Tidying her hair with her hand, she waited impatiently at the lift doors, praying that the bandage she still wore on her abraided leg would be sufficient passport for her to get, unquestioned, to Tully's floor. Thereafter, she knew things would prove more difficult, for she had heard on the local radio that the photographer was still under police protection, for fear another attempt might be made on his life.

She smiled at the thought. Tully deserved to die for what he had done to her and what he had, no doubt, done or planned to do with others. But, right now, she had every interest in his staying alive. And the receptionist's good news was exactly what she wanted to hear. For an incapacitated Tully would be no good at all for the plans her fertile and vengeful brain had now devised for him.

No one questioned her right to be in the lift and she pressed button '2' in the assumption that hospitals were like hotels and numbered their rooms to align with the floors they were on. Once out on the second floor, she looked around for any signs that might tell her what direction to take to room 217. But unlike hotels, there were none. Just an abundance of arrows to various wards, carrying famous Devon names, such as Drake, Widdecombe and Dartmouth. A nurse passed her in the corridor and she was tempted to ask for a room next door to Tully's, such as 216 or 218, but was fearful they might also contain patients with restricted visiting hours. So she took a chance and turned down to the left. It was not very long before she knew her decision had been the right one. For rounding the second corner, she spotted the dark figure of a policeman at the end of the corridor. He was seated on a chair, with his back to her and seemed to be looking out of the window.

She stopped and bent down, pretending to be adjusting the bandage on her leg. She needed time to think. But before her mind could come up with a way to circumvent the law and get into Tully's room, she felt a tap on her back, that scared the living daylights out of her.

'Bettina Blair, isn't it?'

She instantly unbent and whipped her head round.

'It's me, Dr Stride. Sorry if I surprised you.'

Over the pounding of her heart, she stammered, 'No,

no, that's all right, Doctor. I was just adjusting my bandage, that's all.'

He looked down. 'Hurt your leg?'

She nodded.

'Not badly, I hope.'

'No, no. I just fell off my bike, that's all.'

To her consternation, he knelt down to inspect her injury. She moved her leg away.

'No, no, that's all right, Doctor. It's much better now. Really.'

Stride pointed down to the bandage and frowned.

'Did they do that in Out Patients?'

'No. Not in . . . er . . . Out Patients.'

'Didn't think so,' he smiled. 'If you don't mind my saying so, they're usually neater than that.'

She blushed.

'Anyway,' he went on, 'what are you doing on this floor? Lost your way or are you visiting somebody?'

She floundered. 'I'm . . . er . . . lost. Lost my way.'

Stride took her arm. 'Well, let's see if I can help. Where do you want to get to?'

'Well . . . er . . . out. I'm trying to find my way out.'

He laughed. 'You'll hardly find your way out on the second floor. Unless you've got a parachute.'

She smiled nervously. 'That's all right, Doctor. Don't you bother yourself. I'll find my own way, don't worry.'

She started to move down the corridor, but Stride caught up with her.

'Hey, Bettina, if you didn't come in about that leg and you're not visiting someone, is there some other reason you're here that I might be able to help with.'

'No, really.'

'It's not, by any chance, about what I prescribed for you the other day, is it?'

She shook her head. 'No, Doctor, it's nothing to do with that.'

He noticed now the scared look in her eyes.

'Bettina, there's something wrong, isn't there? Why don't you tell me?'

But as he spoke, she ran off down the corridor and disappeared round the corner.

Stride waited a moment, then shrugged and turned back. It was not until he passed the policeman outside Tully's door that a possible reason for Bettina Blair's perplexing behaviour flashed into his mind.

'Well, Miss Pike,' the Reverend Meek smiled, peering over his half-moon glasses, 'that's about all I can tell you about the arrangements for the big day. We're all ready for Bobby Quick. And I'm quite sure he's all ready for Hallowes.'

Sue Pike flicked over another page of her note pad.

'Oh, there's just a few more things, Vicar, if you can spare the time.'

He consulted the scratched Timex watch on his blue wrist. 'I see I still have over half an hour until I have to go out, Miss Pike, so I'm all yours, as they say.'

'Tell me, Vicar, do you really approve of . . . well, evangelism of the sort that Bobby Quick seems to be such a master. For instance, I read recently that the Bishop of Tavistock does not really approve of all the show business style and razzmatazz of American TV preachers and questions their whole motives and the validity of instant conversions, triggered by such an atmosphere.'

Reverend Meek cleared his throat. Really, he would rather the sweet girl stuck to facts and not probe opinions – especially his own. For he had reached the time of life when tranquillity was infinitely to be preferred to controversy. And opinions voiced too often only caused the latter. Besides, there were enough problems in Hallowes right now without adding to them with his private thoughts on the likes of Bobby Quick.

'Everyone is entitled to their own opinions, Miss Pike. As for me, I'm delighted we in Hallowes have been chosen as the first audience in Mr Quick's first visit to this country.'

Sue Pike could see she would get no further with that question, so changed tack to the second and more intriguing reason for her interview with the vicar – a reason she had deliberately not revealed to him beforehand.

'Can I turn to another subject, Vicar, that seems to be even more of a talking point right now than the big rally. I'd like your views on it. As pastor of a parish, you must get to hear quite a cross-section of Hallowes' worries, troubles and tribulations.'

Meek made a church steeple with his fingers.

'I can guess to what you are referring. The twin subjects of the weather and the newfangled telephone system. Am I right?'

She nodded. 'You read my piece about poor Mr Tully the other day?'

He shook his head woefully. 'I did indeed, Miss Pike. What a dreadful thing to happen in Hallowes. Oh dear, oh dear and it was such a happy place until . . .'

He stopped abruptly.

She leaned forward in her chair.

'Well . . . er . . . perhaps I shouldn't say this, but my parishioners seem to be saying it more and more, so . . .' He shrugged, then went on, 'Well, it was one of my loyal ladies, Thelma Rickett – she does all the flowers for the church, you know. Wonderful little woman. Never stops – who first pointed it out to me.'

'Pointed what out?'

'She's a great one for keeping a diary. She has done it, apparently, ever since she was at school. And she states quite categorically that all the bad weather started the very day the new Telephone Exchange was officially opened. I remember it well, now she's reminded me. The poor Mayor nearly got struck by lightning as he unveiled the plaque.'

He took down the steeple of his fingers and went on, 'And it wasn't long after that we began having the trouble with the phones. It's probably all a silly coincidence, with no meaning whatsoever, but the idea certainly seems to be catching on amongst those I meet. They're even starting to say that if the weather and the telephone troubles don't clear up soon, they will want to press for an official enquiry into the whole matter and, maybe, even try and get the Exchange closed down. Deary me, you know how wild people's talk can become sometimes.'

Sue Pike looked back at her notes and then asked, 'Do you believe there's any connection?'

He lifted his eyebrows to the heavens. 'Well, logic certainly says there can't be. But who knows? As our great bard says, "There are more things in heaven and earth . . ." '

'Vicar, you've lived in Hallowes some long time, I believe. Therefore you must know the area pretty well.'

His blue face blushed purple. 'Well, there are many more, I'm sure, who know it better. But go ahead with your question, Miss Pike and I'll answer it to the limit of my knowledge.'

Her eyes flicked down to the list of questions that Dr Stride and herself had worked out.

'The piece of land that the Exchange is built on. What was it before?'

The vicar frowned. 'Why, just a field, Miss Pike. Starlings Meadow. Why do you ask?'

'Yes, I gather it was a field. But I overheard someone in the market say that it might have been a burial ground of some sort.'

The vicar smiled. 'Oh, that old story. Well, if it ever was a burial ground, it must have been centuries ago. I went into all this, you see, many years ago when I first heard this old wives' tale. I went through all the church records and that of St Edmund's at the other end of town and then all the parish records. Both here and in Exeter. I could find no mention of Starlings Meadow being used as a burial ground or any land near it, for that matter.'

'What about Widow's Field?'

He shook his head. 'No, no mention of that either. So I'm afraid, Miss Pike, the tale must be just another Devonian myth. The county is full of them, as you must have realised.'

'Napoleonic wars?' she tried. Again she received a shake of the head.

'No. That little story can be totally disproved, as we actually do know where some of the men killed at those conflicts were buried. That's over Plympton way. Not here in Hallowes at all. So I'm sorry, Miss Pike, to throw cold water on your theory. Would have made good copy for your paper, I admit.'

She smiled. 'Never mind. Worth a try. So both Starlings Meadow and Widow's Field have always been agricultural land? Nothing more?'

'That's right, Miss Pike. Oh, I believe during the war American troops requisitioned quite a lot of the land round here for storing ammunition and equipment for the D-Day landings. And I've heard people tell of the lines of jeeps, guns and stacks of shells and so on that there used to be in that general area. But other than that, no, both fields have always been just that. Fields, plain and simple.'

Sue Pike shut her note book.

'Thanks anyway for giving me so much of your time.'

He rose from behind his desk with a benign smile.

'I have enjoyed the little break from my normal routine, I assure you.'

She got up and followed the vicar to the study door.

'Oh, by the way,' she said, 'I forgot to ask you whether you yourself have experienced any trouble with the telephone.'

He hesitated, then, blue fingers crossed behind his back, replied, 'Not really, Miss Pike. Nothing to mention.'

For he certainly had no intention of telling a newspaper reporter, of all people, his concern as to how the rotund Mr Homer Friend had got wind of his Bishop's scathing comments about the Bobby Quick organisation – comments that he was certain the Bishop would only have made when he telephoned the vicarage the day of Friend's first visit.

For once it dawned fine, with not the hint of rain or stormclouds gathering over the distant moors. Indeed, it proved hot for late September and the protest marchers were soon divesting themselves of the sweaters and anoraks with which they had started out.

The town of Hallowes itself was certainly not a marcher's paradise, for nestling as it did between steep hills – ten miles to the north, Dartmoor, ten miles to the south, the sea – one did not have to walk far before meeting an incline that called for stamina, determination and a healthy pair of lungs. Thus it was, not long after the start, that Enid Drench noticed, to her concern, that a few of the more elderly of her band had begun to drop by the wayside.

However, with the sterling and soul-stirring help of sympathisers, notably Thelma Rickett from the church and Priscilla Marsh from the Hallowes Health Farm shop, the mass of the marchers kept up their spirits, despite the heat and hills and carrying their protest banners aloft like true crusaders, continued along the designated route which would take them through at least two thirds of the town and culminate in a rally outside the ivy clad Town Hall.

William Drench watched the procession pass from his estate agency and was thankful that his windows were still intact, when the last of the motley gang of 'greens, gays and ga-gas', as he was to describe them in the bar of the Crown Hotel that night, had disappeared from sight. As he was about to go back into his own office, a large white Mercedes pulled up outside. He smiled to himself and went to greet his visitor.

'Thought you might be standing guard,' Craven

grinned, as he came into Drench's inner sanctum.

'Do you blame me?' the estate agent asked, rather irritated by the developer's flippant tone.

'Nope. Would have done the same myself with that weird mob shambling past my door.'

He took the seat Drench offered him and went on, 'Still, have to admit, your old mother has attracted more to her cause than I was expecting. Reckon there are around two hundred and fifty or so, from what I could see from the car.'

Drench went over to the window which faced towards the railway station. In the gaps between houses, he could just see the marchers turning into Flags Lane.

'All right, George, to what do I owe the pleasure of your visit? Or have you just come to gloat over my discomfort about my potty mother leading that dotty gang?'

Craven laughed. 'Not gloat, William, never gloat. Sympathise, perhaps. My own mother is almost as batty as yours seems to be. But at least her last few years are being spent in what Dame Edna Everage would call "a maximum security Twilight Home for the Bewildered". Yours, unfortunately, is still on the loose. Still, she'll have shot her bolt after today, thank the Lord.'

Drench turned back to his desk. 'So why have you come, George? We weren't due to meet up again until tomorrow.'

The property developer shrugged his substantial shoulders. 'Just passing, that's all.'

Drench smiled. 'You have to really, don't you?'

'What do you mean?'

'Oh, come off it, George, you have to pass here to get to the Health Farm.'

Craven sighed. 'Oh, so you know about Penny?'

'I should have thought everybody but her husband does by now. If you want to keep your amours secret, old love, buy a less conspicuous car than a brilliant white Mercedes with all the go-faster trimmings.'

Drench sat down at his desk, then leaned forward confidentially.

'Taking a bit of a chance, aren't you?'

'How so?'

'Well, couldn't it complicate your quiet little divorce, if dear Annabel decided to get nasty about your new inamorata? I mean, I know you've told me you've both agreed to split amicably, fifty-fifty and all that, no fuss, no fury, but that was all before you'd hopped into the well ploughed bed of the old Hallowes Health Farm.'

Craven got up from his chair and came over to the desk.

'Now look here, William,' he said firmly, 'that's enough of that. The fact we're business partners doesn't give you licence to criticise my private life or make scathing remarks about anyone I might choose to associate with. Anyway, I'm well aware that Penny has had other affairs before me and it doesn't worry me in the slightest.'

Drench waved his hand. 'Calm down, George. I was only trying to warn you, that's all. We don't want anything else queering our pitch right now. Least of all, scandal. Not until that Widow's Field development is finished, anyway.'

Craven glared across at him, then somewhat grudgingly resumed his seat.

'Don't worry. Annabel won't kick up.'

Drench was silent for a second, then remarked, 'Perhaps you're right and she won't dare to, considering . . .'

Craven looked up. 'Considering *what*?'

Drench grinned. 'Considering she's having it away with her own bloody lawyer, or didn't you know?'

Extract from the report on the Protest March, written by Sue Pike and published in the Hallowes Gazette, 29 September of that year.

FIERY END TO ENFLAMED PASSIONS

The much heralded Protest March against the proposed development of Widow's Field reached a fiery climax outside Hallowes Town Hall yesterday evening.

A crowd estimated at nearly five hundred blocked the High Street to hear the organiser of the march, Mrs Enid Drench, 82, of Black Lane, deliver a tough and uncompromising condemnation of both the developers involved – one of whom happens to be her son – and the Town and District Councils for giving their assent to what she described as 'another monstrous rape of rural Devon' and 'a satanic thrust into the hallowed soul of our precious town'.

But the most dramatic fireworks of the event were not contained in any of the speeches or in the four-hour-long march itself. But were to erupt as the enthusiastic applause for Mrs Drench's final words began to die down.

As Mrs Thelma Rickett of Rickett's Nurseries described it afterwards, 'There was suddenly a rumbling sound. The ground beneath my feet seemed to shake and then I heard the explosion. I ducked, then saw the flames. They seemed to almost reach the sky. And where the telephone box had been standing, there was now nothing but a huge smoking hole.'

Another member of the crowd, who wishes to remain anonymous, described his own reactions. 'Jagged pieces of the telephone box were falling everywhere. I thought, "My God, we're all going to get killed or injured." It was just like Normandy, when I was in the army in the battle for Caen. But when we all looked around afterwards, not one person had even been scratched. I tell you it was a ruddy miracle.'

Many present reported that immediately after the explosion they had seen a rainbow form an arc across the town, though the evening was cloudless and, for once, no rain had been reported in the area all day.

The fire was soon put out by the Hallowes brigade, led by Steve Moffat, who attributed the telephone box explosion to a gas main that had probably been disturbed when the new box's foundations had been dug . . .

'I don't like her being out almost every evening,' he muttered.

Maggie Blair looked across at her husband and put a finger to her lips.

He resumed watching the TV soap opera, a particular favourite of his wife's, but his mind was elsewhere. Though he had now more or less recovered from the shock of finding the bloody and battered Tully, he still harboured doubts about his daughter. That she might have been Tully's attacker, he no longer really believed, now that the trauma of the whole affair had receded, but he still could not quite accept her assertion that she neither knew, nor had even met, the photographer. For if that were true, then why should a schoolgirl have chosen him as the subject of her fake phone call the night of the storm? Surely she would not have pulled some name out of a hat? No, in his book, Bettina knew more than she was letting on. And if it weren't for his wife's stubborn defence of their daughter, he would have persevered with his questioning, until she would have been forced, sooner or later, to confess the truth of the matter.

He wondered where his daughter was right now. She had claimed to be going to the cinema with a school friend to see the latest Tom Cruise film, but once he had started to doubt her words, then . . .

His eyes flicked back towards the television, as the vertical hold seemed to be slipping and the soap stars' legs and feet were appearing above their heads and torsos.

'Damn and blast,' his wife grumbled. 'Trust the ruddy set to act up right now. Come on, Walt, can't you do something? It's ruining the whole thing.'

'Oh, I don't know,' her husband smiled, 'half the cast seem to have their legs above their heads most of the time anyway.'

He got up from his chair, as he saw his wife's savage frown. Not that she did not have a sense of humour, but like a lot of women, her humour had never embraced any joke with a sexual content.

He went over to the set and adjusted the vertical hold control at its back.

'That better?' he asked.

She shook her head.

'No, it's bloody worse. Now it's gone all snowy. Can't see a rotten thing.'

He adjusted the control to its previous position.

'Can't be our set then. Must be their tape. We will just have to wait until they can get it right.'

He came around to the front.

'What on earth have you done, Walt? It's still bloody snowy. It was better before you started mucking about with it.'

He peered at the blizzard on the screen and was about to go around to adjust the control once more, when vague shapes started to emerge through the snow.

He smiled across at his wife. 'There you are, love, it's coming back. Not me, see. It's them.'

He turned and walked back towards his chair.

'But Walt, it must be you. Look, you must have changed channel or something. This isn't . . .'

He instantly looked round, as he caught the inflexion in her voice. She was sitting rigid in her chair, as if paralysed, with her hand held over her mouth. He shifted his gaze to the screen and his joke about legs over heads seemed to have come only too starkly true.

'My God, Maggie, what on earth are they playing at? Hell, it looks like we've picked up some porn satellite station or other. The Italians . . .'

'Bugger the Italians,' his wife exploded. 'Can't you see who the bloody girl is . . . ?'

Now thoroughly embarrassed, he concentrated his attention back on the coupling on the screen. And as a grotesquely tight close-up of a phallus ejaculating over a shaven crotch faded, it was replaced by an equally tight close shot of a girl's face, her eyes closed and her tongue licking her smiling lips, like some giant cat who has just swallowed the cream. Despite the fuzzy quality of the image, there was no doubt of her identity.

It was his daughter, Bettina.

A split second later, the soap resumed, as if it had never been interrupted.

Priscilla Marsh watched until the Griffon's van had disappeared round the corner at the top of the High Street, before she went back into the shop.

'Help me tip some of these potatoes out, will you?' her boss demanded immediately.

Priscilla knew precisely what Penny Seymour-Jones meant. Her 'help me's' never unfortunately included herself; and many a time Priscilla had found herself risking a hernia or a heart attack, lumping great sacks or cartons on her own. But this time, she was determined not to jump instantly to her boss's command.

'Penny, I'd like a word with you, before we get down to unpacking and stacking.'

Penny said nothing, but put her hands on the counter and waited with pursed mouth.

'I think . . . er . . .' Priscilla began, hunting for the most tactful way of introducing a most vexed question. 'I think . . . er . . .'

'You thinka. You thinka,' Penny mimicked. 'You sounda lika an Italian shopkeeper. Now hurry up and get on with it. I want all this delivery unpacked and . . .'

For once, Priscilla threw all tact to the winds and even surprised herself with the vehemence of her interruption.

'Penny, will you stop going on and listen to someone else for once in your life.'

Her boss stepped back from the counter with a look of mock horror on her face.

'Lordy, Lordy, what's got into you, Priscilla? Tired after your long march with the Enid Drench gang yesterday? Or are you still shocked from that gas main blowing?'

Priscilla picked a potato out of one of the fresh sacks, came over to the counter and held the vegetable under her boss's nose.

'See that, Penny?'

'Yes, my dear,' she yawned. 'It's just a common, or rather garden, potato.'

'That's exactly right, Penny. You're telling the truth for once. It's just an ordinary potato.'

'Oh God, Priscilla, are you going nuts or something?'

She laughed. 'Nuts are another thing, now you mention it.' Her trembling fingers now began pointing one by one to the rest of the still unpacked sacks, trays and cartons.

'So are those peaches. Those sprouts. Those cauliflowers. Those onions. And no doubt, those apples . . .'

Her catalogue was abruptly terminated by a hand that knocked the potato clean out of her grip.

'Priscilla, for God's sake, if you're not feeling well, go home. Go home now before you drive me round the bend too.'

Priscilla smiled back at her employer, suddenly enjoying her unfamiliar centre stage role.

'I will go home, Penny, but only in my time. And only after I have seen you mark all this produce here with the prices it warrants and not the exorbitant prices you like to charge.'

She watched as her employer's expression slowly changed from anger to concern.

'Getting my message, Penny?'

There was silence, then Penny said, 'Is that why you wanted to go out and speak to the Griffon driver?'

She nodded. 'I tackled him. I told him what I have heard now four times over the phone. In the end, he admitted everything. And it's even worse than I thought. That over half of what Griffon sells is definitely non-organic, half of the rest is a question mark whether it is or isn't. Which leaves only a quarter of their produce that justifies anything like the prices you like to charge.' She took a deep breath. 'And what's more, my dear health and fitness friend, you've known about this all along. That's why you changed suppliers in the first place. You went to Griffon's for one reason only. The profit reason. To buy more cheaply, but sell at the same exorbitant prices. You are nothing but a cheat, exploiting the gullible of Hallowes, who have trusted you over the years to . . .'

Priscilla suddenly stopped, as she saw Penny's eyes shift towards the door.

'Please do go on, Priscilla,' the elderly lady customer smiled, as she put her purse back in her basket. 'I'd like to hear the end of this sorry tale, as I'm sure would the whole of Hallowes.'

Chapter Eleven

'For the Lord's sake, Walt, stop pacing the ruddy room,' Maggie Blair said at last. 'It's not going to solve a thing or bring Bettina back home quicker.'

Reluctantly, her husband obeyed and subsided into his usual chair.

'Damn it all, Maggie, I had enough trouble getting the bloody afternoon off work, so that we could both talk to Bett quietly and calmly after school and now she's obviously taken it into her silly head to go off somewhere with God knows whom.'

His wife looked at the cuckoo-clock on the wall - a souvenir of a bargain basement holiday in Switzerland many years before.

'She's only three-quarters of an hour late, Walt. Stop fretting. You're driving me barmy.'

'You should have let me talk to the girl when she came back last night, like I said.'

'What?' she exclaimed. 'At well after midnight? You must be out of your mind. As I told you, if we want to get to the bottom of this, we all need the clear head of day and to keep our tempers, and not to charge in like a ruddy bull at a gate.' She sniffed and looked away. 'Besides, you know what I think. You were right first time. The ruddy BBC transmitter must have picked up some awful foreign station or other. And because you are still so obsessed with that damned phone call and obviously have no faith in your own daughter, you immediately jumped to the conclusion that the girl in that disgusting film was Bett. Lots of girls must shave themselves. God knows why, but there you are. I never felt the need.'

'It wasn't just because of that, Maggie, and you know it. You said yourself the girl looked like our Bett.'

'I know I did. But I never said it *was* our Bett, did I? It was just the shock of seeing something like that in our own home, on our own screen. Besides, you couldn't really see who it was until that last shot of a face. And remember, it was so close, it was all fuzzy. Not like the rest at all. Mark my words, you're getting all lathered up for nothing. It was just some other poor unfortunate girl, who looks a bit like Bett, that's all.'

'Wish I'd been able to see the man's face,' he muttered, 'then that might have settled it.'

'God, Walter, can't you leave it all alone until we've had a talk with Bett?'

She rose from her chair. 'You're never ruddy happy unless you're worrying over something. You know Bett would never do anything like that, let alone be filmed while . . . well . . . you know. And last night you seemed quite reassured after you'd phoned the BBC in Plymouth. Why don't you believe what the ruddy experts say? After all, they back up what you thought in the first place. Atmospherics, they said. Over the South Hams and Hallowes, they said. We weren't the only ones to have rung in, they said.'

'But we were the only ones to see what we saw.'

'Can't be sure of that. Just because you asked some of your mates at work and I checked on a few of the neighbours, doesn't mean much. Hardly a Gallup poll, was it? Besides, they *did* all say there'd been more interference on their sets last night than they can ever remember. Maybe our TV is just a bit more sensitive than theirs, that's all. Hey, didn't we pick up something weird once before, now I come to think of it?'

Her husband thought for a moment. 'You mean a few months ago?'

She nodded. 'Yes, it's coming back to me now. We

were watching Spotlight. They were showing the opening of the new Telephone Exchange, in all that terrible downpour. I felt sorry for the Mayor and all. And suddenly, there was a flash and . . . soldiers were running up a beach . . .'

'. . . and then it was gone. Back to the poor Mayor. He looked like a drowned rat, despite his big hat. But that was only an accidental change of channel, love. I checked next day. On "2" they were showing *The Longest Day*. You know, that old war film with all the big stars in it, Robert Mitchum, John Wayne, Henry Fonda, all that lot.'

His wife held up her hands and smiled. 'Well, there you are. Last night's was a kind of change of channel, wasn't it? Only if it was Italian or French, the station was across the Channel, see what I mean?'

She went to the door. 'Anyway, I'm going to put the kettle on for a nice cup of tea. Bett can't be much longer. And then she'll put both our minds at rest, you'll see.'

Walter Blair watched his wife go out. He knew only too well that her words were actually braver than her thoughts. Throughout their marriage, she had been the one to bottle up her worries out of sight and put on a broad grin, where tears would often have been more appropriate. It was her way of keeping both her own sanity and that of the family. Many times in the past they had all benefited from her restraint and wishful thinking. He prayed from the bottom of his soul that such would be the outcome on this dreadful occasion.

'This has just come by hand for you, Mr Tully,' the blonde nurse grinned and handed him a letter.

He took it from her and glanced at the handwriting on the envelope. The letters were large and rounded and somewhat immature.

'From a girlfriend?' the nurse teased. 'Can always tell a feminine hand, I can. Would you like me to open it for you?'

He waved his hand. 'No, thank you.' His speech was still somewhat laboured, as the cuts and bruises around his face and mouth, not to mention the plasters and one remaining bandage, made even the slightest facial movement a painful effort.

'All righty,' she smiled. 'I'll love and leave you, Mr Tully. Don't forget to ring if you want anything, will you?'

She went out and Tully saw her wink at the police constable, who still sat guard outside.

He looked back at the envelope. Though he had never had occasion to see Bettina Blair's handwriting, he had a feeling the letter must be from her. In fact, he was surprised that she had not contacted him before. Certainly since she must have heard that he was now considerably improved and even able, now that he was off the last of the drips, to take the odd few steps around the room without assistance.

He inserted a forefinger underneath the flap and slit the letter open. The second he had unfolded the single sheet enclosed – a page that seemed to have been torn from a school exercise book – his eyes went down to the signature. It was from whom he thought.

He smiled to himself and started to read. But almost immediately the smile vanished from his face and the hand holding the page started to tremble.

It did not take long to read, for the message was only too simple and devastatingly direct. When he'd finished reading, he collapsed back on to his pillows and closed his eyes. But almost immediately he sat up again and reread the letter.

But this time, upon finishing, he lifted aside the bedclothes and painfully swung his legs across the bed and to the floor. Then holding on first to the bedside table and then to a chair, he stumbled across to the window that looked out over a small lawn to the side entrance road to the hospital car park.

He saw her almost at once. Her pink cardigan,

flamingo like, against the rhododendron bushes. He shut his eyes tight, as a wave of nausea came over him and he grabbed for the window-sill. When he looked up again, she had moved forward on to the lawn. Over in the distance, he could see her bicycle propped up against a 'No Parking' sign.

She gave no sign of greeting or even that she had seen him. She moved a couple of yards nearer his window, then stood, legs astride, hands on hips, staring up at him. He felt as if he were going to be sick and put his hand to his mouth. The sharp pain of that contact somehow brought him round and, holding on to the window frame with his left hand, he slowly raised his right and waved three times.

Immediately, she turned on her heel and walked back briskly to where she had left her bicycle. He watched her cycle away without a single backward glance and then he hobbled back to his bedside table and instantly pressed his buzzer.

The little blonde nurse was back with him in seconds.

'My, my, Mr Tully, get straight back into bed. I can see by your face you've been overdoing it while my back's been turned.'

But instead of obeying her, the photographer grabbed her roughly by the hand and shocked her by stammering, 'My clothes. My clothes. Where are my bloody clothes? I've got to get out of here.'

She quite unexpectedly stayed his hand.

'No, not now, really George . . .'

His fingers persevered and managed to get the front clip of the brassiere unclasped

Penelope suddenly sat bolt upright and his hand slipped out of her silk blouse.

'Oh come on, Penny. What's wrong? It's our last chance for a bit, with your blasted husband flying back tonight.'

Her long, red tipped fingers clipped her brassiere and

then proceeded to fasten the buttons on her blouse.

'Because, that's all,' she said firmly. 'Can't you men ever take no for an answer?'

'I'm not "you men", remember? I thought I was someone special. Or have all the "Darling George's" suddenly flown out of the window?'

Craven readjusted his tie and got up from the settee.

'You've been funny all afternoon, Penny. What the hell is the matter?' He went over to a mirror on the sitting-room wall, where he tidied his hair with his fingers. 'Is my novelty wearing off – that it?' He saw her reflection, as she turned away. He instantly went back to her, but now she was curled up away from him on the settee, like some foetus afraid to be born.

He leant down and whispered, 'Penny, I'm sorry. I didn't mean that.'

Neither spoke for quite some time, until she said quietly, 'You've been pretty weird yourself, you know, this afternoon. Getting touchy at my slightest remark and being about as subtle as a cartload of monkeys.'

He sighed and reached for her hand. 'Okay. Okay. I admit it. I'm not exactly my usual self.'

She turned her head slightly to look at him.

'Well, right now, two are "unusual" selves. Welcome to the club.'

He squeezed her hand sympathetically.

'What's wrong, Penny? Tell me. Is it because your husband . . . ?'

'It's nothing to do with my bloody naïve husband. The day I get upset over him, is the day I die, I assure you.'

'So?'

She uncurled herself and sat upright.

'You tell me your little problem first, my love. Mine may take quite a while.'

He shrugged. 'Oh, I don't really want to bother you with it, especially if you . . .'

'Bother me,' she cut in.

'All right. But don't say I didn't warn you.' He took a breath. 'It's my everloving Annabel.'

'What about her?'

'She's . . . well . . . I don't know for sure . . . but it looks like . . .'

She suddenly relinquished his hand. 'Oh, for God's sake, George, get on with it. Don't imagine I'm going to get upset over anything your vacuous Annabel does or doesn't do . . . except perhaps, if she's changed her mind about letting the divorce go through.'

'No, she's not done that. Quite the reverse. She seems, as they say, to have taken unto herself a lover.'

Penny raised her carefully lined eyebrows. 'Joining your club, eh? Don't blame her. Who's the unlucky man?'

'You'll never guess.'

'So don't make me.'

'It's Sebastian Fanshawe. You know, that hifalutin' lawyer fellow of hers.'

Penelope sat back amongst the cushions and smiled for the first time that afternoon.

'So aren't you a lucky man, George?'

He frowned. 'Lucky?'

She turned to him. 'Of course. Bloody lucky. Now you've every reason for not going ahead with that bloody silly fifty-fifty divorce settlement.' She prodded him in the ribs. 'More for little Georgie Porgie, here. Hell, don't you see? It's heaven bloody sent, you idiot.'

'But Penny,' he protested, 'if I try that on, she'll just quote "us" back at me. After all, your husband must be about the only person in Hallowes who doesn't know we're . . .' He hesitated and she jumped in raunchily.

'Screwing our arses off?'

He got up and went over to the fireplace.

'Well, you know what I mean. It'll be the bloody pot calling the kettle black.'

She rose too and joined him. 'Which one's the pot?' she grinned, prodding him in his incipient middle-aged spread.

'It's true,' he persisted. 'It's better to leave things as they are. I don't want any more scandal about the affairs of Craven Enterprises. After all, even in business, there's a limit to how much mud can be thrown around before it starts gumming up the works.'

Her smile suddenly vanished. 'Don't I bloody know it?' she said bitterly, then proceeded to tell her lover of Priscilla Marsh's dramatic and destructive mud throwing of the morning.

'I don't believe it.'

Craven took her by the shoulders.

'Penny, you can't close down the Health Farm just because some old biddy heard that woman shooting her mouth off.'

Penelope closed her eyes. 'That old biddy just happens to be Mrs Beatrice Smith-Masterson. She is not only just about my best customer, but she is chairwoman or president of just about every "do-gooding" society in the South West. So by now, Priscilla's allegations will have been spread like bloody manure right across Hallowes and the South Hams. So what else can I do but close down? It isn't as if I can prove any of what that perishing Priscilla said is untrue.'

'Oh, come on, Penny. It's not like you to give up so easily. All this will die down in time, you wait and see. Just issue a denial that you knew anything about the real quality of Griffon's produce. Say they told you that everything you bought from them was organic and organic food has its own natural price level.'

She shook her head slowly, her long hair now almost obscuring her face.

'It's no good, George. I've thought about it.'

'Why is it no good? Fighting is always worth it.'

She sat down once more on the settee, her head now in her hands.

'It's the telephone calls.'

'Telephone calls?'

'Priscilla has had phone calls. And she claims she's

heard my voice talking to Griffon's and making it quite plain I know exactly what I'm getting from them.'

'But that's impossible. She must be lying.'

'I thought that at first. And that she must have just overheard me on the phone. But two of the things she recounted me saying, I know were said in conversations when she was away sick and couldn't have overheard me.'

He came over and sat by her once more.

'So what are you saying? Someone is recording your conversations and playing them back over the phone? What sense would there be in that . . . ?' He stopped suddenly, then resumed, '. . . unless it's some vindictive customer or some idiotic attempt at blackmail or . . .'

She looked across at him and for the first time ever, he saw tears in her eyes.

'. . . or . . .' she murmured.

He suddenly took her in his arms and stilled her mouth with his hand. For he did not need to hear any more, as he remembered what William Drench had told him about the mysterious call he had intercepted at his mother's cottage.

By the time Tully had stuffed some clothes and toiletries in his lightweight airline suitcase and packed his cameras and lenses into their engine-turned aluminium container, he had to sink back on his bed, as his vision blurred and the room had started to revolve like some terrible surrealist nightmare.

As he lay there, he was half tempted to return to the hospital. For he realised he had seriously overestimated his own strength and pace of recovery and that the medical staff and the ambulancemen who had driven him home, had been only too right. He was not yet fit, by a long way, to check himself out of their care.

But after a few minutes, his determination returned with the clarity of his vision and the stabilising of the room. He told himself that he had been dead right to react as he had and get out of the hospital. For what he hadn't disclosed to the medical staff was that he wasn't just leaving their tender care, but getting the hell out of Hallowes – which, in his view, was a stinking little nothing town that had brought him nothing but tragedy and trouble. And it wasn't just Bettina Blair's note that had triggered this reaction. There was something about the town, an aura of self-satisfied, holier-than-thou complacency, that had irked him long before that dreadful evening.

He slowly raised himself up from the bed and sat on its edge. The first thing he had checked when he had let himself in, was whether the . . . thing . . . was still there. The 'thing' that still made his heart race, his mouth go dry at its very mention. But it had gone and was, no doubt, now in some police laboratory. Only the wires were left in the wall to remind him.

He looked round his bedroom and caught his reflection in the wardrobe mirror. For a second, he panicked, for he was still unused to the sight of his own face. Or what little of his own face still showed amidst the plasters and white crepe bandaging.

He shut his eyes, then opened them again, being careful not to look towards the wardrobe. Somehow, as he sat there, a feeling grew that someone else must be in the flat there with him. He shuddered. It was the same feeling that had come over him that terrible evening, when he was in the middle of his call to Soho.

He got up too quickly from the bed and had to hold on to a chair to prevent himself falling to the floor.

'Oh God,' he shouted out and the sound of his own voice seemed to echo round the room. He tried to pull himself together, telling himself over and over again that the police and the hospital staff were right and he had been wrong. Telephones just could not up and attack someone all on their own and that it was just a figment of his delirious imagination, a post-product of shock and his head injuries. But now he was back in his flat their reassurances, that he had begun to believe in the cosseted safety of his hospital room, seemed paper thin and certainly no protection against the panic he now felt.

Tully suddenly reached across for his case and lugged it to the door. In his weakened condition, it felt like a ton weight, as did, subsequently, his camera equipment. He had to make two trips to get both cases down the stairs and to the back door. But by the time he was outside and locking up, he felt a little stronger. For now, at least, he was starting on his way out of the damned town of Hallowes, and all the horrors it now represented. What's more, he was leaving behind a sixteen-year-old schoolgirl who, overnight, seemed to have changed into a surprisingly mature and shocking predator.

He opened the boot of his Camaro and stowed away the two cases. Breathless after his exertion, he had to hold on to the rear wing for a moment or two to let his vision clear once more. He prayed his strength would last out on his long drive to Scotland, where he aimed to stay at a small inn he had used once before on a photographic trip to Loch Ness. He planned to hide away there until he'd had a little time to work out his future plans. For at that moment, his forward thinking had only got as far as saying a thankful goodbye to Hallowes and all it represented. For even if the police were right in their assertion that the telephone must have been wielded by some assailant, then he was a damned sight safer hundreds of miles away from the scene of the crime, than sticking around in the godforsaken town, waiting with baited breath for another attack.

Tully looked at his watch and then up at the sky. Although it was late and the light was starting to fail, at least it wasn't raining or stormy and he felt pretty certain he could make Bristol before having to stop off somewhere for the night.

He moved round to the side of the car and was about to insert his key in the lock, when he noticed the denting and scratches around the catch.

'Hell and damnation,' he muttered to himself, as he realised the car must have been broken into while he had been in hospital. He tried the handle and the door, as he suspected, opened without the need of his key. Sliding into the driving seat, his eyes went immediately to the stereo fitting in the console. To his relief, it was still there, as were the speakers in the doors. With some difficulty, he turned his head so that he could see the rear shelf. The angled speakers mounted at each end had also been ignored by whoever had broken into the car.

He checked the mileometer, in case the car had been taken out for a joyride. But as far as he could remember, the figure of fifty eight thousand five hundred and forty was about right and the fuel gauge showed an almost full tank.

With a sigh, he inserted the key in the ignition and started up. The V8 motor rumbled into life instantly and a moment later he had reversed into the High Street and, slamming into Drive, roared away up the hill, heading towards the A38 and the M5 to Bristol.

It was just before the Ashburton turn-off that he first noticed it. And a shiver went up his spine. Telling himself not to be such a damned fool, he pressed on. But just after the signs to Newton Abbott, the feeling came again. And this time it was almost overpowering, like it had been that dreadful night.

His foot slackened its pressure on the accelerator and he looked round to the back seat.

And, as his reason told him must be the case, there was no one there. But even so, he couldn't rid himself of the feeling and almost immediately, his head started to pound and his vision to blur.

'Come on, Tom,' he muttered to himself. 'Pull yourself together. You've only got to get yourself to Bristol and then you can rest up . . .'

He blinked rapidly for a second or two in an attempt to clear his vision and the tactic seemed to pay off. Now the trees and hedgerows, silhouetted by his headlights against the twilight of the sky, had sharp outlines once more, but the throbbing in his head still persisted.

The Camaro ate up the next few miles in smooth style and despite the drummers pounding at his brain, Tully started to relax a little. He reached forward, chose a cassette, Michael Jackson's 'Bad', and inserted it in the stereo.

As 'Man in the Mirror' started to fill the car with its own beat, Tully glanced up into his own mirror. And, for a split second, imagined his blurred and double vision had returned. But then, slowly, another head seemed to emerge from behind his own. He blinked, then looked again.

'My God,' he screamed and almost lost control of the wheel.

'Not your God, you fucking bastard,' the head replied, 'more an avenging angel . . .'

Tully slammed on his brakes and the car slewed across to the slow lane.

'Keep driving,' she shouted, as she clambered over to the front passenger seat.

'We can have our little talk while you turn right round and drive me home.'

He looked across at her, as she deliberately refrained from pulling down her school skirt over her bare, down-covered thighs.

'Bettina, what the hell do you think you're doing?'

She smiled and switched off the Michael Jackson.

'Keeping tabs on you. What did you think I'd bloody do? Let little Tom slip out of my fingers, just as I've got him right where I want him?' She laughed. 'I guessed you might do something like this once you'd got my note. So I kept watch on the hospital, saw you get into the ambulance and I cycled after it as fast as I could.'

Tully reached into his leather jacket.

'I promise I wasn't running out on you, Bettina. I have

every intention of paying up.' He took out his wallet and handed it to her.

'Look, there's sixty pounds or so in there. Take it, it's yours.'

She carefully removed the ten-pound notes and wagged them in his face.

'That's just the first instalment, you bastard. As I said in my little note, I want half of everything you earn from now on, or I'm going straight to the police.'

Her fingers returned to the wallet and started to extract his credit cards.

'Perhaps I should keep one or two of these, just to make sure you don't try to run off again, eh, Mr Tully?'

'No, no, no. We can work things out, really.' He put his hand out towards her, but she slapped it away. 'No, please, Bettina, I'm sorry. Terribly sorry. I should never have done . . .'

'No, you shouldn't, should you?' she sneered. 'But you have and now you've got to pay the penalty.'

She selected a Visa card, then replaced the others in the wallet.

'I'll keep this one,' she grinned. 'You can call it my visa to your bank balance, if you like. Oh, and my guarantee that you'll get that fucking tape back from whoever you've sent it to.'

'I will, I will,' he stammered, not admitting to her there would be thousands of copies of it by now, circulating around shady video stores and shops, not only in Britain, but very soon, no doubt, across the world.

She waved the credit card in front of his face.

'You'd bloody better, you sod.'

The throbbing in his head had now become unbearable and he had difficulty in coping with the dazzle of the headlights from the traffic in the west-bound lanes.

'Want to know how your little Bettina found out?' she asked teasingly, turning her body sideways towards him and opening her legs as far as the fascia would allow.

Tully hardly heard, for now his vision had deteriorated to the point where he could hardly discern the lines marking the edge of the roadway. But somehow, try as he might, he found he could not raise his foot off the accelerator and the Camaro seemed almost as if it were being drawn forward by some giant magnet.

'Heard you, I did. Talking to your filthy pornographic friend. You're just a dirty, stinking bastard. No wonder somebody tried to kill you. I wish they'd succeeded.'

'Heard me?' he said softly, as if in a trance.

'Yes, bloody heard you.'

'How on earth . . . ?'

'How? On the bloody phone, of course. I must have got a crossed line . . .'

But Bettina Blair never had a chance to finish. Suddenly Tully screamed and the steering wheel seemed to wrench itself free of his hands. He felt his right foot slam the accelerator to the floor, whilst his left remained as if paralysed just above the wide brake pedal.

The Camaro's big V8 roared out its power and the speedometer needle swung from sixty, through seventy and eighty to over the ninety mark.

'Tom, what the bloody hell are you doing?' Bettina screamed at him. 'Trying to kill us both?'

She threw herself across the console to try to get some control over the wheel, but the rim felt like a burning brand and, with a scream, she let go.

'TULLY . . .' Her shout died in her throat, as she felt the car hit the grass verge with a sickening thud. Then suddenly there was nothing but the screaming of the V8 as it wildly over-revved during the car's brief flight into the air.

She looked up just in time to see the telegraph pole that would snap as they struck it, then spear the car as if it were some giant kebab.

Chapter Twelve

Bobby Quick switched off the television, then relaxed back, stretching his long legs out in front of him.

'Not a mention,' he muttered gruffly to his companion, who, sitting next to him on the Cadillac limousine's broad rear seat, looked like some portly puppet compared to the long and lean limbed evangelist.

'They did you proud when you arrived at Heathrow the other day.' Homer Friend smiled nervously.

'The other day is the other day, Homer. Why no mention of my leaving for the West Country, tell me that?'

Friend fidgeted on the seat. 'That's all arranged, Bobby. You'll get big coverage when we arrive at the hotel in Hallowes, you'll see.'

'National media or just local?' He turned to face his aide. 'I'm a national figure, Homer, not some local hick, who's a local hero for twenty-four hours.'

'Right, right. Well . . . er . . . there'll be Spotlight there and TSW and all the papers . . .'

He hastily looked out of the window at the passing, rather flat Somerset countryside, hoping Quick would not realise that the two television stations he had mentioned were only local, as indeed, in all probability, would be the newspaper journalists. National coverage would have to await the big night of the rally.

'Well, they had better be there, my friend,' the evangelist threatened, 'or we ain't going to fill that . . . great field you've chosen or even start to recover our expenses, let alone make our movement a profit.'

'Right again, Bobby. We'll fill it, double fill it, you'll see.'

Quick played with a vast gold ring on a lean and tanned finger. Square and chunky as a nut, it looked robust enough to have fallen off a solid gold Cadillac.

'Weather permitting,' he smiled grimly, 'as I'm told the inhabitants of this pompous little country always say about outdoor events.'

Homer Friend cleared his throat. 'Oh, they'll come to hear you, Bobby, come rain or come shine.'

'Or come hell and highwater. I doubt it, Friend. What's more, I read a piece in *The Times* this morning about the weather in the Hallowes area of Devon acting up real weird. Storms seem to be bubbling up like there's no tomorrow. If that's true, we may be in big trouble. Don't kid yourself.'

The aide played with his fat little fingers.

'Well, let's pray for a dry spell. They must be real overdue for one now.'

The evangelist snorted. 'Noah prayed, my friend, and a lot of good it did *him*.'

The aide decided to change the subject. For he knew the weather was, indeed, the only unreliable element in the elaborate plans for the great evening. He ferreted in a wine-coloured leather briefcase resting beside him and produced a clutch of papers.

'By the way, Bobby, I've finished the revise to your opening speech.'

The evangelist reached across and took the papers from him without comment. He perused them for a couple of minutes, then turned back to his aide, his look clearly indicating his displeasure.

'Leaves a rotten great hole, still.'

Friend held up his hands. 'I know, Bobby, I know. It's a real shame they asked you to take out all reference to your being in Hallowes during the war. Made a great opening. Are you sure you . . . er . . . can't just slip it back in?'

Quick sighed. 'Yeh, I'm sure, I'm sure.'

'But those Army Veteran friends of yours,' the aide persisted, 'they'll never know.'

The evangelist turned on him. 'Look, my naïve little Friend, you should know damn well by now that our organisation cannot risk offending anyone to do with the government of our dear old US of A. And the Army's the government. And "those Army Veteran friends" of mine are not exactly corporals or down the line troopers or even one star generals. They're top brass. You have to use all the fat little fingers of one of your hands just to count their stars. So if they say forget it, I forget it. You forget it. We all forget it. And most of all, make damned sure that little old lady, who you were going to get to say remembered me during the war, will silence her mouth with a dollar gag, right?'

'But what's their reason . . . ?' Friend began, then seeing he was on a hiding to nothing, stopped.

Quick smiled. 'Ours not to reason why, my dear Homer, but like the army, do or die.' He tossed the papers back into his aide's lap. 'So get about it. That revise just ain't filling the gap.'

She noticed his eyes lingered longer on her legs than quite befitted such a religious crusader. But she did not resent it. For Sue Pike guessed her good looks had probably been the only reason she had been given an extended private interview with the evangelist and, what's more, in his hotel suite.

'Have you got any more questions for me?' Quick smiled his most Hollywood smile. Indeed, he had played the whole interview, angling his tanned face so that she only caught the most photogenic side of him.

'Not about you or the rally itself, no.'

'But you *have* more questions?' he asked, hopefully, for even a dumb reporter with good legs was better company right then than any of his many aides, or particularly the rotund Homer Friend. For Bobby Quick was not a man who relished solitude. His ego constantly needed reflation by others. Without a constant injection of flattery and servility, his soul seemed to become as parched and leathery as the skin on his face.

She nodded. 'Well, it's a bit parochial, but I'm sure the people of Hallowes would like to know what you think of their present . . . problems.'

'Problems?' He leant forward in his chair.

She blushed slightly. 'I'm afraid all this may sound very silly to you . . .'

He reached forward and touched her hand.

'No, please go ahead. That's exactly why I'm here, why God is with us. To help us solve each and every problem, however small or trivial they may seem to be.'

His physical proximity now rather unnerved her, but she could not push her chair further back from him without causing offence.

'Well, Hallowes is, I suppose, going through it a bit now. It started with the onset of the dreadful weather, I suppose . . .'

'Yes, I read a little piece on that this morning. In your *Times* newspaper.'

'. . . the constant storms are starting to get everyone down. But it's not just that, unfortunately. There's something else . . . something that's very difficult to explain away, at least, in natural terms.'

He got up from his chair, came over and put his arm on her shoulder.

'Perhaps the timing of my coming was heaven sent,' he said quietly.

Trying to ignore both his remark and his touch, she went on, 'Let me explain as best I can. I have interviewed a lot of people in Hallowes now, about this phenomenon.'

'Phenomenon? Don't tell me there's been some sighting of the Blessed Virgin or . . .'

She shook her head. 'No, no, nothing like that. It's just that everyone now is becoming afraid to . . .' She stopped suddenly, as she realised how ridiculous her next statement was going to sound.

'Yes?' he urged, the pressure of his fingers on her shoulder increasing.

'. . . afraid to answer the telephone.'

At least her remark made him relinquish his hold and take a step back from her.

'What's that, Miss Pike? Or can I call you Susan?'

She smiled nervously, which he took to be her acquiescence.

'I know it sounds silly, but somehow or other people are getting calls that clearly are not really intended for them to hear.'

Quick frowned and was now starting to regret having singled out this particular reporter, however attractive she might be. For in his book, she was clearly some kook.

'I'm afraid you've lost me.'

'I thought I might. You see, we have recently had a whole new telephone system installed in Hallowes. New automatic exchange, new fibre optic lines, new telephone receivers, the works. And ever since, the system has been acting up. Not all the time. Just sometimes. And not with everybody. But with enough to cause considerable concern.'

He went back to his own chair and sat down, now not caring about the angle of his face.

'I reckon that's more a problem for the big chief of the Telephone Company, than for our Big Chief in the heavens.'

'I don't think so,' she said hastily. 'At least, I don't think it's a fault in the telephone system. It's more like a . . . well . . . a fault in people.'

'A fault in people,' he repeated. 'What exactly do you mean by that?'

'It may all sound crazy to you and maybe it is crazy but, you see, the telephone seems to be only repeating calls that people have actually made. But it seems, as far as I can tell, to be repeating them only to those for whose ears the calls were obviously not intended.' She hunted for the right words. 'It's like . . . well . . . it's like, somehow, its only intention is to cause trouble, to hurt and offend and . . .'

'You mean, it's evil?' he cut in. 'Acting like the Devil? Is that it?'

She shook her head. 'I don't know. I don't know. Is it evil to repeat what one has already said? That's all it seems to be doing. From all accounts, it doesn't make things up at all.'

'But it stirs things up, right?'

'Yes, but . . .'

He suddenly rose from his chair, his piercing eyes now bright with enthusiasm.

'Miss Pike, you don't know how mighty pleased I am to have met you today.'

'You are?' she muttered in disbelief.

'Yes indeed, Susan.' The hand returned to her shoulder and this time she couldn't restrain a shiver. 'Now tell me more. Tell me about it and I'll guarantee you a good quote. If something is worrying Hallowes, however strange or silly, it worries Bobby Quick, oh yes, indeedy.'

The evangelist refrained from telling her the real reason for his enthusiasm. That she had just given him the perfect substitute for the now deleted army references at the start of his Grand Rally speech.

The rear tyres of John Stride's Bristol scattered gravel as he turned fast into the small forecourt of the nursery. As he pulled abruptly to a halt, he saw the mean figure of Thelma Rickett waiting for him at the conservatory door. He grabbed his bag off the rear seat and ran from the car to her side.

'Where is he?' he asked breathlessly.

She said nothing, but pointed a thin finger to the inside of the house.

Stride found Rick Rickett in the kitchen, slumped over

an old scrubbed wood table. Beside him was an almost empty mug of what looked like tea. He immediately took his right wrist that was stretched across the table as if reaching for the tea. There was no pulse.

Putting his own arm under Rickett's armpit, he had some difficulty in lifting the nurseryman's torso up from the table. As he did so, a piece of paper fluttered to the floor. But his attention was on Rickett's head that now rested limply against his chest. He didn't need to reach over for his bag, for he had seen death often enough to recognise it when he saw it again.

Stride deliberately stayed with Thelma Rickett until the police had left and the ambulance had taken away the body of her husband.

'I'm afraid there is bound to be a post-mortem,' he said as sympathetically as he could.

'Oh,' was her only reaction to his remark. 'Like a cup of tea?' she asked.

He shook his head, amazed at her apparent coolness after finding her husband had committed suicide. 'No, thank you very much. I ought to go in a minute. I only stayed . . .'

'Good of you, Doctor. You're a man who still thinks of others. There are not many of your like left, more's the pity.'

He got up from his chair and came over to her at the old-fashioned, grey enamel stove.

'Mrs Rickett, about that piece of paper that was under your husband's body.'

She looked him coldly in the eye. 'What about it, Doctor? Police have got it now.'

'Yes, I know. I just wanted to ask you if you had ever seen it before.'

She looked back at the stove and, taking a box of matches, lit one of the back burners.

'How could I have? He wasn't likely to show me his suicide note before he'd . . . now would he?'

She placed a blackened kettle on to the flames.

'No, of course not. But I just thought it looked as if it might have been torn from something else. Maybe another note.'

She moved away from the stove and sat down at the table, her back now to him.

'Don't take no notice of those torn edges. My husband never wasted a single penny on new notepaper, he didn't. Always tearing bits off other bits, he was.'

Stride came around the table to face her.

'So you've never seen it before, Mrs Rickett?'

'Never. 'Course not. 'Ere, what are you insinuating, Doctor?'

'Nothing, Mrs Rickett. It's just that, well, that piece of paper said nothing about taking his own life, did it? Only that the business wasn't going at all well and that he felt like chucking it all in.'

Her eyes flared her anger.

'So you *are* insinuating. That's why you've stayed behind, isn't it, Dr Stride? Nothing to do with kindness of your heart, like what I thought. No. You're just the same as any other man. If you can think dirty, speak dirty and act dirty, then you ruddy will. Now get out of my house.'

He tried to grab her by the shoulder, as she turned away, but she eluded his grasp.

'Mrs Rickett, I found the rest of the piece of paper.'

She stopped in her tracks.

'You can't have. I burnt it in the . . .'

She spun round as she realised her mistake.

Stride slowly moved towards her.

'It was the telephone, wasn't it?'

She closed her eyes tightly.

'She wouldn't stop, you see . . .' she began, as if speaking not to him, but to spirits of the air that only she could see, '. . . day after day, she phoned me . . . with her obscene talk, her foul-mouthed slaverings . . .' She shuddered. '. . . and she thought she'd got me beat, the stupid little whore. But I was too clever. Oh yes, I soon found out who she was and I phoned her back. Day after day, day after day. But she wouldn't listen . . . so I had to . . . I just had to kill him . . . didn't I? It was the only way to get her to stop. If he was gone, there'd be no reason for her to ring no more . . . It was all so easy. He'd written that letter some days before to his sister and never posted it. And we've got enough paraquat in the conservatory to kill the whole of Hallowes, let alone . . .'

She suddenly stopped and then would have certainly collapsed to the floor, had Stride not caught her in his arms.

As he carried her out to his car, she clung to him with the tenacity of a baby ape to its parent. And with her eyes still closed, from her lips came the thin high voice of a small child chanting, 'Ring-a ring-a roses, pocket full of posies. Atishoo, atishoo. We all fall down.'

Inspector Dudkin looked up at the sound of Stride's bleeper.

'I'm sorry, Inspector, I had better phone in, just in case.'

Dudkin extended his hand towards one of the telephones on his desk.

'Use my cursed instrument,' he smiled ruefully, reminding the doctor of his remarks about the rôle of the telephone in Rick Rickett's death.

Stride dialled his surgery and had a brief conversation with his receptionist. When he had replaced the receiver, he said, 'Apologies once more, Inspector, but I had better go.'

'Crisis?' the policeman enquired. 'I guess your life is much like ours in the police. You dread the phone to ring because normally it can only mean trouble.'

He got up from behind his desk and saw Stride to the door. 'Whoops,' he smiled, 'but right now in Hallowes, we police and you doctors are not alone, eh? The dring-dring of the old phone is becoming a source of panic for quite a few, from all accounts. And yet, as I told you, neither we nor the boys at Telecommunications can find any real cause why the telephones should be acting that way. Let's hope it will all stop as suddenly as it began.'

He opened the door. 'Maybe when the weather settles down.'

'Maybe,' Stride smiled, then, as he shook hands, remarked, 'I wish it was all just confined to those damned errant calls, though.'

The Inspector frowned. 'What do you mean?'

'Well, we've had that telephone box explode into flames the night of the protest march.'

'Oh, now don't go letting your imagination run away with you, Dr Stride. That was a leaking gas main.'

'Maybe. But then there was that attack on poor Tully. He claimed, as you know, that it was . . .'

The Inspector laughed and cut in. 'Mickey Mouse who attacked him. You really don't give credence to such lunatic ravings, do you, Doctor – you a man of science, too?'

'Well, we'll never know now after last night.'

'Ah yes. You are the poor young lady's doctor, I believe.'

Stride nodded. 'That's who I'm going to see now. I asked them to bleep me if there was any change in her condition.'

'Is there? Because if there is, we would like to ask Miss Blair a few questions about the accident. You see, we've been over the remains of the car and can't find anything that would have caused it to swerve off the road like it did. Maybe, when she's a shade better, she will be able to shed a little light on things. It came as a considerable surprise to us that she even knew Mr Tully.'

Stride made no comment on his last remark. 'Well, from what my surgery reports, she has regained consciousness now, but doesn't even know who she is, let alone what happened last night.'

'I hope her memory returns, for, with Tully dead, she is the only witness as to what happened.' He shook his head. 'Dreadful, dreadful thing to occur. I saw him in the morgue. The telegraph pole had gone right through his chest like a giant spear.'

Stride suddenly turned back into the room and the wild look in his eyes rather unsettled the Inspector.

'What did you say? All I've been told is that the car ran off the A38 and crashed.'

The police officer held up a calming hand. 'You were told right. That's what did occur. But it just happened that there was a bloody great telegraph pole right in its path.'

'Happened,' Stride repeated, as if to himself. 'You believe . . .' He stopped suddenly and went back out into the grey and dismal corridor.

'I must go,' he said hurriedly, 'otherwise the hospital will think I'm not coming.'

'Do let us know as soon as Miss Blair is fit to answer a few questions,' the Inspector shouted after the doctor's retreating figure.

When Stride had disappeared through the main entrance, a police constable, who had just entered, overheard the Inspector mutter to himself, 'Overwork. Sends 'em all crazy. No wonder every other suicide's a damned doctor.'

'Hello. Recognise me, Bettina?'

The blue eyes blinked their negative answer.

'I'm your doctor, John Stride.'

He held out his hand and was relieved to feel how firm was her grasp.

'Hello,' she smiled and for all the world looked quite normal, save for the pallor of her skin. For she had been found lying face down on the grass some feet from the crashed car. She had obviously been catapaulted from the vehicle and had, ironically, been saved from terrible injury or even death, by not having worn her seat belt.

'How are you feeling?'

'Bit woozy,' she blushed, 'but better now I've seen Mum and Dad. They've only just left, because the nurse said I should have some rest.'

'Yes, I saw them in the corridor. You recognised them all right?'

She nodded. 'Of course.'

'But you don't recognise me?'

She shook her head. 'I expect I will soon.'

Stride leaned forward and pulling down her lower lids, looked into her eyes. But again, everything seemed only too normal. When he had first examined her, around eleven-thirty the previous night, just after she had been brought in, he could not believe how injury-free she seemed. For someone who had just survived a lethal crash and been catapulted into the air to thud down on to the grass verge, her whole body was remarkably, indeed uncannily, free of major bruising or abrasions. And the X-rays of her head had not revealed any haemorrhaging or damage that could explain her unconsciousness or her now considerable loss of memory.

'Tell me, Bettina,' Stride smiled, 'what is the very last thing you *can* remember?'

She sat up on one elbow. 'Mum and Dad asked me that just now.'

'And what did you tell them?'

'Well, it's kind of funny,' she blushed again. 'I can't seem to remember anything since, but I remember this as clear as a bell.'

'Go on.'

'It was a long cycle ride I went on with Julie - that's a girlfriend of mine at school.'

She grinned. 'It's dreadful, isn't it? Dad tells me that was way back in April. He remembered it because it was the first really warm day of the year, he said.'

'And where did you go?'

'Bifton. Bifton Sands. It's lovely there. Do you know it?'

Stride nodded. 'Longest stretch of beach for miles

around. But it shelves a bit steeply.'

'No problem,' she retorted proudly. 'I've been able to swim since I was four. Mum always used to take me to Paignton pool.'

Stride thought for a moment. 'And you really can't remember anything at all since then?'

'No. Not really. Isn't that awful?'

'It'll come back bit by bit,' he smiled, but secretly hoped that those bits would not include the full horror of the fatal crash, despite his own avid curiosity as to what exactly had occurred. 'Why do you think your ride to Bifton Sands sticks out in your memory so? Did anything happen there out of the ordinary?'

'No. Not really. Julie and I just lay around on the beach. Played ducks and drakes over the water. There was no one else about. We ate some sandwiches that Julie brought.' She grinned. 'I remember turning my nose up at one. It had peanut butter in. I don't like peanut butter.'

Stride smiled. 'The English don't love it the way the Americans do.'

She relaxed back against the pillows and with mock modesty, pulled the sheets up over her bosom.

'Oh yes, that reminds me of something funny. Do you know why we upped and left the beach in the end?'

He shrugged. 'Got too cold?'

'No, though Julie got cold feet all right, but not from the water or the temperature. She had fallen asleep, see, while I read a pop magazine. Then she suddenly woke up screaming and leapt to her feet. Fair shook me, it did. I asked her what on earth was wrong?' She giggled through her fingers. 'You'll never believe what she replied. That a huge tank had just run over her.'

Stride frowned. 'Tank?'

'Yes, you know, army tank. Big thing, she said it was, with dirty great white stars on its sides, like American jeeps have in films. Well, after that, she just couldn't relax at all, so we packed up and cycled home. Crazy, wasn't it? Hey, maybe that's why I remember that afternoon so well. What do you think, Doctor?'

'Maybe,' he said quietly, then got up from his chair. 'Well, Bettina, I'd better get on, otherwise I'll have all my other patients complaining I only like looking after pretty girls.'

She grinned sheepishly, then asked, 'Before you go, Doctor, can you tell me something? Whose car was I in when it crashed? No one seems willing to tell me for some reason.'

Stride hesitated, then lied, 'Oh, we would rather you remembered for yourself, you see, Bettina. By the way, there's one last question from me. Sounds a bit personal, but isn't really. Do you remember who your boyfriend was in April?'

She sat bolt upright, with a fretful look across her young face. 'I hope it isn't "was", Doctor. He's lovely, is Bill. That's Bill Paget. They'll let him pop in to see me after he's finished school today, won't they?'

Stride smiled and left. For he could not reveal that he himself had pronounced Bill Paget dead, his motorcycle crushed by a contractor's lorry on one sunny afternoon last May.

Chapter Thirteen

Sue Pike shut her notepad and looked away from him.

'I'm sorry, Doctor, but as you can hear, I've come up with next to nothing.'

'Don't be sorry,' Stride smiled. 'We had to start somewhere and the history of those two fields seemed a reasonable choice.' He sighed. 'Maybe there isn't a darned starting point. Maybe there's no rhyme nor reason to any of it. Maybe it is just one of those weird phenomena that occur now and again that defy logical explanation. Like the ability to bend spoons . . .'

'. . . crockery flying about rooms for no reason . . .' she added.

'Groans and bumps in the night.'

'Apparitions and ghosties . . . *déjà-vu* . . .'

'Only this is not so much *déjà-vu*, as *déjà parlé*, if there is such a phrase.'

She grinned. 'There is now.'

Both suddenly fell silent, as distant thunder caused the french windows of the sitting-room to fret against their lock.

'Even the weather has a reason,' Stride said at last. 'It's just that we don't quite understand it enough yet. One day we will.'

She looked up at him and knew what he was trying to say.

'You don't believe it's all random, do you?'

He shook his head. 'No. Do you?'

'Well, if it isn't . . .' she began, then suddenly reopened her notebook, turned to a clean page and took out her pen. 'Let's write down as much as we know, ignoring the blind alley of the fields.'

'Okay,' he agreed, and rising from his chair, joined her on the settee. 'Let's begin now, not with land, but with people. Obviously we can't list everyone whose telephone has acted strangely. We don't know them all for a start, so let's just list those we know have personally suffered in some way from receiving those rogue calls.'

'Thelma Rickett,' she grimaced as she wrote down the name.

'Yes. From what the police can gather, she claims her husband used to ring numbers advertised in girlie magazines. Apparently, all it amounts to is recorded dirty talk by girls with come-on voices.'

'And then they started to ring her. Which we know is impossible. Right?'

'Right,' he agreed.

'So in the end, she's driven to murder her husband. Do we know any more?'

'Not really. No doubt, more will come out at the trial, but that's ages away. So let's go on to Tully.'

She wrote down his name. 'We don't know he received any of these calls, do we?'

'No. But Tully's death might well be connected with the phone system in some macabre way.'

She looked at him in surprise, but saw from his expression that he was being serious. 'You believe his claim that . . . the Mickey Mouse attacked him on its own?'

'Well, let's put it this way. The police have discovered no evidence of either a break in at the premises or any trace of an assailant. There were no footprints, apparently, no fibres of clothing, no fingerprints on the telephone, no traces of hair or blood other than Tully's own and no sign of a fight or struggle.'

'But unlike Rickett, he did not die as a result of the phone attack.'

'Not that time,' he said quietly.

She left her question until she'd made some notes,

then asked, 'But he died in a car crash? Went off the road.'

'Correct.'

'So his death was not anything to do with . . .' She stopped suddenly. 'Oh my God, you don't mean to say . . .'

'Well, the car didn't kill him, did it? It was the thing it hit.' He lowered his voice. 'I went to see the body in the morgue earlier this morning. There was almost nothing left of the top half of his body. The telegraph pole had gone straight through him.'

Stride saw the colour disappear from the reporter's cheeks and he reached across and patted her arm reassuringly.

'Sorry for all the grizzly details.'

'No, that's all right, really.' She took a deep breath, then went on, 'But okay, so he was killed by the pole, but even so, think for a minute. He wasn't killed in or around Hallowes. It was over near Ashburton on the A38.'

'Good point, Sue. I thought of that too. So just before you came, I rang up Hallowes telephone people and . . .'

'Ashburton still comes under their control?'

He nodded. 'The town itself actually marks the eastern edge of their area.'

She was silent for a moment, then returned to her note-taking.

'What about that schoolgirl, Bettina Blair? Don't forget she very nearly got killed too.'

'Correction. She didn't "very nearly get killed".'

She frowned. 'But I gather she was thrown out of the car, when the police estimate the car must have been doing well over seventy. If that isn't nearly being killed, I don't know what is.'

'In reality, you're right, Sue. She should have broken her neck or spine, or had multiple injuries of some sort. But when I examined her, there was hardly a mark on her body, let alone a fracture of anything.'

She looked at him. 'But the hospital told me she is badly concussed and has lost her memory to quite an extent.'

'The second part is true. But we can't find any signs of head injury or haemorrhaging. Not even a bruise or a bump.'

'So what you're saying is . . .'

'. . . that from a physical standpoint, Bettina Blair seems as fit as you or I and you'd never know she had been in even a minor accident, let alone a fatal crash.'

'But that's kind of impossible, isn't it?'

He smiled. 'Impossible things seem to be the order of the day - and night - in Hallowes these days, don't they?'

Stride handed her the gin and tonic and sat back on the settee with his Scotch.

'It's not what I say to my patients, Sue, but maybe alcohol will trigger that spark of inspiration we seem to be so sadly lacking right now.' He raised his glass. 'To our brain cells.'

She grinned back. 'To health and happiness.' Then she added, 'For us and for Hallowes.'

Neither spoke again, until the latest rolls of thunder had dissipated themselves amongst the hills around the town and then she asked, 'Now where had we got to? Ah yes, Bettina Blair. But she hasn't had any phone calls.'

'No, not as far as we know. But her father has.'

'Her father?'

'Yes. Walter Blair. Like his daughter, he's a patient of mine.'

'He's had a call? How do you know?'

'I wormed it out of him, after an event occurred that I can't really tell you about. You know, the old oath we doctors swear.'

She wrote down the father's name. 'Well, that does give us a link between Tully and the Blairs, or does it?'

He shrugged. 'I don't know. I have a feeling her father

knows more than he has actually confessed to me, but maybe it's my over-active imagination.'

'And maybe not. Sure you can't tell me?'

'Very sure. Sorry.' He sipped his scotch. 'Next, just write down, "Telephone engineer".'

She did as she was bid and then asked, 'And this anonymous engineer. He's had a call?'

'Well, he had a call of a different kind. To ask him to investigate a suspected fault in the lines near where the Blairs live.'

'Did he find anything?'

'No fault, if that's what you mean.'

'But he found something else?'

Stride smiled self-consciously. 'I didn't think too much of it at the time. It just seemed to me that he'd been working too hard and had suffered some kind of hallucinatory fit or other.'

'But you think differently now,' she said, excitedly. 'I know he's obviously another patient of yours, but can't you tell me what he said?'

Stride thought for a moment. 'All right. But remember you haven't heard this, Sue.'

'Heard what?' She smiled.

'Well, he said that just as he was about to put the cover back over the inspection chamber in the road, the fibre optic lines began to pulse and glow as if they were alive.'

'My God!'

'That's not the end of it. He claimed he felt they were trying to draw him down into the pit and when he wouldn't obey them . . . oh hell, this sounds ridiculous, even now . . . they leapt out above ground and tried to lasso him.'

'Come on, Dr Stride, don't stop there.'

'I have to. There's nothing more to tell. You see, that was when he fainted and was found lying by the side of the inspection chamber by a passer-by.'

'Was he injured?'

'No. They examined him in out-patients at the hospital

and I saw him first thing the next morning. There seemed absolutely nothing wrong with him that a cutting back of overtime or a holiday wouldn't cure. In fact, the latter is what I prescribed for him. Of course, after all that's happened since . . .'

She sipped her gin and tonic thoughtfully, then said, 'Any more hair-raising surprises for me, Doctor?'

'Well, no surprises, but I suppose we shouldn't ignore the Enid Drench protest march and the fact of the telephone box blowing up.'

She looked at him questioningly.

'So you're not buying the explanation of the gas main?'

He downed the last of his Scotch at a gulp and got up from the settee.

'I don't know what I'm buying right now, Sue. But it does sort of fit, doesn't it? Or did, when we thought Widow's Field might have something to do with it all.'

'Widow's Field protest march ending with a bang?'

'Exactly. Another telephone link, if you like. But who knows, maybe it was just a coincidence and the gas main *was* to blame.'

He looked across at her. 'You know, I'm starting to reach the stage with this whole thing that I don't know what's up any more. I even dread my own phone ringing in the surgery, in case I hear . . . oh, I don't know . . . a patient talking about how he or she is planning to murder me, or one of the other doctors in Hallowes contradicting all my diagnoses, or someone telling someone else whose children I've prescribed the pill to . . .'

He stopped by the settee and collapsed down into it.

'That the end of our list?' she asked quietly.

'You got any to add?'

'Yes, I probably have.'

He turned to her, his eyes alive once more.

'Oh? And what have you been finding out?'

She combed her hair back from her face with her hand and he thought how very attractive she looked. But her next words were drowned by a crack of thunder that startled them both and seemed to make the whole room shake.

When she had recovered, she started again. 'It was when I was interviewing about something else, actually. You may have heard the health food shop at the top of the High Street is closing. All very sudden.'

'Yes, a patient mentioned it last evening.'

'Well, I couldn't get its owner, Mrs Penelope Seymour-Jones, to give me an interview at all, so I found out the name and address of her only employee, a very nice widow, named Priscilla Marsh.'

'But what has all this got to do with our problem?'

'Telephone calls. When I tackled this Priscilla Marsh about the rumours I'd heard about the reason for the shop's closure – that most of the produce sold there that was claimed to be organic, wasn't and was no different from what you can buy for under half the price – well, she confessed she'd only found out about the fraud through mysterious telephone calls.'

'Let me guess.' He paused, then went on. 'If the calls follow the kind of precedent we know about, then this Priscilla woman will probably have overheard the owner ordering bog-standard produce from her various suppliers.' He turned to her. 'Am I right?'

'Near enough.'

Stride groaned, then leaned over to look at her list. 'So let's consider, for a moment, what on earth Rickett and Tully and Walter Blair and the telephone engineer and maybe even that Drench woman, and now, what's her name, Penelope Seymour-Jones, can possibly have in common.' He sighed and threw his arms in the air. 'Sweet Fanny Adams, I suspect.'

'Especially,' she concurred, 'as they're all from such different walks of life and of different ages, even different generations. And don't forget, this list is only composed of those people we know about. There are more than a few others, and God knows how different from one another all those are. Still . . .'

Stride looked at her hopefully and she knew she would not be able to turn his suggestion down.

'Still, we ought to have a go at finding something. That the prescription for today, Doctor?'

In lieu of a direct answer, he took her now empty gin and tonic glass from her hands.

'Like a little more inspiration?' he smiled gently.

Almost every pew in St Matthew's church was filled that Sunday. The Reverend Meek could not remember the last time he had seen so many of his flock gathered together for a regular service. Memorial services, yes. Celebratory occasions, yes. He recalled the large congregation on the Sunday of the dear Queen's Silver Jubilee week in 1977. And almost as many attended the memorial service of the two young men from Hallowes who had died when the *Sheffield* had been hit during the Falklands War.

From the high vantage point of his pulpit, he scanned the many rows of his parishioners with a certain pride. Not a pride in his own ability to attract such a large audience, but a pride that so many in his town of Hallowes, in this strange time of stress and turmoil, seemed to be turning to Christ for guidance and comfort. He only prayed that when they had finished singing the present specially selected hymn, 'Oh God, our help in ages past', he would be able to reward their faith and satisfy the wishes of his own great Maker, by delivering a sermon that would, indeed, both guide and comfort.

For after the dreadful news of poor Rick Rickett's death had spread through the parish – whose murder by someone who appeared to be amongst the most loyal and devout of God's servants, had shocked his flock to their very souls – he had been besieged by requests for a sermon today that would address itself solely and exclusively to the recent, inexplicable events in Hallowes.

As a result, the Reverend had discarded a general homily on the meek inheriting the earth, that he had actually written years ago whilst still at theological college and had stayed up all night penning the oration that he was now about to deliver.

The organist brought the hymn to a triumphal close and the congregation resumed their seats with the usual slap of shutting hymn books, the shuffling of feet and a varied assortment of coughs, sniffs and clearing of throats. While the cacophony was dying down, the Reverend Meek arranged his notes out on the magnificent lectern carved in the shape of an eagle – a gift from a late parishioner, who wanted to be sure of a reserved seat on his flight to Heaven – and then, when he was sure his audience was at last with him, he cleared his own throat and began.

'Dearly beloved, we are gathered here today – and I am truly gratified to see how great a number – we are gathered not in some great celebration, nor in sombre commemoration, not to pray for salvation from the onslaught of some foreign adversary or for strength to combat and overcome the overwhelming numbers of such a foe.

'I well remember that during the war, our churches were filled every Sunday with those who had sons or loved ones away fighting in the war; those who, perhaps, had already been bereaved or knew someone in their family who had suffered such an unspeakable loss. Then there were those who prayed for deliverance from the terrible bombing, those who prayed for our nation's salvation and ultimate victory. There were those who prayed for peace; then, I'm sure, there were some, perhaps fewer in number, because that, alas, can be the nature of man and womankind, who prayed for our enemies too, for *their* bereaved, for the countless mothers and fathers who had sons and daughters on active service. For those dying in the deathly grip of a Russian winter or those who went down in the *Bismark* or died in the *Graf-Spee*. Or crashed in a Heinkel or a Messerschmidt.'

He stopped and sipped a little water from a glass, as was his wont, when attempting a sermon that was not, at least in part, derived from his bank of tried and tested Sunday homilies.

'You may be asking yourselves,' Meek resumed, 'why I have started my address to you all today by going back in time. Back indeed, almost fifty years now, long before many of you, I'm sure, were born.'

He leaned forward over the lectern. 'I'll tell you why, my brethren. Because the Second World War was probably the last time that the people of Hallowes have felt such a desperate need for the love and guidance of our great Saviour, Jesus Christ. All churches were full during those harrowing years, because the arms of our Lord always offered us His loving protection. His almighty love never failed us, never shut us out. He alone could hand each and every one of us a torch to lighten our darkness, to illuminate the right path for our earthly salvation.'

He took a deep breath and continued. 'When I look out upon you all this Sunday morning, I see the same look upon your faces as must have been worn by those worshippers of fifty years ago. I see the same kind of questions on your lips, the same worries in your eyes, the same yearning for an answer, a sign, a signal, some beam of light . . . some divine explanation. But this time we in Hallowes are not facing a physical enemy. An enemy we can identify by uniform, weaponry or national insignia. An enemy from outside, from another land, another culture, another world . . .'

He paused for a moment and looked out over the sea of faces and Sunday hats. For once, he could not detect even one who had nodded off and even the few children in the congregation seemed to be looking up at him rather than down at some secret game they were playing with hymn book or hassock.

Glancing back at his notes, he resumed; his voice demonstrating his increasing confidence in this first time sermon.

'Indeed, right now in our beloved town, we are not even sure what, if anything, we have to fear. And aye, there lies the rub. An external enemy we can easily identify; and by identification, channel our fears and restrict them to one clear source. Thus we can, by the same token, channel and direct our hopes, our prayers and thereby, find a degree of solace and comfort.

'But today, we in Hallowes . . .' Meek spread his arms wide as if to embrace his audience, a device he had learnt to be effective as far back as his student days, 'know not the cause of our unease, our discomfort, our fears. Oh yes, some of us have experienced strange events that seem to defy logic and, thus, explanation. And all of us have been set on edge by the storm clouds that so often, of late, have drenched us with their rain, alarmed us with their electrical energy and deafened us with their thunder.

'For this unprecedented spate of storms, we look for explanation to the weathermen and their answers seem not to satisfy some of us. "We've always known," we say, "that the many hills amongst which our town is set, attract more thunderous activity than most other places in the South West of our country. But we have never experienced anything approaching the present rate and spate of storms." Their answer to our comment is simple. Weather records of all kinds are constantly being broken right across the land. Sometimes for rainfall, other times for temperature, for wind strength, for drought, for hours of sunshine, snowfall or frost. Indeed, they are right. How often have we heard them announce yet another record has fallen? So this autumn, my friends, perhaps it is just our turn in Hallowes to write a new entry in the great book of records.'

Meek paused once more to turn over to the last page of his notes, where, in contrast to the previous pages, almost every line was underlined in red ink.

'Now let me turn to what seems to be the greatest cause of concern amongst more than a few of us – a concern highlighted and intensified, it would seem, by the tragic rumours that have been circulating and, indeed, magnifying, since the shocking death of Mr Rick Rickett, husband of one of St Matthew's most industrious and devout parishioners, a lady known to so many of us over so many years.

'In our search for a logical explanation for what seems such an inexplicably shocking event, some of us have picked on the one seeming element in the press coverage of Mr Rickett's death that appears to us to link up with those other disturbing happenings of recent weeks. I refer, of course, to our newly installed telephone system and the strange and unsolicited calls it seems to be connecting, as if, as one of you so graphically described it to me, "it had some evil and malicious mind of its own".'

He put his hands together and raised them high, as if in blessing of the assembled townspeople.

'Beloved brethren, have no fear. Do not let us sink back into the wild beliefs of long ago, of witchcraft, of demons stalking the land, of the devil incarnate, of avenging apparitions, of evil wizardry. Why, I have been quite dismayed, nay, shocked, by some of the explanations and notions that I have heard in Hallowes in the last few days and hours. Has it not occurred to those who, if they are not very careful, will spread panic like a biblical plague, that these calls have only apparently occurred since the brand new telephone system has come into operation? And that whilst the telephone engineers at this moment cannot trace the fault, that they undoubtedly will, given God's good time. For after all, did we not know from the first mention of the new service that it would have, already built in, a very advanced and complex memory facility, to be activated at a later date, together with the option even later on of a video extension, so that we will be able actually to see on our televisions to whom we speak?

'So what more likely than that memory facility and nothing more sinister, lies behind these reportedly disturbing calls? Of course the engineers in charge of development will deny that anything has gone wrong.' He stabbed a long, blue finger across his audience. 'So, would I suggest, would you . . . and you . . . and you were you responsible for the design and development of such an electronic miracle as our new telecommunication system. We are all too frail, too proud to admit our every mistake, I'm afraid . . .'

He paused again, but this time because his mouth was dry. After a long draught from the glass beside him, he went on, 'So have faith, my dear friends. Don't be stampeded into mumbo-jumbo and black magic for your explanations, just because you are afraid. Down that road lies only more fear, more dread, more panic. So that, in the end, your trembling fingers will not be able to pick up that receiver at any time, however legitimate the connection. That way too, your direct line with the true God, our omnipotent Saviour, will be cut as surely as by the Devil's knife.'

Meek held up his right hand. 'One last word, my friends. Last but perhaps most pertinent to all our fears at this time. Just reflect for a moment on the reported nature of every one of those strange calls. At least, every one that has been reported to me.'

Now he prodded the air with his hand, as if in beat to his words. 'There is no real horror in any of these calls. No horror, that is, unless we regard our own actions, our own words with horror, when they are repeated to those other than we have chosen. If we do, then surely we have more to fear than the fact of these calls or their content. We are afraid of what lies in the depths of our souls. We are so afraid of our feelings that we hide in lies and hypocrisy in our human communications. And by that, I don't just mean on the telephone, my friends. I mean in all our dealings with our fellow men and women. If we are afraid when that phone goes dring-dring, dring-dring, then perhaps it is for one reason and one reason only. Our conscience. Our guilty conscience. We are afraid because somewhere, sometime, we know we have said or acted in a way that is, quite literally, unrepeatable. Unrepeatable, that is, to all but the person to whom we made that free choice to confess it in the first place. Surely, as true Christians, we should not harbour secrets of this kind. Our faith teaches us the sin of such hypocrisy.

'Thus, I would say, beloved brethren of Hallowes, that, to quote Franklin Delano Roosevelt during the Depression, we really have nothing to fear but fear itself. Nothing to fear but fear itself.'

His voice now moderated to little above a stage whisper.

'That is, unless we live in mortal fear of our very own selves. Our very own thoughts. Our very own desires. Our own past actions. Our own consciences. Then it could well be that the cause is dramatically simple. We are obstinately and wilfully refusing to answer the most important call we ever receive in our whole lifetimes – the calls from our great Saviour, Jesus Christ. The call that costs us nothing to receive, but which cost Him His *life* to put through to us . . .'

Chapter Fourteen

Mark Stride pointed up towards Dartmoor.

'Oh, hells bells, Sophie, and we've only just got here.'

The ten-year-old girl looked in the direction in which he was pointing. Clouds were building up high over the hills and the characteristic anvil shape was, by now, only too familiar to her.

'Maybe it'll just stay over the moors,' she remarked hopefully. 'Don't let's go home yet.'

'Well, we ought to watch it, just in case,' he sighed. 'We daren't get home sopping wet, otherwise . . .'

'. . . our mums and dads will know we didn't just stay around the houses like we promised,' Sophie Fanshawe said in a mock baby voice, a big smile on her face.

'All right,' Mark shrugged, not to be out-bravadoed by a girl, even if she was almost two years older than him. 'So what's the big deal if we do get wet? We're old enough to be allowed to cycle where we want, I reckon. 'Sides, 'tisn't as if Widow's Field is miles away, is it? Lots of kids play here on their own.'

Sophie looked around. 'No one here now,' she grinned.

'Well, maybe they've only just gone. Bet there were hordes of them this morning. Always are on Sundays.'

'Doesn't really bother me,' Sophie bragged. 'My mum's been acting a bit funny recently - bit dreamy, I suppose. Sometimes she hardly seems to hear what we all say. Especially dad. So I wouldn't be surprised if she didn't even notice if I came in a bit wet. Especially if I rushed upstairs and dried myself off a bit.'

A wind had sprung up and Mark pushed a lock of blond hair off his forehead. 'I think mine still would. Though, I must say, my mum and dad have been acting a bit strange recently too. I keep catching them whispering together and then they shut up as soon as they spot me. Funny –'tisn't as if it's Christmas or my birthday or something. They're often whispering then. 'Bout my presents, I suppose.'

Sophie pointed towards her glossy blue bicycle. 'I knew about that long before my birthday. I found it in the back of the garage hidden under an old sheet.'

'Were they cross you found it?'

'No,' she grinned. 'Didn't tell them. My dad says "What the eye doesn't see, the heart doesn't grieve over." '

Mark made a face. 'You were lucky. My dad discovered I'd found out about my radio-controlled aircraft last birthday. Got quite cross. Said I'd been ferreting around.'

Sophie looked towards the telegraph lines at the side of the field. 'Was that the Hurricane?'

He shook his head. 'No. One before that. A silver Mustang with big American stars on it. Looked great.'

She removed a turquoise clip and tried to gather her long, blond hair more tightly back from her face. But it was a losing battle against the now quite strong gusts of wind.

'Can't remember that one. Did I ever see it?'

Mark laughed. 'Don't suppose so. I lost it on its first flight. Went out of control at Hargreaves Point. Must have crashed into the sea somewhere off Bifton Sands. Least that's dad's guess from where it was headed.'

'Cor. You don't have much success with your old things, do you?'

'You can talk,' he sneered. 'The chain's always coming off that bicycle of yours. And the gears are wonky. And how many times has that computer your dad gave you for Christmas been back to the shop?'

She got up from the grass and looked away from him.

'If all you're going to do is jolly well argue, I'm going home.'

Mark got up and went over to her.

'Come on then, let's find something to do.' He scanned the field, then exclaimed, 'Hey, look over there.' He pointed to where a bulldozer had obviously now dug a second trench at the opposite end of the field to the first.

'Tell you what, Sophie. Let's both get back on our bikes and try to jump them over those trenches. Got to jump both, mind. Then first one back here is the winner.'

She looked towards both the piles of red earth, then back at him with a frown. 'But you'll win easily. Yours is a BMX.'

But Mark had not waited for her objections and was already picking up his bicycle from the grass.

'And you're practically two years older than I am. So what?' he laughed and she knew she would have to play along. As she ran towards her own bicycle, the first thunder rumbled towards them from the hills.

To the children's delight, both trenches proved narrow enough for them to soar over with ease, the rear wheels of their bicycles comfortably clearing the far edges. But the two hundred yard gap between the two trenches, unexpectedly, proved to be the real decider between them. And here, despite his giving Sophie nearly two years in age, Mark clearly established his ascendancy; part through sheer muscle power and stamina developed over the many school sports at which he excelled and part through the thicker wheels and deep ribbed tyres of his BMX, which made lighter work of the bumps and thick tufts of grass.

As a result, after three jumps and three lengths of the field, where Mark proved first home every time, Sophie lost heart and interest and got off her bike.

'Oh, come on, Sophie,' Mark pleaded, 'just one more go.' He held out his arm towards her. 'We'll switch bikes, if you like.'

She shook her head and once more rearranged her windblown hair within the hairgrip. But Mark was determined not to give in and looked around the field. The two piles of red earth at the end of each trench suddenly gave him an idea.

'Hey, Sophie. Here's something you'll be able to do as well as me.'

She did not even bother to look up. 'Oh yeh?'

'Yeh,' he went on eagerly. 'You're just as good at the jumps as I am, aren't you? It's just those skinny tyres of yours that are letting you down over the grass.'

She glanced up at him suspiciously. In her brief experience, when boys started to be kind of nice and kind of considerate, they were after something.

'So?'

Mark walked his BMX over to her. 'Well, let's forget the grass bit. And just do the jumps.'

She looked disappointed. She had been expecting something a little more adventurous than just repetition.

'We've done the jumps. There's no fun in just doing them again.'

He shook his head. 'No, you don't understand. I don't mean jump the holes. I mean jump the piles of earth.'

She looked from him to the red mounds and back again.

'Don't be daft,' she sneered. 'How can we jump them? They're too high.' She looked down at her beflowered Laura Ashley frock. 'Besides, if I fell into that stuff, my mum would half kill me. She's always telling me you can't get red soil marks off clothes and how lucky we are to live in the only part of Hallowes that has ordinary brown soil.'

Mark laughed. 'Oh you're not going to fall, Sophie. You're too good at jumps.'

'Still leaves . . .' She stopped as a peal of thunder

drowned her words, then went on, 'Still leaves how we can jump something that high.'

Mark thought for a moment, determined not to let such a mundane problem stand in his way.

'We'll make a ramp,' he said.

'Oh great,' she scoffed. 'We'll make a ramp, he says. What from, idiot?'

He looked round him, then back towards the entrance to Widow's Field.

'Hey, remember when we came in? All that building material, bricks and scaffolding and stuff that they've now dumped by the gate, ready for when they start on the houses?'

She nodded.

'Well, then. We'll just borrow some bricks and two of their long scaffolding boards and hey presto, we've got a couple of ramps.'

He immediately saw her frown. 'It'll be all right, Sophie. We won't damage anything and we'll put it all back when we've finished.'

He got off his own bike and picked hers up from the grass.

'Come on. It'll be fun. If we hurry, we'll have time for a good few jumps before it starts raining.'

It all worked splendidly, as Mark had described. The bricks made steady foundations for the far ends of the boards and after a certain amount of experiment, provided just the right angle of elevation for their bicycles to clear the piles of earth with about an inch to spare.

Sophie was amazed at how much she was enjoying Mark's suggestion, though she would not let on. Even, after one jump, when she landed with a jar on her front wheel rather than the rear, and the handlebars almost twisted out of her grip, she did not complain, but immediately cycled round again for the next leap.

So absorbed were both the children in what Mark described as their 'dare-devil display' that neither paid much heed to the now rapidly approaching storm clouds. And it wasn't until the first stab of rain on her arm that Sophie shouted across to Mark. 'Better make this the last jump. Or we'll be soaked before we can get home.'

He braked to a stop and looked up at the black and ominous clouds. Instantly, he had to close his eyes against a searing flash of lightning that zigzagged to the ground over towards the centre of the town. When he looked again, he saw that Sophie was pointing to something in the distance.

'It's the church,' she shouted. 'It must have struck the steeple. Look, the weather vane is all broken and hanging down.'

He pulled round to focus towards the grey silhouette of St Matthew's. The familiar shape of the rooster weather vane was certainly no longer proudly upright atop the steeple, but swinging broken in the wind.

'Never mind,' he urged, 'let's get on with the jump and get home.'

But as he manoeuvred his bike to the start position for the jump, another flash of lightning blinded him and the rain, like ice spears, jagged down out of the sky.

'Come on, Sophie,' he shouted. 'Last one home's a sissy.'

But she did not hear him for the thunder, that made her clap her hands to her ears.

Mark set off at a cracking pace across the now glistening grass but hit the end of the ramp slightly too far to one side. He twitched his handlebars in a frantic effort to correct his line. But the front tyre lost grip on the wet board and slewed off wildly to the right. He twitched again, but far too late. The wheel went off the side of the board. The back of the BMX reared up like some crazed bronco in a rodeo. He felt himself being thrown upwards off the saddle. The handlebars wrenched completely out of his hands, as the front wheel, hitting the side of the earth pile, flipped through a hundred and eighty degrees. A split second later, bike and rider were carving separate trajectories. The bike to clatter back on to the grass, the boy to thud into the raw, red soil, which then seemed to open up and enclose him like a grave.

Sophie screamed and throwing her bike to the ground, ran to the now sodden pile of earth. Kneeling beside it, she started frantically to scrabble with her hands. But as fast as she made an impression, it filled up again with sticky rivulets of red mud, like coagulating blood.

'Mark!' she shrieked, as, momentarily, she saw some fingers appear. But then they were gone again. Now emitting one long scream after another, she tore at the soil until she knew the red on her fingers was not all due to Devon earth. But now the rain was merciless, stabbing at her back, blurring her vision and turning the pile into a thick red soup.

Suddenly, around her, there grew a sound other than her screams and the crashing of the storm. And her hands started to tingle as they touched the earth. She spun her head around. To her horror, the whole of Widow's Field was erupting with flashes of light. As she watched, now shocked into numbness, they grew into hundreds of crackling, sparking, zigzagging pulses of electrical energy, like a sea of embryonic lightning struggling to leave the earth and reach the heavens. And the sea was moving inexorably towards her across the field.

Now wild with panic, she looked back at where Mark had disappeared. The blood red earth now began to bubble and then slowly dissolve in front of her eyes. Too shocked to do anything but stare open-eyed, she watched as, bit by bit, limb by limb, Mark's red stained body started to emerge. First the fingers and hands, then arms thrust upwards towards the black and booming sky. Rivulets of molten soil flowed off a knee as it was raised, then off another knee. Then the whole earth beneath her own knees seemed to quiver and rumble, as if hit by some terrible earthquake. She flung out an arm to try to save herself, but was thrown sideways on to the soggy slope of the soil. Out of the corner of her eye, she saw that the vast sea of lightning flashes had now succeeded in arcing towards the sky, like the Devil was presiding over some hellish laser show. In abject fear, she pressed herself back against the slippery slope of the soil, and held her hands to her ears against the now deafening crackle of their zigzag arcing.

But to her amazement, the dreadful sea suddenly halted its progress and then from its very centre a single gargantuan flash leapt high into the sky, illuminating all around as if it were day. When she dared look again and her eyes had recovered from their blinding, she saw that the lightning was now curving back down to the ground, but now its head formed four separate spears of crackling intensity.

The spears suddenly snapped from their mother charge and changed course . . . but towards her.

Too petrified even to scream, let alone attempt to escape, she shot a quick glance down to where Mark had been lying, still half covered by the red and running earth. But now, inexplicably, astoundingly, his red stained body lay flat out on the surface of the soil, his legs tightly together and his arms flung out wide at right angles to his body.

A split second later, the four separate spears of lightning found their four separate targets. And Mark, his eyes shot with terror and a silent scream on his wide-open mouth, was lifted up as if by a giant hand and thrown into the bottom of the trench that he had only so recently exulted in leaping.

Mary Stride moved away from the french windows and winced as a thunderclap resounded almost overhead. Its reverberation throughout the house caused her to hesitate no longer and she made straight for the telephone. As she picked up the receiver, she listened intently, just in case . . . But, to her relief, there was no one already speaking, just a dialling tone. So she punched up the number she wanted.

'Prue?'

'Yes. That you, Mary?'

'Yes, I . . .'

'That's funny. I was just about to ring you myself.'

'About the kids?' Mary asked hopefully.

'Yes.'

'You got them?'

She heard a sharp intake of breath.

'No. No, I haven't. I was hoping they'd come over to you.'

'No. They're not here. Oh God, I hope they've got the sense to shelter somewhere.'

'I told them to stay around the block.'

'Yes. That's our standing instruction to Mark too. But there's no real shelter around here for them, except our two houses, that is. I'm very surprised they haven't turned up.'

Prue Fanshawe sighed. 'Do you think we ought to go out and look for them?'

Mary looked back out the window and she could not see even the end of their garden for the driving rain.

'Look, Prue, I'll go. I know you haven't been feeling too well recently. The last thing you need now is to get soaked through.'

'Are you sure? It's no trouble to get the car out.'

'Sure, I'm sure. If they're not sheltering in someone's doorway or garage round here, where might Sophie have got to? Do you know of any haunts or anything?'

'Well, she likes going up to Widow's Field, but we don't ever let her go alone. Really, I can't think of anywhere else. Where does Mark like?'

'Same place. And I've caught him on two occasions cycling down to the sweet shop in East Lane. You know the one. It sells all the comics. That's why he likes going there.'

'Perhaps they're both sheltering there, then. Let's hope so.'

'I'll try that first, Prue,' she said hurriedly, now

anxious to start her search. 'Don't worry. I'll drop Sophie back to your place the second I've found them both. Bye.'

She replaced the receiver before Prue Fanshawe could prolong the conversation further and went out to the hall cabinet, in one of the drawers of which they kept the car keys. But as she slipped the drawer open, she heard the sound of voices outside the front door, almost immediately followed by the dring of the door bell.

She pocketed the keys and swore to herself. Whoever it was calling right then would receive pretty short shrift. With a sigh, she opened the front door, all prepared to say sorry, but she was just on her way out. But what met her eyes made the words of apology in her throat turn into a strangled scream.

Mary clutched at the doorjamb to prevent herself falling.

'It's all right, Mrs Stride,' she vaguely heard someone say. But by then she had recovered enough to reach forward and clasp the seemingly blood-covered figure tightly to her.

'My God, my God! Darling, what's happened to you?'

'It's all right, Mrs Stride,' the voice repeated more strongly. 'That's not blood. That's just earth. Your son is all right. He's just a bit shaken, that's all. Plunge him in a hot tub and he'll be as right as rain.'

Mary looked up and, for the first time, recognised the dark and shapeless figure in the background.

'Mrs Drench?' she asked falteringly.

'Yes, that's right. I was walking up by Widow's Field and got caught in the storm. That's where I found your son. Lying near one of the mounds of earth those devils have started excavating. He must have fallen off his bike.'

Mary Stride knelt down and held her son at arm's length. But she could see no sign of injuries on his red stained features; just tears starting to roll down his cheeks.

She felt tears well in her own eyes and once again, she hugged her son to herself, her dress now imprinted with the red from Mark's stained and sopping clothes.

'I've got his friend in the taxi,' the old lady went on. 'She's all right too.'

'Sophie?'

'Yes. She's told us her address. The taxi driver has been generosity itself. He was just coming back from a job when he saw me trudging out of the field with the children and the bikes. Stopped instantly and picked us all up – despite the mess we must have made in his car.'

Mary rose to her feet, but did not let go of her son's hand.

'Look, Mrs Drench, I can't thank you enough for finding Mark and bringing him and Sophie home. Do come in, whilst I find something to cover the taxi and all the trouble . . .'

Enid Drench waved her hand. 'No, thank you, Mrs Stride. I'm very wet and dirty and I don't want to ruin your carpets and furniture. Besides, I ought to get Sophie home. Her mother is probably worrying about her in this weather. By the way, the driver has put your son's bike by your gate.'

'But I must get something for him.' Mary made to go indoors, but Enid Drench restrained her.

'No, please don't, Mrs Stride. I'll take care of that. I'd have hailed him myself, anyway, I expect, to get me home. The storm's a bit fierce even for an old battleaxe like I'm supposed to be.'

She smiled and Mary Stride suddenly saw a warmth in her she had never noticed before; for on the few times that they had met during her childhood in Hallowes and since her subsequent return two years ago, Enid Drench had seemed to Mary no more nor less than her reputation – of being an oddly irascible and eccentric recluse, who had a peculiar penchant for lost causes.

'But he has had to go round the houses,' Mary persisted, 'to bring these two home. Can't I . . . ?'

'No, you can't, Mary Stride,' she retorted firmly, then added, 'But if you feel you are somehow beholden to me, there is something you *can* do.'

'Anything. Really. Please tell me.' She tried to dry her eyes with her only free hand. But the effort only succeeded in smearing her mascara into a red streak of Mark's mud that had rubbed off on her cheek at their first embrace.

'Anything?' Enid Drench's eyes narrowed and her look became a challenge.

Mary suddenly hesitated and she herself wasn't quite sure of the reason. 'Why . . . er . . . yes . . .'

The old woman wagged an arthritic finger. 'Don't ever say anything you don't mean, young woman. The world is too damn full of people whose mouths are a sight bigger than their actions.'

Mary blushed and brushed another tear from her eye.

'No, really, Mrs Drench. Do let me know what you would like me to do.'

A rumble of thunder echoed over the hills beyond the houses and Mary noticed that while they had been talking, the rain had eased considerably.

'Believe, Mary Stride.'

She frowned. 'Believe?'

'Yes. Believe.' Enid Drench reached out a hand and placed it on Mark's head. 'When your son tells you what happened over in Widow's Field, believe him, Mrs Stride.'

Mary looked down at her son, then back up at Enid Drench.

'I don't quite understand. You said just now that he must have fallen off his bike. If he tells me that, then of course I'll believe him. My son is not a liar, Mrs Drench.'

She waved her hand. 'Now calm down, Mrs Stride. I didn't say he was, now did I?'

'Then what are you saying, Mrs Drench?'

'I'm telling you to accept every word of what your son says happened in Widow's Field. Every word, Mrs Stride. However difficult you may find doing so.' Then she added, 'You, of all people, must have faith.'

A shiver of fear went through Mary Stride, as she suddenly realised what the old woman may be hinting at. But the relevance of the last statement certainly escaped her. 'Something . . .' she hunted for the right word '. . . dreadful happened up there, didn't it? And you saw it, didn't you, Mrs Drench? And what do you mean, I, of all people, should have faith?'

Getting no reply, she knelt down by her son.

'What happened, Mark, tell me? You must.'

But instead of replying, Mark clamped his eyes firmly shut to avoid her gaze, then hid himself in her arms. When she looked up again, the ominous black figure had disappeared. A second later, she heard the taxi accelerate away down the road.

It wasn't until Mark had taken off his red-stained clothes and got into a warm bath, that she saw it.

'Mark, what's that on your hand?'

He took his now clean hand out of the water and looked at it.

'No, the other side.'

He turned it palm upwards and stared, uncomprehendingly, at what he saw.

His mother reached across and took his hand in hers. With a trembling and tentative finger, she touched the blood-red spot in the centre of his palm.

'What's this, Mark? How on earth did you get it?'

A shake of his head was his only response. She inspected the mark more carefully.

'Why, it almost looks like a nail or something must have somehow . . .'

She stopped suddenly, then said quickly, 'Mark, show me your other hand.'

He relinquished the soap and turned his other hand palm upwards.

Mary Stride gasped, as she saw an identical red spot.

The boy, sensing the fear in his mother's reaction, immediately hid both hands under himself.

'Mum, what's the matter?' he pleaded. 'Please tell me what's the matter.'

But Mary Stride hardly heard his voice. She was now looking down the bath to the bare feet of her only son.

Chapter Fifteen

Prue Fanshawe watched from the window as her husband reversed his silver Jaguar XJ6 out of the drive, then swooshed off down the road, without a backward glance, to take their daughter to school on his way to his office in Hallowes.

She stayed at the window for some time, watching the steam rising from the sodden grass of the lawn, as a rare glimpse of September sun did its best to mop up a little of the inch or more of rain that had fallen during the previous day's storm. She just prayed the day would also help evaporate some of Sophie's strange fears. Fears she had expressed at length from the moment Enid Drench had brought her home in the taxi.

Her husband, Sebastian, as she might have expected, coldly dismissed the whole of his daughter's weird tale of sparks and lightning and forked heads, as just an elaborate fabrication to cover up her disobedience in not staying around the houses; and to explain the disgusting condition into which she had got herself and almost every stitch of her clothing. When Prue had pointed out that Sophie was not exactly given to being a liar and had suggested that she rang the Strides to see if their son's story corroborated their daughter's, he had laughed at her naïvety in not having worked out that the tale had undoubtedly been concocted by both the children in an effort to save their hides. Therefore, of course Mark's story would be the same and, if anything, further proof that the whole damned thing was an elaborate fabrication.

Whilst there was a certain logic in her husband's view, Prue herself could not believe that Sophie had been lying. First of all, she had obviously suffered from some kind of shock up there at Widow's Field, for she had been trembling when she had first come home and almost incapable of coherent speech for quite some time. But again, dear Sebastian had a simple explanation for that too. 'Children naturally get terrified when they're caught in a violent storm, my dear. I'm not doubting lightning may well have struck somewhere close. Indeed, both kids may be very lucky to be still alive. But I'm not falling for all that mumbo-jumbo about the field coming alive with flashes and boiling mud and all that nonsense. Really, my dear, we're not living in the dark ages and we haven't burned a witch for donkey's years . . .'

Prue sighed and turned away from the window. The Widow's Field affair, whatever the truth of the matter, had come at a most regrettable moment for her. For Prue Fanshawe had other plans for that morning. Plans she had devised only after deep soul searching and long hours of sleepless night and restless day. Plans she had felt she must not postpone, whatever her worries about her daughter. Indeed, she had only agreed with her husband's assertion, that Sophie was fit to go back to school that morning, so that she would have the freedom to carry them out.

She went out into the hall and sat down beside the telephone. But suddenly her hand froze as she was about to dial. She waited, almost afraid to breathe, lest she prevent what she knew was about to happen once more. And sure enough, within a few seconds, she heard the dreaded 'dring-dring'.

She did not hesitate for a second, after she had replaced the receiver. Her call to Mary Stride would now very definitely have to await her return. She went straight to her husband's desk and took her car keys from a small vase on its top.

The house was considerably grander than she had been expecting. She passed and repassed it a number of times before she had the courage to pull up and park, about ten yards or so from the stone pillared gates. Even then she did not get out of her car immediately. But sat behind the wheel, rehearsing the speech she had written and rewritten in her mind a thousand times over the last weeks.

At last, after crossing herself – an act that she could not ever remember herself performing before, as an adult – she opened her door and swung her legs to the ground. After a quick glance towards the house to make certain no one was coming out or watching her, she turned back to lock the car. But as she touched the metal-work of the door, she had to stifle a scream, as a powerful shock of static shot up her arm and the car keys fell from her hand to the ground.

It took some seconds before she felt able to bend down and pick them up. As she locked the car, she realised that somehow, the shock had emptied her mind of everything she had so carefully prepared to say. But to her amazement, she felt neither horror nor disappointment. Quite the opposite. She felt curiously elated, almost light-headed, as if the shock had freed her of inhibition and stimulated cells in her brain and psyche that, before, she had not really believed she possessed.

She smiled, then with a purposeful step, she strode out towards the house. It intimidated her no longer.

The look of shock on Annabel Craven's somewhat over-made-up face when she opened the door only served to further heighten her confidence.

'Mrs Fanshawe . . .'

'Yes,' Prue smiled and brushed past her husband's mistress and into the hall, before she could be stopped. 'With emphasis on the *Mrs*,' she added, turning back to face the property developer's estranged wife.

But by now, Annabel had recovered from her shock and snapped angrily, 'Mrs Fanshawe, what on earth has given you the right to storm into my house . . . ?'

'*You* have,' Prue cut in.

Annabel put a hand to her not inconsiderable bosom. 'I have? Have I heard right, Mrs Fanshawe? Surely not. I can assure you, my use of your husband's legal services does not give you a passport into my home.'

Prue laughed out loud, then her eyes narrowed as she spat out, 'Your use of my husband's legal services may not, Mrs Craven. But your use of my husband's sexual services certainly does.' She took immense pleasure in seeing Annabel Craven's sensually arrogant look change to one of shocked dismay. Suddenly Prue Fanshawe found to her surprise that she was actually starting to enjoy this dreaded encounter. Indeed, she felt a degree of confidence in herself now that she had not experienced since . . . well, since she had married Sebastian Fanshawe.

'What on earth are you talking about, Mrs Fanshawe?'

She came towards her, but Prue backed off until she was in the centre of the large wood panelled hall.

'Sex, dear Annabel, sex.' She pronounced the word with heavy emphasis, as if it ended with an 'a'.

'Look, I must ask you to leave immediately or I'll call the police.'

Again Annabel tried to get behind her, but this time Prue moved sideways and into the doorway of what was obviously the main drawing-room.

'I don't think you will, Annabel darling.'

She glanced back into the room, then cast her eyes up the wide and splendidly banistered staircase that led up from the hall.

'What a terrible shame,' she smiled back at her adversary, 'that with such a splendid house as this, you have to slum it in some Formica and chipboard motel, when you want to take the pants off my dear husband. Or rather, motels, with an "s".' She started to count on her fingers. 'Now let's see, there's been Exeter. There's been Bristol.

Then God knows how many in London. Then wasn't there Taunton? Now don't be shy, Annabel, you must know much better than poor old me. Mistresses always know more than little old wives, don't they?'

This time it was Prue who moved forward and with a beckoning finger.

'Come on, Annabel. I'm sure you're not shy with my husband. Or used to keeping your mouth so steely closed.'

She stopped, her hands now on her hips, then laughed as she saw Annabel's incredulous expression.

'Don't look so shocked, my sweet. After all, shouldn't wives know their husbands a wee bit better than their mistresses can ever do? I know what he likes too. What turns him on.' She looked reflectively up at the ornate ceiling, then back at Annabel. 'I wonder if he's ever told you he actually prefers watching to . . . I expect you call it, screwing. Oh yes. But I can tell from your expression that he hasn't quite got on to that subject yet. But he will, he will. Just as he did with me years ago . . .'

'Get out! Get out, you bitch!' Annabel screamed, her eyes full of both fear and hatred and made a lunge at Prue that she neatly sidestepped.

Swinging round, Prue went on, her voice now as calm as if she were telling a child a bedtime story. 'He's a dear man. He wanted me to . . . screw . . . with an old school chum of his, whilst he just sat and watched. Then there was a time when we were staying at Skindles in Maidenhead, when he actually made an arrangement with a man we met in the bar. Actually brought him to our bedroom . . .'

Annabel Craven suddenly turned away and swept across the hall to a small table on which stood an elaborately enamelled gilt phone.

Prue held up a hand. 'Ah, ah, ah, ah. I wouldn't toy with that, if I were you, my dear. You see,' she smiled, 'the telephone seems to be on my side, not yours.'

'What on earth are you raving on about now, you

stupid cow?' Annabel ranted back, a scarlet-tipped finger poised over the press buttons.

And so Prue Fanshawe had not the slightest hesitation in telling her.

'They're no different this morning.'

John Stride looked up from his son's hand to his wife's face and went on, 'They did not look like burns last night and they don't look like burns today.'

His wife turned away, her hands clenched tightly together in front of her, betraying her anguish.

'Then what are they, John? And how the blazes did he get them? I refuse to believe that . . .'

Stride patted his son on the back to reassure him.

'Don't worry, Mark. They'll go away. They look three quarters healed already.'

'They don't hurt,' his son smiled weakly. 'Never have. That's why I didn't even notice I'd got them yesterday, with all the mud and everything.'

His mother turned back to him, now forcing a smile across her own face.

'That's all right, darling. As Daddy says, they'll soon be gone anyway. So don't let's worry about how you got them, eh?'

'Why don't you pop back to your own room, Mark, and get dressed,' his father suggested. 'After all, you don't want to waste the day we've let you off school, now do you?'

He grinned. 'All right, Dad. Then I'll put "Phantom Force" on the computer. I've only ever got past the first two stages and I just have to complete stage three. It's called "Devils' Dungeons". The boys at school say it's the best.'

They watched their son run out of their bedroom and along the landing. Then when she was sure Mark was out of earshot, his mother said wearily, 'Well, I suppose we might thank God he seems as fit as he does this morning. After yesterday's . . .'

She sat down with a sigh on the side of their bed. Her husband came over to her and put his arm around her shoulder.

'He's fine physically, Mary. Even those marks look as if they'll be gone in a few days.'

She looked up at him and he could see the fear in her eyes.

'What are they, John?' Her voice was hardly above a whisper.

'I don't know.'

Neither spoke for a moment, then Mary asked, 'Those marks . . . they're not . . . really physically possible, are they?'

'In that they're already almost healed?'

She nodded. 'You say they look as if whatever caused them, happened like weeks ago.'

'They do. The scar tissue, though still red, is not comparable with an injury sustained ten days ago, let alone a few hours. And whatever Mark says, they're not burns.'

She suddenly clasped her husband's hand. 'Oh God, John, what's happening to us all?'

He did not reply, but asked, 'Tell me again what Enid Drench said to you last night.'

She took a deep breath. 'Well . . . she just said that there was something I could do for her . . . you know, to thank her for bringing Mark home.'

'To believe Mark?'

She nodded. 'Believe everything he said happened up at Widow's Field.'

He sat down beside her on the bed.

'Well, I have no idea where this will get us, but let's go over Mark's story again, in case we're missing something.'

Mary wiped a tear from her eye. 'All right.'

'Mark said everything was normal up at the Field, until the storm came. They jumped the trenches on their bikes and all went well.'

'Yes.'

'Then he said that soon after they'd made the ramps and had started to jump the piles of earth, the rain started.'

'Right.'

'Then he and Sophie agreed they had better go home after the next jump. Mark starts off across the grass, hits the ramp, his front wheel skids off the wet board and he is thrown off into the pile of earth.'

'Yes. That's the bare bones of it. But darling, don't you remember, his actual words were something like, "It was funny, but I didn't feel scared when the wheel skidded. Or when I was thrown off the bike. And I didn't really feel a thing when I hit the earth . . ." '

' ". . . it just felt warm and soft".'

'Warm and soft,' she repeated to herself.

'And then, how did he go on? Something like, "Everything went black and I knew the earth was covering me . . .".'

' ". . . but I wasn't frightened, Mum, not for a second . . .".'

' ". . . it was almost like I was in bed . . .".'

' ". . . looking up at the poster on my wall . . .".'

He stopped her. 'Hang on a minute, he said everything was black, didn't he?'

She shivered. 'Well, everything would be, if you're covered in earth.' Then she went on, 'Then he said the next thing he knew was that the earth seemed to sort of move and he could suddenly see what looked like . . .'

'. . . little lightning flashes all around him. Then a giant flash and then blackness again.'

'Until he saw Sophie and Enid Drench standing over him.'

'And Enid Drench helped him up, etcetera.' She looked at her husband. 'Have we missed anything?'

'Don't think so.'

'Well, it's not too hard to believe all that, except perhaps the little lightning flashes, but strange things happen in storms. So what do you think Enid Drench was getting at?'

'Maybe she's as dotty as a lot of people think she is.'

Mary shook her head. 'Enid Drench may be eccentric, but she's not out of her mind.'

'Perhaps Mark embroidered his story a bit, when he told her about it, coming home in the taxi.'

'Maybe. But even so, why should she go out of her way to say I must believe every word he said?'

He shrugged. 'Could be she saw Mark playing about far more dangerously on his bike than just jumping piles of earth. And she didn't want us to probe too deeply.'

She thought for a moment, then said, 'There was something else Enid Drench said, now I remember.'

'Which was?'

'That I, of all people, should believe.' She looked questioningly at her husband. 'I of all people?'

He frowned. 'What does Enid Drench know about you? She knew you, I suppose, when you were growing up in Hallowes, before nursing took you away.'

'Knew of me, rather than knew me. Of course we had met a few times. Everyone in Hallowes came across Enid Drench sooner or later. But you couldn't really say I knew her or she knew me.'

'Does she know anything about your family? Your mother, for instance, or maybe she knew your grandmother.'

'Maybe. She's old enough.'

'And what about your grandfather?'

'Oh, from what I can gather, even grandmother only knew him for a short time before he went off on D-Day and was killed. So I doubt if Enid Drench had even heard of him. Besides, I can't see someone like her hanging around the GIs, that were camped around the town, can you?'

'Or they hanging around her, if she did,' he smiled. 'Is that more what you mean?'

She blushed.

'So you can't think of anything that would have prompted Enid Drench to say "you of all people"?'

She shook her head.

'Well, then, I guess there's only one way of our finding out. Ask her to her face.'

Mary looked surprised. 'Think she'll come clean, even if we do?'

'Who knows? But it's worth a try.'

'By whom?' she grimaced.

'By me,' he reassured her.

'Thank God for that. I've seen enough of Enid Drench for a day or two. By the way, do you think she knows about Mark's . . . ?' she hunted for a word, which he instantly supplied.

'Stigmata.'

She recoiled from him. 'God, don't say that, John. You know all that's a load of rubbish. No one's had stigmata. Ever. It's all just hysteria.'

He did not comment, but said, 'I'm not going to go out to see her. I haven't the time today. I'm going to get her on the . . .'

Instead of finishing his sentence, he got up from the bed and left the room. As he walked along the landing on his way downstairs, he popped his head around his son's bedroom door. To his surprise, Mark had not yet even dressed but was lying back on his bed, arms behind his head, staring at the pop poster on his wall.

At first Stride thought Enid Drench must be out and he was about to hang up when the phone was at last answered.

'Hello, who's that?' said a gruff and suspicious voice, after a moment's hesitation.

'Oh, I'm sorry. Have I got a wrong number? I dialled Hallowes 37376.'

'This is 37376. You'll be wanting my mother, I expect. But she's not here at the moment. Can I leave a message? This is her son, William.'

Whilst John Stride had never actually met William Drench, he knew enough of his personal and professional reputation to tread warily.

'Thank you, but there's no message. Just say Dr Stride rang and that I'll ring again later. You don't happen to know when she's likely to be back, do you?'

'Before lunch, I would imagine.' Then he chuckled. 'I have only just arrived myself, but I can smell the oven is on from here.'

'All right. Thank you, Mr Drench. I'll ring later.'

As Stride put down the receiver, his wife came down the stairs behind him. He looked round.

'It's all right. I heard. She's out,' she sighed. 'Now I'd better use the dreaded instrument and ring Prue yet again.'

Which she proceeded to do. But with no more luck than on the three other times she had tried that morning.

Directly he had replaced the receiver, with some difficulty, over the yellow and blue duck's arm, Drench resumed the task that Stride's phone call had interrupted.

For whilst he had, at first, been incensed to find his mother out, for it completely negated his plan to finally have it out with her over the drawing up of the new will, her absence did, at least, enable him to search the house for clues as to whom she now intended to leave her estate.

For, to Drench's acute disappointment, Sebastian Fanshawe had not yet bowed to his veiled threats of blackmail over his partner's estranged wife, Annabel Craven. And not a word or a hint had he yet spilled as to the character of those mentioned in the rogue telephone call he had interrupted on his last visit – those whose 'names and addresses may be hard to trace'.

Drench looked at the watch on his thick wrist. It was eleven thirty. He knew he did not have long. For his mother, so forgetful of time most of her day, had always been a stickler for having meals at set hours. Twelve thirty was her very latest time for lunch, come hell or high water. Besides, he knew from the smell issuing from the gaps around the oven door that the fish pie inside would be overcooked if it wasn't taken out soon.

There was one more place to search downstairs. He had already been through her small bureau and chest of drawers in the sitting-room, the hall wardrobe, the understairs cupboard and the drawers in the dining-room dresser. And that was the rickety top of the twenties style cream and green painted cabinet, which was now screwed to one of the walls in the kitchen to prevent its rotting framework from collapsing.

Not that he really expected to find what he wanted there. But he so clearly remembered from his childhood his mother's practice of popping on to the recessed top of the cabinet absolutely anything that, in her view, might come in useful on a rainy day.

Taking a bentwood chair from the kitchen table, Drench placed it beside the cabinet and, rather shakily, climbed on it. He could feel its simple framework deform under his weight and he held on to the leaded light doors of the cabinet to steady himself.

Bowing his head slightly to miss an ominous bulge in the crumbling horse-hair and plaster ceiling, he peered at the amazing jumble of bric-a-brac his mother had stored up there over the years. But to his disappointment, there seemed to be nothing obviously new. For everything, from old newspapers, pieces of brown wrapping paper and lengths of string to bits of broken crockery, an egg-cup commemorating the King's coronation of 1937, old postcards and even a chipped plaster bust of Winston Churchill, was covered in a sticky film of dust and grime.

He rummaged about with his hand, just in case something might be concealed under or amongst the yellowing pages of newspaper (which, to his amusement, even included an old *News Chronicle*), but discovered nothing other than a bill dated the seventh of June, 1953, for plumbing repairs to a bathroom pipe and a 1946 handbill announcing a Victory Parade through Hallowes.

Muttering an expletive, Drench was about to descend from his precarious perch, when his eye caught sight of an old envelope lying under the plaster bust of Churchill. He would have taken no notice of it, dirty and almost brown with age as it was, had it not been that it seemed to be still sealed with a blob of red sealing wax.

Pulling it out from under the bust, he turned it over. It carried neither address nor postage stamp. From its weight and feel though, Drench doubted it contained anything that would give any clue to what he was after. And he was almost about to put the envelope back, when just plain curiosity got the better of him.

Very carefully, he picked at the wax seal with his finger nail, but it proved as protective as when it had been first applied with burning match. Losing patience, he pulled at the flap. It tore away from the seal almost instantly and he reached inside the envelope with his hand.

Whatever was inside was wrapped tightly in tissue paper, but there seemed to be no letter or papers accompanying it. He withdrew the slim package that was almost the length of the envelope, but under half its width. As he started to unwrap the soft tissue, a musty smell arose from it that, somehow, instantly made him feel giddy. He leaned forward to rest an elbow on the framework of the cabinet door, but, with the wobbling of the bentwood chair, only succeeded in cracking one of the diamond panes of glass in its leaded lights.

Emitting another curse, he fumbled angrily with the tissue paper until it fell like a falling leaf to the floor, leaving what looked like some old and discoloured animal tag in his hand. He prodded the thin metal chain with his finger, To his surprise, it felt warm, not cold. Now somewhat timidly, he picked up what was clearly an oval name disc, and started to turn it over to read what might be inscribed on it, if anything.

Suddenly, before he could actually decipher the

engraved words that appeared on the other side, the disc grew red hot in his fingers. Horror stricken, he instantly released his grasp, but the disc now seemed to be welded to his forefinger and thumb.

Drench screamed and clinging on to the cabinet with his one free hand, frantically shook his other in an attempt to dislodge the disc. But the more he flailed, the more unbearable the pain became, until looking down, he could see the flesh on his finger tips actually starting to melt on to the surface of the disc.

Crazed with fear and pain, he tried to clamber off the rocking and creaking chair. But as he floundered, another noise drowned out all others. A noise he instantly recognised as the frenzied flapping of wings and which he knew, with a terrible certainty, had to be yet another element in this gruesome nightmare. Now kneeling on the seat of the trembling chair and screaming with pain, he looked behind him just in time to see the blue and yellow telephone flying directly towards him. He cowered down and the sudden weight transference unbalanced the chair, which toppled sideways.

Drench flung out an arm to save himself, but to no avail. He fell heavily on to the stone-flagged floor and his head struck the point of an old army shell-case that he had been given as a boy and which his mother had always insisted on putting to good use - as a kitchen doorstop.

Chapter Sixteen

Mary Stride was both relieved and surprised to see Prue Fanshawe's car in the drive outside their large, but severely anonymous house. She parked by the gates and was somewhat amazed when she did not encounter some degree of static when she slammed the car door shut.

After at least half a dozen abortive rings of the door-bell, she left the porch and walked around the crazy paving path to the back of the house. Here the path broadened into a patio area served by the large french windows of the drawing-room. Shielding her eyes from the light, Mary peered in through the panes and scanned the room. Though the interior was grey and shaded, she could just see Prue Fanshawe's figure in an armchair at the far end of the room.

She knocked on the glass and waved her hand, but the figure did not respond. She knocked again but to no avail. She tried the handle of the french windows, but it would not turn. Now somewhat alarmed, she ran back along the path to the front door and put her hand to the large cast iron ring that served as both knocker and handle. Thankfully, it turned easily. She let herself in and made her way straight through the hall to the drawing-room.

Prue Fanshawe was slumped in a chair just inside the door, her eyes closed and her breathing hardly perceptible. Beside her was a small table on which stood a bottle of whisky, an overturned cut glass tumbler and a half-empty bottle of paracetemol.

On her lap lay a sheet of their headed notepaper, upon

which, in a barely decipherable hand, she had scrawled a telephone number.

Sue Pike leaned forward and took a copy of that morning's *Planet* from her enraged editor.

'Look what *they* bloody do with it, Sue,' he fumed. 'Makes your pieces seem like kindergarten stuff.'

Sue ran her eyes over the boldly bannered article.

TEN THOUSAND IN STORM
OVER WEATHER AND WITCHCRAFT
Freak Storms and Ghost Phone
Calls afflict Devon town

> 'It's like the devil's got it in for us,' is how an ex-mayor of Hallowes sums up the recent extraordinary happenings in this, up to now, sleepy and peaceful Devon town. 'I've never known the townsfolk so jittery and on edge. Certainly not since the war. You ought to hear some of the wild rumours going around.'
>
> And the cause of all Hallowes's fury and frantic speculation? An unprecedented spate of thunderstorms that has hit the town over the past weeks. Plus – and this is what has really electrified the townspeople – a series of freak phone calls . . .

She did not bother to read any more of the popular national's article, but put the paper back on her editor's desk.

'I didn't think the *Hallowes Gazette* was that kind of newspaper,' she remarked quietly.

He leaned forward across his desk.

'*What* kind of newspaper?'

'Sensational and scaremongering.'

He slapped his hand down on the paper. 'And you consider that sensational and scaremongering?'

She stood her ground. 'Yes, I do. The *Planet* is always

after a sensation, even if it has to invent the facts to back its headlines. Look at the number of stories it's had to retract recently. That Neil Kinnock is about to get a divorce. That the head of the civil service's secretary is a call-girl. That Joan Collins . . .'

He held up his hand. 'Okay, okay, we all know about the *Planet*. But it doesn't alter my point. I want to know why you've been pussyfooting over what is a big, big story. After all, the other day in my office, you yourself were dropping wild enough hints about the attack on that photographer fellow, Tully. So what's got into you, Susan Pike? When I took you on, I thought you were an aggressive newshound, not a timid news kitten.'

Sue Pike had both suffered and witnessed similar tirades before and therefore stopped herself rising to his taunts. Besides, there was a certain amount of truth in what he was saying. She had been pussyfooting. Deliberately. And would continue to do so until she had finished her present lines of investigation.

'I'm not ignoring the potential of this story, believe me. It's just that I'm working on several theories at the moment and would rather not find refuge in fantastic fiction like witchcraft, instead of getting at the real facts behind . . .'

'And what do you reckon *are* the real facts, my dear?' he cut in. 'Hallowes readers are not going to wait for ever for their own local paper to have a bloody point of view.'

'I know they're not. And I have to confess I haven't unearthed any significant leads yet.'

' "Unearthed",' he repeated with a thin smile. 'I love it. Had you bothered to read the whole of the *Planet's* article, you would have come across that word more than once. Sensational or not, at least their reporter's come up with a theory. And as far as I'm concerned, all the dead from the Napoleonic wars that were buried round here are a damn sight better than sweet Fanny Adams.'

She looked at him coolly. 'Even if it's not true?'

He shrugged. 'Maybe it is true, who knows? It was all so long ago.'

'I do. I've been through all the local records and there's no mention of any dead from those wars buried around here. What's more, I've discovered where they were actually buried. And it's miles away from here. Near Plympton.'

Her editor looked away and found refuge in fingering his unkempt moustache.

'All right, so the *Planet* didn't do its homework. But at least it provided its readers with a titillating thought. We're providing our readers with plug nothing right now.'

'We've given them all the facts we know.'

He turned back to her. 'Facts don't sell newspapers, Miss Pike. It's what you do with them, how you dress them up that pulls in the pennies. Now you'd better get out of here and do some more damn digging and then get dressing mighty fast.'

She rose from her chair, but turned as she reached the door.

'Can I remind you of something you said to me the other day?' Not waiting for a reply, she went on, 'You said something like, I'd be a complete idiot if I came out with anything I didn't have any evidence for. You said, if I did, I would only be fit to work for something like the *Planet*.'

He shuffled some papers on his desk and muttered, 'That was yesterday, my dear. And I thought you would know how we regard yesterday in the newspaper business.'

Mary Stride was at the front door before her husband had a chance to put his key in the lock.

'How is she?' she asked him. 'When I rang the hospital, they were very cagey.'

He leant forward and kissed her, then led her forward into the sitting-room.

'She's fine. I'm really only keeping her in overnight so that Sebastian can't get at her until, at least, tomorrow.'

He collapsed into a chair and grinned up at his wife. 'Been quite a day, hasn't it?'

She came over and sat on the arm. 'Suppose so. It isn't every day, I guess, that you think a best friend has just tried to commit suicide. And coming after last night . . . By the way, has she said any more about it? I'm terribly intrigued to know whose telephone number that was on the bit of paper.'

'Yes. We had quite a chat when I was with her. Could hardly stop her talking. It's like she's on some fantastic high. In fact, that's how she herself described it.'

Mary frowned. 'High? When you've just had your husband's infidelities confirmed by his mistress. Hardly, surely?'

He nodded. 'You wouldn't have thought it of our quiet, self-effacing old Prue, would you? But that's the way it is. As I told you earlier on the phone, she hadn't drunk all that amount to drown her sorrows at all. Quite the reverse. She said she was celebrating. Claims having Sebastian's affair with Annabel Craven confirmed, somehow set her free. "For the first time in my life," she said, "I feel free to be myself and no one else".'

'She's just trying to hype herself into acceptance of it all, I would imagine. Postpone the awful moment, when she has to accept the terrible truth.'

'I don't think so. Her high is genuine, I'll swear it. She's a different woman, really, Mary. Totally different. Confident and optimistic and somehow, years younger. It's amazing.'

He took his wife's hand. 'By the way, she apologises profusely to you about it all. Says that if she'd been used to that much booze, she wouldn't have been so daft as to take paracetemol to try and kill her hangover headache. Oh, and she says thanks for looking after Sophie and picking her up from school.'

Mary pointed upstairs. 'She's in Mark's room right now. They're playing his latest pop cassettes, as you must be able to hear.'

He grinned. 'Be a little difficult not to. Prue says she'll pick her up from school herself tomorrow and take her back home.'

'Think that's okay?'

He nodded. 'More than okay. Desirable. She'll need Sophie and Sophie will need her, now that she's banning Sebastian from the house.'

'He's there tonight. I know because he rang here, when Prue wouldn't see him in the hospital.'

'Did he want to pick up Sophie?'

'No. He asked if it was all right if she could stay tonight, because he was going to be working late.'

'On dear, Annabel Craven, no doubt,' he sighed, then went on, 'You know, I had no idea he was carrying on with anyone, let alone George Craven's wife. And she a client of his too.'

'Nor did I. Though I must say I've never really trusted Sebastian. He's just . . . well, too smooth altogether. Always has an answer for everything under the sun. But I suppose that's what lawyers are supposed to have.'

'His heyday as a legal beagle may be coming to an end.'

'What do you mean? The scandal won't do him much good?'

'That, and the investigation by the Law Society or whatever his professional body is called.'

She looked at him questioningly. 'They've heard about it already?'

'Prue rang them and told them all about it, before she took the paracetemol. It was their number she had written on that paper. She'd got it from Directory Enquiries.'

'Wow,' Mary Stride gasped. 'Prue didn't waste any time, did she?' She was silent for a moment and then asked, 'By the way, she hasn't confessed to you how she found out about Sebastian and Annabel Craven, has she?'

He nodded, then suddenly got up from his chair. And

she could see from his expression that she was not going to like his answer . . .

'Which shall we play next?'

Mark shuffled through his pile of cassettes, as Sophie looked on. He stopped at the latest Michael Jackson tape and withdrew it.

'How about this? It's even cooler than his last. You ought to hear . . .'

'I've heard it,' she interrupted unenthusiastically. 'And I don't like all that stuff going on in the background.'

'What stuff?' he demanded indignantly. 'You mean the drummer, do you? Why, he's deadly.'

'No, I don't mean him. He's all right. I mean all that, well, what sounds like lots of people sort of murmuring. If you've heard it, you should know what I mean.'

'Oh,' he smiled, 'I know the sound you mean. I like it. After all, the tape is called *Underground Voices*. That's what they're meant to be. Voices coming up from below . . .' he adopted a broad American accent 'the mean streets of Manhattan.'

She shrugged her indifference, climbed on to his bed and sat, legs crossed in front of her, Red Indian style.

'Still don't like it. Sometimes you can't even hear his voice for the silly noise.'

She leaned forward and started to sort through his tapes herself. After a moment or two, she stopped and held up the latest Bananarama single.

'How about this?'

He shook his head.

'No. Don't like Bananarama anymore. Wonder they're still going.'

She resumed sorting through the tapes but, in the end, could not find a single one that suited them both.

'Oh, come on, Sophe, let's have the Michael Jackson, like I said. Maybe when you heard it before, you'd got too much bass or treble or something.'

He made to take out the last tape they had played. 'Anyway, I like all that murmuring.' He suddenly froze and looked at her. 'Hey, Sophe, I've been meaning to tell you. You know up at the field . . .'

She made a face. 'Don't mention it. I got into enough trouble trying to tell my parents what happened, without you starting it all up again. They didn't believe a word I said – especially about all that lightning and stuff. Let alone about the big flash.'

Mark surreptitiously looked at the mark in the palm of his hand. For he had not yet had the courage to show any of the marks; not only because he was nervous how she would react, but because he had become very self-conscious about them and very near to being ashamed. He had decided that should Sophie spot them, he would say something about having got the marks from his bicycle handle bars when he was jumping the trenches.

'No, listen, Sophe. That's why I haven't told mum and dad about this, 'cos I don't think they'd believe me.'

She grudgingly looked up and remarked disbelievingly, 'All right. So what's the big secret? Though I can't see how *you* can have seen or heard much buried in all that soil.'

He moved closer towards her on the bed. 'That's the whole point, Sophe. Why I haven't told anybody about it.'

'What's the point?'

'I shouldn't have heard much, should I? But I did. I did, Sophe.'

'Big deal. So you heard the thunder. We all heard the thunder. You'd have to be at least . . . well, twenty foot under, not to.'

'No, not the thunder. 'Course I heard that. No, this Michael Jackson tape has suddenly reminded me of it. I heard voices, Sophe. A bit like on that track. Kind of murmurings, they were, all around me . . . But it wasn't scary at all. It was just like, you know, I wasn't alone . . .'

She frowned at him. 'No wonder you think your parents won't believe you. I jolly well don't, for a start.'

He grabbed her wrist. 'No, honest, Sophe. I haven't made it up. There *were* voices.'

She wriggled free of his grasp. 'Oh come on, Mark. It doesn't matter now, anyway, does it?' She leaned across, flipped the tape door shut and pressed the Play button.

'Let's hear Sherman and the Yank Tank again.'

And as the heavy metal beat started to reverberate once more around the room, she lay back on the bed and stared up at the pop idol's poster on the wall – depicting Sherman riding with his rock band atop the star-blazoned World War II tank that had inspired the group's name.

'Peculiar, don't you think?'

John Stride looked back at the lifeless hand, the tufts of black hair on the fingers in macabre contrast to the white and now almost translucent flesh.

'The burns on the fingertips?'

Inspector Dudkin nodded.

'That's why I called you in.' He smiled. 'As a kind of third opinion, if you like. Our chaps and Drench's own doctor, McKenzie – you will know him of course – say that they're very recent. And probably occurred while he was at his mother's house. What's your view?'

Stride stifled his distaste – he had a morbid fear of handling corpses that had developed in his student days and had never left him – and reached for the forefinger and thumb once more.

'It's not the fact that he's got burnt that worries me, Doctor. It's the type of burn. And its obvious intensity. Look at the way this fingertip seems almost to have melted.'

Stride tentatively felt the burnt flesh with his own finger. Its feel and look reminded him somewhat of the plasticine he'd played with as a child.

'He must have been gripping something, I would

think. Rather tightly, by the looks of things.' Stride let the hand fall back alongside Drench's body that lay, obscenely naked, on the mortuary slab. He turned back to the Inspector.

'Maybe he burnt himself somehow at home, before he left for his mother's place. Like on a toaster or even an iron. After all, he did live alone.'

'Maybe. But I don't think so. Constable Deakin reported that when he arrived at the cottage in answer to Mrs Drench's phone call, he noticed a funny smell near her son's body in the kitchen – a smell that, he said, could well have been that of something like, well, flesh burning. Now I know Mrs Drench had her oven on while she was out, but he said the smell from her cooking was quite different.'

Stride went over to the window and looked out over Hallowes. The sight of living, breathing people in the streets helped stem his nausea.

'Perhaps he opened the oven for some reason and touched the metal grid of the shelf.'

The Inspector rested back against the far end of the slab, seemingly entirely oblivious of the naked feet only inches from his hands. 'Just possible, I suppose.'

Stride looked round at him. 'Inspector, you told me an hour or two back that Mr Drench's death was accidental. That he must have fallen off a chair and struck his head on the iron doorstop.'

Dudkin smiled. 'I didn't say "iron", Dr Stride. That's your interpretation. All I said was "doorstop". It happens to have been an old military shell. From World War II. His mother told us she had used it as a doorstop for donkey's years. "Putting a thing of violence to a peaceful end", as she put it.'

Stride thought for a moment, then said, 'All right, but it doesn't alter the fact that he died accidentally, does it? So why are you so concerned over these burns to his fingers, if there's nothing sinister about his death?'

The Inspector shrugged. 'Frankly, Doctor, I'm not

quite sure. It's just a little, nagging worry I have, that will probably go away. We policemen, you know, get so used to having to be suspicious, that I often think we're in danger of seeing devils, even where angels tread. But the other thing is, of course, that the deceased was not exactly the most popular man in town, as you must realise. I mean even his own mother had raised Cain about his latest plans for Hallowes. There were a lot of people on that protest march of hers.'

Stride frowned. 'You don't think that Enid Drench . . . ?'

Dudkin laughed and as he raised his hand to wave it dismissively, it flicked the tip of an ice-cold toe.

'Glory be, no. Mrs Drench may be a bit eccentric, but she's no murderess. Besides, she was clearly in a state of shock when we arrived. Her grief over her son's death was only too genuine. I feel very sorry for her.'

'But the fact remains, you're not a hundred per cent sure that Drench's death was accidental?'

'Ninety-nine per cent, Doctor. Let's leave it at ninety-nine.' He moved away from the corpse and came over to the window.

'Well, that's about it. Thank you so much for coming, Dr Stride. As I say, I just wanted a third opinion, just in case we had missed something. But it seems we haven't.'

Stride shook the extended hand.

'If only the dead could speak,' Dudkin smiled, as he glanced back at the cold, white form on the slab.

'Er . . . er . . . yes,' Stride muttered and made quickly for the door.

The cottage was different from her mental picture of it. At least, from the outside, it seemed more kempt, less tumbledown. More welcoming and homely and less the forlorn abode of a witch-like recluse.

As a result, a little of Mary Stride's reticence and nervousness left her and she felt somewhat easier about calling on Enid Drench, so very soon after her terrible tragedy.

To her surprise, the door was opened almost immediately after she knocked and she could see Enid Drench was dressed to go out.

'Oh . . . it's . . . er . . . you, Mrs Stride. I was just about to . . . er . . . get some fresh air.'

She stepped back from the porch to let the old lady come out.

'I'm sorry, Mrs Drench. Maybe you would rather I came another time. I know it's very soon after . . .'

Enid Drench shook her head, then removed the long pin securing her hat.

'No, come in. Please. My hesitation was only because I thought you might be the police coming back.'

She beckoned Mary into the narrow hall.

'They stayed so long. I thought they would never go.' Closing the front door, she said, 'You had better come into the sitting-room.'

Mary bowed her head to miss the beam atop the door and went ahead of her into the room.

'I won't take up too much of your time. I only came really to express my husband's and my own heartfelt sympathy at your terrible loss.'

She took the chair she was offered and Enid Drench, having first picked up the wary cat, sat down opposite her, the previous occupant now glaring at Mary Stride from her lap.

Eliciting no comment, Mary tried to hide her embarrassment by adding, 'I tried to ring you. Several times. But I just couldn't get through.'

For the first time, Enid Drench's face showed some emotion. 'It's broken. I had to go to a neighbour to ring the police. The damned thing's kaput. I don't know why or how, but thank God. If I told William once, I told him a thousand times that I didn't want the damned phone in the first place. But he kept on and on. "Mother, living alone up here at your age, I won't know whether you're dead or alive, without it".' She looked up at the heavens. 'Dead or alive. Huh! Now who's dead? And who's alive?'

'I'm terribly sorry,' Mary said softly.

Enid Drench looked at her, her eyes now glistening with moisture.

'You shouldn't be sorry,' she said coldly. 'No one in Hallowes should be sorry. My son was no friend of Hallowes, no friend of any of you. There was only one person he loved. Himself. And only one thing he loved. Making money and more money. Money he didn't even need . . . didn't even know how to spend.' She stroked the cat with feverish fingers and he stared up at her, taken aback by the unaccustomed roughness. 'Until, in the end,' she went on, 'he went too far. I warned him. Oh yes, I warned him. Time and again. But he wouldn't listen. It was like the devil was driving him . . .'

Mary listened wide-eyed, not daring to interrupt this totally unexpected tirade against a son only hours dead.

'. . . and maybe he was. Sitting on his shoulder, goading him with a satanic fork.' She cackled at the image she had created. 'Prod. Prod. Prod. Dig, dig, dig. Get out your little spade and dig your own grave, William Drench.'

She subsided back into her chair. 'And he got out his little digger and did just that.' Her voice trailed away and her hand ceased to stroke the cat.

Mary Stride fidgeted nervously in her chair, uncertain quite how to react to the enigmatic outburst; let alone how to steer the conversation round to the subject that had, in reality, prompted her call.

Neither spoke for quite a few moments. At last, Mary decided to try and pick up the thread from Enid Drench's last words.

'But I thought your son had his accident in your kitchen, Mrs Drench. Fell off a chair and hit his head against . . .'

The old woman suddenly sat up straight in her chair, unsettling the cat as she did so. With an insolent yawn, he jumped off her lap and disappeared out of the room.

'. . . an army shell,' she cut in. 'Isn't that ironic, Mrs

Stride? An American army shell, too. From the big ammunition dump that used to be up on Widow's Field, remember?' She shook her head. 'No, you wouldn't remember, would you? I forget, you're far too young. Even your poor mother would only have known of it by hearsay. But your grandmother . . .' She sighed. '. . . now your grandmother. She knew it well. Now if she'd only known . . .' She stopped suddenly.

Mary leaned forward in her chair. 'No, go on, Mrs Drench. What about my grandmother? Tell me, please.'

The old woman closed her eyes and said very quietly, almost as if she were in a trance, 'She was very pretty, your grandmother. All the young fellows used to think so. Hung about her like bees round a honeypot. She could have had any of them, just for the asking. But no, once she had seen that GI corporal . . . there was no turning back, then. I used to see them strolling arm in arm through the town. By the river. I couldn't have been much over thirty-five myself then. And still unmarried . . . I can remember so well being a mite jealous of their obvious happiness. Little did I know then that their time together was destined to be so very brief . . .'

'I know,' Mary said, in little above a whisper. 'My grandfather was killed on the D-Day beaches.'

Enid Drench's eyes suddenly opened. 'He was killed on the beaches, but . . .' Again she stopped in mid sentence.

Mary instantly got up from her chair and came over to her. 'But what, Mrs Drench? You've got to tell me.' Getting no answer, she persisted, 'You know something, don't you, Mrs Drench? Something that affects me. Or my family. Is that why you said the other night that I, of all people, should believe my son about the happenings in Widow's Field?'

Again, she could get no response. She knelt down in front of her and grasped her hand.

'Please, Mrs Drench, you've got to tell me. Why did you say I'd got to believe? Believe what? Believe it all happened? Mark's jump with his bike? That he had an accident? Or is it what happened afterwards? His being covered with earth. The sea of lightning? Or the big, blinding flash?'

She shook her arm. 'Which is it, Mrs Drench? Please, please, if you ask me to believe, I must ask you why . . .'

Enid Drench gently removed her wrist from Mary's grasp, then clasped her hand.

'Is that all he told you, Mrs Stride?'

'Why . . . er . . . yes . . . I think so.' She suddenly shivered and looked down at their linked hands. 'You've seen the stigmata?'

Enid Drench nodded and a hint of a smile flitted across her grief-stricken features. But then she went on, 'Ask him what he heard, Mary Stride.'

'Heard? What do you mean . . . the storm . . . or what?'

'Just ask him,' she repeated softly. 'Ask him.'

Mary Stride looked up at the tired eyes and knew Enid Drench would not tell her any more right then.

'I'll ask him, I promise.'

'Good.' She smiled. 'You know, you're so lucky to have such a beautiful boy.'

Mary suddenly found herself crying and lay her head against the old lady's lap.

As fingers softly stroked her hair, she heard Enid Drench whisper, 'If you will play with fire, my son, you will only get your fingers burnt.'

Chapter Seventeen

The surgery receptionist looked up as John Stride's head appeared round his examination room door.

'If there are no more, you can go home now, Daphne.'

'But Miss Pike . . .' she protested. 'Shouldn't I wait until she's gone? I don't mind, you know.'

'She's not a patient,' he smiled. 'I'll see her out.'

Daphne Pringle, despite the round-and-barmaid-bounciness of her appearance, held straight and narrow views on life – unlike so many in Hallowes – and rather frowned on leaving an attractive, married man alone with any young woman, if it wasn't for strictly professional reasons. Not that she really suspected her esteemed boss would actually succumb to the undoubted charms of the young reporter, let alone within the white and antiseptic walls of his surgery. Nevertheless, as her mother had always advised her, 'you can't give in to temptation, if it's never put your way'. What's more, this Miss Pike had not been willing to give a decent reason for her visit to the surgery. Just a 'Could you tell him I'd like to see him? He'll know what about.'

'Are you sure, Doctor? It's no bother, really.'

'I'm sure. See you tomorrow. Goodnight.'

Stride smiled to himself as he closed his door and returned to his desk.

'I suspect my receptionist thinks you and I might be up to no good.'

Sue Pike blushed. Not at the thought, which she had to admit was quite attractive but at the doctor having voiced it.

'Well, I'm sorry to come round at such short notice. I did ring you at home, actually, but your wife said you were still here and why didn't I try to catch you before you left? It would save me a journey.'

He sat down at his desk. 'No, don't worry. That's fine.' Leaning forward over his desk, he went on, 'Now come on, Sue, don't leave me in suspense any longer. I'm sure you must have found out something, or you wouldn't have called me.'

She pushed her hair back from her face. 'Now don't get too excited, please. I don't know really that I've discovered anything yet. It's just that . . . well . . . I wanted to chat to you about a few things before I got any further.' She grinned sheepishly. 'Just in case you think I am making a fool of myself.'

'That last I'd never believe,' he smiled. 'Now come on. Out with it. You've found a connection between Rickett and Tully and Walter Blair and . . .'

'. . . the telephone engineer and the health shop lady,' she completed the list. 'No, not really. Well, nothing concrete. Just sort of bits and pieces that might just join together, if we only knew more.'

He tried to hide his disappointment. For the death of William Drench and his son Mark's experiences and stigmata had considerably magnified his already acute fears about what might be happening in their town. And had made acutely urgent his need to discover some link between the recent harrowing and dreadful events. For link there must be, he was certain. Natural or – he blanched at the thought – supernatural. Every fibre in his being told him so. The only question remaining in his mind was whether any human mortal would ever have sufficient intelligence or sensitivity to divine it.

He patted the top of his desk. 'Okay, Sue, lay your bits and pieces on the table and we'll see if we can fit any of them together.'

She took a notebook out of her shoulder bag. 'I won't take up your time by going into every little thing. I'll just give you the bits I think might be important.'

'All right.'

'I'll start with Tully. Comes from a South Hams family. Only child. Father apparently had a bicycle repair business in Paignton. Died soon after Tully was born. It's all still a bit hazy further back than that. But I did discover his grandfather got into a bit of trouble with the police towards the end of the war.'

'What kind of trouble?'

'Seems he was had up for stealing.'

'Did you get this from police records?'

Sue shook her head. 'No. From some people who claimed to have known his grandfather during the war. They said they thought the police wouldn't have any record of it, because it became a military matter. You see, they said he stole from a GI stationed in Hallowes.'

Stride looked up with interest; his wife's description of her time with Enid Drench still fresh in his mind.

'A GI?'

'That's right.'

'What exactly did he steal?'

'They mentioned a watch. And a ring. Or maybe two rings, they weren't sure. And there might have been some other stuff too. But all personal, it would seem.'

'And the American military police handled the case, you say?'

'From all accounts, yes.'

'So he wasn't prosecuted by the British?'

'Doesn't sound like it.'

Stride thought for a moment. 'Would figure. I read a book once about American GIs in Britain during the war. The British and Americans bent over backwards to try to hush up any unpleasantness between them. So . . . any more about Tully?'

'No, not of any significance. Except that his extensive love life seems to have been pretty common knowledge. If the stories can be believed, he seems to have made passes at almost every pretty woman who came through his studio door.'

'Yes, I've heard that too. So that brings us neatly to the Blairs. Young Bettina and especially her father. After all, he seems to be the one who received the strange calls.'

Sue turned over to the next page of her notebook, then asked, 'By the way, how is Bettina Blair now? I gather she is out of hospital.'

'Yes, she's back home now.'

'Memory any better?'

'No. Still can't remember anything that's happened in the last few months. Her memory seems to stop dead in April. The last thing she can recall clearly is a cycling trip she took with a schoolfriend to Bifton Sands.'

Sue Pike looked up. 'Bifton Sands?'

'Yes.'

He watched as she flipped over some more pages of her notebook.

'What have you just thought of?' he asked anxiously.

She pursed her lips. 'Well, oh, it's probably nothing. It's just that . . . ah, here it is.' She started to read from her notes. 'Samuel Roderick suddenly came into a lot of money at the end of the war. Sufficient to retire and close his undertaking business . . .'

Frowning, he interrupted, 'Who's Samuel Roderick?'

'Oh, sorry. I should have explained. These are notes on the health food shop lady. Penelope Seymour-Jones. Her maiden name was Roderick. Samuel was her grandfather and he was an undertaker in a fairly modest way in Kingsbridge, though he actually lived at Crossways.'

'Crossways is just up from Bifton Sands, isn't it? Is that the connection?'

'No. Not really.'

'Then what . . . ?'

'Well, you remember I said he suddenly seemed to have come into money?'

He nodded.

'Well, gossip in Crossways is that he got it somehow from the Americans.'

'The military, you mean?'

'Yes.'

'Why? Did they employ him? I mean, as an undertaker?'

'Must have, I suppose. Why else would they have paid him money?'

Stride sat back in his chair. 'I don't know,' he said quietly. 'Anyway, go on.'

'Well, it seems that during the war he had to leave his house in Crossways, as did all the inhabitants on that bit of the coastline. Tney weren't allowed back until almost the end of the war.'

He looked up. 'Come to think of it, I remember my wife telling me once that the whole area around Bifton was evacuated. To enable the various armed forces to practise their landings for D-Day and the assault on Normandy.'

'That's right. I've checked on it in the back files of *Hallowes Gazette*. Quite a fuss it caused, as you can imagine. Apparently the Bifton Beaches are almost identical to those chosen for their landings in France.'

'So what are you saying, Sue? That this man Roderick must have got some massive compensation for being turfed out of his home?'

'He may have, I don't know. Obviously everyone living round here must have been compensated to some degree or other.'

He leaned forward again. 'So what else are those old gossips saying?'

'They're hinting that more Americans actually got killed on the D-Day landings than the Army was willing to admit at the time. And that they may have shipped Roderick over to France to dispose of them secretly.'

'Bit far fetched, isn't it? I mean why should they bother to ship this Roderick over there, when they could just use some local French fellow? Much less bother, I'd have thought.'

She shrugged. 'Well, I did warn you that all I'd got was a jumble of bits and pieces. I didn't promise any of them would make a great deal of sense.'

'I'm sorry. I didn't mean to sound dismissive. You've done very well. At least now we might have some kind of American connection. God, we've just got to find something.'

'If not French,' she smirked. 'Anyway, sorry for drifting off at a tangent after you mentioned Bifton Sands.' She flipped back through her notes. 'Let's get back to the Blair family. Here I can't see anything really interesting or promising at all. Originally the Blairs seem to have come down from the Midlands. Just before the war, it was. One of Walter Blair's work colleagues says he claims his grandfather had been a clock repairer in Birmingham. Walter's own father, who is still alive, was a milkman. Had a round over Brixham way. Long retired now. Wasn't in the war because of a spot on a lung. Now in an old people's home in Torquay. Mother died years ago, it seems.'

She ran a finger quickly down her notes. 'Walter himself has lived in Hallowes ever since his marriage. Has had various jobs, including being a waiter in a Paignton hotel. Now a manager in a warehouse, as you no doubt know. That's it, really.'

'Mrs Blair?'

'Even less exciting,' she sighed. 'She came to Devon as a child, from where I haven't been able to discover. Met Walter at a dance, so they say. Like her husband, she has had quite a few different jobs. Waitressing, cleaning. Even worked as a groom over Ashburton way.'

She held up her hands. 'End of the Blairs. Oh, except for Bettina, I suppose. I made a few enquiries at her school. Again, nothing sticks out. All much as you'd expect. They say she is an average pupil, liked by the other girls and popular with everyone.'

'Meaning the boys?'

'Guess so. But schools are always very guarded when

they're asked questions about their pupils.'

He sighed. 'So we seem to have drawn a blank with the Blairs?'

'Guess so. Shall I go on to the others?'

He nodded. 'Give me Rick Rickett. Surely there's more to his background than the blandness of the Blairs'?'

Sue turned back two pages and began reading. 'Rick Rickett. Family lived in Devon from way back. Mother for years a maid for the Beechwoods.' She looked up. 'Apparently they were a wealthy family who lived near Dartington.' She read on, 'Father rather a ne'er-do-well. Had a multitude of jobs, all of menial or labouring variety. Inveterate gambler when he had a bean. But good looking when young. Great lad for the girls. Exempt from serving in Forces during war due to working on the land. Died in 1958, after fall from back of haywagon, when reputedly drunk.'

'Charming. And the poor soul he took as a wife?'

'Mrs Rickett senior. Talked to several people about her. I've got here: worked in factory making components for Spitfires during war. As much one for the men, as her husband was for girls. Had several local boys in tow before GIs arrived in Hallowes. Then went American mad. Always hanging around the camp. Even got engaged to one. Name of Shoemaker. They remember the name because it was such a funny one. But broke it off when she met Rickett. He just bowled her over. Apparently, the GI was mortified when she left him. They said it was almost like she knew Shoemaker would never come back from D-Day.'

'Another possible American connection,' Stride commented. 'But pretty tenuous. Go on.'

'There isn't much more on the Ricketts. Further back than that, no one seems to know much about them.'

'Anything on Rick Rickett himself? Or Thelma?'

'Nothing really that we don't know already. Confirmation that the nurseryman was a pretty obnoxious individual, highly unpopular with everyone. People say they only bought flowers and plants from him because they felt sorry for his wife. Oh, and there is a rumour that he once interfered with a little girl who came into the nursery to buy a flower for Mother's Day. But there seems to have been no proof of that.'

'And Thelma herself?'

'Just that people are sorry for her. Especially now that she's in gaol awaiting trial. I don't detect any great liking for the woman, though. Just sympathy. Mainly, I suspect, because she had to put up with her ogre of a husband all those years.'

'Too religious to contemplate a divorce, I suppose.'

'I guess so.'

Stride sighed and sat back in his chair. 'So that's it, really, isn't it?' He counted on his fingers. 'Rickett, Tully, the Blairs, the health shop lady . . .'

'There's the telephone engineer,' she interrupted, 'but I haven't got round to him yet. You forgot to give me his name.'

'Don't bother right now, Sue. His wife came in a couple of days back to pick up another prescription for his tranquillisers. They've taken my original advice. They've gone on holiday. Left on a package tour to Spain yesterday.'

She closed her notebook and replaced it in her shoulder bag.

'So that looks like it then,' she grimaced. 'Sorry it doesn't add up to very much, but . . .'

Stride got up from behind his desk. 'Not quite it, Sue. You see, I've discovered a little more since we last met. Another of my patients has admitted to receiving one of those phantom calls.'

She looked up at him, as he came round to her side of the desk.

'Oh? All right for me to know the name?'

After a moment's hesitation, he said, 'I think things are looking far too ominous now for me to pull the

Hippocratic bit. Her name is Prue Fanshawe. Wife of the legal beagle.'

'You mean the solicitor in the High Street?'

He nodded. 'Sebastian Fanshawe's wife. I won't go into all the circumstances, but she has certainly received two or more of these calls.'

She frowned. 'Any obvious connections with all the others?'

'No. Not that I can see. But then I don't know anything much about the Fanshawes, really. They just live fairly near us and their daughter goes to the same school as our son, Mark. They're only dinner-party friends, if you know what I mean?'

She smiled. 'I know exactly. I hate dinner parties too.'

Stride warmed to her reaction. 'Doctors are expected to hold dinner parties, more's the pity. Part of being accepted by the community. Anyway, there's something else, Sue, something that may or may not have a bearing on all this. Have you heard about William Drench?'

She looked at him in surprise. 'Yes, of course. But from what my editor has told me, there's not much of a tale there, is there? He, apparently, fell off a chair and struck his head on a doorstop. That's why my editor put our new junior on the story and not me.'

'There's a little bit more to it than that. May not be important, but, somehow, with Drench's being so involved with the development of Widow's Field . . .'

'Come on, Doctor, don't tell me you've found out Drench had been having these calls too.'

'I have no idea about that, but there is something rather uncanny about his death.'

'Uncanny? Please go on.'

Stride recounted his time in the mortuary with Inspector Dudkin.

She did not react for quite a few moments after he had finished, then asked, 'The shell being used as a doorstop. You said it was American?'

He nodded. 'Yes. From the ammunition dump the

Americans had in Widow's Field. Drench was given it as a child.'

She looked at him. 'Another possible American connection?'

'Yes, I suppose it could be. I hadn't thought about that until you came up with your findings this evening. No, it's the burnt fingers that bother me. That and the fact that Drench died, when he did. Like, right now. When he and that George Craven are just about to send in the bulldozers to develop that site.'

'I know what you mean. But you say the Inspector is almost positive his death was accidental?'

Stride shrugged. 'But so, apparently, was Tully's.'

'Rick Rickett's wasn't,' she observed. 'But we know his actual death wasn't supernatural either . . .' She stopped abruptly and looked at Stride.

'Or do we?' he said quietly, then suddenly exploded. 'Oh God, Sue, we don't really know a damned thing, do we? We're just floundering about, clutching at every damned straw that's blown about in the wind.'

He slammed his fist down on his desk top. 'There's only one certainty in this whole terrifying affair. And that's that something is happening in Hallowes that, if we're not bloody careful, can destroy the whole damn town and send even those of us who may survive, screaming to the nearest mental asylum . . .'

Stride ran out of breath and stared into space. After a moment, he said, 'I'm sorry, Sue. I shouldn't have sounded off like that. After all, I'm supposed to be a man of science, aren't I?' He looked back at her. 'And men of science should not be tempted into hysterical outbursts about ridiculous things like fire and brimstone and plague and perdition, now should they? Men of science should, above all, be men of reason.'

She reached out sympathetically for his hand. 'Don't feel sorry, please. What's happening right now in Hallowes seems to defy all reason. All natural explanation. All logic. So I feel exactly the same way you do. So do many others in Hallowes now. The town is becoming, well, almost afraid of itself.'

He clasped her hand with his own. 'Thanks. But hysteria is not going to help anybody.' He took a deep breath. 'Now let's try to think positively. Let's go back to Drench for a minute. If his death was not wholly accidental and was somehow connected with his part in the Widow's Field development, then . . .'

But Sue Pike had raced ahead of him and cut in, 'What about George Craven?'

'Exactly.'

'You mean, he might be next?'

'With Drench gone, his death would probably put an end to the development of Widow's Field. At least for the time being. I doubt if anyone will be too eager to take on a project that would then be so tainted by controversy and death.'

She looked at him enquiringly. 'So what are you saying?'

'I'm not quite sure. But somehow, I feel we ought to find a way to warn George Craven. God knows how and God knows what we'd say to him. But all the same . . .'

'He must know about Drench's death by now,' Sue pointed out. 'Maybe that will stay his hand. In any event, it will delay things a bit, won't it? While they sort out Drench's affairs?'

'I suppose so,' he agreed, 'but I still feel he should be warned.'

She pointed to the telephone on his desk.

'Maybe you should ring him. Try to set up a meeting or something, so that you can outline . . .'

But her words were cut short by the sudden ringing of the desk phone.

Both caught their breath and looked at each other. Stride's mind raced, as he tried to think who might ring the surgery at so late an hour, well after all knew it was closed.

'Maybe it's my wife,' he muttered, 'wondering when

on earth I'm going to be home.' But as he stretched out a faltering hand to pick up the receiver, he somehow knew the call was no domestic affair.

'Hello, Dr Stride speaking.'

He looked across at Sue Pike, who sat motionless, holding her breath.

'Seems to be no one there,' he began, then held up his hand. 'No, wait a minute . . . I can hear a noise . . . it sounds like . . . well . . . like waves . . . on a shore.'

Sue frowned. 'Waves?'

Stride continued to listen intently, too absorbed to even announce himself again.

'Now there's a grinding sound . . . and more waves . . . and now there's shouting . . . men shouting . . .'

Sue got up from her chair and rushed over to the phone. He held the receiver so that both could now hear. And she was just in time to hear the first explosion. She stared at him in panic.

'My God, it sounds like a . . . war.'

Stride said nothing, but held the receiver further from their ears, as explosion after explosion resounded through the phone; and the shouts of the men turned to unearthly screams that seemed to fill the very surgery with their terror and pain . . .

As George Craven came down into the hall, he heard a key being inserted into the front door. Before he could get to it, his estranged wife had already let herself in.

'George, where are you going?' she demanded. 'I've tried to get you all afternoon. Didn't your office pass on the messages?'

'Yes, my love,' he replied irritably. 'I got the messages. I just didn't choose to react to them, that's all.'

He tried to brush past her, but she grabbed his arm. 'George, I've got to see you,' she pleaded and he could see unfamiliar panic in her eyes.

'Well, I haven't got to see you.'

But he could not brush off her grip.

'George, I'm frightened.'

He laughed out loud and looked down at her, enjoying her sudden dependence on him.

'Of what, my love?' he sneered. 'Of being alone, now that darling Sebastian's wife has found out all about you and her husband?'

She looked startled. 'How on earth did you . . . ?'

He laughed again. 'My dear, the whole of Hallowes now knows about you and that la-de-dah lawyer. I guess his unassuming little wife has seen to that.'

She swallowed hard, then pleaded, 'But George, that's not it. That's not what's frightening me.'

'Really?' he grinned. 'It should do. After all, your name is going to be trodden in the mire for months to come. Especially when Prue Fanshawe brings her own divorce proceedings. By the way, my love, who are you going to get now to handle your divorce? My lawyer says you'd be very silly to think Fanshawe can continue with the action.'

'For God's sake, George, shut up and listen,' she shouted.

'My, my,' he smiled. 'Always the little charmer when you want your own way, aren't you?'

She suddenly slapped his face. 'Oh . . . I . . . er . . . didn't mean that, George. I really didn't. I was just trying to get you to listen, that's all. I'm sorry.'

He whipped round and his strong fingers prised open her grasp on his arm.

'All right. I'll give you two minutes, Annabel. Out with it. What the hell is frightening little Miss Fire-proof?'

She rested a hand back against a carved oak settle to support herself.

'Prue's been here, George.'

He raised his heavy eyebrows.

'Very frightening,' he mocked.

'No, it's not that. It's what she told me . . . how she found out . . .'

'Like me,' he grinned, 'bending an ear to the gossip?'

She shook her head, her usually immaculately groomed hair now falling about her face. 'She heard it on the . . . telephone.'

He grinned again. 'Someone rang her.'

'No. No, George. The phone did it . . . the phone rang her. You know, like's been happening all over Hallowes.'

He pursed his lips. 'You mean, Prue had one of those calls?'

'Yes,' she whispered. 'More than one.'

'Who was actually speaking?'

'Sebast . . . her husband seems to have been making a call to me.'

'All lovey-dovey. She must have adored that.' He put a hand on Annabel's shoulder. 'You know, I feel suddenly sorry for the little woman.'

'George, don't you see . . . ?'

'See what? See why you're frightened? Oh yes, I see that. But it's not because of any joke talk about phantom phone calls.'

She grabbed his arm once more.

'It's not joke talk. How can you say that? You know the feeling in Hallowes right now. Lots of people have been receiving all sorts of calls.'

He looked away. 'My dear Annabel. Some hysterical people may well have imagined they've received calls of this nature. I'm not denying that hysteria can produce phenomena of all kinds. Look at Lourdes. Visions of the Virgin Mary, signs of the crucifixion on hands and feet. You name it, they've heard, seen or suffered from it. But don't forget there are other pathetic idiots – especially in a loony town like this – that will *say* they received calls just to show how special they are or to draw attention to themselves that they'd never normally get. And don't tell me that self-effacing little Prue Fanshawe isn't in their number. She's just the type. Besides, she'd be cute enough to know it's about the only thing that would frighten a hard-boiled case like yourself.'

She closed her eyes and tears started to smear her mascara.

'George, you weren't there. You don't understand. She was telling the truth, I know it.'

He shrugged. 'So? What does it bloody matter? You haven't received any joke calls.'

He made to go, but she ran round him and stood with her back to the front door.

'Don't go without me, George, please. I don't want to be left alone.'

'So go to a pub. You won't be alone in there. If you wear the right dress, your boobs might well pull you a Sebastian substitute, who knows?'

She put her arms out in front of her to keep him away. 'Why, where are you going? Can't you take me?'

He guffawed. 'Are you kidding, my pathetic little love? Two people just about to be divorced, seen out about town together. That would set tongues a-wagging even more, wouldn't you think? It's bad enough your still being in the same house.'

She stood her ground. 'But tell me. Where are you going, George?'

'All right. If you want to know, I'm going to see the Chief Planning Officer and check on what difference, if any, poor Drench's death may have had on things up at Widow's Field. I'm planning, now, to take over the whole deal myself.'

Annabel thought hurriedly. 'All right. All right. How long will you be?'

'I don't know. About an hour and a half, I expect. Two hours at most.'

She glanced at her Piaget watch, that was thin enough for Midas to have painted on her wrist.

'George, it's eight o'clock now. How about you dropping me at the Devil's Friend and then picking me up on your way back. I'm deadly serious. I don't want to be alone tonight.'

'In case the phone rings?' he sneered, then beckoned with a thick finger. 'Okay, okay. Get out of the way and I'll take you to the pub.'

'And pick me up?'

'And pick you up. Though God knows why I should.'

She held out her hand. He shook it reluctantly and could feel the cold sweat of fear on her palm.

The big white car swept out of the drive and accelerated up the hill away from the town, whose lights now pinpricked the valley with stars.

Neither occupant spoke at first, but then Annabel ventured, 'Terrible about poor William Drench, isn't it? Won't you miss him?'

He shrugged. 'Miss his beady eye for an investment, yes. But he was hardly a buddy. He was just too damn stroppy and selfish to bother about friendships.'

She looked across at him, as he swung the big car round the curve. 'Doesn't his death worry you a bit though?'

'Why?' He smiled across at her. 'I can always get another partner.'

She stifled the inclination to bring up the subject of Penelope Seymour-Jones. For to have an argument right then about his rumoured new lover would hardly help her cause just when she so needed him.

'No, George, I meant that . . . well . . . you know, all the present fuss about Widow's Field and the strange things they say are going on up there.'

'So?'

'Well, it's almost like . . .' She hesitated, as she tried to find the right words and her husband cut in.

'Like the gods up above are trying to tell us never to build another house in Hallowes. Oh, come on, Annabel. You used to have your feet on the ground. That is, before you, no doubt, raised them in the bloody air for your smarmy Sebastian. You can't be falling for all that shit about heavenly signs and portents and what not.'

He shifted into low to pass a rusty Datsun, that was

struggling in a cloud of smoke up the rise.

'Jesus, you know what people in Hallowes are like,' he went on. 'They're as gullible as all get out. Why, they sell more tarot cards here than playing cards. More books on Zen Buddhism than Christianity. And more herbal remedies than they did in the Dark Ages. Hell, I wouldn't live here, if they weren't so bloody green in every sense of the word, that it's so dead easy to take money off them. No wonder they're all wetting their knickers about Widow's Field and the telephone system. You name it and they'll get in a panic about it . . .'

But his homily was suddenly cut short by the bleeping of his car phone.

Annabel gasped and he looked across at her. 'What's the matter with you? Got phonaphobia, like the rest of those loonies? Heaven help us all.'

He picked up the handset.

'Hello,' he grunted.

She watched him intently, her hands gripping her seat belt so tightly, white showed on her knuckles.

He shook the phone.

'Hello. This is Craven. Who's calling?'

Suddenly, he pulled the set away from his ear and now, she too could hear the violent explosions that had so startled him.

'Bloody hell, what the . . . ?'

But his shout was cut off, as the car telephone flew up out of his hand. Annabel screamed and watched with horror, as the phone described an arc in the air, like some demented rocket out of control, then crashed into the dashboard. But instead of falling to the floor, it suddenly started to glow, then punch out at the controls on the fascia one by one.

'My God, Annabel,' she heard her husband shout above the continuing thud of explosions. 'Can't you bloody do something?'

Terror stricken, she closed her eyes and reached out to where she had last seen the jabbing instrument.

Almost instantly, there was a deafening explosion, but this time not from the phone, but from the car itself. The fascia, windscreen, everything in front of them suddenly disappeared. Now in total darkness, both the Cravens found themselves flailing against a vast amorphous demon marshmallow that seemed to want to smother them.

As she pummelled with her fists and fought for breath, Annabel heard the scream of tyres as her husband slammed on the brakes and she felt the car snake across the road.

'George,' she shrieked out, but any last words her husband might have uttered were drowned in the death throes of the car, as it crashed through a fence, then flipped over and over, until it rested upside down in a mass of still unspread silage.

Chapter Eighteen

Margaret Blair's eyes showed a certain alarm as she opened the front door.

'Oh, it's you, Dr Stride.'

'I'm sorry to call on you at this hour, Mrs Blair,' he said quickly to reassure her, 'but don't worry, there's nothing wrong. I was on my way home when I remembered there was something I would like to ask your daughter, if I may.'

She opened the door wide to let him into the hall.

'That's all right, Doctor. Bettina's up in her room, I think. We bought her her own telly after her . . . accident.' She smiled. 'Wish we hadn't now. We hardly ever see her downstairs of an evening.'

She went to the bottom of the stairs and shouted up, 'Bettina. Dr Stride has popped round to see you. Are you decent?'

Turning back to Stride, she explained, 'Better give her a minute or two to tidy herself up a bit or she'll give me what for, when you're gone.'

'Fine,' he agreed. 'I'm sorry not to have given you any notice I was dropping by.'

She cleared her throat. 'Er . . . would it be rude to ask what you want to see my daughter about? I mean, if it's about her health . . .'

'No, it's not about her health. Other than her memory, she seems to have recovered remarkably. No, it's just that she mentioned something the other day that may just have a bearing on something else that I'm looking into just now.'

'And what might that be, Doctor?' Margaret Blair enquired, somewhat suspiciously.

'Oh, nothing very important,' he parried 'just something she said about a girlfriend of hers, that's all.'

Detecting Stride's reticence, she commented, 'This girl is another patient of yours, no doubt. Well, I won't ask any more. I know all about you doctors and your Hippocritic oaths, you know.'

She pointed upstairs, then shouted, 'Bett, Dr Stride is on his way up now.'

Acting immediately on her invitation, Stride made his way past her to the staircase.

As Sue Pike rounded the bend in her Mini, she saw the pulsing lights of at least two police cars that were pulled off the road two hundred yards ahead of her. She braked and changed into third. But it wasn't until she was only fifty feet or so from them that she saw the skid marks on the road, the broken fencing and then, way across in a field, upside down, the ghostly white shape of what had once been a forty-five-thousand-pound car.

Once past the police cars, she pulled the Mini into the nearest gateway, parked and ran back to the scene. But a police patrolman blocked her path.

'Sorry, Miss. I must ask you to move on.'

She reached into her bag for her press pass and flashed it at him.

'*Hallowes Gazette*. Sue Pike.'

He took it from her and compared her face with the stiff and unnatural passport style photograph.

'All right, Miss Pike, but I must ask you not to go past the broken fence for the moment. We are still examining both the car and its wheel tracks.'

She put away her pass and took out her notebook.

'Can you tell me whose car it is?'

'Yes. It's a Mr George Craven's.'

He heard her sudden intake of breath.

'You know him?'

'Er . . . I know of him, if he's that property developer in Hallowes.'

'Yes, he is. Or sorry, was, Miss. You see, Mr Craven was already dead when we arrived.'

She closed her eyes and held on to the patrolman's arm to steady herself.

'You all right, Miss?'

She nodded and after a moment or two, let go of his arm.

'Crushed by the car?' she asked in a voice now betraying her fears.

'No, Miss. Not so it would seem. There was hardly a mark on him when we got him out.'

She looked back down at the mangled and deformed shape of the vehicle.

'But the car is almost unrecognisable.'

'Yes, does seem strange. But you see, none of us have seen a crash like this before. Not with a car fitted with an air bag, we haven't. That's what must have cushioned the impact.'

She looked up at him. 'Air bag?'

'Yes, Miss. It was fitted with one of those air bag things that are supposed to inflate in a crash. Only before she was taken away in the ambulance, the lady who was with Mr Craven, his wife, I believe, told one of my colleagues that the air bag came out while they were just going along, like. For no reason, it would seem. Though, delirious as she was, the poor lady claimed the car phone must have set it off. Seems he was using it when it all happened.'

Sue Pike snapped her notebook shut. 'Oh my God, Constable, are you sure that's what the lady said?'

'Well, as I say, she was a bit incoherent. Hysterical really. So it was a bit difficult to make head or tail of it all, but . . .'

'Is she badly hurt?' she cut in.

'Not according to the ambulance men. Mainly shock, it would seem. And no wonder, turning over and over like that, even with a strong car like that.'

'Which hospital has she been taken to?'

'The nearest. Hallowes. Now if you get hold of a doctor there, he will no doubt be able to tell you far more than we can.'

'Thanks.' Sue made to go, but suddenly turned back. 'By the way, you said there was hardly a mark on Mr Craven. Then what actually killed him?'

He held up his hands. 'None of us rightly know, Miss. Although one of the ambulance lads hazarded a guess that the air bag exploding like that might have done it.'

'Done what?'

He cleared his throat. 'Well, Miss, given him a heart attack, like. After all, air bags aren't given to exploding out in the normal way of things, now are they?'

Mary Stride looked at her watch, as she heard the deep throated thrum of the V8 Bristol, as it pulled into the drive. She was at the door before her husband could insert his key in the lock.

'Darling, Sue Pike has just phoned.'

He stopped taking off his raincoat, as he saw the fear and anxiety in his wife's expression.

'Mary, what's happened? What was Sue ringing about? I've only just seen her in the surgery.'

Instead of replying right away, she took off his raincoat and led him into the sitting-room.

'You had better sit down, John, whilst I give you a stiff drink.'

But he remained standing and grabbed her arm. 'Mary, for God's sake, just tell me what's happened.'

She looked at him. 'It's Craven. He's dead. Sue Pike had just come back from the scene of the accident.'

'Accident? What accident?'

She sank into a chair. 'Craven and his wife were apparently out together in his car . . .'

He snapped his fingers together. 'So that's why I could

get no reply when I phoned him tonight. I tried four times. Sorry, go on.'

'From what Sue could glean from the police at the scene of the crash – the car went off the road and overturned umpteen times – it appears that that safety device plusher models sometimes have . . .'

'An air bag?'

She nodded. 'It seems to have blown up for some obscure reason, all on its own, right out of the blue.'

He frowned. 'And they think that's the cause of the crash?'

'It seems so, from what she says. But Sue's not so sure.'

His wife looked away and Stride instantly went over to her.

'Come on, Mary. What did she say? Don't be afraid to tell me.'

She suddenly put her arms around her husband's waist. 'Oh God, John, I'm scared. So very scared.'

He knelt down beside her and took her hands in his.

'I know, my darling. And so am I. But we have got to be brave somehow, and face up to what is happening. Only then will we even start to be able to understand it, let alone find a way of . . .' His voice died away, as he took his wife's head in his hands and gently kissed her on the forehead. After a while, he said softly, 'Tell me what Sue said.'

Hesitantly, she began. 'You see, George Craven was not alone in the car. Annabel was with him.'

'She killed too?'

Mary shook her head. 'No. Hardly hurt, apparently.'

'Like Bettina,' he whispered, almost to himself.

His wife went on, 'It's what Annabel is reported as saying, as she was being taken away in the ambulance, that Sue thought we ought to know right away.'

He forced the words out. 'Go on, Mary, tell me what Annabel said.'

She buried her head against his chest. 'She said . . .

she said . . . oh God . . . she said the car phone had set the air bag off.'

Stride stopped half-way up the staircase. 'But surely he will be asleep by now?'

She sighed. 'Probably. But I didn't want to ask him without you there. I'm sorry, John. But I wasn't to know you'd be so very late home tonight.'

He took her hand. 'No, that's fine, darling. Don't worry. If he's gone to sleep, we'll leave it until the morning.'

'But the way Enid Drench described things, it might be so very important.'

'Look, if we go and wake him, it could well frighten him into silence. After all, he obviously hasn't felt able to tell us before, so the timing has to be right for us to coax whatever it is out of him now.'

'But there's so much else you plan to do tomorrow. See Sue. Then the Inspector. Then Meek. Then God knows what else, depending on what you manage to get out of them. And time is running out, John. Fast. I can feel it. So can you.'

He squeezed her hand. 'Well, it's my day off tomorrow. But there's one thing I can do tonight, whether Mark's asleep or not.'

He turned and mounted the rest of the stairs, his wife following close on his heels.

'What's that, John? You must tell me.'

'I will,' he whispered, 'once I've checked that what I remember is right.'

He stopped outside Mark's door and listened. But there was no sound. Very carefully, he pressed down the handle on the door and opened it just sufficiently to let enough of the landing light in for him to see the walls of his son's bedroom.

'What are you looking for, John?' Mary whispered.

He went half into the room, then pointed at the large poster on the far wall.

'That,' he breathed. 'It's as I remembered.'

'The poster?' she frowned.

She peered at it through the dim light and then, in a flash, understood.

'You mean, what Mark said about lying there in the earth . . . ?'

He nodded. '. . . was somehow like lying in bed, looking up at the poster on his wall.'

She went further into the room and now stared up at the poster.

'The tank . . . the stars . . . my God, it's just like . . .'

He put his finger to his lips, as he saw their son stirring in the bed. Only when Mark was still again, did he whisper back, 'I know. Just like Bettina reaffirmed tonight. You only need the gunfire and explosions and you have her friend's nightmare that day on Bifton Sands.'

Bobby Quick put down his coffee cup as he heard the knock on his door.

'That you, Homer?' he shouted, without getting up from his lavish room-service breakfast.

'Right, Bobby. Am I too early?'

Muttering his annoyance at Friend's arrival in mid ham and eggs, Quick put aside his napkin, got up and unlocked the hotel door.

'You're early,' he snapped, letting his aide in. Homer consulted his oversized and overgilded watch. 'Only three minutes, Bobby. And we've a mountain to get through today.'

Quick prodded his rotund colleague in the stomach. 'Correction, Friend. *You* have got a mountain to get through today.' He pointed to himself, as he returned to sit at the breakfast table. 'Now *I'm* ahead of *my* game. Finished writing my address last night and I plan me a spot of relaxing today. Get my mind in a tranquil and contemplative state, so that I'm good and rested and on a spiritual high, as you might say, for the rigours of the morrow.' He plunged a fork into a thick slice of ham and waved it in front of his aide.

'Right now, as you can see, Homer, I'm taking on a little physical fuel, so that I have the stamina to put up with those who have about as much idea of tactful timing as the Japanese at Pearl Harbour.'

The beads of sweat on Homer Friend's forehead – no one could remember ever seeing him without them – doubled in number and he turned back towards the door.

'I'll come back when you've finished . . .' he began, but Quick cut him off.

'You will come back right now. The damage is done.'

He plunged another forkful of ham into a fried egg yolk and lifted it dripping into his mouth. Between hefty chews, that betrayed the falseness of his teeth by their clicking, he went on. 'You weren't, by any chance, going to tell me you have arranged some other damn fool engagement for me today, were you? Lunch with the tinpot Mayor of this crummy place is hardly going to be uplifting. Let alone that . . . what did he call it? . . . 'parishional party' of the very Reverend and almighty boring Meek, this evening.'

'Parish get together,' Friend offered hesitantly. 'I don't think it's a party. Just a chance for his flock to . . .'

'Go baa . . a . . a . . a,' Quick guffawed and almost choked on the last of his ham and eggs.

His aide smiled weakly. 'Yes, well, Bobby, no . . .'

Quick wiped his mouth with his napkin and pushed his chair back from the table. 'Homer,' he cut in once more, 'nobody but a totally uneducated moron begins a statement, "Yes, well, Bobby, no". For everyone's sake, can't you speak decipherable English?'

Friend mopped his brown. 'All I was going to say was that, no, I haven't laid on any more engagements for you today.'

'What about the media? Made sure they'll be there, when I'm with the Mayor?'

'Right, Bobby.'

'What about when I'm with Meek and his gang?'

Friend cleared his throat. 'Well, the Reverend Meek made a special point to me about not turning what he calls a "quiet get together" into a big thing. I think we ought to . . . er . . . respect his wishes. You know, we don't want to offend anybody right at the start of our tour.'

Quick muttered under his breath, then looked up. 'Hadn't you better get on, Homer, if you've got such a busy day? By the way, have the boys got the sound system working properly now? Yesterday you couldn't hear a damn thing from the back of the field.'

'Yes. It's almost fixed now,' Friend lied. For one thing he didn't dare confess was that their one hundred thousand dollar sound engineer – who just happened to be Homer's cousin – was still having difficulty eliminating curious and unidentifiable interference in the relay of the sound.

'Okay. But what about the projection on those big screens? Can't you get it any crisper? Faint and fuzzy images are hardly going to wow even the dear, unsophisticated people of Hallowes.'

'That's because you saw it in daylight yesterday, Bobby,' Homer said quickly. 'They all say, when it's dark, it'll come across just fine.'

'It'd better,' Quick retorted. 'Now one last thing. What about the weather? What do those Met boys say?'

It was the question Homer Friend had been dreading.

'Er . . . well, they say it'll be . . . er . . . a mite cool, but winds only force three or thereabouts.'

Quick rose irritably from his chair. 'Quit stalling, Homer. You know what I'm getting at. Is Hallowes going to be blessed with one of its crazy storms again, or are we going to be given some divine exception to the rule?'

Homer hesitated. 'Well, it's like this. They are not actually forecasting any storms, but they say they can't absolutely rule them out in this area of the South West.

Seems they've been bubbling up recently with little notice.'

Quick threw up his hands. 'That's all we need. Thunder, lightning and a downpour to add to lousy sound and fuzzy film.'

'All we can do is pray that, if they come at all, they happen after ten o'clock. Doesn't matter then. Except for those going home or packing up.'

'Let us pray, indeed,' the evangelist observed dryly. 'That all, Homer? Because if it is, I have one or two calls to make before I settle down to running through my address again.'

'When you're through, ring down and my secretary will type it for you and make some copies. Then I'll come back and put in a few cues for the sound and lighting guys.'

'Doesn't need any cues,' Quick observed sharply. 'I intend to deliver it without any gimmicks at all. Just arrange for a single spotlight to kinda carve my lone figure out in light against the blackness of all the rest.'

'Yeh. I can just see it,' Friend enthused. 'That's great, Bobby. You alone, the light in the darkness, the light they must follow to find the love of our Lord. That's a heap more dramatic than the way we usually open, in a blaze of lights and the swelling sound of a hundred organs. What inspired you, Bobby, to think of changing it?'

Quick strode over to the window and looked out at the town of Hallowes.

'Homer,' he began in his deepest and 'most sincere' of his many theatrical modes of delivery, 'the little people in this town are sorely troubled at this pregnant point in time. Many, indeed, confess quite openly to being frightened. Of what, they really know not. Maybe it's just of themselves. Of their sins. Their commissions. Their omissions. Their lies and deceits; deceptions and half truths. Over the years, I detect, their guilt has built up in their souls, until they cry out for some catharsis to wash their souls clean. I see it here, as I have witnessed it so often back home in California. In their guilt and agony of self doubt, they flail around to try to find some external source of their unease. Something other than themselves, that they can blame for their distress.'

Quick turned back from the window and deliberately stood so that his strong profile was silhouetted against the morning light.

'Some imagine, poor misguided souls, that they have found it in the vagaries of the weather. In the storm and thunder. In the zigzag flash of lightning. Others, equally lost, condemn the advances of science. In Hallowes, it happens to be the newly installed telecommunication system and they imagine that the telephone has somehow become the instrument of evil. But when you probe, you discover that all the so-called phantom calls are only conveying what has been said already. Said rashly, perhaps. Said wrongly. Said maliciously. Said deceitfully. Said lustfully. Said wickedly.'

He wagged his finger towards Friend. 'But said, all the same. Spoken down the line in the hearing of our great Saviour, Jesus Christ. And my guess is, Homer Friend, that Hallowes, right now, is pleading for a way for its sins to come out in the open. To be aired and atoned for before that dreaded Judgement Day, which we all know must come and which only the truly righteous anticipate with a calm and benign heart.'

Quick paused. But Friend knew that were he to interrupt what had clearly become a rehearsal of part of the rally speech, it would be at considerable personal peril.

'So,' Quick resumed, 'to my dear friends in Hallowes, I will say very quietly and very simply, "Come to me. Come to me now. Let me show the Light. The one and only true Light in this dark and frightening world." ' He suddenly pointed at his aide. 'Now hear this, Homer. When I come to that sentence, that is the only place I want a lighting cue.'

'Okay, Bobby. You're still in the single spotlight,

right? Now what do you want to happen?'

Quick sat down at the table and picked up his coffee spoon. 'Imagine that's me in the spotlight.' He pushed back the linen cloth and inserted the spoon in the gap between two of the oak boards that formed the top of the old table.

'Okay. Got you. The spoon's you, Bobby,' the aide rushed to observe.

'So . . .' Quick reached across for a fork and inserted it in the next gap in the boards in a direct line behind the spoon. '. . . the fork's our No. One Cross.'

'No. One Cross. Fifty Foot high. Gold and enamel. Filigree or plain?'

Quick glowered. 'Plain, of course. This is Britain, not Vegas.'

'Right. No. One Cross. Fifty foot. Gold and enamel. Plain. Now, with or without Christ figure?'

Quick thought for a minute. 'Without, I think. After all, I'm there.' Then he quickly added, 'In the spotlight, I mean. Don't want to confuse them. Anyway, we're using the Christ figure in the finale. Right?'

'Right again.' Friend pointed back to the table. 'So the spoon is you. The fork's the Cross. Now what do you want done?'

'When I say that line, I want my light to be slightly dimmed. Remember my exact words, Homer. I said slightly.'

'Got it.'

'Then I want another spotlight to catch the Cross at its tip, then gradually grow to spotlight the whole Cross.'

'Right. So then there's the two of you.' Countless more beads sprang out on his forehead. 'Sorry, Bobby, I mean you and it. I mean you and the . . .'

'I know what you mean, you dummy. So you can get all that arranged?'

'Yeh. Sure. Simple. No problems that I can see. Instead of our usual opening, right?'

Quick waved his arm impatiently. 'So get going. I told you I've got some things to do.'

Homer Friend made for the door, then suddenly turned. 'Sure you need the number one size?' he asked nervously.

'Sure I'm sure. Why? Afraid if there's a storm, a high wind will blow it down?' he scoffed.

'No, no, no, it's not that, Bobby. It'll be secured strongly enough for a tornado. Remember that time in Kansas . . . ?'

'Quit the reminiscing. What's your worry?'

'Well,' Homer cleared his throat, 'you see I've just remembered about the pylons in the field. Do you remember yesterday, I pointed out how the wires tend to sag between the poles? I actually pointed it out to that Inspector guy – what's his name? Dudkin, that's right – well, I said to him something like that just wouldn't be allowed back home. Wires sagging that low. Nossir. And he just laughed.'

Quick glowered at him. 'Which is more than I'm doing right now, Homer. I remember those wires and you're not going to tell me they're only fifty foot from the ground. Why, they must be close on a hundred.'

Homer Friend held up a tentative finger. 'Remember the Cross has a base and then there's the stage.'

'Okay. So the Cross, base and stage will still give us over thirty foot clearance. So what are you bleating about?'

'Well, okay, Bobby. You could well be right. But I was thinking more of them spoiling the image of the Cross. You know, the spotlight can't help picking them up.'

The evangelist slammed his fist down on the table and the spoon fell down, but the fork remained standing.

'That's your problem, Friend. That's what I pay you for. Now for the last time, get out of here and give me some peace.'

The Reverend Meek at last looked up from his blue

hands. 'Dr Strike, I must admit that what you and Miss Pike are putting forward, well, it simply amazes and confounds me.'

'I'm not really surprised, Reverend,' Stride admitted. 'The whole concept amazes and confounds us, too.'

Meek shook his head. 'No, you haven't quite understood me, Doctor. What I mean to say, I suppose, is that your *believing* such a wild hypothesis to be sustainable amazes me. You, a man of science, putting any credence in . . . I have to say it, I'm sorry . . . the supernatural.'

Stride got up from his chair, impatient at the vicar's reaction.

'Reverend, don't you do exactly the same? Every day of your life?'

Meek looked most affronted. 'Do what, Doctor? Really . . .'

'Believe in the supernatural? Isn't religion supernatural? Isn't your God a super being, over and above our natural experience, our natural world? "Beyond our humble understanding" is the quote I remember from my churchgoing childhood days.'

Meek fidgeted in his chair, like a schoolboy caught out by his teacher.

'Well, really, Doctor, you may see some similarity, but oh, no, we're talking different languages here.'

Stride came over to him. 'Look, Reverend , don't let's waste time getting into some semantic war. We didn't come here to try to convince you that we are right in our theory. Only to enlist your help.'

Meek looked back at his now steepled fingers. 'Naturally, I am only too willing to give any help I can to anybody, Dr Stride. But really, you've picked a most unfortunate day to come round. I told you on the phone how hectic today is for me, with all the final preparations for the big rally tomorrow. The choir rehearsals. The final seating arrangements for the infirm and disabled amongst my parishioners. Their transport to the rally field. Oh dear, oh dear, that reminds me. I've forgotten to ring Thomas's about adding an extra coach. Then I have the great man himself coming round this evening to meet some of my flock. Now, if you came round the day after the rally . . .'

Stride looked across at Sue Pike, who raised her eyebrows in desperation. 'Okay, okay,' he cut in. 'I've already had that story once today, Vicar. From the police. They too don't want to know about anything right now but the preparations for this damned rally.'

He stopped as he saw the look of shock on Meek's face.

'I'm sorry, Vicar. I shouldn't have used the word "damned", but I just can't believe that half of Hallowes is shutting its ears to anything right now but the coming of the Quick road show. Can't any of you see that the day after tomorrow may be . . .'

He hesitated and Meek asked blandly, 'May be what, Doctor?'

Stride waved his hand dismissively. 'Oh, never mind. Don't let me waste any more of your valuable time, Vicar, in speculation. Let's get on to some facts. There are some things I and Miss Pike would like to check with you.'

Meek looked at his watch. 'Fire away, Doctor. I still have twenty minutes or so before I have to leave for the final choir practice.' He pointed to the chair in which Stride had been sitting. 'But please, do sit down. I'm afraid my nerves are none too good today and . . . er . . .' He watched as Stride resumed his seat, '. . . er . . . thank you, Doctor. Now what are these matters you would like to check out with me? But I had better first warn you that, though I was brought up around here,' he smiled thinly, 'I'm not quite as old as I probably look to you two, comparative youngsters. I was still only fifteen when the war ended.'

'That's fine. We understand,' Stride said quickly. 'So that would mean you were fourteen in 1944. And boys of that age must have been interested in all that was going on around Hallowes at that time.'

'Oh yes. It's terrible to confess it, but many of my

parishioners of a similar age to myself say that the war, with all its death and destruction, was still the most exciting period of their whole lives.'

'So the presence of the American military in and around Hallowes must have caused great interest and excitement . . .'

'. . . and resentment too, I'm afraid. You've no doubt heard the phrase, "oversexed, overpaid and over here".'

Stride nodded and raced on, 'Two of their main encampments were in Starlings Meadow and Widow's Field, I'm told.'

'That's correct. But a lot of the officers and senior NCO's were billeted in the town and around the neighbouring villages, like Staverton, Dartington and so on. And they had another large encampment the other side of Hallowes. Now this was . . .'

'No, it's just Starlings Meadow and Widow's Field we're interested in right now,' Sue Pike observed, to prevent the Vicar from another digression.

'Ah, well, so be it. Yes, I remember, as a boy, the rows of Nissen huts around the edge of Starlings Meadow. And I gather they must have had a parade ground there. Oh and a baseball pitch or some such. We used to hear their shouts when they played.'

'And Widow's Field? What was there? I've been told that by 1944, it had become mainly an ammunition dump.'

'Yes, as I recall, that's right. In the run-up to D-Day, that would make it from around January '44, they tightened the security a lot round Widow's Field. There were big notices everywhere warning people to keep their distance, even from the wire. I vividly remember the perimeter was patrolled by burly military policemen with fierce-looking dogs. We certainly did not venture very near with those around.' He rubbed one set of blue fingers against the other, as if to improve their obviously poor circulation.

'Mind you, come to think of it, somewhere around

that time they also tightened security around the Starlings Meadow encampment too. And they kept security tight on both sites until well after the war. Right up, in fact, until they finally closed the camps around 1949.'

Meek noticed Stride shooting a glance at the reporter.

'Oh, come now, Dr Stride, I saw that look of yours. Now what I've just said about security changing at the Starlings Meadow site too, does not indicate in the slightest way that the military were trying to hide anything of the terrible nature you described when propounding your wild theory this morning. No, it was quite natural at such a time when secrecy was paramount in case the Germans discovered the extent of our preparations, let alone the timing for D-Day, that every possible precaution should be taken.'

'All right,' Stride conceded. 'I can see your point. Now let me go back to Widow's Field. Weren't the people in Hallowes a little disturbed at having what would have been such a very large ammunition dump quite so near the town?'

The Vicar smiled. 'Oh yes. I remember quite a lot of talk about that at the time. The Mayor even had a long meeting with the camp commander about it. It was his reassurance that finally calmed the town down.'

'Which was?' Sue Pike queried.

'That only part of Widow's Field was actually used for shells and ammunition storage. Thus even if the whole thing blew up, the town of Hallowes would be most unlikely to suffer to any degree.'

Stride thought for a moment. 'So what were they using the rest of Widow's Field for?'

The Reverend Meek glanced at his watch, clearly irritated by Stride's continuing insinuations.

'Now how could I know, Dr Stride? Or any of us in Hallowes? If you had been around in those days, you'd have heard the slogan "Careless Talk Costs Lives". People just did not query what the military did. They just accepted everything as being in the country's best interest to win the war.'

He pointed a finger. 'But you can be certain they did not put the rest of the land to the use you and Miss Pike have conjured up out of the blue.'

'It's not out of the blue, Reverend,' Sue pointed out sharply, now as angry as Stride at the Vicar's refusal even to consider their reasoning. All because it dealt with concepts that his religious training and calling had obviously excommunicated from his imagination, and thus from the realms of the possible.

'Surely we have detailed enough evidence this morning to show you this is no wild and woolly idea that we've pulled out of the air?'

Meek leaned forward in his chair. 'My dear Miss Pike, I don't wish to sound rude. But this so called evidence you quote. Really, looked at in the cold light of day, it doesn't amount to more than an earnest and well-meant wish by both of you to try and make some sense of a lot of, ah yes, disturbing but nevertheless disconnected phenomena.' He lowered his voice. 'Some of which, indeed, like the deaths of poor Mr Drench and now Mr Craven, can in your own admission be explained readily without recourse to the fanciful or supernatural.'

'But my son's experiences,' Stride protested, 'the voices and murmurings he now admits to hearing, the tanks he saw, the marks on his hands and feet . . . ?'

Meek held up a hand. 'I can readily understand your deep concern about your son's experiences that terrible night in Widow's Field, but you should not react . . . well . . . quite so, er, hysterically . . . I'm sorry to have to use such a word to a man like yourself, Dr Stride. But to try to represent to me that your son, Mark, may bear the marks from the cross, when perhaps all that may have caused them was shock and his own hysteria that night.'

Seeing Stride about to protest, he quickly went on, 'Now don't get upset, please. Just let me tell you that over the years I have seen what shock and resultant hysteria can produce, amongst my own congregations.

Indeed, a poor lady, alas long dead, once stood under a tree to protect herself when caught in a storm and lightning stuck the tree. She was found unconscious amongst the fallen limbs. The next morning, I was called in by her husband, as he imagined the marks on her hands and feet might be stigmata. But the best medical opinion in the town at that time, Dr Saunders, alas now dead himself, pronounced the seeming scars as just the product of intense shock at her close call with death.'

'She was a religious woman? Correct?' Sue Pike immediately asked.

'Yes, indeed. But why . . . ?'

Stride picked up the reporter's thinking. 'The point, Vicar, is that your parishioner must have heard of stigmata and thus may well have caused them or somehow willed them to appear on her body. But we haven't brought up Mark in any religion. Mary and I are agnostics, so he's never heard of such a phenomenon as stigmata.'

'Besides,' Sue Pike went on, 'whatever actually happened to Mark, there's still all the rest that keeps pointing to the Americans in Hallowes. There's the Tully connection through his grandfather. The Health Farm shop lady's father – the undertaker. Don't you think it somewhat strange that he came into all that money during the war? Then there's Rickett and his father being had up for stealing from some GI. There are the tanks with the stars on them. It's not only Mark who saw them. But Bettina Blair's friend, remember, on Bifton Sands? And what about the phone call last night? We both heard it. The sounds of waves. Gun fire. Shouts. Screams. Explosions.'

She got up from her chair. 'It all fits, can't you see? Dr Stride and I are not hysterical idiots. We're neither of us the kind to let our imaginations run away with us. We've just done the best we can to make some sense out of all the strange and horrifying things that seem to be happening around Hallowes right now. And the conclusion we've come to – which we both feel in our very bones must be the right one – is that something terrible happened during the war that no one knows about. Or, correction, that no one cares to remember or confess to. And that something terrible must somehow be connected with the Americans who were encamped in Starlings Meadow and Widow's Field. Now what that something terrible was, at this stage, if you'll pardon the expression, Vicar, God only knows. Our guess that it might have something to do with the Americans trying to minimise the number of deaths inflicted on the Normandy beaches by bringing some bodies back to Devon, is just that. A guess. I have rung the American Embassy four times this morning before we came over to you. And I asked them about the war and Hallowes and Bifton Sands. But they kept putting me through to yet another department and yet another person who couldn't comment or wouldn't help. So my next move is to ring the States. Lord knows who, at this stage. Maybe even the Pentagon. Or perhaps, it would be better to alert the media – the *New York Times* or the *Washington Post*. Whichever way, Vicar, Dr Stride and I aren't going to give up just because you and the police and, no doubt, ninety-nine per cent of the people even in a green and gullible place like Hallowes won't allow their minds to stretch to . . . to . . .'

She ran out of breath and the Vicar stepped in the breach, his voice betraying both his impatience and his disbelief.

'. . . calls from the dead, Miss Pike. That's what, in reality, you are asking us all to believe, now isn't it?'

Chapter Nineteen

She reached forward to touch him, her long, scarlet-tipped fingers caressing the dark hairs on the back of his hand.

'You'll keep your promise, won't you?' she whispered.

He nodded. 'Of course, darling. If I say I'll be in New York in under a week, then that's where I'll be.' His dark eyes flitted nervously around the departure lounge.

'What's the matter, Ahmed?'

He turned back to her. 'Oh, I don't know,' he lied. 'I just don't like airports, I guess. Especially when they're crowded like this. You'd think London would have built an additional terminal to cope with it all by this time.' He squeezed her hand reassuringly.

'You know us British,' she blushed. 'We're a little backward sometimes.'

'You, Rachel, are certainly not that.' He flashed the broad smile that his organisation had found so effective over the years in co-opting young female recruits to their cause and in lulling others to their true purpose.

'I love you, Ahmed.' She leaned forward across the table and kissed him lightly on the mouth. But to her disappointment, he made no effort to respond. He could not tell her that her gesture had suddenly sparked the very first feeling of guilt he had experienced during his very deliberate relationship with her over the last months. And also reminded him of how very true his last comment to her had been. For the seemingly reticent and quiet young Jewess had proved quite the opposite, once he had managed to get her into bed. Memories of their abandoned and frequent lovemaking and insidious, naked images of her slim and sinuous body, her small but wide set breasts and never ending legs pervaded his mind. A body that was so soon to be . . .

'What are you thinking about, Ahmed?'

He shook his head, not in answer to her question as she imagined, but to clear his brain of the last terrible vision.

'Oh, nothing.' He sighed and looked across at her. She blushed once more, the blush, as always, heightening the dramatic appeal of her beauty.

Pushing her long, black hair back from her eyes, she said, 'I'll be counting the days until you come. Each one will seem like a year.'

Suddenly, for the very first time in his ten years with the group, he felt the urge to grab the hand of his victim and confess. But almost as soon as the impulse had struck, it had vanished again, as the hard professional training of his youth proved its worth.

'You'll find things will go much quicker than you imagine,' he said quickly. 'It will all be over in no time.'

She frowned. 'Why do you say that? You know how much I love you. Every moment will seem to last for ever.' She stopped abruptly, then asked, 'Why? Won't time seem a bit endless to you, without me?'

'Of course. Of course it will.' He pushed his cup of coffee to one side and pointed to her Campari and soda. 'You ought to drink up now, Rachel. They'll be calling the flight any minute.'

She closed her eyes. 'Oh God, will they? If I pray, do you think they will cancel it for me?'

'You'd have to go sometime soon,' he said softly. 'Your parents have been expecting you to join them for weeks. I don't want them to think ill of me, before we've had a chance to meet. After all, I'm not exactly the first choice for a good Jewish girl, now am I?'

She tried to smile, as tears started to well in her eyes. 'They'll understand,' she said, more in hope than in expectation. 'One day, surely, all this tragic enmity between Arab and Jew must die, mustn't it?'

He looked away. 'One day,' he repeated, 'one day . . .' He rose from the table as the cold and anonymous voice of the airport announcer called the TransAmerican flight 806 to New York. 'Got your things?' He pointed down to her TransAm bag and two small parcels that he knew contained presents that her parents would never actually receive.

She got up and hugged him to her. 'I've got everything, except what I want the most. You.' Then reaching down for her packages, she remarked, 'I hope I don't have any trouble with US customs about the things for mother and father.'

'You won't,' he said, looking out across the tarmac to the TransAmerican Boeing 747, where he could just see ground staff loading the last of the passenger luggage containers.

'It's not these I'm worried about,' she added. 'It's the one you had packed for me. In my suitcase. You know, that expensive television and cassette recorder I bought cheaply from your friend.'

'I know,' he said, lowering his voice, 'but if I had to make a guess right now, Rachel, I'd say they'll never even get round to looking at it.'

'Why do you have to go at all?'

Stride turned back from the window and looked at his wife.

'You know why, Mary,' he said quietly.

She came up and put her arms round him. 'I don't know. All I know is what you *say*. That you think that . . . something . . . might happen at the rally.' She looked up at him, pain and fear showing in her eyes. 'But that's no reason you should be there, John. Don't you see? It's quite the opposite. If something awful happens there tonight, God, I don't want you involved. Besides, if you are right, whatever will be, will be, whether you're there or not.'

He hugged her to him and longed to be able to concede and say, 'Yes, my darling, I'll stay. Stay with you and Mark until this dreadful curse on Hallowes is finally lifted, the skies clear and all is at rest and peace once more.' But he knew he could not. Must not. Especially tonight. For ever since he had received that terrifying telephone call in his surgery, when he had been with Sue Pike, he had felt somehow drawn inexorably to Quick's rally, despite his own personal distaste for popular religious crusaders. It had become a magnet whose power he knew he could no more ignore than the ultimate beckoning finger of the Grim Reaper.

'I'll be all right, Mary. Please try not to worry. But I just know, somehow, I have to be there . . . I'm sorry.'

She pulled away from his arms. 'Hell, John, you're so bloody stubborn sometimes. But this time your stubbornness could be the d . . .' She stopped, as she realised the horrific implications of what she was saying, then went on, 'God, haven't you done enough already? You've warned the police that you think something might happen. And they more or less laughed in your face. You've warned Meek and the same thing happened. You had warning letters delivered to Quick and the Mayor, when they wouldn't even see you. And you've heard nothing back. I'll tell you this, John, for nothing. If the rally passes off without incident tonight, we're going to look like the biggest loonies in what is to many people an already pretty far-out town. And I suggest your partners in the practice will get most of your patients. Overnight.'

'I'd rather look a loony than keep my mouth shut,' he said firmly. He looked at his watch. 'I'd better get over there. Otherwise I'll never be able to park, let alone get a good vantage point . . .'

But his words were cut off by the dringing of the phone. Mary instantly grabbed his arm.

'I'd better answer it,' he sighed. 'Sometimes, I detest being a doctor.'

She followed him out into the hall and waited, with baited breath, as he picked up the receiver. The seconds before he reacted seemed like light years.

'Oh, it's you, Sue,' he said at last, with immense relief.

'Well, what did she say? Has she found out anything?'

Stride shook his head. 'No. Unfortunately. She said her visit to the Embassy was almost a complete waste of time. Apparently, she got passed from official to official, department to department and no one seemed able – or willing – to give her any information about anything to do with the American forces in Hallowes during the war. They referred her, however, to several books on the GIs in Britain and various war histories and so on, but the nearest she got to what we want was a pamphlet they'd produced to commemorate the forty-fifth anniversary of the actual D-Day landings. And she says she's read that cover to cover and there's not one single mention of even the American forces' presence in this part of the South Hams.'

'So a blank?' she sighed, but then remembered, 'But didn't you say Sue's verdict on her visit was "*almost* a complete waste of time"? What gave rise to the *almost*?'

'Just that the last person she was shunted on to was fairly high up in the US army. Due for retirement, she reckons, by his liver spots and white hair.'

'And what did she get out of him?'

'She's not quite sure. But she took it as a warning.'

'Warning?' Mary frowned.

'That's what she thinks. Apparently, he wouldn't really answer any of her questions. Just went on about "the war being now long over". And "it being time people stopped raking over the coals of such an old fire". That kind of thing. Then she says he commented as he saw her to the door that "things sometimes happen in war that are best forgotten, at least until all those involved at the time have passed from this earth". And that it was his recommendation that such a young and attractive girl should bother her head about the present momentous changes in the world and not bury herself in the darkness of the past, or words to that effect.'

Mary thought for a moment. 'Is that what prompted you to offer her the fare to get to Washington?'

He took her hand. 'You don't mind, do you? She has next to no money of her own, I know, and we can just about afford it.'

'Won't her editor raise Cain when he hears about her disappearing off across the Atlantic?'

'She says she has already rung him. And at last got him to agree purely on the promise that she'll bring him back a story that will make the *Hallowes Gazette* the envy of every national paper in the land.'

'And if her trip to Washington proves as unrewarding as her trip to Grosvenor Square?'

He grimaced. 'Then I'm afraid he says she's fired and unfortunately, his lack of confidence in her is shown by the fact that he adamantly refuses to dub up for her fare.'

'So when is she leaving?'

'She hopes to get a plane tonight. She tried to cheer me up by saying if it passes anywhere near this area on course for its Atlantic crossing, she'll wave down to us at the rally.'

Mary closed her eyes against the thought of the imminent event, as the evening's first roll of thunder rumbled its discontent among the Devon hills.

'Why, Doctor, I didn't realise you would be a Bobby Quick fan.'

The cheerful voice startled him as he was locking up his Bristol, in the vast area of rough grassland alongside the rally field, allocated for parking.

He looked round. 'Oh, Mrs Blair. I . . . er . . . just thought I'd come along and see what all the fuss is about.'

The couple, arm in arm, came over to him. 'Don't

know how we're all going to find our own cars,' Margaret Blair went on, 'when it's all over. There are only a few hundred here now, but we're over an hour early. There'll be thousands and thousands by the time the rally starts.'

She nudged her husband. 'Then how yer going to find your precious Cavalier, then, eh?'

'Should have numbered the ranks,' he grumbled, looking at Stride. 'Don't you think, Doctor?'

Strike mumbled a 'yes', but his mind was on slightly weightier problems than the typical omission of the Hallowes authorities to number the rows in the parking area.

'Looking forward to it, Doctor?' Mrs Blair beamed. 'Me and my hubby can't wait, can we, Walter? Bobby Quick is just what Hallowes needs right now, don't you agree?' She grinned self-consciously. 'He's just what the doctor ordered, as you might say, Doctor.'

'Yes, could be . . . now, if you don't mind, Mrs Blair . . .'

But she wasn't going to let Stride get away so easily. 'Where's Mrs Stride and young Mark?' she asked. 'You should have brought the whole family, you know. After all, things like this don't happen every day of the week. Now, our Bettina . . . well, we tried to persuade her to come, but she said she had a terrible headache. And well, seeing as how it's no time really since that terrible crash, it's no wonder . . .'

'No, I suppose not. I . . .'

'Here. I know what it is. Why you left them at home. You are here officially like, right, Doctor? On duty, as you might say. Silly me, of course you have to have medical people around when there's a huge crowd of people. Well, let's hope you lot are not needed.' She laughed. 'After all, this Bobby Quick's here to heal our wounds and cleanse our hearts – I heard him say that on telly – not cause us to have heart attacks in all the excitement or be trampled in any great rush.'

Her husband at last succeeded in getting her attention.

' 'Ere, Maggie, I don't think we should all hang around in the car park talking, otherwise we'll never get a good position.'

'Quite right,' Stride remarked with alacrity. 'Now if you'll excuse me, I'd better . . . get on with . . . er . . . why I came here.'

He thankfully watched them hurry away towards the rapidly filling rally field, at the far end of which was arranged a vast dais, decorated with massed banks of flowers and strewn with elaborate lights of every kind and intensity. At each end of the dais stood magnificent silver screens, that shimmered under their own individual spotlights.

To prevent any unauthorised invasion of the platform, countless four foot high crosses, in gold and silver and studded with coloured stones, stood side by side at its front edge. But provision was made, a third the way along from each end, for some of the crosses to swing aside to allow dignitaries to come up and meet the great evangelist, or rally converts to ascend to 'give themselves to Christ'.

When the Blairs had finally disappeared into the throng, Stride moved quickly, his plan being to take up a position near the platform, but well to the right, where he could see the large police communications van.

Even at this early hour there were ranks of people, at least a hundred deep, standing behind the seats reserved for the dignitaries and the disabled immediately in front of the dais. And Stride had completely forgotten the space that would be occupied by the television towers that stood at each side, their scaffolding, control boxes, cabling and monitor vans virtually dominating the area he had chosen for his vantage point.

As he negotiated round a coil of cabling, a voice shouted down from one of the towers, 'You from Spotlight West?'

He looked up and into the face of a red-haired and ruddy-faced TV technician, who was climbing down from the tower beside him.

'No. Sorry.' Then he added, as he saw a possible opportunity, 'No, I'm a doctor.'

The technician, now on the bottom rung of the ladder, looked at him hard, then said, 'Oh, sorry, Doc. I'm expecting a camera Johnnie. He's supposed to be on his way from Plymouth. One of our butter-fingered crew dropped some lenses. Always happens, doesn't it, on the big night.' He laughed. 'Sod's Law.'

'Right,' Stride smiled back. 'Sorry, I can't help you. But you might be able to help me, though.'

The technician frowned. 'How's that, then? Always one to lend a hand. If I can, that is.'

'Well, you see,' Stride lied, 'being a doctor, I really need to have a bit of a view of things, if I'm to spot anyone tonight who might need my help. So I was wondering if I could . . .'

He did not need to finish. 'You mean, you'd like to go up there?' He pointed to the top of the tower.

'Well, not all the way up. That would be in your crew's way, wouldn't it?'

The man scratched at his mat of red hair. 'Well, yeh, it might. But there's a little ledge . . .' He pointed to some planks just below the main platform. '. . . where we've put the camera boxes and that. I dare say no one will mind, seeing as how you're a doctor, if you sit yourself down on one of those.' He grinned. 'Always providing you stand up again, if we want anything out of them, that is.'

'Sure that'll be all right?'

'Yeh. Sure I'm sure. Got to help out a doctor now, haven't we?' He shepherded Stride towards the ladder. 'After all, never know when we'll need the help of guys like you ourselves.'

From such an elevated position, Stride now enjoyed a perfect view of not only the platform, but the crowd, almost the entire area of the field, and could well have seen some of the surrounding countryside, had it also been illuminated. As it was, he could just see the lights from the new telephone headquarters in Starlings Meadow and the tiny pin-prick of stars from houses on the outskirts of Hallowes. His only distraction was the never-ceasing talk and banter from the television crew above him. But even this, very soon, started to interest him, much to his surprise. It began when he heard one man remark, 'Look at that bloody lightning over Dartmoor. That's all we need.'

'Yeah, well,' another retorted with a chuckle, 'it may not be our only bloody problem. Heard a rumour earlier that some crank's been running around saying he reckons something weird and horrible is going to happen tonight.'

'Like your focus pulling!' the first guffawed.

'No, seriously, Pete. He's told the police. He's told the Mayor. He's tried to tell everybody. Something about, you know, the stories you hear about the Hallowes telephones.'

'Not surprised,' his colleague sniffed. 'I'll be glad to get out of Hallowes. Full of cranks it is. Never known such a place for panicking loonies. Why, it's so far-out alternative, it's almost on its way back.'

They both laughed, then the second added, 'You can say that again. Tell you a story. I was in a local pub last night, drowning my sorrows and got into conversation with a long haired bird in a kind of kaftan. Not my type, but her boobs looked a bit of all right. And you know what she said? Well, after about ten minutes of my chatting her up, she said that I came over as very tense. Me, tense? God, well, she claimed it was probably my job that was doing it and that she knew a great way to get me to relax.' He gave a dirty laugh. 'Well, I said I know a way too, but I'd listen to hers first. Well, she then said, I should try the Alexander Method. I said, what? And she repeated, the Alexander Method. So I asked, "What's that then? Where you get gang-banged by the whole of the joker's Ragtime Band?" '

But the crew's badinage was suddenly drowned by an explosive burst from the tannoy, as the thunderous sound of a hundred organs accompanied choir after choir on to the platform. And spotlights picked out the crosses that bordered the platform, one by one.

Stride looked at his watch. It was already ten past the hour that the evangelist had been due to make his entrance and even above the stridency and volume of the organ music, he could hear the restlessness in the vast crowd that was now filling and spilling out of the rally field below him.

Then suddenly, as if orchestrated – he discovered later that it had been, Quick rallies always started that way – a chant of 'Bobby Quick . . . Bobby Quick' rose amongst the gargantuan congregation. Rose, indeed, to such a fever pitch and intensity, that it almost drowned out the recorded tracks of the organs. It was not until the chant had been at its deafening peak for at least five minutes that all the lights on the platform were doused and a single spotlight shed a pool of light in front of the fifty-foot cross. The chant gradually died away to nothing and then, from the black behind the cross, emerged the lone, lean figure of the evangelist.

Even from his lofty position, Stride could sense the indecision amongst the crowd as to whether they should applaud and cheer, as was their desire, or reverently accept his coming in silence, as was their practice with preachers in their normal places of worship. However, after a few seconds, the decision was taken out of their hands, as the organ track died away, to be replaced by a stentorian voice, as if from Heaven which announced, 'Please kneel for Bobby Quick to lead us in the Lord's Prayer.'

And fifteen thousand people did as they were commanded, seeming totally to ignore the damp ground that played havoc with nylon stocking and knee of Sunday-best suit alike. When the multitude had recited the final 'Amen' and the few had regained their seats and the mass their feet, the same Heavenly Announcer proclaimed with timbreful sincerity that stifled any attempt at applause, 'Bobby Quick, our beloved soldier for Christ, now brings his healing to Hallowes in his first crusade through the great British Isles.'

Stride leaned forward as the lanky figure of the evangelist started his address, his arms spread high and wide, as if to enfold the whole of his audience within his embrace.

'Good and worthy people of Britain. Good and worthy people of this your beautiful South West. But especially, tonight, the good and worthy people of Hallowes.'

He stopped and lowered his arms and looked out across the hushed crowd, his own sudden silence now riveting their attention. After a calculated pause, he continued, 'Yes, you are, my friends. Good. Yes, you are, my friends. Worthy. Every man and woman in this world is born good and worthy. And with our Lord's great guidance and strength, we can rejoice all our lives and for ever more in the perfect happiness of our own worth, our own goodness. And there is no happiness greater on God's earth, my friends, than believing in our own selves. For only with that belief will any one of you . . .' Quick stretched forth his right arm towards the audience '. . . ever find a paradise on this earth, let alone a paradise in God's heaven.'

Quick paused and gazed out across the crowd. When he spoke again his voice was lower in tone and almost husky in its intimacy. 'Now don't imagine that I, Bobby Quick, a humble preacher from way across the water, have not heard of your troubles here in Hallowes, in my parish of California. Indeed, I have, my friends, believe me; for all man's troubles are my troubles. All man's cares and worries are my cares and worries. God's love knows no frontiers. No boundaries. No customs official can ever declare, "You can't bring God's love into this country or that country." No, sir, my love and care, the love and care of our Lord and Saviour know no bounds on this planet of ours. No limits. And are infinite and inexhaustible in their plenty.'

Quick placed his hands on his hips and surveyed his audience – a stance and gesture that reminded Stride of film footage he had often seen of Hitler addressing rallies of Nazi faithful.

Then the evangelist continued, the fire of his rhetoric now starting to enhance his transatlantic accent. 'No, my dear friends of Hallowes, I, Bobby Quick, have heard much of your troubles. Your worries. Your fears.' His voice rose. 'Yes, fears, my friends. Fears. Indeed, many of you have confessed even in the brief time I've stayed in your beautiful town, confessed quite openly that they are frightened. But of what, they really know not.'

As he broke off yet again, a loud crack of thunder filled the hiatus, as if on cue.

Quick's arm instantly pointed to the heavens. 'Is it of that? The flash of lightning? The roll of thunder? Oh yes, my friends, I've heard of your recent weather. And the savage anger of the storms that have lashed at your poor town, almost day after day. But I suspect it is not the storms of which you are really afraid. Or indeed, of the rash of inexplicable phenomena you believe these tempests may have created. No, dear people of Hallowes, I suspect you must look elsewhere for the origin of your fears. Much nearer home. Your home . . . you must look into your very selves.'

He raised an arm. 'For your fear may truly be of . . . yourself. Of your sins. Of your commissions, perhaps. Or of your omissions . . .'

Stride hardly heard the remainder of the evangelist's opening address, his eyes scanning the hills around Hallowes, as lightning zigzagged a course inexorably nearer to the rally field. Stride was starting to regret now that he was sitting on a metal box, high up on a steel tower, surrounded by enough high voltage cabling to burn him to a crisp, without any uncalled for help from the heavens above. It was not long before the lightning's electrical charges started to make themselves heard on the loudspeaker systems and Stride noticed that when the crackles occurred, Bobby Quick's expression somewhat deviated from that of the sublime evangelist with the key to solve all life's problems, major or minor. By the time his initial address had climaxed, his voice was sometimes drowned by the ensuant claps of thunder.

Stride's attention, however, soon returned wholly to the platform, as immediately upon the end of the evangelist's address, the spotlight on the preacher faded somewhat, as the giant cross at his back was highlighted by an even brighter arc. Simultaneously, the rally field was filled with the penetratingly shrill sound of a trumpet fanfare, and upon the giant screens at both ends of the platform appeared in red the words, 'BOBBY QUICK – SOLDIER FOR CHRIST'. The fanfare ended and the deep heavenly voice, that had first announced the evangelist, started the commentary to what was obviously intended to be an inspiring film account of Bobby Quick's life – from cradle to his present eminence in what the more scurrilous of journalists termed, 'the God Stakes'.

Stride adjusted his fastly-numbing backside on the hard camera case and settled back to what he imagined would be, perhaps, the most tedious and embarrassing part of the whole rally.

'Bobby Quick, our great soldier for Christ,' the voice rang out against the final rumblings of the last thunder. 'Bobby was born in the then modest backwater of Walnut Creek, situated not all that great distance from the hustle and bustle of the hilly city of San Francisco. His father had been a travelling shoe-salesman, who had met his mother, as Bobby always proudly describes, when acting as usher in the tiny church of St Bartholomew, where they both worshipped with their poor but hard working families . . .'

The film pedestrianly cut from sepia still to sepia still, depicting the subjects mentioned in the commentary, with little variation in pace, little inspiration in the layout or emphasis. Even the folksy music that backed the voice seemed to lack any real sense of rhythm or drama and seemed a pathetic let-down after the spirited, if raucous, fanfare of the film's introduction.

Stride tried to shut his eyes and ears to the banalities and sat with his head in his hands. But every now and again, a sentence or two would nevertheless come through.

'. . . delivered papers from six a.m. to eight-thirty every morning before he went to school, donating every cent he earned to the poor box in his modest church. For even then in Bobby Quick . . .' The voice and film droned on.

'. . . his teens, he had little time for the life-style of many of his high school pals, who idly cruised about town in their Model T jalopies or hung about bars, cinemas or dance halls. When Bobby Quick wasn't working late into the night to make his parents proud in his school examinations, he was doing his own style of cruising around town. Yes, sir, you bet. On a two wheeled bicycle. And he wasn't on the look out for girls to impress, oh no, not our Bobby Quick . . .'

Suddenly, lightning, with the tearing shriek of a billion arcing volts bleached out every other light on the rally field and thousands of throats gasped their horror and surprise. Instantly following, and virtually overhead, a thunderclap seemed to rock the very earth and heavens with its unleashed power. Stride held on to the nearest tube of scaffolding and it reverberated through his fingers.

Then, equally suddenly, all was silence and the rally field was as before, but to Stride's surprise, the voice delivering the film's commentary had changed. From the Olympian male to what sounded a very earth-bound female. But the screens, seeming oblivious of the track, continued to portray what were obviously yet more scenes from the evangelist's childhood.

'. . . Bobby, don't say that, lover,' the rather whining female pleaded. 'I couldn't not phone yer, you know that. Besides, who's going to hear us in that silly little town of Hallowes? Why, you told me it's only a one-horse place. Well, one horse-places have one-horse people with half-arsed minds . . .'.

Stride heard a murmur start in the crowd, as it began to realise what it might be hearing.

Then abruptly, they all heard a voice they recognised cut in, 'Get off the goddamned line. Right now, you hear? They've had enough trouble with telephones down here, without you putting us all at risk with your prattle about . . .'

While the screen now portrayed what was obviously a shot of a teenage Bobby Quick holding the hand of a young, demure and virginal looking girl of around the same age, the female voice on the soundtrack became anything but demure and virginal.

'It's not prattle, Bobby,' she pleaded huskily. 'It's real. I can hardly close my legs at night for thinking of our last time together. Why, how many times was it now? And gee, just how many places did you try it in? Now I bet with your wife, you don't . . .'

Suddenly, both screens went blank, but after a crackle from lightning flashing in the distance, the soundtrack continued on its own, but now with an almost hysterical male voice, that at first, because of the American accent, the crowd imagined to be still that of Bobby Quick.

'I've told you, damn it . . . it's not anything I'm doing . . . You should be up here in the cockpit . . . God, what the hell's happening now? I tell you I'm trying everything and she's still veering far too far south . . .' The voice now started screaming. 'She's going, God, she's going . . . I can't hold her . . . Feels as if the rudder's locked solid . . . now we're swinging west . . . Hell, it's like a magnet drawing the bloody plane. I've no control

. . .' Then the voice was drowned by a deafening explosion that suddenly was cut off as if by a knife.

Stride stood up and held on to the scaffolding, his whole body trembling with fear and anticipation. For he knew only too well that what he had forecast for that night was, in reality, happening. And what was worse, that what he had so far heard, might well be only the overture.

Without warning, all lights were doused across the length of the platform and the murmurs from the bemused audience grew into excited chatter. But in under fifteen seconds, the spotlights illuminating the ranks of the massed choirs were switched on. A rather harassed looking conductor appeared, obviously out of schedule and led the hundreds of voices into the singing of 'Oh God, our help in ages past, our hope for years to come'.

The cacophony from the crowd eased and a few joined in with the singing of the famous hymn. But just before the second verse, the air was rent, not by lightning, but by a series of thunderclaps that resounded around the rally field, seemingly unannounced by any electrical discharge from the storm clouds above.

Looking down, Stride saw many in the audience clap their hands to their ears and peer fearfully upwards. The fear in their eyes grew more wild as they, with Stride, suddenly started to realise that no storm that had ever vented its fury on this earth had ever sounded quite like this onslaught. Each thunderclap being a sharp and violent explosion on its own, with no trace of any rumbling or reverberating tail.

Suddenly the significance of the terrifying sounds and the complete absence of lightning struck Stride. His eyes were instantly drawn to the two giant screens, upon which vague shapes were now forming, through what looked like rolling mist or some kind of smoke screen.

He heard a voice above his scream out, 'Forget the

bloody choirs . . . focus on the screens, for God's sake.'

The conductor on stage was making violent attempts to keep the massed voices together for the rest of the hymn, but in vain, as one after another, members of the choir started to pick up the sense of shock and panic that was now spreading through their audience.

The explosions were deafening and all around; and a peculiar and disturbing odour was being carried by the gusts of wind that each one seemed to generate.

Stride kept his eyes riveted to the screens. But was now certain what dread armour would clothe the strange, ghostly images, as they emerged from the swirling fog and smoke.

They erupted on the screens like iron dragons belching fire to consume all that would stand in their way. Instantly the huge audience cowered down, screaming and shrieking in their frenzy of fear. Within seconds, Stride saw great panic-stricken groups turn their backs to the platform and try to climb and claw their way through those still too stunned to move.

Stride's first instinct was to descend from the tower to try to bring some calm, at least to a few, but knew his task was absurd and that he would undoubtedly end up being crushed to death by the growing stampede. He remained where he was, clutching on to the scaffolding which rocked with every deafening explosion.

The huge Sherman tanks, their guns belching fire, could now be seen clearly on both screens. Big white stars on their sides. Behind them crouched countless ranks of helmeted soldiers, guns at the ready. But their heads were not turned towards the tanks or the direction in which they were inexorably heading. Some looked upwards, others backwards, but all had shock and incomprehension written on their young faces.

Stride suddenly found himself hanging half off the scaffolding, as a massive explosion rocked the rally field. As he frantically tried to regain a foot-hold, he could see below him scores of figures climbing and clambering through the maze of high voltage cables and scaffold poles, in their mad rush to escape.

The instant Stride managed to swing himself back on to the planks that had been supporting him and the camera boxes, he looked back at the screens. Now they no longer depicted khaki tanks belching yellow tongues of flames, but khaki human beings, their uniforms and flesh torn asunder and their veins belching red blood and gore to seep into what looked like sand.

Then abruptly, the terrible images changed. On the left screen a close-up of a young man in American naval uniform, his face somehow strangely familiar. On the right screen the silhouette of a World War II destroyer off shore. The officer seemed to look at his watch, then bark an order, but it could not be heard over the now all pervading screams of those desperately trying to flee the rally field.

As Stride continued to watch, his hands now bleeding from clutching at the rust-rough scaffolding, spouts of red and yellow erupted from the destroyer's gun turrets. Instantly, yet again, the images changed. Back to what could now clearly be recognised as a beach. But a beach running with the blood of those who were being blown to smithereens by the destroyer's shelling. And now, even those in the Sherman tanks were not spared, as explosions lifted the mighty vehicles high into the sky and blew them apart, as if they were no more than matchwood. In the background, Stride saw a landing craft, its front loading ramp lowered, about to disgorge its troops on to the shore. But as the first khaki clad figures emerged, it too was struck by a shell and the whole air around was rent by soldiers' screams, as severed limbs seemed to fall like rain from the shattered darkness of the sky.

'Christ, al-fucking-mighty!'

Stride looked up to see the red-haired technician climbing down to him.

'You all right, mate?'

Stride nodded.

'Hell, that crank who said something would happen tonight wasn't so mad after all.' He pointed upwards. 'I'd better get back. We're all going spare up there. Only came to see how you were.'

Then suddenly, he pointed a trembling finger down towards the platform. Stride whipped his head round to look back at the screens. But, to his relief, they were both now blank and he realised that the explosions had also ceased.

'Not over there. Look by the big cross.'

Stride shifted his gaze to centre stage. And he instantly saw what had so transfixed the technician. The telegraph wires that spanned the field from pole to pole had inexplicably sagged to such an extent that they were now flicking the top of the cross with each gust of wind. At each flick, an electrical arc crackled and leapt between them, like some deadly, darting snake of light.

Then, as they watched in horror, the sagging wires seemed to weld themselves to the top of the cross. Instantly, with a searing scream, the arcing flashed along the wires from pole to pole, leaving each one now burning bright with light in the shape of the crosses of Calvary.

Before Stride and his companion had time to absorb the incredible phenomenon of what was now becoming legions of burning crosses leading far out of the rally area and down towards the town of Hallowes itself, a huge fireball materialised above them, glowing and spinning and streaking a fiery track across the dark and deathly sky towards . . .

'My God,' the technician screamed, 'what on earth . . . ?'

Stride closed his eyes and prayed, for now he suddenly understood the nature of the Last Act, that the whole of the rest of the terrifying drama had been but a just and long overdue preparation.

Chapter Twenty

'It's like . . . it was never here.'

Sue Pike turned away from the huge depression in the ground in which gangs of men were still working feverishly in the vain hope of finding bodies.

Stride put his arm round her shoulder. 'I know. They've been hard at it here ever since it happened. But besides minute pieces from the 747's fuselage, they've found nothing at all.'

She swallowed hard. 'Nothing? I mean . . . ?'

He shook his head. 'If you mean bodies, no. They seem to think both the people in the plane and those few still left in the Telephone Exchange must be . . . well . . . I suppose, vaporized.'

Sue looked back at the hundred and fifty foot long scar in the ground where the Telephone Exchange had stood, that appeared as if some giant foot had descended from the heavens to stamp its indelible impression upon Hallowes.

'Ground into the ground,' she whispered to herself, then looked up at Stride. 'Oh God, John, if only we'd been able to find out sooner.'

'Maybe it would have made little difference. All the evidence points to the fact that there was a bomb on that plane and, on the news, I heard that an Arab terrorist organisation has already claimed it was responsible. So maybe the wreckage would have come down somewhere, even if not here.'

'Maybe, nothing,' she retorted somewhat sharply. 'I've checked on what you told me you heard at Quick's rally about the pilot saying he couldn't hold the plane on course and that he felt it was being drawn like a magnet. Well, at Heathrow, those who should know maintain that the fuselage of that 747 could not have ended up so far west, especially as the prevailing winds were against it doing so. As they rightly point out, they've found large sections of both wings scattered over an area only some fifty miles off its course, not nearly two hundred.'

Stride looked at her and she suddenly realised what he had been saying.

'You mean . . . that there would probably have been casualties on the ground anywhere the fuselage hit?'

He nodded. 'So if we had found out sooner . . .'

'We wouldn't have necessarily saved lives.'

'I don't know. Oh God, I don't know.' Grimacing, he went on, 'There's only one thing we can be sure of now.'

'What's that?'

He pointed back to where the men were starting to bring in bulldozers to the crash site. 'That Starlings Meadow will never be misused again.'

Completing his thought, she went on quietly, 'But will for ever remain a memorial to the dead. Preserved to commemorate the two great tragedies in the twentieth-century history of Devon.'

'The three hundred and eighty who died in the plane crash . . .'

'. . . and the seven hundred and seventy Americans killed on Bifton Sands, when shells crashed upon their company . . .'

'. . . fired from their own supporting ships, one dreadful night of rehearsal for the D-Day landings.'

He stared at the deep red soil now being disturbed by the first of the excavators, then added fiercely, 'Fired on the order of one Lieutenant Franklin Stewart Quick, late and unlamented brother of Bobby Quick, the now hopefully disgraced evangelist, who, mistakenly, started the softening up bombardment one bloody and horrendous hour later than planned. Hell, Sue, how could he have lived with the knowledge that he had slaughtered his own troops in the very act of landing?'

She turned and put a finger to his lips. 'Please . . . don't say any more. Don't forget I'm still partly subject to the secrecy laws of the great US military machine, until they make their formal admission of what really happened that bloody May. They said they had to have time to notify those involved first to save them further suffering. That's why I agreed to their terms.'

'I know. Don't worry. I won't breathe a word until you say. Let's just pray, though, that they won't take for ever to atone for their heartless cover-up. It's been nearly fifty years too long already. Besides their own dead, the people of Hallowes deserve it too.'

Sue looked at him. 'Do you think that now the dead have at last succeeded in bringing their massacre at Bifton Sands to the attention of practically everyone in the world – let alone taking their revenge on families who had been involved – they'll . . . ?'

She paused and he stepped in. 'Leave Hallowes in peace?'

She nodded.

Stride glanced back at the scarred site. 'Maybe,' he replied quietly.

'You don't sound too convinced. Why, what more can those poor dead want from Hallowes?'

'I don't know,' he sighed and went on, 'It's just that you could also interpret the deaths of Tully, Rickett, Drench and Craven and what seems to be the punishment of people like his wife, Annabel Craven, and Penelope whatshername of the health food shop and . . .'

'. . . Sebastian Fanshawe,' she added quietly. 'By the way, we haven't discovered any link between him and those events in '44, have we?'

'Yes. I have now. I went over to see him yesterday, when you were flying back from Washington.'

'And the link?'

'His father was, apparently, the British army officer responsible for liaison with the American forces stationed in this area. So it is reasonable to assume he may have known of the Bifton Sands tragedy and even, perhaps, have helped in the cover-up. After all, the Americans would need some kind of British co-operation in the whole affair, if only to get permission for the burial of such a huge number of bodies on British soil.'

'So that accounts for everyone we had suspicions about?'

'But there may be many more, we know not of, Sue. Anyway, my point is that you could interpret the deaths and punishments we do know about, as not simply a terrible revenge for deeds long in the past, but perhaps, verdicts on those individual's contemporary actions, sins and omissions, now couldn't you? After all, none of those people we've been investigating seem to have exactly saintly reputations.'

'So what you're getting at is that . . . ?' She stopped, suddenly, as the full implications of Stride's observation came through to her.

'That's right,' he frowned, 'that they may be acting as judge and jury on the present, as well as on the past. And if that is so, then Hallowes may well not have heard the last from Starlings Meadow and Widow's Field.'

The gull soared silently over their heads, riding a thermal from the steeply shelving beach.

Enid Drench looked up. 'Beautiful, isn't he? Little does he know how fortunate he is. To be able to leave the frailty and troubles of this earth behind and feel the freedom of the air beneath his wings.' She looked back at Stride and then at Mary. 'You may laugh at me when you hear what I'm going to say.' She chuckled. 'But then, I suppose, everyone laughs at dear old Enid Drench these days.'

'No, that's not true,' Mary protested and took the old lady's strong but wrinkled hand in hers. 'Especially since everyone now knows what you've known all along.'

Enid Drench smiled sadly. 'Well, anyway, what I feel is that,' she looked back up at the gull who now hung motionless above them, 'the whole trouble with people is that they can't fly. Oh, I know they can, imprisoned in those metal tubes they call aeroplanes, but that's not what I mean. I mean *fly*. Really fly. Like that bird. Like every bird in the whole wide, wide world. Wouldn't that be truly marvellous? Just think of it. Their cares and hatreds and squabbles and worries and evil thoughts and machinations would seem all so very pointless and would just drop away the moment they spread their arms to the wind and shrug off the heavy burden of the land.'

She stopped and waved her hand. 'I'm sorry, I didn't mean to go on so. Forgive me.'

'There's nothing to forgive,' Stride smiled.

She looked at them both. 'Oh yes, there is. Maybe not my passion for birds, perhaps, but . . .'

She abruptly turned, then walked on and they followed in silence. Off the fine shingle of Bifton beach now, and back through the tough, weatherbeaten grass that topped the wide expanse of sand dunes separating the beach from the one and only approach lane.

Enid Drench, though visibly tiring, did not stop again until she had crossed the narrow strip of tarmac and come to a clump of trees that bent away from the prevailing south westerlies, like so many children flinching from their parent's wrath.

Then resting back against one of their trunks, she said quietly, 'It was here. In the shelter of these trees.'

Stride looked back towards the beach and sea, both of which were still in clear view.

'I used to hide myself away here week after week, watching the birds. My father's old binoculars weren't as powerful as they tell me you can buy nowadays, but they did me perfectly. One season I counted sixty-seven different species of birds in just this one area.'

She sighed. 'But that's not what you've come here

with me to know, is it? The tally of my winged friends.'

'But when they evacuated this whole area early in '44 and closed it all off . . . ?' Mary queried.

'Hardly a problem,' the old lady smiled, 'for someone who knew every single tree, every blade of grass, every rise of a dune and fall away of the land. Not that I wasn't nearly caught once or twice, mind you.' She chuckled at the remembrance, then went on, 'No, they couldn't keep me out. Even when they had doubled the guards patrolling the barbed wire and even installed an elaborate system of trip wires and alarms. I studied them all, you see, while they were doing it. Knew their little tricks backwards. And their guard routines. Even though they changed them once in a while, they only seemed to alternate between three basic formulas. So all you had to do was learn them.'

'But weren't you worried that one day you might get killed?' Mary asked. 'I mean, not only by some trigger-happy guard, but by a shell or a bomb or something. Or even a mine?'

'Not really,' Enid Drench shrugged. 'If I did, I pushed it firmly to the back of my mind. The birds were all I cared about at that point in my life. You see, I was still unmarried then and only had myself to worry about.'

'And the night of the massacre?'

She rested her head back against the tree trunk and closed her eyes.

'Don't make me relive it now. Please. There's hardly a day or night that's passed since, that hasn't been filled with terrifying visions of the carnage I witnessed then. At first, you see, I imagined it was yet another practice landing like quite a number I had watched before. With carefully staged explosions and whatever firing that took place being over the troops' heads, if it were live ammunition, otherwise they all seemed to use blanks. But then, I should have known, shouldn't I? I saw the destroyers off the shore, but thought they were just there to protect the landing-craft from any possible enemy action during the rehearsal – you know, like submarines or perhaps, an air attack . . . But when I suddenly saw those belches of flame when they opened up . . .'

She stopped and Stride could now see the tears running from under her closed eyelids.

'It's all right, Mrs Drench, please. Don't go on for our sake. Please.'

She slowly opened her eyes. 'What do you really wish to know, Doctor? Why I've kept silent all these years?'

He nodded, but then said quietly, 'But only if it costs you nothing to tell us.'

She smiled weakly. 'Cost? No, it costs me nothing to tell you why. You see, I was injured by one of those shells that night.' She suddenly took off her black woollen hat and parted one side of her hair with her fingers.

'There's still a scar there, Doctor, where the shell splinter knocked me unconscious. The next thing I knew I woke up in a bed in a bare, white room, looking into the faces of men in white coats and others in khaki or blue with more pips and braid on their uniforms than I'd ever seen in my life.'

'The American top brass must have been worried out of their minds when you were brought in,' Stride commented.

'They were. One after another they interrogated me for hours on end. And for days they wouldn't accept my story about Bifton Sands being just about the best bird sanctuary in the whole of the South West and me being just a nut of a spinster who still wanted to watch them. I'm sure they thought I was some devilishly clever Fifth Columnist simply posing as a nature lover.'

'But they believed you in the end?' Mary queried.

Enid Drench sighed. 'I don't know whether they ever really did. But they certainly knew they could not keep me incarcerated in that room for ever. I even had to ask every time I wanted to spend a penny. So they could escort me to the "john", as they called it, and back again. Then "click", I was locked in again.'

'How long did this go on?' Stride asked.

'Over a month. I was starting to think I would never get out of that place alive. Oh, forgive me, I haven't said what place, have I? It was a kind of annexe to a Nissen hut on Starlings Meadow. It was like a prison. It had only one window, high up on one wall. And that was barred. When my head wound was better, I used to climb the rails on the end of my bed and then stand on tiptoe to see out. That's when, one day, I saw them . . .' She closed her eyes once more, '. . . disinterring the bodies from Starlings Meadow and loading them into trucks.'

Strike frowned. '*Dis*interring the bodies? But I thought . . .'

She shook her head. 'No. Starlings Meadow was only a temporary resting place for about a third of those killed. For they reckoned they could safely lose about that number scattered over the fields of Normandy, without causing too many questions.'

'They shipped those men back?' Mary said in amazement and disgust.

'Yes. So I wormed out of one of the orderlies. But the shipping of almost eight hundred would have been impossible to hide.'

'And the rest are still buried in Widow's Field,' Stride remarked and turned back to look once more at the beaches on which they had fallen.

Enid Drench opened her eyes and smeared the tears away from her cheeks. 'But not for much longer, I pray. Thanks to all your inspired work.'

'So how did you get them to release you?' Mary asked.

'They said that if I didn't promise on the Bible never to divulge anything I knew of the tragedy, then I only left them with two options. Either to have me charged and tried as a spy, where they guaranteed they would see I was found guilty and hung. Don't forget they still weren't really certain I wasn't one. Or they would have to fly me secretly back to the United States in one of their DC-4's, where my fate would be in the hands of those who held the successful outcome of the war to be way above the rights of any one petty individual.'

'I can see why you had to agree,' Stride sympathised, but Enid Drench instantly took umbrage.

'*That*'s not why I agreed. Personal threats I have always regarded with extreme contempt. And it wasn't the bribes they eventually offered me. Seems money had kept a lot of other mouths shut. It was what one of the doctors attending my wound said that swayed me in the end. He pointed out that would not the grieving relatives of the fallen prefer to think that their loved ones had been killed in the heat of battle with their enemies, than slaughtered by accident by their friends? Then he ended by saying, "One day, perhaps, their tale can be, indeed must be, told. But the day is not now, whilst the war is still not yet won. And indeed, may not come for many, many years, until those who must grieve most, have actually themselves rejoined their loved ones".'

Enid Drench suddenly plunged her hand into a pocket of her long, black dress and produced a small packet wrapped in tissue paper.

'This is for you, Mary Stride. The time has now come for you.'

Hesitantly, the doctor's wife took the package from her and slowly unwrapped it to reveal an identity disc on a silver chain.

Enid Drench added, in a voice little above a whisper. 'I saw your grandfather fall not far from these very trees.'

As Mary Stride looked down at the disc to read the inscription, the setting September sun painted it red with its reflection.

On the morning of 5 May in the following year, a large but impressively simple, stone memorial in the shape of a Sherman tank emerging from waves was unveiled amongst the dunes at Bifton Sands.

Amongst those present at the ceremony were the Vice President of the United States, the Prime Minister of

Great Britain, the Duke and Duchess of York representing the Queen and many distinguished leaders from the Armed Forces of both the United States of America and the United Kingdom, together with nearly a thousand relatives of those killed in the tragic accident of 5 May 1944.

At the close of a short service of remembrance, conducted by the Archbishop of Canterbury, the Mayor of Hallowes presented Dr John Stride and Miss Susan Pike, previously of the *Hallowes Gazette* and now with BBC Television News, with miniature bronze replicas of the memorial, in heartfelt thanks for their inspired work on behalf of both the dead of Bifton Sands and the community of the Devon town of Hallowes.

More Terrifying Fiction from Headline:

NIGHT TERRORS

EDITED BY

CHARLES L GRANT

—— ALL ORIGINAL STORIES BY ——

DAVID MORRELL
JOSEPH PAYNE BRENNAN
KARL EDWARD WAGNER

As I looked into its glaring fiery eyes, I glimpsed the depths of hell itself. If it was something that had once been human, it was now nothing more than a tangible concentration of fury, lust and inexpressible cruelty, a fiend escaped from the pit. Its red eyes held me like two malign magnets. Its face – if such it could be called – was a mottled, wattle-like mass of bloated flesh in which individual features were almost too blurred to discern. A thing of indescribable darkness, it swayed there in the half darkness of the night, riven with rage, a famished predator cheated of its prey . . .

A new collection of twelve original tales of terror from three of the top writers in the genre: David Morrell, Joseph Payne Brennan and Karl-Edward Wagner.

Follow them to the darkest edge of fear, where the sound of horror is not always a scream . . . Enter with them the kingdoms of the damned, where demonic creatures haunt by night, where the chill, dank wind howls through the shadows, and where the clammy hand of death reaches from the crypt to drag its prey into the nightmare . . .

Also from Headline
NIGHT FEARS
Introduction by CLIVE BARKER
All original stories by DEAN R KOONTZ, EDWARD BRYANT, ROBERT R McCAMMON

FICTION/GENERAL 0 7472 3440 X £3.99